LENS of the WORLD

R. A. MacAVOY

Lens of the World
WORLD

WILLIAM MORROW AND COMPANY, INC.
NEW YORK

Library of Congress Cataloging-in-Publication Data

MacAvoy, R. A.
    Lens of the world / R. A. MacAvoy
        p.   cm.
    ISBN 0-688-09484-8
    I. Title.
PS3563.A25316L46   1990
813'.54—dc20   89-48414
                                                         CIP

ɪ rinted in the United States of America

First Edition

1 2 3 4 5 6 7 8 9 10

BOOK DESIGN BY PATRICE FODERO

You are the lens of the world: the lens through which the world may become aware of itself. The world, on the other hand, is the only lens in which you can see yourself. It is both lenses together that make vision.

My king,

I have ruined three clean sheets and broken a pen nib in writing this salutation of two words. I had not thought I was nervous, but how can I deny this image the world throws back at me: four smears of black ink and one broken bit of brass?

I have been used to writing histories at your command, sir, such as that of my first visit to the court of the Sanaur Mynauzet of Rezhmia, where the king is a demigod and the court spends half its time trying to kill him. This narrative, set in its climate of rolling grass, high mountains, dusty spices, murder, and roses, seemed to have an intrinsic interest beyond my ability to spoil in prose, but I am not so certain that the story of my own forty years of life will stand so well.

If the subject of an autobiography is insipid, the narrator can only be the same, and where does that leave me? I imagine you yawning behind the reading lens I ground for you fifteen years ago. Still I scratch by your own order, so yawn away, King of Velonya; though you are a courteous monarch, the paper takes no affront, and my refuge is in true obedience. In this thing at least, complete obedience.

•   •   •

Seeking a beginning that might attach interest, I consider the incident of the wolf that might have turned into a man, or the man with the nature of a wolf, since that episode was astonishing and full of proper theater, but though it was bloody it was also ambiguous, and it occurred after my childhood and schooling were over.

My initiation into the ranks of the peculiar and rightfully unpopular Naiish nomads is more instructive in the usual sense of the term, and it has its share of blood, battle, and unexpected changes of allegiance, but it also happened much too recently.

I must first retreat to a time where I may describe the disinterested craftsman Powl and what he made of an odd-shaped piece of material. This, too, is ambiguous; I begin to see that the theme of this whole story is ambiguity, but I must start somehow.

I will try to describe myself.

My first memory is dimness and movement: the heavy boots of soldiers and the great, white, flailing limbs of a cook in my uncle's kitchen. They grunted and heaved and she cried out, not in terror but in weary disgust as they flopped her onto the rough wooden chopping table.

This interpretation is the redraft of the incident, through the mind of Nazhuret, forty years old. At the time, the collected sounds had no more meaning to me than the cries of animals outside the door at night.

Those cries can terrify children, too.

When some waggish man-at-arms lifted me off my feet and made to drop me on her belly, on the piled wet and dirty skirts, I almost peed onto the poor woman, and my screams were much more the usual sounds of outraged innocence than her own.

Of that house I remember no more than this. Of my uncle—I was told I had an uncle—nothing.

. . .

My first real memory of myself was that of my own remarkable ugliness, revealed in the great, badly silvered practice mirror at school.

It surprises me always, how early children learn what they
look like. Had I not had the name Zhurrie the Goblin thrown
into my ears every day I think I would still have known I
looked like one. You, sir, have been kind enough to deny that
there is anything daunting in my features, but then you are a
very liberal man in matters of taste, and I have known you
to show enthusiasm over the lines of a camel. And then,
remember that I have grown into my face, as all men do, until
now it is more my years than my birth I expose to the world.

In the mirrored wall I saw a white oval wider than long,
widest just below the great, staring, lashless eyes. My nose,
which would someday arc out and then tilt up (like water
frozen on a windy lake), hardly existed in those years, and my
mouth was very small. My ears attempted to make up for the
inadequacies of my lower features, however. They stood out
so wide that I looked as though I had my hands cupped behind
them, straining for some sound. My hair was pale, pelty, and
weightless, like the down of a day-old chick.

Even then I was undersized, though mostly through having
short legs, slightly crooked by some infantile disease. It was
only later I discovered how unambitious my growth was to be.

As a boy I spent many stolen moments staring at my
reflection, hating it but fascinated, as many people are by
spiders. I don't remember any particular feeling of self-pity—
self-pity is not one of the original flaws of children—but rather
I hugged my repulsive peculiarities to me. Unlike many young
boys, I knew who I was: Nazhuret of the goblin face, Nazhuret
of no family, Nazhuret of Sordaling School.

My king, I know you will grow angry merely to read again
that the Royal School at Sordaling has had masters and even

boys who used the youngsters sexually. The school is under your own sponsorship, certainly, and was founded by your family, but still no king can be responsible for human nature being what it is. Your own education was very noble, good, and private, and I remember your saying that your greatest stumbling block as a child was that your tutors couldn't wallop you as you needed.

Most of us are not princes-heir, and we have to come by our learning in any way we can. We have different stumbling blocks, and randy masters were one of mine.

In Sordaling, all sorts of boys and men meet, most not staying beyond a year or two, and I have spent so much of my life there that I cannot judge its good and evil as simply as a stranger might, though I knew both very well. Being the youngest boy at Sordaling for my first four years and the smallest for two more, I was frequently held down and brutalized. Had the drillmaster (usually it was the drillmaster, ironically) done this to me in exchange for favors, or had he petted or praised me, I probably would have had my honesty or my independence of spirit ruined, but although there was buggery in my childhood, there was very little catamitery.

I disliked being buggered, but I also disliked being bashed about the head with wooden swords by boys twice my size. No one ever led me to think the two experiences were of different quality, and when I finally learned to avoid them, it was in the same manner.

By the time I was nine years old, it was rare for any but the most proficient students to be able to rap my skull with the practice bat, and the masters found whatever enjoyment my small form provided (thank God I was ugly) unworthy of the struggle.

The yellow brick buildings of the military school make a sort of city within a city, and the fact that students are denied the rest of Sordaling is of minor interest, especially to the young. To spend eight of the ten months of the school year in a loose confinement made up mostly of boys one's own age is no hardship, as long as one does not carry the mark of the victim on his brow. The usual two years spent in training and study are a bright memory for many of the most boring lords of Velonya.

Of course, I spent not two years but fifteen years at the school, but the routine did not wear as thin as might have been expected. The fact that I was as much a servant as a student meant I had frequent access of the outer city, and even when there was no errand to be run, I knew a dozen inobvious ways out, and could be trusted to carry messages from students to young-cock town-bred rivals, or to these rivals' sisters.

I was never betrayed, though the hotbloods were frequently caught. That says something about the character of the students at Sordaling. Or perhaps of their recognition of my usefulness. Or of their fear of me.

Can a strapping young lord be afraid of an undersized boy without family whose job it is to change the young lord's sheets? Yes he can, when the boy has friends among both schoolmasters and cooks. Especially among cooks. And when the boy is so habituated to use of the stick that he can strike his enemy up the crotch in full view of the class in such a manner that all the students and the master will miss seeing the illegal blow and mock the injured fellow for self-dramatization.

This is a very poor thing to be proud of, isn't it, sir? Perhaps I was not proud of it; that I can't remember.

I can hear you saying that there is no such thing as a young lord at Sordaling School, since all students are treated equally, called by their prenom only, and forbidden to tell anyone their lineage.

This rule is a beautiful one, my king, and your great-grandfather did nobly in devising it. It is sometimes even

11

obeyed, at least in public, but I reply that there was rarely a boy whose right name and titles I didn't know by the threshing frolic of their first year.

Except my own name, of course. About myself I knew only that my uncle had convinced the headmaster that my birth was genteel enough for the school's standards, which are moderately high. Unless this unremembered uncle returned to claim me or the headmaster broke the king's rule, I should never know more than I knew when I came, which was that my name was three odd syllables in a row, accent on the first: Nazhuret.

Heimer, friend of my years ten through twelve (my friendships were neatly packaged in two-year intervals), said that my name sounded like the sneeze of a cat.

Sometimes I dwelled upon the idea that my birth was quite exalted, but that my parents could not stand the sight of me and so stored me away at Sordaling until the time I might grow into (or perhaps out of) my features. It was as useful a daydream as that common one of being switched in the cradle.

When visitors of some grandeur toured the school, I watched carefully to see whether they were looking at me out of the corner of their eye. Often they were, of course. It was hard not to look at something so exceptional.

Later, when my unremembered uncle stopped paying, this fantasy of birth became harder to maintain.

By all rights the bursar should have sent me home when I was ten and the tuition did not appear, but the death of the headmaster, combined with my own ignorance, meant they had no idea where to send me. Six years had passed since my arrival at school, and my tenure was longer than that of many young masters, trainers, and deans. All were very used to my presence, and I had drifted into the role of school orderly before anyone could decide how to show me the door.

The next year the money resumed, along with a lump of delinquent tuition, so I was paid for a whole year's worth of cleaning and carrying and sitting up with young fellows whose crying awoke the dorms.

With this money I began to swagger a bit myself, and visited both the bakeries of King Gutuf's Street and the entertainments of Fountain Park. I was very fond of the swanboat ride down the slanting canal shunt, which has in the past few years (I find) been dismantled and replaced with a mill. I was also very fond of Charlan, daughter of Baron Howdl, whose honors surround Sordaling and who owns a number of the commercial buildings as well. Charlan did not act like a baron's daughter. She scarcely acted like a girl at all, but I rode the swanboats with her and tossed old bread to the real birds.

For a fee of a tuppence I taught little town-boys how to spring over the old broad sword and the bonfire (which activity is considered very dashing and auspicious among their set), and I taught basic rapier work to Charlan free.

Unlike many students, I did not fight with the townies. I was too jaded with sparring in the halls to do it for sport, and the satisfaction of flattening ten burghers' sons would not have been worth the inconvenience of a single split lip.

But the money I had been given ran out, and Lady Charlan was deemed too old at twelve to be a boy-daughter anymore and was locked away. I moped around the river for a few weeks until Howdl's old nurse took pity and told me how things were. I spent another week dreaming mad escapes in which I would spring the girl from her father and her fate and we would take to the woods together and live—I don't know how. As brigands, I suppose. Luckily I did not have much free time for mad dreaming and so never attempted to carry out the scheme.

I returned to the more sedate life of the school and when, two years later, the money stopped again, there was no talk of sending me away. I was recognized as a son of Sordaling School itself: part master, part servant, part imp.

Remember the school with me, sir, as the bricks glow in evening sunlight, or the snow of the drill field lies etched with diagrams of war. The buildings are solid and they loom with a certain presence. The quadrangles are restful, arbored, and well planted, regularly mowed by junior boys and sheep.

All my duty at school was reasonable and regular, though not exciting, and the food was good. I'm sure I would have grown tall on the meals dished into our tin plates if I had that growth within me. Most of the masters were very companionable, at least to me. I learned two languages; a simplistic geography; a minimal art of courtesy (which I have now lost again, my king is well aware); skill with the broadsword, the rapier, and the spear; the cleaning and maintenance of the powder catapult and harquebus; practical horse ménage; the making of beds; the sanitation of latrines; wrestling and pinching and threatening other boys to good effect; and a hundred other martial skills, which I will never use. I also developed a manuscript hand that is better than I deserve and an accent in speech purely Old Vesting, owing nothing to the Zaquesh-lon influence, which has sullied the pronunciation of most of the people of Velonya.

(Or should it be said that your Vestingish ancestors, sir, have imperfectly imposed their language upon a people largely Zaquash by birth? And does it matter which of these explanations is true, or both? The accent has served me well, and I digress again.)

In short, I had the education of the usual rural lord. I was no lord, however, and had only my acceptance long ago into Sordaling School to testify that my birth was more or less gentle. My destiny was the common one—to be remitted as knight-contract into the forces of whatever school donor came to the school to recruit and who fancied me.

I was eligible for such remission when I turned fifteen, but at that time I looked twelve, and as I felt a great reluctance to enter into the service of Baron Howdl, Sordaling's most intimate neighbor and patron, I stood at attention with the younger boys and no master betrayed me.

Howdl was a handsome man—though he had not so good a face as his daughter—and he sat a fine figure on a horse, but he was a black and surly employer who refused to follow the government of Velonya into the modern age and who made himself tyrant to his dependents. Though his honors were all near Sordaling and therefore secure both from Rezhmian incursion and the coast raids of the Falinkas, he was always recruiting, because he could not hold on to his men. I disliked the thought of owing allegiance to such a man and feared he would someday find out how I had aided his daughter to misbehave.

Howdl was either fooled by my tactics of concealment or, as is more likely, found that my personal inadequacies overcame the good reports of my instructors. He did not look at me more than once.

The following summer a rumor came that he had killed his daughter in a fit of rage. Grief and fury nearly led me to challenge the man when I heard that, but he would merely have had me thrown into prison for my temerity, and I'd be digging the baron's own fields in a checkered burlap coat with a chain around my leg. Besides, it was only a rumor. Another rumor had it that she was not dead, but had been spirited away to deliver a bastard baby. A third had it that he had killed her because of the bastard. I did not know which of these was more probable; it had been three years since I had seen her, and the years between thirteen and sixteen are very long. Whatever had happened to take Lady Charlan out of our sight, it made me very grateful to have escaped Howdl's winnowing and more resolved against falling into any lord's power at all.

After this event, Headmaster Greve, who was a kindly man and much more lenient than the headmaster who had originally admitted me, made me sure to know that I could not stay on as student past my twentieth birthday. Nor could

I hope to change my role into that of skills master, because all masters at Sordaling School had proven themselves either in war service or state work (or were placed there as a cheap and honorable retirement by one of the noble donors, but the headmaster never admitted as much aloud). Nor would any of the deans or masters hire me on in any capacity of service, for the graduates of Sordaling School were not to be common servants, or at least not within sight of the present students. In short, I must be gone.

From the ages of sixteen to nineteen, I lived unhappily in the knowledge that I would have to take employment somewhere. I suffered anxiety that I would never be picked, and would leave the school trotting on shanks' mare, with sixpence and references, unemployable at my own trade and fated to become a drudge somewhere far from home. I had frequent bad dreams to this effect.

Each time the school was winnowed, however, I did my panicked best to be invisible.

The Earl of Docot Dom came with his ranks greatly reduced from his unwise incursion against the Red Whips in the South of the Zaquashlon territories, and he took three fourths of the eligible young men back with him, amid excitements and toasts and gold gratuities all around.

He did not take me.

Baron General Hydeis came the next spring, to take twenty good, reliable men-at-arms of no particular gentility, to be coastal sheriffs in the West. Though this position was all I could hope for, and though I was field-ranked third out of a school of two hundred, still I played the blinking fool in front of the man and was not chosen.

For this bit of clownishness, Rapiermaster Garot, my longtime patron and personal friend, knocked me backward over the bricks of the dormitory court. I deserved the blow, but at the next recruitment I made no better impression.

It was not fear of battle that drove me to behave so badly,

though I have a strong dislike of battle. It was not dissatisfaction with the status of a knight contract, for that estate carried with it many times the power and honor I had ever known and could lead to high advancement. Nor did I cherish dreams of personal liberty. I had never considered the possibility of such liberty.

My panic came from an utter inability to decide—to give myself over to any one person. I had been everyone's for so long.

Perhaps I was too much a child, kept so by living among youngsters, and at the place where I had been living since the age of four. Perhaps it was that my own odd face had driven me foolish. Perhaps I was waiting for Powl. But that is all to say the same thing, for who but a fool and a child would have been of any use to Powl?

To encapsulate years as tightly as I have been doing here is by necessity to lie. To speak of a year's events in any manner is its own sort of untruth, for a year has no more unity than the broken nib at the left corner of the table; the sound of thunder; and the flight of the bird outside the window, which has just now stolen my eye from the paper. It is a thrasher, I think. (They are all over here in early autumn.) The nib is stained a thin black, which has dribbled onto the porous wood of the tabletop. The thunder is only in my memory. What is the set, pattern, or entirety of these three things that I should speak of them together, or of the events of my early life, for that matter? Perhaps you know, sir, for you have eyes to see me, and mine exist only to look outward from myself.

I awoke before dawn for the whole week before Baron Howdl's next winnowing. It had been explained already that my name had been brought up before his sergeant-steward, and that gentleman was interested in a contract. Allegiance and obedience for five years, renewable at the discretion of the noble or his representative. Three years was the standard first graduate's contract, but at nineteen I was already as old as many who were entering their second contract.

I have a memory of the stripe of violet that opened the sky that day, broken by the bulk of the square clock tower and the peak of the headmaster's house, as I saw it from the dormitory window. This memory may well be overpainted by visions come before or since. It may be totally false, for the mind creates with as much talent as the eyes perceive, but still—I have it. (The dewy, young-girl colors of dawn make an ugly picture against the mustard-yellow squareness of Sordaling School, even in the frame of recollection.)

On the day before Howdl's descent upon my life I awoke from a very strong dream, which I remember with more assurance than I do the skyline. I was walking in a woods, which was odd enough for one of my background, and had managed to lose the path entirely. It was midday, and I found myself climbing a round, bare-topped hill. Near the top of it was a hole—a cave entrance—and out of this entrance a cool wind was blowing.

I knew I had to go into this cave. I also knew I would be killed within. I entered darkness, very cold.

Once I had kicked myself awake, I felt no need to delve for the meaning of the dream. It echoed my waking feelings perfectly. I was left with a chill of dread that the late-summer morning could not overcome.

I hung from the second-story window, swung sideways onto the sharp-peaked little snow roof of the main entrance, and slid down to stand before the locked dormitory door.

This was my method for leaving my quarters too early or too late. (It was more difficult to return.) Though my body now is in most ways a more serviceable tool than the frame of that Nazhuret, still I think if I tried such a stunt immediately after springing out of bed in the morning, they would have to carry me back into it. The difference between nineteen years and forty.

I went barefoot to the practice field: six enclosed acres of coarse grass, chewed earth, and horse droppings, where a few unkempt sheep wandered, badly shorn and painted in unsheeplike colors each year by teams of students. Three of them were indigo-stained, my own victims, for indigo was the team color of my dormitory and I had a pronounced talent for sheepcatching. The more sheep colored after one's team color, the greater the prestige of the dormitory.

This summer had been a good one. We had three indigo sheep for North House and I still bore as much of the pigment as any woolly creature. I drifted over the field that morning in such early light I could not tell Indigo-North from Madder-East, and I said good-bye to the scene of a life's play, like a wistful ghost in theater.

I touched the armory and the better-kept drill field in the same manner, but by the time I reached the refectory, I was little ghostlike enough to strike a conversation with the night scullery and cadge a piece of cheese. He, like everyone in the school except the self-involved freshers, knew that Zhurrie the Goblin's future had been disposed of, and so sympathetic he was, he probably would have given me a whole beef joint on request.

I had planned to be back at the dormitory door just before it was unlocked for the day, but time had betrayed me or I it, for the last of the boys were stumbling or swaggering out to breakfast as I returned. Someone whose name and face are lost to me told me that I had been sent for by the headmaster. I remember only that the fellow expected me to be terrified at the news, and even in my lowering mood, I was amused by that.

What more could the headmaster do to me?

The headmaster then was no older than I am now, strange

to think. A young man for such a position. He came to his office door not to greet me, but to stare at me.

"They said you had run away," he told me.

"They were certainly not correct," I replied, explaining no more.

Of his office I remember only that he had on a table a clock that worked with dripping water at almost the accuracy of the usual spring-weight variety, except in exceptionally dry, hot weather. I don't remember if it made a sound.

He was very kind to me, once he had overcome his surprise. He told me that I would be missed, and he excused me from all classes and duties that day so I might enjoy myself in the city and get my wardrobe ready.

My instructional duties had already been relegated to another the week before: not another student, but a minor instructor, who would be paid a living wage for what I did free. My classes—I had not really attended much in the way of classes for years, since I knew the lectures by heart. My wardrobe consisted of the padded suit I was wearing, drill uniform and day uniform, as well as one set of coat and britches handed down to me by a boy in North who had grown four inches during his first year as a student. All these but the hand-me-downs would revert to the school, to be given in turn to the next ten-year-old arrival, or slow-growing adolescent. I had the rapier I had bought the previous year, but no saddle, bridle, or other horsegear. The noble who wanted my services had to do without dowry entirely.

It is a great deal of fun to do nothing in a place where everyone else is working very hard, but even that amusement paled soon. I went out into the sun. I donned my civilian clothing and buckled on my rapier, just like any underbred burgher gentleman of Vestinglon. I showed my pass at the door (unusual behavior!) and walked out among the cobbles and shops of Sordaling.

My elegiac mood deepened as I wandered into the flower

market by the swanboats, remembering dirty little Lady Charlan, who despite her lack of skill had possessed a very fine though not overdecorated dueling rapier. Dubious ornament to a virgin girl. Dubious virgin girl. That spring the air had been rich with tuberoses and narcissus.

Now Lady Charlan was dead or pregnant—or both, perhaps. Now the only flowers for sale were asters, which had no odor. The young man who owned the shop, hauling the bags of bulbs and the heavy earthen pots, was one of those I had taught to leap the bonfire. He was eighteen, I was nineteen, and he probably could have lifted me off the ground on one straight arm.

I envied that youth: his flowers, his day-long view of the gliding swans, his day's income, his bulk, and his inches. Most of all, I envied him his simple independence. Only the simple can *be* so independent.

Of course, I may have misunderstood him. Perhaps he was crossed in love. Perhaps Howdl was his landlord.

I think it was in the park that day that the townie stopped me. It was either that day or another close to it. He had a red face, brown hair, and three attendant loungers. He accosted, followed, and insulted me, using no originality of expression at all. He was not interesting. I suppose it was my rapier that drew him on—burgher's sons are frequently excited at the sight of a rapier. It might also have been that the indigo stains on my neck resembled a disfiguring birthmark. With my unusual appearance, however, there is no need to look far for the stimulus to his behavior. In the end he spat at me, forcing me to wipe my shoe. In the end his chatter drove my steps out of Sordaling and onto the sunny road.

Unhappiness either overwhelms beauty or heightens it. So does joy, now that I reflect on it. It is my fortune that both extremes of emotion tend to increase the quality of all I see, leaving me bright visions of the natural world.

The suburban air was sharp and the earth was gold and

the maples that mark Sordaling's banner were beginning to brighten with autumn. Even the busy road's horse manure, preserved by the cool, dry air, seemed perfect and necessary to complete the picture.

This may be last autumn I am visualizing, my king. How can I know?

I had never had much business outside the city. If there was in me any instinct for venery or for botany, residence in a closed school had given it no soil in which to grow. So it is not really surprising that by the time I had walked two undirected hours or so, I did not know where I was at all, but only that in my finery I was too hot.

Examining the flat, well-planted, and sparsely peopled landscape, I spied in the distance a dark line. It looked like trees: a planting of some kind, or a river with willows. I made for the coolness and for the water.

That is how I came to be stomping through a woods without any sign of path, tangling my rapier in mannerless briars, climbing out of the trees on the domed side of a hill, and recreating every step of my fatal night vision in the bright light of noon.

I exaggerate for the sake of effect. My dream was not manifest literally, for at the top of the hill there was no cave. Instead there was a building of mundane brick: red, squat, high-windowed, surmounted by a dome like that of the civic house at Sordaling but less impressive, and in that dome was stuck a huge pike or spear . . . a large tube of metal, at any rate, pointed at the horizon.

My words make the thing too romantic. It was a dull and commercial-appearing building. I thought at first sight that it was some sort of lumber mill or foundry.

The irony of this: to have a nightmare made real and then turned into a lumber mill. It only served to dispel the last traces of unease from my mind. The moment after I had seen the hill, I could no longer swear that this hill was the one I had dreamed of, rather than the real sight of a hill replacing an imperfectly painted memory. The mind is like that.

I walked around the squareness of it. I was thirsty.

Obviously a mill or foundry would be accessible by road. Easily accessible, moreover, and close to the city. Now, at this remove, it is easy for me to see this. Either my fatigue that day, my ignorance, or some other factor kept me from understanding the anomaly of this undecorative structure at the crown of a pathless hill. Perhaps once I had decided not to be afraid of it, my mind was unwilling to admit anything uncanny concerning it at all.

There was a door of wood and metal, with a small open grille at the top, out of which poured a welcome cold air. I knocked with open palm, calling halloo, calling mercy for a drink of water.

I waited in the shadow of the bricks for a long time before I had an answer. I had given up, I think, and would have walked on had I any better place to go, but then I heard a bolt drawn.

From this point on, sir, I have no doubt of my memory.

It was an iron bolt holding the door I leaned against that was shot open. There was no sound of footsteps before or after. No voice answered mine. My weight caused the heavy, reinforced door to swing in.

There was a hallway, dark and ordinary and smelling of earth, and beyond that a large central room, such as one would, of course, find in a foundry, and this was lit by small windows up at the base of the dome. From the ceiling dangled numerous cords, each of which ended in a brass button.

This dome base was decorated—I thought at the time it was decorated—with a frieze of crenellated wood in what is called a key pattern. It was massive. In the corner of the room nearest the dark hall stood a tall machine of gears, equally massive. In the middle of the room, where the penetrating

23

shaft reached its end, stood a platform with stairs. There was a glint of brass. Over the newel post of the rail serving those stairs was draped a gentleman's overcoat of boiled wool.

This much I perceived in a glance, and as I still stood blinking, a human figure was added to the scene. A man stepped from the concealment of the near wall of the central room into the passage and stood as a black outline.

I should have spoken again. Perhaps I did, but I doubt it, and I am sure if I spoke it was not coherently. From him also I heard nothing, but there were some yards between us, so it might have been that he bid me enter before turning on his heel and proceeding toward the central platform.

He had not the back of a foundry worker or the clothes of a miller. He was dressed in a bright brown that went well with his smooth brown hair, over which I could barely espy the glint of his incipient baldness. He was not a large man. Not a small man. The keen eyes of nineteen noticed that his tailcoat was piped at the seams in gold and that thin rims of gold edged his rather tall, square boot heels.

Trusting that he had spoken me in and that I had only missed hearing the words, I entered, and the cold of that passage was marvelous and the draft hardly to be accounted for, considering the lack of ventilation this block of bricks had seemed to possess. I was intimidated against my will, and the cold upon my sweaty back drove me forward.

At the end of the passage I stood blinking for the very oddity of the room around me. There were benches with a great shimmer of glass, and mounted on sticks protruding from the coarse brick wall were bits of animals—not heads and skins as a hunter will mount his trophies, but out of a more twisted fancy: a hawk's leg, with weights on its toes; a dog's jaw, still hinged; and a suspiciously human-appearing set of hipbones and thighbones.

Suddenly I recognized the geared apparatus in the corner as nothing other than a torturer's rack.

My hand flew to the handle of the rapier, and my dream was alive and flooding again through my senses. The man who was neither foundryman nor miller had faced me, this time full in what light the place afforded.

I remember his face less well that the rest of the scene, for other, similar encounters have superimposed themselves. I can state truthfully that I thought it a smooth face, a round face, a face of less than average beard and more than average grooming. His eyes were pale for his coloring and set far apart, not unusually deep. The receding hairline gave him a bit of the flat look of an egg. He was not plump, but there was something about the neat, small hands and feet that suggested he *could* be plump, or that one day he would be.

His eyes were open wide, but they were ironical. His hand was raised to one of the many hanging strings.

"I had hoped," he said in the perfect accent of the court— the accent drubbed into every boy of Sordaling School, with more or less success—"I had hoped for a young girl with porcelain hands." He pulled the cord and I heard behind me the slam of the door I had used to enter, followed by the thump of a bolt driven home.

I started, my ears popped, and my rapier rattled in its scabbard. I put my hand to the hilt—to quiet it, to draw it out; I didn't know then my intent and don't know now.

The problem with carrying a weapon as part of one's costume is that one is thereby inclined to use it, and when one's hair is rising and crackling about one's head and all one's tooth enamel exposed like that of a frightened dog, that is exactly the time one is most inclined to use it, and that use may well be murderous.

This man had done nothing to me but to tell me he'd rather had a visit from a pretty girl than from me. That was no affront. Was it his fault his dwelling had found itself in my dream, or that his style of furnishing raised the hair on my head? I let my hand slide, hoping he had not noticed, and

25

explained my situation: I was lost, I was hot and I begged only water.

He cut my words short. "All in good time," he said. "Water, work, sleep, study, food, argument, extinction . . . all in good time." He loosed the hanging line and let the brass button swing. He turned his tailored back to me and walked to a table, where were laid three flat disks of something that shone, a pot of reddish paste, rags, boxes of sand both white and gray, and what looked like a hedge sickle. It was the last that took my attention.

"What is your name?" he asked me, and I told him the full of it: not Zhurrie, the boy's nickname, but all three ungainly syllables, leaving off only the title "the Goblin." Hearing it, he stopped as still as a fly in amber. I could see the corner of his gray eye as he looked over his shoulder at me.

Time passed, and the brass buttons swung.

"Nazhuret," he repeated, pronouncing it oddly, and then he added, to my mystification, the words "Warrior, poet, king of the dead."

I stepped to where he originally had greeted me, and from here I was more convinced than ever that it was a hedger that he had taken into his hand: a sharp-bladed hedger with a hook in the handle.

"My name is Nazhuret, yes." I spoke slowly to avoid misunderstanding, for the manner in which he now regarded me was more unsettling than the manner in which he had closed the heavy door. Perhaps he thought I was mad and speaking gibberish and he needed the tool to protect himself. More likely he was mad himself. Whichever, he had his hand on the hedger, and the door to the outside was bolted against me.

The brass button swung in shorter arcs now, and nothing more had been said by either of us. I was wondering whether the pull cord opened the door as well as closed it. It seemed more practical to essay this than to run screaming and clawing at the oak (my first impulse). I caught the button and gave it a yank.

He shook his head, between contempt and pity. "Things do not work that way, lad. How could the same vector of force move a thing in alternate directions?" He had stepped away from the table very quietly while I was making my futile try at the cord and he held the hedger. It looked scandalous in his manicured hand.

"I just thought it might," I replied. I sounded silly even to myself. He smiled at me.

"Nazhuret, you are well named"—the pity on his face grew and overspread the contempt—"for I believe you will have to die now, before we can do anything else with you at all."

As he spoke, my rapier was out and at ready, though I have no memory of drawing it. My mind was filled with the horror of his madness: madness with a hedge sickle in its hand. But the man with the smooth face and the pretty coat made no move to engage me. Instead, he smiled even more sweetly, grabbed another of the hanging cords with his left hand, and dangled from it, like a big brass button himself. His fine shoes swayed left and right in the empty air. There was a scraping from all the walls of the room, and he began to sink slowly toward the floor.

It was the windows. He was closing all the shutters of the clerestory windows together, and the light was failing in the room. It would be dark in another moment and I would be locked blind in a strange room with a madman brandishing a crude blade. I sprang for him as the last light went out, trying to grab the hedger from his hand.

I met only empty air.

Spinning my sword around me in a vain effort to find the man by touch, I crouched low against the stone floor. The flagstones gave off cold; I was chilled in all my sweat. I told myself that if I couldn't see him he couldn't see me, no matter how familiar he was with the chamber itself. Surely a sane

27

man could be more silent than a mad one, especially if the sane man was fighting for life itself, as I was. I resolved to make no noise.

It was amazingly quiet in that stone-walled block of a building: no traffic of feet or of wheel nor song of bird nor cry of dog, cat, horse, or ass in the distance. I heard my breathing only, and the alarming percussion of my heart. A drop of sweat fell from my hair to the flags, impossibly loud. I held my breath, but my heart only beat louder and more erratically. It seemed to me that my body was making such noise I would not be able to hear it if my enemy ran full tilt over me, swishing his agricultural implement in the air. I felt self-betrayal and a touch of panic. I would run for the entrance hall at any moment, not knowing at all in which direction to find it.

While my brain was giving way in this manner, my long-trained body remained in posture of defense, and so when the foppish madman whispered "Here I am, Nazhuret. In front of you. Engage me," my rapier began the deed just as I had been commanded. But halfway in the motion I remembered that this was a naked blade, noble-sharp and without cork or button, and that my enemy was no enemy at all but some mere mad burgher in a frock coat with a tool that could not touch me at my fighting distance. My attack, which began lustily, ended as no more than a tentative, chiding prick.

Which met nothing. "Misplaced condescension, lad. Or are you merely inept?" The words seemed to come from my left. The stinging, flat-bladed blow across my face came from a different direction. I spun toward the source of the attack and lunged.

This time he took my impetuous sword against his hedger, and I felt the weight of his body as we came hilt to hilt. "Better," he whispered, and he kicked my leg out from under me.

I fell in a clattering pile and bounced up again. My useless eyes were open so wide I felt my eyelashes brush against my eyebrows—sir, this is the sort of thing one *does* remember—and I felt around me with my rapier as a blind man does with his stick. He cleared his throat most graciously behind me so I would know his position. "Are you blind as well as crazy?" I shouted, "that you can see in the dark?"

"I am not as blind as you," he answered. "Nor half so mad."

And he laughed at me. Sir, I did go mad with that laugh, on top of all my terror. I lunged for blood—to kill. I would have run him through again and again had I had my way, though the man had countered my attacks defensively and done me no more affront than to slap me across the face with a garden tool.

Again my blade met only metal and we engaged, rapier to hedger, but this time he dropped his blade to the fourth quadrant and took the slim rapier into the hook at the guard of his weapon and it broke. I heard the point of my blade skitter across the floor, and I thought inconsequentially that this was the sort of blade one gives an untried noble's son to wear with his signet belt: not a meaningful blade, no great loss.

And Nazhuret: not a meaningful young man, no great loss. My last thought.

The heel of a boot took me across the jaw and my head hit the flagstones and I felt cold opening my throat.

I was above, hanging in the black dome, looking down at my body and at the man who had killed me. The darkness was no obstacle.

The killer indeed had a bald spot beginning on the back of his head; from above this was very noticeable, especially as he was bending over the small, shrunken body with the yellow hair. He went away and I was left with nothing to see but the dead boy with one smear of blood across his face. His eyes were closed, as in sleep. He looked very young and hopeless. I felt a distant pity, not too sharp. Then the killer came back, dragging a bench, upon which he sat and leaned over his victim. His patch of pink scalp gleamed.

The importance of this scene was soon exhausted, and it began to recede and grow smaller. It became nothing but a spot of light in the middle of an emptiness that expanded without limit.

Decide, was said to me. Grab on to this that is passing, or let it go. Madness or death.

This was not a comforting choice, and with it came no instruction or clue. But all comfort was past anyway, along with Nazhuret and the ten stubby fingers on his hands and the two splayed feet that moved him from place to place. Out of what instinct or guidance I do not know I turned from that shrinking light amid the darkness and let go of Nazhuret and of all of the first-person-singular pronoun as well.

My king, this is a memory of a memory, but I speak as truthfully as I know how. Try to follow me, no matter where.

The darkness was not darkness (is not darkness, even now) but light, and in every reach was knowledge, content and endless. So, too, was time (that thing which we know only through its being gone): content and endless, not a river but a sea.

Yet there was a voice, and it said, "Tell me about Nazhuret."

Amid infinite light nothing is hidden, not even Nazhuret, so the answer came easily. "Nazhuret looked often into the mirror, yet he was not vain."

"What else?"

"He made third in the ranks at Sordaling School, and would have been first, but for his background."

"What was his background?"

"He had none."

"Tell me more." The voice was familiar. Ironical.

30

"Nazhuret loved the Lady Charlan, daughter of Baron Howdl. But she is gone."

This, although true, had never been said aloud.

"Go on."

"So is Nazhuret. Gone."

The voice amid the light was no stronger than a draft through a cold hallway, but it could not be escaped.

"Was Nazhuret a good fellow, as men go?" it asked, and after slow rolling time came the answer.

"Yes. He stayed out all night sometimes, but he was a good fellow."

The voice laughed: not an annoying laugh. "Good fellows are not everywhere, these days. Nazhuret could be useful. There is even a need, perhaps And perhaps he will come back to us."

The reaches of light were moving. There was a haze, a glaze, a network of brightness through them. "Nazhuret is dead," it answered, but the voice continued, "Nazhuret can come back, if he chooses. If he cares."

The light ran into veins, coalesced, leaving dark and unknowing around it as it shrank.

"Will he come back? Will you come back to us, Nazhuret? Back to the world and the cold stone floor?"

The light spun cobwebby fine, tighter and tighter until it extinguished its own inner radiance. I became aware that it was I. That I was. I. First person singular.

Oh, grief and loss and straight necessity, that light and time and knowing be pressed down until it is matter, until it is I.

"Why must I?" I said. "Nothing is worth this. Not this. This is terrible."

And he answered, "You are not compelled to return. Yet I have a use for you here. I ask this sacrifice of you, Nazhuret. Will you return?"

I opened my eyes, saying, "Yes. Enough. All right, damn it," and there, leaning over me, was the smooth face of the man with the hedger and the bald spot and all the fine tailoring. "Nazhuret," the voice said as he lifted my head and put white linen on my bleeding cheek. "Welcome. My name is Powl. I am your teacher."

I can scarcely believe it has been four weeks since I began this manuscript, sir. I am appalled to have been so slow in fulfilling a command of the king, but believe that I have not been merely desultory; along with the local haying we have had epidemics both of summer fever and dueling, and they have kept me tolerably occupied. I hold the pen now in a hand neatly silk-stitched from knuckle to wrist to prevent the flesh from gaping.

No, I mislead you. It is an injury from a grass scythe. I lent a hand (this hand) to replace a sick harvestman. I could try writing left-handed, but it is not fair, sir, that you should be the sufferer in such an experiment. I will proceed slowly, but I will proceed.

In the garden of your city palace at Vestinglon, where I hazard the guess you sit to read this—that is, if the weather remains fine and I do not continue writing on into the winter—there you have a very clear pool. Rise if you will, take this page with you, and go to the bank of it. I remember the day we played colt games by this water, and His Royal Majesty went in, rearmost foremost, and seven members of the Privy Guard were dissuaded only with difficulty from filleting His Majesty's wrestling partner like a trout. Doesn't this water appear to be scarcely shin-deep, though we both have reason to know it is deep enough to float a sizable monarch?

Not even the bulk and bustling of a submerged king could muddy this pool, which rises from unknown depths and issues out through a marble dolphin mouth at your left hand and settles there back again, unnoticed amid the reeds to your right, far enough from the kitchens and offices to take no stain from them. I could count the red pebbles on the bottom and the blue ones and the white even as we hauled you out, dripping.

Look into this depth, so much clearer than air and so much colder and heavier, and keep it in your mind as you read of my first day of return, after my death at Powl's hand. For I was sunk deeper and more silently into the confines of my body and into the airs of the world that day than the blind, translucent fish are sunk in the water of this pool.

The bench he laid me on was rough and porous. The wood had absorbed the wet and the smells of night, and now it issued them against my face, and the touch against my broken skin was full of sparks. The wall of bricks glowed with the terrible colors of its kilning: flame-red, blood-black, and the yellow of sulfur.

The fortressed door stood open again and yellow light poured in, along with the endless song of a bird. I sat up and stood up and Powl came with me. He led me through the blossoms, traps, and snarls of the September grass, which might otherwise have held me for all this second life (I was so bemused), and he sat me in the green glow of a maple tree.

"If finally I am damned," he said, "it will be for this, lad. Forgive me."

His words were lightly spoken, but I considered them for a ridiculously long time. At last I answered him, "It was not murder, but a fair duel. I had the better weapon, the longer reach. And a lifetime of training."

He smiled. His teeth were white and even and did not quite meet. "No, Nazhuret. Between you and me could be no fair duel. But I did not mean damned for that, but rather for dragging you back again, to this"—he touched my head in two places—"to where your skin is split and there is at the back of your head a lump that you will feel soon, and to where

33

you were thirsty and I presume still are, and . . . and all that is to come."

In my mind the constellations wheeled slowly. No intelligence, mind you, but very many stars. "You could not drag me. I came," I told him, and I was very sure of myself.

His pale, ironical eyes, colorless themselves, caught the sun. "Back to a world that is full of pain and confusion? Yes, so you did. Do you know why?"

I shook my head, and he was right: It was going to hurt soon. "No," I said, "you have to tell me why."

Powl leaned forward, into shadow. He pointed a neat and delicate finger at me. "Because, Nazhuret. Because the world is full of pain and confusion. That is why I called you. That is why you came." Then he rose and lifted me by the back of the collar and marched me back through the door of oak, where I was given water and strong coffee with cardamom and the end of a very fine cheese. I slept and dreamed not at all, and when I awoke, the coat of boiled wool was over my shoulders, the moon was streaming blue through the high windows, the door was cracked open, and the fine gentleman was gone.

I went out to relieve myself, ate the rest of the cheese, played with the disks of glass, worked the mechanisms of bone, and ascertained that the torturer's rack was actually a gear-and wheelwork that somehow connected with the wooden crenellations edging the dome roof. I climbed the platform and peered up at the slot in the roof through which the hinder stars of the Great Hog could be seen, and I wondered how the rain was kept out. By then I was chilled and headachey, so I returned to my bench and the gentleman's coat.

Not once through that afternoon and evening did I spare a thought for Sordaling School, or for Baron Howdl, or for the dream that had brought me away from both. For the rest of the night I slept like a dead man.

• • •

The next morning I was still on my hard bed when Powl opened the door and walked through to the central chamber. "Still asleep, I see," he said, but it was obvious he meant "still here." He was carrying a bundle.

I got up, shook out his felted coat, and followed him.

In the morning light he was smoother than ever: smoother and cleaner and more pink-scalped. His plumpness was an illusion brought on by small features and the delicate joints of his fingers. While his dress was conservative, everything he wore had a little bit of gold about it, including his teeth. He put down the bundle on the boneworks table, where it clattered. He took back his coat, examined it—for fleas, possibly—and said: "The rules, Nazhuret:

"First, never piss against the walls of this building."

I started to interrupt, to explain it had only been the outside wall, and on a structure this massive, that could scarcely matter, but it occurred to me to wonder how he could possibly have known, and in the face of his inexplicable knowledge, my protest died.

"It is unhygienic, it stinks, and it only encourages dogs. I find it an unappealing habit, and you will not do it. Further, for the sake of my sensibilities if not your own, you will wash every day—yes, of course you do, but I mean head to foot. Neatly. Cold or hot. You will launder your shirt every evening."

At this I must have gawped, for I had never heard of anyone except the clergy living with such nicety, and among those, only such who had servants with time to waste. Powl paid my expression no mind, or perhaps he answered it indirectly, for he continued, "This training would be easier if you had been fifteen years instead of nineteen. You're now at an age to balk, to challenge everything I say."

Indeed, I was about to challenge his rules as time-consuming and inappropriate considering my station in life, when I was overcome by a feeling of uncertainty amounting to pure dizziness, for I no longer knew what my station was nor in what voice I was about to answer this man.

The student of sixteen years training in obedience was dead, as dead as if the body still lay cold on the cold stone flags. The perfect detachment of yesterday also was gone; I had awakened without it and not noticed the change. The fellow who had tried twice to object to very minor inconveniences was neither of the Nazhurets I knew. I heard him squeak my own confusion and I did not recognize the man. I was nauseated. I lost my balance.

I think I fell to my knees, for I remember Powl holding me up, stronger than he looked, with the small hands with little gold rings about the fingers. He put my seat down on a bench.

"Boy," he said, "I understand. Don't worry about it. Such moments were not made to be held to. What is necessary is simply . . . faith. Or obstinacy. That what happened did happen." He let me go then and began to pace, his shoes with their lacquered heels making surprisingly little noise against the floor. "That, actually, is the only legitimate meaning of the much-abused word 'faith.' It is the . . . the cussedness . . . to insist that what we knew to be true remains true, in the face of confusion and distraction. When it is hidden from us. Because . . ."

And he looked sharply into my face. "Because we were not made to live constantly in a glow of divine illumination."

He sighed and rubbed his lips with the tip of a finger. "Most people, I think, experience all the inutterable perceptions of a saint, a sage, or a scholar in their own times. Burghers, smiths, soldiers like yourself: all ripe for blinding illuminations. But these perceptions can't be readily communicated, called for at will, or stored in a jar against future need, so . . ."

He paced. "The perceiver first classifies them as undependable and later, useless, and finally, unreal. Most ordinary people are so practiced at this negation that by the time they are in their midteens they suffer their sudden understandings as though they were bellyaches and are quickly over them. The sage or the ecstatic, on the other hand..."

His face tightened. "Do I have it right, Nazhuret, or am I previous, and you were only swooning from insufficiency of food?"

I told him he had it, and that as Zhurrie the Goblin was certainly dead, and peace-filled Nazhuret the Revisitor seemed to have disappeared also, I had no idea who was talking to him at all. I stared not at the floor but at his gleaming shoes, soiled by September dew and forest mulch only a bit on the sides of the toes, and he patted me on the head, where I would have been bald had I been Powl.

"That is a very good beginning," he said to me.

The clothing in the bundle—that I was to wear and wash out nightly—was a coarse handweave shirt as well as woolen knee breeches, stockings, and wooden clogs. "I am to dress like a peasant and wash like a lord?" I asked him, trying not to make it sound like a protest.

"Yes," he replied, with his grin turned away from me. "And eat like a lady and talk like a scholar with a long gray beard. All these things, you see, are perfection in their own variety, and perfection is what we strive for."

I was grateful for the lack of mirror in the room, not because I thought I looked so much worse in the poor clothes but because I was very much afraid I would find they looked more appropriate on me than my frock coat. "Peasant shirts are more perfect than... than linen and pearls, Master Powl? Then what about—"

"No 'Master,' Nazhuret. Just 'Powl.' And as for my own dress—if it is any of your business—I am in disguise."

Powl glanced over me with satisfaction as I stood before him in my rude finery, and I was more and more certain he thought it the right clothing for the sort of person I was. I was tempted to remind him about Sordaling School and its rules for admission, but among the lessons I had learned at that school was that many things were for sale that were not supposed to be salable, and how could I say that admission for a low-born or bastard son was not among these? I held my peace. He fed me more cheese, bread, and beer, until the natural man in me began to climb out of his stupor.

"Do you remember why you came here and why you stayed, Nazhuret?" Powl ate more slowly than I and far more delicately, so that I had been waiting across the table from him for five minutes.

"I remember. . ." I began, and then memories that had seemed perfect and coherent as long as I didn't look directly at them began to behave alarmingly. "I came because of a dream," I answered at last, "and I stayed because you. . ." and here I became unsure of myself, wretchedly so, so that it was almost impossible to continue. Powl prodded me. "Because I what, lad? Speak."

"Because you called me back. From death."

Powl skinned an apple. Its fragrance filled the air, even overwhelming the cheese. "Called you back from death? Now, how could I do that?"

I don't know where my anger came from, but I was shouting, "Don't make fun of me that way! You were only an hour ago saying that I must believe my own memories, that it required cussedness that was actually faith, that—"

He waved me down with a light gesture. "No, I'm not making fun of you. It was a legitimate question. By what power could I call a man back from death? I'm not God, I assure you, nor some prescientific notion of a wizard."

This outraged me, for although I didn't confuse the man with the Almighty, yet he was exactly my "prescientific" idea of a wizard. "And yet you did it."

"I don't think so," answered Powl, so very mildly I was ashamed for my temper. "Examine your memories again. In all honesty."

I could not; what had been so coherent the day before had become as cluttered and handleless as the dream that brought it about. "I don't remember. I don't even remember why I'm here."

"You can leave again." Ever so coolly, Powl began to eat the skin he had carefully excised from the apple.

This left me utterly blank. "Leave? But you said you would be my teacher."

"So you remember something, then. But what is it I am to teach you?"

I thought mightily but could remember nothing of the experience relevant. Except how easily he had beaten me at my own skill. "Swordwork, I imagine. Isn't that it?"

Powl laughed outright, which I doubt a proper lady would have done with a mouthful of apple. "You are asking me? Like that? You have no idea, yourself, and yet you've sat here and chided me . . ."

I could only shake my head.

He put his knife and his tine sticks down and wiped his fingers with a clean handkerchief. "We could certainly begin with that, Nazhuret. If it's swordwork that interests you, I can teach you to be the most deadly deulist in all of Vestinglon and the Territories."

I blushed to think how easily taken in he thought me. "I'm not really so interested in it—"

"So much the better."

"It's only that since you have reason to know you're so much better than I am, I naturally thought—"

"Naturally."

"But Master—Powl—I have to be honest. I have ranked third out of two hundred at Sordaling and after all these years I'm as good as I'm going to get. I work the rapier hours each day and I know I have reached my limits."

His wide, colorless eyes had no expression as he answered, "That would be too bad if that were true, but I don't think it is."

I sought to excuse myself, for calling myself third of Sordaling had not been my idea of a pitiful confession, and Powl's "that would be too bad if that were true" really rankled. Still, the man had played cat and mouse with me. "I have been fighting with wooden swords or steel ones since I was four. Though always the smallest in my sessions, I had to stand there and take it and take it until I could figure out how to turn it aside—and I did learn, despite my years and despite my size. That is the school system. Can you think of a better, more realistic one for producing able fighters?"

I was quite amazed to see Powl lose his temper, even though it was only revealed with a sneer and a slap to the table. "I can think of none worse!" He rose, and his lacquered heels glinted in the light of the high windows as he strode in high energy to and fro, striking the hanging buttons from his path so that they swung to and fro in the air like reapers' blades.

Silently, I began to clear the table. I kept back the bread heels and the scraps of cheese and the rest of the apple skin in case he was about to toss me out, for I had no idea where I would go in that event.

Not back, certainly.

Powl returned to me and in his hands he held something in a sheet of flannel. I sat on the stair of the platform beside him as he unwrapped the item.

It was the size and shape of the bottom of a small bucket and about a thumb's length in thickness. It was clear, perfect glass, with only a touch of green in its makeup when examined along the diameter. "It's a lens," I said, fairly sure of my information.

He propped it on his knees, and his round face looked like a happy cat's. "It is a lens. I'm glad we can start with that understanding. Now, do you know exactly what a lens is?"

His brightness dimmed a little when I could only say it was something made of glass. "To help see things," I added, and that cheered him again.

"Yes. This is to help see things. Everything taught is merely to help us see things. Nazhuret, I will teach you the arts of conflict, since that is your background, and as I have heard said, one can only teach a person what he already knows. I will also teach you five languages, two of which are dead and one of which has—for you—what are called magical properties. Together we will study dancing, too, and a sort of history more accurate than that fed you poor brutes at your school. But the only perfect teaching—the only treasure I have—I can give you in a few words, right now.

"You, Nazhuret, once of Sordaling, are the lens of the world: the lens through which the world may become aware of itself. The world, on the other hand, is the only lens in which you can see yourself. It is both lenses together that make vision." He paused, terribly still.

"Do you understand me?"

I listened, and I looked into the cool clearness of this immense glass, which showed me magnified the fine pink fingers of Powl and the glint of gold and the blue-rose-colored drop of a discreet ruby on one of those rings, and superimposed over all this the ghost of my own face, turned upside down and thus unknowable to me. I had to put both hands over my face and retreat into darkness.

He asked me again, "Do you understand me, Nazhuret?"

The words, meaningless to me, were locked in the dark box of my head, and like powder charges, were set to go off. I knew about handling powder charges, and knowing they were locked in with me and the fuse ignited, I began to sweat.

For a moment I saw myself from above as I had briefly the day before. For a moment I felt the blackness that preceded death. Then I remembered more.

I opened my eyes again and let go of Powl's words.

"I don't understand at all, Powl. Not at all. And I can't think. My head fills instead with memories of . . . of before I knew I ought to come back."

"Good." He nodded forcefully, as though I had said something profound instead of failing the test completely. "Knew *you ought* to come back. No nonsense about my calling . . ." He nodded and nodded. To himself.

"Good, Nazhuret. We have a very strong beginning."

Memories only remain connected, so that they make a tale that moves from third hour to fourth hour to noon, in situations so utterly new that our minds cannot otherwise catalog them. Once we have begun to feel comfortable—to understand or to give up understanding all things around us— we group memories in clumps of like experiences. (I am told, however, that it is not the same for idiots, who remember each incident of their unsuccessful lives as sequential, unique, and inexplicable. Though I have been called a simpleton all my life, I am glad my memories have not been so drearily particular as this.)

My recollection of my first whole day with Powl switches from the first mode of memory to the second at about the time just described. Sometime later in the afternoon he took a set of keys and led me through various doors into the odd-shaped rooms that made up the rest of the volume of this round building within a square one.

There was a spare but perfectly comfortable bedroom that boasted a fireplace not set into the wall but pounded out of what seemed to be pieces of old body armor (both of horse and man) and served by a flimsy exhaust pipe, and a storage room where grain was kept very tidily in glass and ceramic with rubber gaskets and where wooden crates rose almost to the low ceiling, along with a far more interesting collection of sabers, rapiers, disassembled pistols, lance cannons, caltrops, and other instruments to eviscerate, maim and otherwise discourage one's friends. The room at the third corner smelled of fuller's earth; it had certain of the flags lifted, and a great displacement of the earth beneath them was scattered over the remaining floor. Atop the hole in the flags was a thigh-high iron box with a matching hole in its top. The entirety was described to me (reluctantly, it seemed) as a "work in progress."

The fourth corner was a fairly up-to-date kitchen, complete with an oven of iron similar to but heavier than the affair in the bedroom. It did not appear to be used.

Why Powl had left me the night before on a hard bench when there were battens and blankets so near at hand puzzled me for a while—he certainly had not used them himself, and it didn't seem he feared my personal cattle would infect his property, for now he gave me the ring of black keys with no hesitation. I can only suppose he had wanted to give me every opportunity for walking out, if my instincts had run in that direction.

That afternoon he gave me the second of my regular defeats at arms, this time simply saber to saber, but it did not appear that the exercise had his full attention, and before evening he left me again, with food to cook and wood to cut and a very serious charge: I was to discover the central purpose of the building in which I now lived, and I was to be able to operate it competently by daybreak.

He left me paper and pen for figuring, if I should need it, and beer for solace. Everything but candles for light he left me, and when I pointed out the omission he walked out the door, laughing, saying that the building operated best without candles.

My king, I know it seems ridiculous to a man of your

43

breadth of experience that I did not know in what sort of place I was, but remember the single-purposedness of my up-bringing, and remember also that it was twenty-one years ago, and many things that are ordinary now were marvelous then, or even unknown.

First, because it had been so much in my thoughts, I approached the "rack" in the corner. It possessed a great oak wheel on an axle of iron, and protruding from the rim of the wheel was a handle also of oak and iron, parallel in line to the axle itself. I had difficulty turning this wheel, both because of the resistance of the machinery and because the wheel stood so tall that at the handle's highest point I could scarcely reach it and could put almost no force into the rotation. Below the mechanism I placed a box from the storage room, and by stepping on and off once for each revolution I worked the thing with a will.

It seemed it did nothing but creak and cause the building to creak. I stopped my efforts and regarded the contrivance again. To the best of my knowlege, nothing had changed. Since I could not lubricate the wooden wheels, I lubricated myself instead, and sat upon the steps of the central platform with a mug of warmish, still beer.

The buttons were moving on their strings and the sun shone its last light through the fault in the ceiling. Beer is not conducive to mental exercise but rest is, and when I rose again I went to the kitchen stove, took from its belly a damp piece of charcoal, and smeared lines over all the meeting places of the gears within the machine, or at least all that could be reached. I worked the thing again until it was growling all around me, and then I observed what progress I had made.

None of the lines met anymore. Some had moved only slightly, and some bore traces of having run their circle through more than once. The bigger gears seemed, in general, to have moved least.

This ought to have been most significant, but my brain refused to lead me any farther. Gears existed to speed movement, to slow it down, or to change the direction of it. These gears were of many sizes and moved up and down, sideways, and in both diagonals, but seemed to be connected to nothing except each other. And the building, of course.

It had grown dark during my last flurry of pumping, and I had suddenly in my mind an even darker vision of myself slowly pushing this square shell of bricks and mortar over the crest of the hill it sat upon, until it would overbalance itself and crash into the trees below. It seemed the sort of joke an inexplicable man like Powl would find humorous. In sudden panic I ran out through the hall and out the heavy door, to find the sun was still in the sky, and the path exactly where I'd left it that afternoon.

I was inspired to leave, to return to Sordaling School with a story of sudden illness, amnesia, attack from townies. Now that I think back, sir, I doubt there was a day in my peculiar education that I was not overcome at least momentarily by an impulse to drop the effort and run. Except for three days, which I shall describe after this is done.

I went back in and poured another beer. It was very dark inside now, and only the swinging brass buttons of the ceiling caught sunlight through the clerestory windows. I glanced out through the crack in the roof and beheld the first stars, and only then did it become obvious to me that the pole, the slot, the entire roof of the building had moved—that the squat dome, the crowded clerestories, and the clumsy key frieze were no chance ornaments of a builder without artistic taste but instead the inevitable concomitants of a roof designed to spin like a top.

A very slow, cumbersome top.

Questions are never really answered, but only replaced by larger questions. Why on earth would a man want to move the roof of his house in a circle? That under certain circumstances he might want to move the house itself over the ground I could accept. That he might want to replace the roof to the left or the right according to rain or wind direction also was comprehensible, though practically speaking it was enough that it merely cover the floor well. This pierced, flawed, and ponderously mobile dome seemed beyond reason.

Yet one thing had led to five or six others in my researches, and I was inclined toward faith in the reasonableness of this ugly brick building. I left off beer and conjecture and mounted the platform.

The great tube ended in a smaller, polished tube, which in its turn was completed by a round lip of brass like the neck of a bottle. It occurred to me that perhaps Powl's intent was to capture dew or rain, but when I inserted my finger into the hole I thought I felt it blocked by something hard. It was a tiny opening anyway, and hard to feel with the fingers. The tube itself rang hollow to knuckles; it made a shivery, almost sweet sound.

On the Zaquashlon southern coast, at Morbin Harbor, there stands a cannon as long as this very tube, and like it, the cannon is made of brass. It can carry a ball of iron for three miles out to sea, and its purpose is to terrify the pirates of Felonk, who harry the shores.

Though the Felonkan are a round people, however, their ships are light and wasplike and balanced on wasp-legged pontoons, and never has this fearsome weapon managed to hit a ship clean on or even to swamp one, though I am told men have been washed off the decks and drowned. If ever it did hit a ship, I'm sure the destruction would be total.

On its way to emplacement on the harbor cliffs, the Morbin Harbor cannon was paraded through Vestinglon and afterward Sordaling, pulled by thirty chestnut brewery horses. We of the school were brought to examine it, and I remember that the barrel of the cannon was very heavy, so that it made little ring when beaten by the fists.

There was a chair on the platform, placed not under the tube but to one side. Its brocade seat was well and particularly worn, as by the posterior of a single man applied many times. I sat on that chair (feeling a slight sense of sacrilege) but found no virtue in the act, nor was there anything to be seen or heard there. Of course, the chair was not attached to the tube but to the platform by its own weight. If the tube moved (as it must) with the roof...

I sought a stick or a pencil and could find nothing but the piece of charcoal I had sharpened against the gears of the roof-engine. I inserted this into the lip of the tube and found it was actually blocked by something hard. In an effort to discover whether the blockage was complete, I managed to break the charcoal in the declivity and fill it, whether-or-no. I peered into the brass ring stuffed with gray dirt and was no wiser. Most heavy guns, the Morbin Harbor cannon among them, are barrel-loaders, and this thing had no obvious juncture between the large bore section and the end section. But it was possible that strength inherent in the unbroken nature of this instrument was worth the extra trouble inherent in a long muzzle-loader. Perhaps such a cannon might be easier to drill to specifications. More accurate.

Though a ladder would be very necessary. . . .

Powl's parting words, that this place operated better without candles, now seemed heavily significant. The man certainly didn't want to give me any opportunity to shoot off the huge gun at random, or to blow up the emplacement. I began to consider breaking open the crates in the storage rooms in search of black powder or gun cotton.

Destroying things seemed beyond the scope of my assignment here, and though I was more and more alarmed each minute and less at one with the purposes of a man who kept a dog with such terrible teeth, still I could not be sure. I determined to go slowly and be certain.

Next I discovered something that excited me strongly, and

that was that the single attaching strut of the tube to the platform was no mere support, but a complex levered pipe that would raise and lower the tube along the slot in the roof. To prove true sane intent in the construction of this mad machine, nothing more was necessary than to find that there was an awning of canvas that followed the tube down, covering the fault in the roof entirely, so that if the thing were laid flat against the bottom of the dome, the roof was impervious to rain and dew, if not to wind.

It seemed likely that the blockage in the end of the tube was a fuse, broken off below level, as so often happens with fuses. The endpiece did seem to be threaded, but I did not manage to get it entirely off to check my suppositions, and I feared to break such an intricate piece of machinery—whether good or evil as I feared, it was obviously quite expensive.

There remained one more test for what was becoming a fond theory: If the building was a huge, immovable cannon, it must be aimed at something.

In the last light of the sun and the first light of the moon I went out again to examine the hill's horizon. It was trees and blackness, except in one direction: the direction of the road whence I had come. I returned to the "rack," worked prodigiously, and looked again.

The next morning I was awake when Powl arrived, for I had not slept. He clearly did not expect the accusation written in my eyes. He dropped a large pack, under which he had been sweating.

"So you know?" he asked me, dry and ironic.

"It is fearful," I replied. "It is fearful and traitorous and I wish I had not seen it pointed straight for my city and home."

"That's where I thought you had pointed it," he answered. "It is what I would expect from a lad your age—to look straight at the lights of the city. There are higher targets, believe me."

I was very angry. "Higher? There is Vestinglon itself, and

the palace, I suppose. But to have a cannon this size pointed at the second city of Velonya and its military capital is enough. I had hoped"—and here I was stuck between anger and a strange embarrassment—"I had hoped that you had only found this place, had overcome the traitorous element and—"

Powl's jaw dropped and his eyebrows rose commensurately. "As a matter of fact, I had no hand in this construction. It was Adlar Diskomb himself who had it built, and who hanged himself from this very ceiling, though whether he was a traitor to do so is more than I can say. But for the rest of your accusation, Nazhuret, son of—of Sordaling School, I am totally bemused.

"A cannon? Do you think you are living in a gun bunker of some kind?" He climbed the platform in two steps and dragged the chair over to the end of the tube. He looked closely into the brass lip and cried out like a bird.

"Deity! What have you done, boy? Idiot! Hooligan! You've broken the eyepiece, and how I am ever going to remove it, let alone grind a replacement. . . ."

I was about to tell him I was glad if I had, but his attitude was so much that of outraged innocence that I was losing faith in my own inductions, and I merely stood stubborn. If this were not a brass gun aimed at Sordaling, I could not guess what it was.

Then the charcoal fell out from where I had wedged it and Powl gave a great groan of relief. He put his eye to and made the sort of face one makes when looking hard. He twisted the adjustment.

He began to laugh, with great good humor. Then he bade me look through. At last he told me what an astronomical observatory was.

So I failed my first test and failed it spectacularly, and by all rights Powl should have booted me out the door then and there. He was always an inexplicable man, however, and as

soon as he assured himself that my monkeying had not destroyed either the telescope nor the roof mechanism, he sat
down on the platform steps and asked me to explain to him
how I had concluded that the thing was a cannon aimed at
the city. I remember, sitting lower, as I was, that his shoes
were glossy, caramel brown with gold threads in the laces.

I showed him the marks on the gears and explained how
the sun's disappearance from its obvious path of descent had
clued me to the dome's movement, and how the blockage
(opaque, once past the test of charcoal) had led me to understand that the tube was hollow but closed at this end, and
how the geography of the hill conspired to allow the tube to
point straight down at the lamps of Sordaling and almost
nowhere else, except at the empty sky. It had seemed obvious
that no man would build such an enormous thing to look up
into the empty sky.

Powl congratulated me at having been so brilliantly wrong.
In this he seemed (most unlike him) not ironical at all. That
morning he set me the task of sitting still and thinking seriously
about the twin concepts of what was obvious and what was
empty.

Perhaps if I had been easier to live with, Powl might have
stopped more in the observatory with me, but I was nineteen,
and the joints of my body were so fluid (so it seems, looking
back) that it was less difficult to keep moving than it was to
pause. Besides, I was totally unpracticed in the art of sitting
still and very used to being kept hopping. I would begin the
morning before light, getting wood for the stove, and by the
time my teacher came to the five-hundred weight door, I would
have bathed and had breakfast ready—Powl's second breakfast, I suspected, though I did not dare ask.

Then he would set me to some bodily endeavor: sword
forms or dancing strapped with meal sacks fore and aft or

beating three over four on my knees, while he sat in the doorway and read a book brought with him for that purpose. Afterward, with the noon sun squeezing in through the high windows to whiten the dusty air, he would lecture on the subject of optics. I was not to take notes, but to remember.

My responses to this branch of his curriculum were predictable. First I would twitch, then I would wiggle, and finally I would fall asleep. If free, I would paw the prisms and sample blanks from hand to hand and roll them down my knees until they were so covered with finger grease and woolen lint they were useless for illustration, and if tied (Powl resorted to tying me to the platform banister), I found myself subject to loud, distracting spells of asthma.

My teacher was alarmed, and though I do not blame him, I think he must have had very little experience with boys. By the end of the first week he had shelved optics in favor of teaching me to sit still and listen. Another few days and he decided to concentrate further: on sitting still.

"Nazhuret, I have a simple assignment for you," he said. "I can guarantee you success in it." We had been sparring with sword balks wrapped in rags when a sudden shower had caught us and driven us indoors.

Though I had looked forward to the bout, I was equally glad to be distracted from it, for there is only so much satisfaction to be won being rapped silly or knocked down repeatedly. I told him I was at his service.

"This is not my service, but your own. I want you to sit down here—I'll carry the chair into this corner here, facing right in to the bricks. Now I will lash your wrists to this very finely carved ornament and your feet to the little lion feet."

Having trussed me to his satisfaction, he leaned his head over my shoulder, ascertaining that my view was dull indeed, and clapped me on the shoulder. "There. Now I will leave you for exactly half an hour there, and you can shuffle and pant and wheeze to your heart's content. I will trust to God you don't stop breathing, but after all, that's your business." He turned to leave.

"Wait, sir," I called after. "What about my assignment? What is it I am to *do* while I sit here and wait for you?"

I couldn't turn enough to see Powl behind me, but I could hear him clear his throat. "Your assignment?"

There were some moments of silence, and then he spoke. "You remember the country tale about the black wolf of Gelley that had nothing in its belly? Good. Well, your assignment is to consider all things in nature and without nature, but not the black wolf of Gelley. Understood: You do *not* think about that tale at all—anything else is acceptable. Pretty easy, hey?"

I had one more question: "What if there's a fire while you're gone?"

"Then you are a martyr to science," said my teacher, and he walked out into the rain.

I was tied in that spot every day for three weeks. The period of time was supposed to be half an hour, but I doubt it was ever that short. The observatory boasted no clock except the heavens. I can still close my eyes and see bricks before me, though at this remove I cannot say they are the same bricks. My breathing panics came and went, outlandish hungers came with their concomitant growls, spots wandered before my eyes, and always, always my thoughts made a regular, endless revolution around the black wolf of Gelley.

I saw this ludicrous nursery rhyme as a large dusty thing, with a triangular face, many white triangular teeth, and a ballooning stomach, clear and hollow like sausage casing. Sometimes it was being outmaneuvered by the old wife, as in verse two, and sometimes being chased by the young smith with the pincers, as in the penultimate verse. Usually, however, it had already eaten the dickeybird, which was now peck-pecking a hole out of its glassine stomach. I felt a strong sympathy with this shaggy, unsuccessful beast, for every day Powl hauled up a day's fresh provisions on his back or in a satchel under his arm, and every day it was not quite enough to fill me. He always seemed surprised.

In my third week of residence I admitted my total failure to keep the damned black thing out of my thoughts, and suggested that extra nutrition might help me to concentrate. If it were the exchequer that was short (I felt diffident about suggesting this), I could gather and sell wood in the nearby townships.

But Powl wanted me in the observatory for the next little while, he said. He would make the task easier. I need only avoid thinking of that hard, clear, and empty stomach itself; the rest of the wolf was free to me, along with the old wife, the young smith, and the dickeybird.

Such riches.

One morning I found I had ceased to care whether I was bound to the chair or not, for it was all the same by the end of the half hour, and as though at that signal, Powl stopped tying me. But I had no such luck as far as the essentials of the study were concerned. From the moment I applied buttock to brocade, my attention dove into the thwarted empty stomach of the black wolf. I strove against it, and the experience was not restful. I rose from the chair ready to sit myself right down again, but free of the wolf's stomach.

At the end of another week my hands were shaking. Had I had a mirror that was not concave, I'm certain it would have shown me looking much older. Then Powl, with a great show of concern, admitted he had misspoken himself and probably caused all my confusion. What he had meant to say was that I was forbidden only the nothing in the belly of the wolf; the membrane itself was fair play.

In this manner I learned to sit still. It was a frightening thing, but I learned to live in the belly of the wolf. Ofttimes I wish there was still someone who would tie me up.

. . .

We had an early winter. It seems all the large changes of my life take place at the year's failing.

Rain ate away all the colors of the leaves. The ground beneath the trees turned soggy black and then white with frost. I wore both my peasant shirts at once and was still blue-fingered, for no ingenious stove could heat a place with a slot in the roof covered only by canvas.

Powl would come up the hill with his lantern like a small star through the woods. It might be as late as eight and a half o'morning, but it would still be dark in here. That yellow star was nearly the only one we saw that first season, as he was teaching me the nature of lenses and of the sky. I had to take his lessons (all his lessons) with a great deal of faith.

He ground lenses in the weak daylight and I watched him, and then I ground mirrors for him (they are easier) as he lectured. I found it easier to grind and listen than just to listen. We tested the glass I worked by its spectra and con-vergence against a sheet of white paper glued to the wall, and sometimes my work ended as a telemetric mirror and some-times it was a paperweight. Either way, Powl packed it all up and took it away again, down the hill, where I couldn't follow.

My first foreign language under Powl's tutelage was Allec, the language of the arts, which (he explained) is the language of no one alive and therefore equally unfair to all students. I had thought I knew some Allec, since all the vocabulary of armory and court ménage is in that rusty tongue, but to Powl Allec was not a series of identifying nouns but a language like Zaquash or Modern Velonyie, in which one might haggle over fish, or describe where one found the bird sitting, which was not native to these inland hills.

For three months we spoke nothing but Allec in the ob-servatory. Powl became a different person in that language. Where in Modern Velonyie he was smooth and ironical, when he spoke Allec he became quick, rattling, pressing, acquisitive, even rapacious. One might sell carpets, having an intonation like Powl's Allec intonation, and make a very good living at it, too.

But Allec is the universal language of studies, and perhaps what was revealed there was only Powl's character as a student rather than as a man of the world.

My Allec personality was mute for many weeks.

After the first few days of trying to translate everything in my mind into the damnable, shower-of-pebbles sounds, I suddenly began to think in Allec, and since I knew so very few Allec words, I could scarcely think, let alone communicate my simple desires. I remember standing in front of my teacher with tears in my eyes and a frying pan in my right hand, trying to tell him I could not get the burned egg off without some of his jeweler's rouge, without knowing the word for egg or for washing. I would have used Velonyie, but at this point I had lost the use of the first language and not gained the second.

It was about then that Powl brought me the bag of colored glass marbles—in illustration of some point of optics, no doubt—and I grabbed on to them with childish fervor. I carried marbles with me everywhere and kept a close record of my successes at eightsie and yard circles. I made charts of distance rolled according to color and to size. When I lost one—a red one—in the detritus of the earth closet Powl had me digging, I went into a panic that all my work would be invalidated.

By New Year I had to be chided for talking to myself. In Allec. I was breaking down.

Remember how alone I was, sir, with no company but that of Powl, and he there only from morning till midafternoon. I had thrown my future away without reflection and now lost the language of my mind as well. In return, what did I have? Only beginnings. I could grind lenses and only half needed to be thrown out. I could dance about seven exotic dances, but only alone, of course. I had a little bit of chattering Allec.

I could listen and remember. Much better. Those, at least, much better.

Now that I no longer writhed like a cat in a bag when I sat in a chair, Powl no longer had to take his half-hour walks in the wintry woods. Mostly I practiced my attention after he had gone. I was very used to it, and in this one manner, at least, felt in command of my own mind. After a few weeks of this routine I felt a cramp in my leg calf and massaged it away, and was bucked up to find I felt as in command of myself in movement as I was on my buttocks. I got up and walked around the telescope platform, feeling very light and free and on top of things. I adjusted the telescope down to the horizon and experimented with observation in this state of mind.

The next day I did not sit down at all, but set the clock to impose the state of attention upon myself and went directly to my Allec studies. After a few days of this I forgot the clock completely, and when Powl walked in on me, late one afternoon right after New Year, he found me on my knees with the marbles again, talking to myself and making noises with every strike.

I felt him beside me just before he spoke. I looked up, feeling alarm and not knowing why; I had so completely forgotten what I was supposed to be doing.

"I was afraid it was a mistake from the beginning," he said. He walked to the storeroom, where he had stored my gentle clothes in a wax-lined box, like perishable fruit. "Take these. Go.

"Out."

I was too shocked to remonstrate. I felt the blood drain from my face and hands so completely I could scarcely stand. Some small part of me wondered where it went. Only when dressed as a town buck again, standing in two inches of snow

56

outside the steel-wrapped door, did it occur to me that I was ill used. That the punishment in no way fit the crime.

I had nowhere to go; I was destitute. I had traded my future away, and if it was a very mediocre future, it was all I had, and had placed myself in that man's power as completely as a dog. After five minutes I was shivering and I hadn't moved.

Enormous disaster. And why? I had trouble remembering. Because I had played marbles when I was supposed to sit still. Had there ever been a dog that did not nose into the trash bin sometime in its life? Did a man throw out his dog just for that?

No, he beat him. Powl beat me daily, about the head with clubs sometimes, and though it was not meant as a punishment, surely I deserved something out of all that beating.

Numbness resolved into self-pity, but then a look at that invincible door shook me into horror again. I sank down against a tree and wrapped myself in my arms. I could not think at all. Images of the city and the school (alternatives to squatting here and freezing in the snow) were forced up but faded instantly, like the colors on a prism when clouds cover the sun. Everything was white and black. My hands were the color of dirty snow.

It got later. Darker.

From behind the door Powl said to get away or he would throw the dishwater on me. He was very calm, and his voice was so cold I could scarcely breathe. I heard the bolt draw back.

I rose, fell, and scrambled up again. I withdrew fifty feet, not along the path but into the woods, and as soon as the shadows hid me I squatted down again. I had nowhere to go and no notion of going anywhere.

I heard Powl leave. His feet went down the path, making dry, ripping noises in the snow. In the last light I went back to the door, hoping he had left it open. Surely he had. I had no coat, and he could not want me to die.

The door was locked. There was a blanket folded on the step, and pinned to the oak was a note, reading (not in Allec): GO BACK TO THE CITY.

I went back to the woods instead. I peeled some pine branches and lay down on them, wrapped in the blanket. After a few hours the moon rose, just past full. It made everything bright black and white: very clear, like the clarity with which I had been dismissed.

I did not sleep that night, but I did a little in the sun the next day. Powl did not come to the observatory. I considered following him down the hill and pleading with him at whatever place he spent the rest of his time, but my obedience had been at least this perfect—I had stayed where I was put and never followed him home. I did follow his bootprints in the snow, but as the hill road met the main road, the going got drier and there was nothing to be seen. I saw no one nor any trace of hearth smoke in the sky. I returned up the hill.

That night was a little warmer, and the slush was harder to bear than the snow had been. I swept the stone step off with branches and curled up on it.

I had considered the matter endlessly. I had eaten snow and listened to my stomach and decided that Powl was right about me after all. I had failed at everything, even at this unheard-of opportunity to become—what? I didn't even know, but unheard-of opportunity nonetheless. I was ugly, undersized, and played marbles when I should be long grown up. Worse, I had returned by special dispensation from death—yes, from death, dramatic as that sounded—to do no more than to play marbles. It was now appropriate that I freeze to death. One more night should do it; I felt dizzy enough already.

All this interior conversation was, of course, in Allec.

Sometime during the middle of the night it occurred to me that it was poor manners to freeze on Powl's front stoop like this. It would look like an insult directed toward him, and I felt no desire to insult him worse. I staggered up, but my feet would not work. I crawled on my knees over the thawing ground and dropped myself in the shadow of the trees. It was too wet to die there. It was unbearable. I turned back to the building, on my feet this time, and decided Powl would have to put up with finding me.

I heard him coughing. I heard the key. "I don't think I can carry you today, Nazhuret," he said. In Allec.

I was spread out on the step of his observatory. An insult to him. How embarrassing. "It was too wet to lie out there," I said in exculpation and then remembered I was supposed to be dead. This stymied me. When Powl began to drag me in over the threshold, I was too confused and clumsy to help.

No amount of sitting before the fire would warm me; I was lowered into a large tub, which was supposed to become part of the earth closet, and buckets of hot water were splashed over. First I roused and then I shivered and by the time I had ceased shivering, I was so sore in every muscle that I felt I had been tied to a post and beaten. This, I find, is the usual aftereffect of near-freezing, but despite my upbringing in snowy Velonya I had never been so cold before. I was put to bed pink-fleshed and wrinkled with water, feeling bright and curious and without a trace of intelligence.

So the autumn produced my first death and the winter my second birth. All through this purgatory I thought in the Allec language, as Powl had taught me. I thought very simple, child-like things.

That day Powl sat by my bed, on the single chair the observatory possessed. He looked gray and old, leaning against the chair's spindly arm. Occasionally he coughed.

"I was too sick to make it up the hill yesterday," he said as I was sitting up, eating the very bad soup he had prepared for me. The stove was sending gouts of smoke out the kitchen door and up through the vent in the roof; Powl was never expert at its use.

I said that I hoped he was better, and he merely sighed. He did not touch the soup himself. He sat wrapped in a large cloak with capes upon it, of gorgeous subdued coloring. Perhaps he was shivering. "It may be . . . that I was coming down with the chill the day previous. It is going around in the city, I hear."

The soup was greasy and lacking in salt, but I had finished it. I was thoroughly warm by now and got up pink and shining from the bed. My town clothes were dry again from being suspended near the stove, but so smoke-smirched that they would need a thorough fullering to be presentable. I threw both peasant shirts over my head instead, and Powl didn't stop me.

I shook out the bedclothes. "Then here. I don't need it anymore, Powl. I'm very warm."

He shook his head, refusing the bed. "I think, Nazhuret, that perhaps my decisions of that day were colored by illness."

As I heard my teacher come so close to apologizing—to me—I began to shiver again. Having gone so far in mind to reconcile myself to disaster, failure, and death, I could go no farther. It was too much that the whole experience might have been simply a mistake. Powl's error. My misery and cold simply my teacher's feverish blunder.

I denied it. I told him I deserved every word and worse. That I only wanted the opportunity to prove I had learned from it. I fixed the stove, added salt to the soup, and put on a hot stone to warm Powl's feet for him. He gave me one sad glance and did not bring up the matter again.

That evening he was much better. That night, when I was alone, the fever descended on me and Powl found me sweating and babbling in Allec the next morning.

I was very sick for two weeks, and for two weeks he slept on wool batts beside my bed.

It was haying season, was it not, when I sent my last missive to you, sir? I remember the envelope was thick enough to chink a good-size hole in a stone wall.

All these walls are wood, and the wet wind is blowing through them now. I am using two stones, a faultily ground lens, and the hilt of an old throwing dagger to hold the paper down, and what drops I flick from the pen travel westerly before hitting back into the inkwell.

In the distance I see the shapes of men tilted against the rain and wind, their great hat brims sodden and heavy. This ought to be the oat harvest, and I ought to help. But in fact there is nothing more useful to do than go watch the rain beat the ripe grain flat, and the peasants can do that without my assistance.

Yesterday evening I was at the local hostelry, bargaining labor against a barrel of summer's ale, and I was forced to step on three physical quarrels aborning. From my own experience I know that tavern fights in autumn are inauspicious omens, like thick hair growing on the horses. It is only September, too.

I can ask no better way to fill these sullen days than with this history. Let me clear autumn from my soul and push the inevitable winter to one side, for in my narrative now the nineteen-year-old Nazhuret has survived one autumn and one winter in his peculiar, enforced hermitage.

I will stare at the glass of the rainy window for a minute and gather memories in place of oats.

Beginning in early spring the weather cleared, and my daily study of glass and of star maps suddenly proved itself. I spent half my days asleep and half my nights adding to Adlar's charts of the Northern Hemisphere.

I took to stargazing as I had earlier to marbles, with a solitary, intricate passion. I had good eyes, even for my age, and the old astronomer's equipment was of the best. Coming to the science with no background at all, I did not have the handicaps of the constellation pictures between myself and the twinkles I saw in the lens. Borlad the Red Eye, of mythological fame, was of no more celestial importance through the lens than the pale bluish dot I called the Midnight Candle and that Powl cataloged as 1904D. (I did not know what the "D" stood for.) The various colorations of the stars intrigued me; why some should be distinctly red and others flickering blue while most were so chaste a silver . . .

I remembered how when serving in the horse-ménage at school, I was taught to heat the coal forge until the flame, viewed from the side, was blue and the shoes heated to dull cherry. I asked Powl whether the colors of the stars could have anything to do with their heat (I was not so ignorant as not to know the stars were hot), and he had no answer for me.

I also tracked the four planets through their orbits with the same scrupulous, star fancier's care. It had been done already by Adlar and years earlier on other, smaller instruments, but I seemed to feel the great bodies needed my own verification before they could be quite predictable.

Also this spring I studied animal movement, spying on the hunting badgers through the frost. Powl stepped up my program of martial exercise, not so much because he seemed to think it an important study but because it was springtime and the sweat was appropriate. He took to jumping out at me from hidden places both at home and in the neighboring woods. I found this habit of his very irritating and for a while it destroyed my serenity completely as I saw my enemy behind every tree and under each shadow. Once I remember, in a brake of dead ferns, spinning at some intimation of assault and punching a two-point buck deer between the eyes.

I hurt my hand, but I knocked the creature cold.

Sometime while I was so occupied, perhaps as the narcissi were blooming on the acid mulch of the forest floor, Velonya declared war against the Falink Islands, in retaliation for their multiplying raids against our coast. Also at this time King Ethelbhel died, some said after hearing of the destruction of the flagship *Bright Banner* within sight of the city of Vesinglon. Of the passage of both these events I was ignorant for over a year.

In these years half my study was stillness, but the complementary half was movement. I cannot teach or even describe the art of movement to you, sir, though I have sat here on a hard seat for the better part of an hour, ruining good paper in the effort. At Sordaling I was taught, "The world strikes back against every blow, and strikes exactly as hard as the blow delivered," but that is not the art of movement but only the science of it; the art I learned from the sly feet and clever elbows of my teacher, Powl. This was also how I learned much about the grass, for sometimes it was more inviting to lie flat and investigate the ragged croppings of the deer than to get up and be knocked down again.

If I give the impression that Powl taught me personal combat by beating me repeatedly, I do him wrong. He disapproved of such teaching, and knocked me down not out of punishment but by way of illustration. Unfortunately, there was so very much to illustrate. By the second year of my instruction I had been rolled over him, thrown under him, tripped, eluded, and simply lost so many dozens of times that upside down was as natural to me as walking. I began to move like a baby monkey, which was perhaps appropriate to my stature and face.

I was also as owlish as a baby monkey, from long unsociability, and in certain things as timid as I imagine a baby monkey to be.

At this time we were speaking in a language the source

and name of which I was not told. It was highly inflected and long in the vowels, with unpredictable diphthong combinations. Powl said it would someday be an important tongue to me and that its power to influence human thought was almost magical. (Almost magical is as close as that old magician ever admitted.)

I will always think of this as a lonely language, partly because I was so alone when it made up my days.

As summer ripened and I graduated from mirrors to prisms and spherical lens grinding and from sword dances to swordplay, Powl spent less time at the observatory: from morning to noon, usually, unless a clear night without moon tempted him to stay over. He also was more cheerful than he had been, that look of appraising worry removed from his oval face. He had lost his incipient plumpness and was more dapper than ever.

I thought perhaps he had taken a new mistress in that place he went to and came from every day, and I almost followed him to see. Almost. I had no hope of escaping unobserved.

I wondered if our eccentric, metaphysical undertaking (he had taught me the word "metaphysical," along with many others equally impressive) had lost savor for him and he was now using me for the sake of his own regular workouts only. I wondered, as I went through my day's schedule of stove, study, combat, delicate optical equipment, brick-beholding, stove again, dinner, wood-gathering, and laundry, whether I still was the Nazhuret returned from the dead or an unpaid servant of less than average mentality.

I felt a fool, and I felt totally in the power of Powl.

Who was he? I had always wondered what history was hidden behind the simple syllable, that very common name. Though in the beginning I had considered him too polite (and too tastefully dressed) to be of higher class than gentry, in this year his natural arrogance had time to shine through the overlay, and I was firmly convinced my teacher was of noble or royal birth. His scorn of anything smacking of birth privilege only gave evidence toward this, for no one can be as contemptuous of the aristocracy as an aristocrat.

Perhaps I thought this way merely to maintain my own self-respect. If I were to be as thoroughly bested by anyone as I was daily bested by Powl, let him be an opponent of the very highest rank. Let him be a baron, a viscount, an earl. . . .

(At this time I had no politics and fair manners. I still have no acceptable politics, but my king knows I have no manners either and can be equally abrupt to the gold cloak and the woolly shirt. Now I don't care who knocks me down.)

Either Powl had an income enough to support his high dress and moderate appetite as well as my enormous appetite and rough weave, or we were supporting us both on the lenses I made. I had no experience with the standard of lens grinding in the city, but I suspected my wares wouldn't run to tailored shoulders with gold piping, or three-inch lacquered heels.

A burgher might easily have supported me as I was, but what burgher would show so little interest in his business as to spend half his waking hours as Powl did? And how would a Sordaling burgher come to be far and away the best man in hand-to-hand combat I had ever encountered, or the smoothest saber fencer, deadly with the Felink tribesman's dowhee (which resembles a hedge trimmer remarkably), and a rapacious scholar besides?

And lastly, what man of any rank could spend so long in communion with another as Powl did with me—to give so much in instruction and so little of himself?

I would go, in the afternoons, along the paths of the woods toward where people lived. The observatory was not in a complete wilderness, certainly; it was only a few hours' walk from the city. There were two households and one cemetery in easy reach. I would prowl the frozen forest mulch in rag-wrapped feet or slog amid the thaw in my clogs until I found myself close enough to a human residence to spy easily, and then I would squat down and peer like an owl.

One place belonged to a turner, and when the weather was passable he would haul his lathe outside and cut his chair legs in the sunshine. I found this activity very entertaining, much like lens grinding and much different. He tied and piled his product under the steep eaves of the house, like cordwood, and once a week a van of one heavy horse came along the road and hauled it all away.

The turner made only one style of leg. I know, for in dry times under the full moon I stole in and examined it closely. It was a leg of three large swellings and three small ones, with a knob for the foot and a square area in the middle for the supporting dowels.

The turner lived alone. He moved oddly on his own legs, like a man in pain.

The other household was larger and contained a market gardener and his family. There was much more happening here: boys and girls chopping sticks, women hanging linen and wool on the line, the gardener himself bobbing in his fields like a log in fast water. Stiff. All of them stiff. But there was a dog at the house as well, a hairy dog of the loud and incorruptible kind, and so my visits were more covert.

One wet afternoon I met the wife in the woods. She was leaning against the bole of a tree, with a sack and a handful of acorns. Her cheeks were weather-red and her headscarf was tied under her chin, giving an impression of roundness to her face. From my direction she was hidden by the tree, so we came upon one another without warning.

The acorns went up in the air and she cried out. "Who are you? How did you get here?" she asked me. I, equally startled, sprang back like a cat with its tail afire. I stuttered an apology, which she could not understand, as it was in a foreign language, tried again and came out with Allec, and then I ran and she ran, in opposite directions. Halfway back to the observatory, it came to me that they might put the dog on my track, so I diverted like a fox, soaking my feet in a stream much deeper than my clogs.

I knew then that I had lost my credentials as a human.

The cemetery was safer, even the small chapel being abandoned at this time of year, and it had enough of the flavor of settlement that I felt a satisfaction in my visits, and the dead didn't care what I said, or in what language.

Through an extended study of the headstones and markers, I realized the extent of the influenza epidemic that had touched both Powl and myself in the previous winter. There were dozens of graves bearing death dates from the first month of this year, most of them of people under twenty or over fifty years of age.

I imagine many of these victims had to wait for spring to be planted, for there can only be a certain number of graves predug before the frost, and no one expects an epidemic. This year the sexton had learned his lesson, and there were rows of empty holes and no one dying.

I took to doing my day's sitting in the chapel, finishing with a short intercession for the dead (my hosts, as it were) to God the Father, God the Mother, and the God Who Is in Us All, but my notion of deity had changed so in the past year that I think this was more a social than a religious exercise. I also meditated in the empty graves, which seemed much more meaningful (like the empty belly of the wolf). The chill I received in my knees from this particular activity still bothers me in some weathers.

Powl found me there once, sitting in an open grave. What could he say? He had never forbidden me to sit in graves. He led me home, for the weather had unexpectedly cleared and he wanted spend the night correcting Adlar's charts for the November sky.

. . .

Winter is the time when people go mad, drink themselves to death, or kill other people. This winter was the time I tried to seduce Powl.

I had had no experience with women, except that wary and childish summer with Lady Charlan so many years ago, and I did not connect such tentative feelings with the physical brutality I had suffered even earlier in my childhood, at the hands of the schoolmasters. My obsession with Powl had some of the feelings of passive disgrace I remembered from my days of being boy-raped, combined with a large share of the entrancement of my puppy love. I analyzed my feelings only when I could not avoid doing so—perhaps three or four times a day. They were, however, very compelling.

From this vantage point, I think the best explanation is that I did not have enough to live on. Though I had conversation and human touch in abundance for six hours each day, that was not enough for the body and brain of twenty years. Perhaps no amount is enough for twenty years. I was in superb health, save the one bout of influenza, and I had nothing to do with eighteen hours of the day but expect the arrival of Powl for the other six.

(Or perhaps all this argument is merely to excuse a part of myself with which I am not now very comfortable. I will try, at least, to be honest.)

I never sat down and admitted to myself that I wanted to encourage Powl to have sexual intercourse with me, no more than any farm girl might when trying to catch the eye of the landlord's son. But my actions were on purpose, as hers are.

I was not aggressive, but instead more docile, tending to go limp in practice, letting his weight rest upon me, trying to fulfill his commands before they were asked. I ceased looking at him directly. I froze under his touch.

Alone, the awfulness of what I was doing (considering my past experience with buggery) would overwhelm me, but the awfulness was part of the attraction. Horror wipes away boredom very effectively.

Powl pretended to be oblivious to all these games for about a week, and then one morning, on the icy turf, when I pulled such a slack, clinging stunt, he threw me away from him, quite forcefully. He went into the observatory and came back with his boiled-wool coat, holding out a gold half regal.

"Here," he said, dropping it into my hand. "Go visit a whorehouse. Make sure she's healthy. I'll come back tomorrow."

I stared at the coin for an hour, and then I buried it under an oak tree. That simply was my spell of randiness broken.

It cannot have been too long after this that the soldier came to the observatory, and my shyness was overcome by necessity.

He was not by any means the first visitor since my residence. Locals passed by the squat building every few weeks, and once a man tethered three goats in the field, without any regard for the rights of the property owner. Boys had come climbing once or twice, and there was a day when I stood below the roof slot by the eyepiece of the telescope, ready to catch young mischief as he fell and either save his life or kill him, depending on whether he had damaged the works, so much had I identified myself with Powl and his interests. But the boy never made it higher than the clerestories, which were too narrow to permit the passage of a good-size body. I never exchanged a word with the passersby. I imagine they were ignorant of my existence.

This fellow was different. He came out of the trees, followed a shadow to the brick wall, and circumambulated the observatory, hunched over and pausing at times to listen.

I had been sitting on the root of a tree at the time, doing my daily self-collection, and so I heard him come from a distance away, and I watched him.

I called him a soldier before, but he was not a man-at-arms as I was, or was to have been. He was instead (I know in retrospect) that unfortunate thing called a campaign recruit, enlisted out of some furrow or gutter for the duration of the Felink excursion and cashiered afterward. By this method many wolves are made out of harmless vagabonds, and this one still wore his russet army jacket, over the white canvas breeches of a kitchen man. He had one woolen stocking but two shoes. He had some excuse for a sword. Like the turner and the gardener, he moved as though it hurt.

Finishing his circuit, he came to the oak door and peered within. Quiet to his eye and quiet to his ear. He pushed the door, which was, of course, unlocked, and went in.

I followed him, not very closely, leaving my high clogs at the door. I found him at the grinding bench, dropping all the lenses and blanks into a sack.

I was far less afraid than I had been in my meeting with the farm wife. I paused to adjust my languages and said, "You will scratch them like that, and they will be worthless."

His sword was a saber, and he drew it out of its cheap board scabbard with both hands, cocked it back over one shoulder, and swung to split me in half at the neck.

I suspected the man was sick, for his movements were lackluster though his face was a grin of hostility. I ducked under the blow, watching him, and as the weapon continued under its own impetus, wrapping his arms to the right, I simply pinned them there and rapped him smartly over the nose.

I picked up the sword as he dropped it.

Fury became fear in his face and he scrabbled for the door, leaving the sack behind. I thought to let him go, but on impulse tried a casual foot trip, which took him down on the flagstones. Holding to his regulation collar and the slack of his liveried breeches, I slid the man over the floor on his knees and locked him in the room with the experimental earth closet, to wait for Powl's judgment. If he dug his way out, he would save me much labor.

He did not attempt to dig, but bawled and cursed me all night long.

Before producing him for my teacher the next morning, I warned Powl that the man was likely sick and possibly contagious. Powl rounded his wide-apart eyes and went to see for himself. He crawled up the wall (much more proficiently than any invading boy) and peered through the tiny window.

"He doesn't look sick to me," Powl said, coming back to earth. "But he has pissed in the corner. What an absurdity, with the facility in the middle of the floor as it is.

"I'm something of an amateur of medicine, Nazhuret. Let us look at your sick soldier." So bright and interested did Powl look that I swelled with pride at having for once been able to give him something he did not already have: an experimental subject.

Now that I examine the matter, I realize he had even that.

I unlocked the door and was forced to knock the man down again as he broke past me for the opening. I brought him forward in a simple hammerlock, and Powl, without a word, examined his ears, gums, and eyelids.

"Why did you think he is sick?" Powl asked me in our current language, as pleasantly as any doctor called by a father to his child's bedside.

"He staggers, of course. He has no balance; he can scarcely stand without help, and then he is confused."

Powl stepped back, appraisingly. "Let him go," he said.

I did so, and the soldier ran to the hall and out the door, skidding on the flagstones. He left behind both his sack and his saber.

"He's not sick at all, Nazhuret," said Powl, washing his hands. "It's just that you have grown unused to people. And if another sneak thief happens by, please boot him out and don't detain him. I want to remain as invisible as possible up here. It's not as though I own this building, after all."

"You don't?"

His glance at me showed he was very pleased with himself. Powl was wearing a new hat over his half-bald head: a russet felt with flecks of red and blue. "Oh, no. It belonged to Adlar and now, since the man's suicide, to his heirs—not that they are likely to have any interest in astronomy."

"The astronomer killed himself?" I had forgotten that.

"Yes. Hanged himself from that crossbeam there. I merely found him."

Very clearly did I remember how that first afternoon I had seen Powl dangling, booted feet in the air, from the window-shade pull, and I felt much more in the stomach at hearing this than I had when the soldier had tried to slice off my head.

Powl put his arm over my shoulder. "Don't go green, lad. We all die. You've done so already, haven't you?" When this had no effect, or at least no good effect on me, he continued, ". . . and by the by, are you aware that for now there is no one at Sordaling School, not master, instructor, or student, and probably no one man of the king's regular forces who could stand against you?"

As I stood gawking, almost offended by such an outrageous statement, Powl went to assay the damage to the lenses in the bag. "Of course, men's skills vary a lot day to day, and then the arts of war are a very minor study. You still have very bad grammar," he added, and I was sensibly relieved.

As the summer of my second year in the observatory drew to a close, I passed some sort of balance point in my studies. It occurred to me one evening, as I was setting up the telescope for a clear night's watch that this period of my life would end as all the others had ended, and unless I got the influenza again, or Powl hit me on the head too hard, there would be time after. I had no notion yet what that time would contain, but the fact that it interested me changed my attitude to my present studies.

I began to decide myself when I should sit, when I should work out, watch, and (of course) grind glass. I faced the bricks in the early morning after feeding the stove. I did exercises after breakfast and studied in the heat of the day.

Within a week after I had passed this point of balance (though I said nothing aloud), Powl started to take me on excursions. He arrived in the morning with a rucksack stuffed with coarse-weave linen, the same as my summer outfit, and I had the educational experience of seeing my dapper teacher make a peasant of himself.

That first day we went nowhere much, just down the deerpath to the road and right, until we came to a knot of men repairing the road, where Powl stopped, sagged against a tree, and gossiped with them, adopting a strong Zaquashlon accent and idiom for the purpose. In this conversation I first learned about the war of the previous year and the death of the old king, and very surprised I was, too. My single attempt to interject myself into the conversation met a startled glance from the smudgy crew and a nudge from Powl that almost knocked me down.

"Don't you want me to talk properly?" I asked him when we had left them behind us. "You have been correcting my pronunciation and grammar for two years!"

"I want you to talk like a courtier and write like a scholar," he answered. "But by choice—not because you have no other language."

"I have three, thanks to you."

"Weel, learn 'tother neuw," said Powl, and for the next two weeks he spoke nothing but South Zaquash and made me do the same.

We went to the Royal Library at Sordaling, and I was flinchy as an owl in my townie clothes, which now were too tight across the shoulders (though no shorter in the legs, alas) and two years out of style. Walking down the River Parade took great courage; though I knew I had broken no laws in leaving the school, had anyone recognized me, I surely would have broken and run. My old life and my new one seemed to batter their realities against one another, and there was only my same ugly face in the reflection of every shop window to tie them together. As we passed the flower market, the sight of Powl moving before the scenes of my young recreation was unnerving, because so natural. A well-dressed and very graceful gentleman strolling a street of gardens and fine shops.

I was the element out of place.

In the library Powl showed a pass that served to admit us both and he disappeared into the history shelves, leaving me to follow my own impulses.

I was not familiar with the classification, since our school library used only ten categories and alphabetical listing within them, but I found a volume of very expert prints, hand-tinted, of tropical birds, and that kept me for some time. After that I found the section called Celestial Mechanics and was amazed to discover that almost all their information was obsolete or simply inaccurate. Most of the telescopes described were of the open refractor variety, consisting of a large spherically ground lens on a pole and a hand-held eyepiece that the observer chased around with until he had found the focal distance for himself. Irritating as squatting in nettles.

Powl had found another book of pictures, and he lowered it down atop my small stack. It was a catalog of military costumes, and that he wanted to show it to me I found amusing. Every sign on my part of interest in the arts of war was met by Powl with denigration or irony, and yet his own preoccupation with the subject ever surpassed mine.

The picture portraying the Velonyan mounted in armor was a very fine etching of a blond man, handsome in face and large in scale, seated on a heavy horse and wearing heavier plate. It was titled "THE DUKE OF NORWESS, IN ACTION AGAINST REZHMIA."

"What do you think?" Powl asked me.

"We studied that campaign. Disastrous. I think he must have been half boiled and half frozen going into the eastern desert in that. Even twenty-five years ago people must have known how to dress for a dry climate."

Powl stared rather sharply, and I apologized for the volume of my voice. Living in total solitude does not encourage modulation.

"The Rezhmian excursion was not in all ways a failure, Nazhuret. And concerning the picture, I meant to show you ...the quality of the reproduction. Look at the fineness of the lines."

I admitted it to be striking.

"Even for talents of twenty-five years ago," he added, with more than his usual irony. "Look at this other one."

The horse was much lighter and so was the rider. He wore no flowing robes and no armor except a leather cuirass, and his black hair flew behind him in a braid. "Also very good, Powl. Mostly artists make the Red Whips look like so many apes. This one looks at least human."

"True, O scholar, but note that the picture is not one of the pony brigands, but a knight of the Sanaur of Rezhmia itself—one of the fellows who made such a disaster of that campaign."

He slammed the book shut almost on my nose.

Walking out of the library, Powl was very quiet—offended, I guessed. I wasn't sure in what way I had blundered, so I kept my mouth shut and waited for him to tell me. He did, before we had reached the gates of the old part of the city.

"It is a provincial, narrow-minded attitude to see another group of people as looking more like animals than our own race," he stated, his face pointed straight ahead.

"I didn't, exactly—"

"*They* say we have faces like horses."

This was a new idea. I played with it for a few city blocks, evaluating each innocent passerby. "For some the idea has merit," I said to Powl in an attempt to be truly broad-minded. "The traditional Old Velonyan nobility is supposed to have a long face with high-bridged nose and straight mouth, though few, indeed, fit that model." I extended my observations to my teacher himself, with his oval face; neat features; and wide, wide gray eyes. I was convinced, nonetheless, that Powl was Old Velonyan nobility. "But I don't think your face looks at all like a horse."

Now he looked straight at me. "Neither does yours," he said without smiling.

I think it was on that same day trip that Powl and I noticed the robbers ahead beside the road. I saw a movement, and by the twitch of his nose, I think Powl smelled them. There were two of them, and I could see at least one heavy club waving brown against the black and white woods as its carrier settled in place for the pounce. Powl and I drifted to a stop a good hundred fifty feet away and conferred.

"There's been a lot of that," said Powl very calmly, facing me to the north but with his attention locked northwest, along the road. "What with the flu and the war and all." He scratched his chin and cracked his back: a very picture of nonchalance.

"So what shall we do about them?" I asked, feeling a youthful eagerness to display myself.

Powl scanned the country, not turning completely away from the twin black humps, which were now motionlessly waiting ahead behind the first row of trees. "I think we might turn off here and come back to the road perhaps a mile farther along. There are some very interesting growths of fungus I have seen in these oak woods that I would like to visit anyway."

76

"Not this early in the spring, Powl. No fungus now. Besides, shouldn't we teach them a lesson?"

He winced. "Nazhuret, I have difficulty enough teaching *you* lessons, without sparing effort for common brute marauders." Powl stepped daintily onto a deer track that crossed the road very near where we had stopped. I plucked at his sleeve and did not follow.

"But if we leave them, won't they attack the next poor travelers and perhaps kill him?"

My teacher looked bleakly down at me and smoothed his smooth hair further. "Zhurrie, lad," he said in heavy Zaquash, "I can see now your life to be a bushel of trouble packed down."

He led me onto the deer track on the other side of the road, the one that ran behind our unwitting criminals.

I had a great deal of fun creeping up upon our enemies. The temperature in these shadows had maintained winter's last carpet on the ground, but it was too warm to crunch beneathfoot. Powl was equally as quiet as I but less amused, being more concerned about the condition of his boots in the soppy, thawing snow.

"I begin to see why you keep me dressed like a peasant," I whispered to him, for my tailored jacket was impeding my movement considerably. He did not answer.

It was not a difficult approach, for our quarry had their ears and eyes fixed on the stripe of road before them. Up until now I had had hopes—fears, actually—that they would turn out to be more road menders, or honest laborers retired for a midday nap. But as we came within thirty feet of them, I could hear them talking, and their subject was our disappearance, and whether it was worth following us along our shortcut for purposes of overtaking. The man to the left (my side) believed it was worth the extra effort, while his partner demurred.

They were no good at waiting; they wiggled constantly,

and I spied the flash of a dagger in the hand of Powl's man. "Should we run at them?" I mouthed to Powl.

"Not unless they see us." He crawled forward on his hands and feet, exactly like a cat, and a feline interest began to illumine his smooth face. He no longer worried about his cuffs.

I kept pace with him, expecting to be noticed at any moment, but much to my surprise we crawled all the way to the men's rag-booted feet without notice. They had meanwhile decided the game was not worth the candle and were setting back to wait for easier prey.

Powl gave me the nod.

I had never hit a man who was down on the ground, or tried to hit one (except, of course, for Powl), and out of sportsmanship I tapped the fellow on the shoulder so he should at least know I was there. He turned without any particular alarm and craned up his head at me, and then with a bellow he floundered up, swinging the knob-headed club at me. I hopped in before it and was at his right side as it swung. From behind him I grabbed his right hand and pinched until he dropped his weapon, and I locked that hand over his left arm with my own left and slid my other hand over his right shoulder, under his chin, and around his jawbone. He struggled, but I had him nicely and I was very proud of myself.

Powl, who had casually kicked his opponent in the jaw before the man could rise, came now and stood before me. "Fine, my lad. But what will you do with him now?"

"Take him to the provincial marshal?" I hazarded. "I don't think the authority of the Sordaling Constabulary extends so far out."

The fellow struggled harder. Though he could not get rid of me, he could lift me off my feet. Powl stood before us and watched for a few moments, one hand cupping the other elbow, chin resting on two fingers. For the first time, he looked amused by the affair.

"Nazhuret, I have spent many years of my life avoiding

involvement with officialdom in all aspects, high and low. It is far more of a grief than simple roadside cutthroats, and if you wish to survive free and happy you will follow my example."

"Then what *do* I do with him?" I asked, my voice bouncing as I bounced. My prisoner next tried to step on my foot.

Powl stepped in and put one hand on each of the fellow's broad shoulders. "Listen to me, assassin," he said in his most arrogantly clean accent. "You will come to a bad end in this occupation. You are not suited for it. You have not the brain."

For a moment the man stopped struggling, and he stared stupidly at Powl, with his ruffles and piping and his snow-stained cuffs. Then, lifting his hand straight from the man's shoulder, Powl cracked him across the face open-handed, and the robber fell senseless from my grip into the slush.

I stuck my right hand into my jacket front, for Powl's slap had glanced off the man's jaw onto the hand, which had gone numb. I thanked my teacher very politely for his help.

That spring, we graduated from the idiom of South Zaquash to the old language itself, though the ban upon its pronunciation in the Kingdom of Velonya still was in effect. Powl said the knowledge of this old mama's tongue would change my way of looking at my own native country.

He was right. All the traits I was taught were typical of the Zaquashlon peasantry were actually built into the structure of their language. In Zaquash questions are asked in a determined (to my ears), descending tone, while declarative statements rise into the sky and stay there. The word for boat is a grammatic variant of the word for man. The word for horse is the plural of the word for woman. Goats driven are called "a braid." The same word is shared by "north" and "black," which in some usages means "left" as well. These are not poetic turns of phrase, sir, but the basic use of the language.

To me, a Velonyan raised, Zaquash sounded incomprehensible, half-witted, and sly. What is our immediate impression of the territories' peasantry? Sly, half-witted, and incomprehensible. Once one begins to understand the tongue, however, their responses seem more consistent, and it is very amusing how they think of us.

They call us "wrapped in maps": astonishing phrase. The actual term for a nobleman, *paitsye* (you hear it every day in the southern territories, even among those who have no real Zaquash at all), is "hut-crusher."

It is a language tailored to survive in secret: a language of resistance. When Powl and I spoke it together, I am not sure we weren't rebels.

I went into Sordaling with my fortnight's product in wooden boxes, packed in milkweed fiber. Powl sent me by myself.

I was surprised at how much such pleasant work brought, even counting the cost of the very clearest optical blanks. One could do better as an optician than as a lieutenant in the King's Horse. Of course, lieutenants don't expect to stay lieutenants. Opticians remain what they are.

I was much less terrified of human society by now, though still I felt alien, and when a man on a horse cantered up the quiet road behind, I took one look to be sure he was not a brigand and then let him come.

He passed politely enough, glancing down his right shoulder at me in my coarse linen. Then he stopped and pushed his mare sideways across the road.

The mare was a fair gray and beautiful, though rather thin. The man was much thinner and dressed in a finery of lace and ruffles dirtier than the skin of the horse. At a distance of ten feet I could smell the man: woodsmoke, sweat, and cheap scent. He was wearing a sword, but that was no military blade. It was a needle with a jeweled, cupped handle. A dagger, also like a needle, was worn jauntily through a velvet chevron across one shoulder.

He was dark and looked as dirty as his ruffles. He stared at me with an intensity close to anger. "Zhurrie," he said at last in the voice of a heavy pipe-smoker, "You have certainly changed."

I don't claim the skill of remembering everyone I have met. The face was familiar, but there were hundreds of boys at Sordaling School while I was there, and the way in which he played the dagger around the fingers of one black-nailed hand was very distracting.

"I don't remember you," I said, and then repeated the phrase in Velonyan, hoping he would not recognize the outlawed language I had spoken in.

He smiled, and his teeth were in better shape than his face. "Because you don't know me, my friend. Only I know *you.*"

Melodramatically, the rider then kicked his mare back into a gallop and left me in a shower of spring mud.

It had been almost three years since I had been recognized. I returned to the observatory in a sweat, heart pounding.

It was a beautiful spring and summer, except that Powl took to hitting me brutally. Three times within a week he knocked me cold and left me on the grass. I would come to my senses and go in (once with a mouth full of blood, from a split lip and a tooth broken and left in the tongue) to find him in the single chair, nose to a book.

Mechanics of the Horse. Savage Art of the Sekret Wastes— in Allec. (Powl had a wide taste in scholarship.) *Civil Mechanics of the Warrior-Poet.*

Powl now was without warmth in our sparring, without pity. I asked him why he hurt me so, and he answered it was because he could.

Of course he could knock me down; he was my teacher. "Your teacher for too long, to be enduring this inadequacy," he replied.

I reminded him he was a head taller and a hand longer in the arms than I. "Excuses disgust me," answered Powl.

I stood before him drooling pink, pressing on my jaw to slow the swelling, and he said to me, "There is something wrong with you, Nazhuret. Not with your skills—I have seen to your skills—something intimately wrong. You should not let me beat you this way."

I agreed with him, but the alternative seemed to be to walk out, in rancor and empty-handed. I did not want to believe he meant me to do this.

The next two days I could not fight, but after that I made a resolution that no attack would get under my guard, and at our next sparring I whipped myself to a trembling alertness. I deflected twenty-two strikes in a row, and then Powl kicked me in the throat.

I squatted down and cried like a baby, choking on the phlegm of my sobs. "I can't block them forever," I said or tried to say. "No one could." Powl brushed past me toward the observatory. "No. I'm glad you finally realize that," he said.

When we were not fighting, he was as affable and as egalitarian as ever.

In the previous dark of winter I had spent many hours sitting or walking slowly, mind open. Now the long days seemed to impress activity on every moment, and Powl decided once more to slow me down.

"This day," he said one very warm morning, "is dedicated to freedom. Not that you are to think about the quality of freedom; you are to realize it, Nazhuret. Go out into the cool of the pines and spend the day in self-collection. Until it is dark."

Cool of the pines or no, it was a sweaty day's work, and my problems—with Powl's brutality, with the man on the road who had recognized me, with my own fecklessness—endlessly intruded themselves. I was too tired to eat supper.

The next morning, earlier than was his wont, my teacher climbed the hill and sent me out again—this time not to think about my own particular and infinite freedoms. I was sure my joints had caught a chill. I was certain I was going insane.

The next day and the next he sent me out without any instruction, and I was in great pain of body.

It rained, and though the trees broke the body of the downpour, the noise in the leaves was trancing. Maddening. It was like the pain in each member of my abused body and the throb in my jaw where the tooth had been cracked open. At the same time the pain, and the shining black-green of the wet needles and the dusty live stink of the forest saved me from the attack of my own thoughts. I had outlived the ability to think and drifted high above the trees, where lenses of water filled the soft air, infinite in number and careless of their own destiny.

Then I fell, too, through and out of my own body. Fell without an end, careless, like the droplets, of destiny. It was an experience like death and unlike it, and it did not upset me in the least.

I noticed I was wet and so I got up, though I needed two saplings to complete the effort. I went back to the observatory, the rain washing my greasy face.

Powl was adjusting the new slatted wooden cover for the telescope slot. It did not work as well as expected, so there were pots scattered around the expensive equipment. Once again the large metal tub from the earth closet had been emptied and called into play.

I helped with the other rattail line. When it was adequately fixed I said, "Powl, I won't be able to use this arms training you have given me. Not occupationally, I mean."

He glanced at me sidelong. I remember his face was pink and his wary eyes glistening. "Why? You're not that bad. You can take on thieves and untrained vagabonds, at any rate."

I sat on the platform chair, leaving my teacher to stand. "Yes, but I . . . It is like a bird that takes off because it is frightened. The dog that feels a wagon wheel roll against its back and is up before the touch becomes crushing.

"You have taught me to be the bird, the dog, Powl. Could the dog be paid to move that perfectly once an hour, for bread sopped in gravy? Would the bird shoot into the sky on command? I think as a man-at-arms I would soon be no different than any other dull, blundering door guard. It would be a waste."

I did not look at my teacher. "And . . . and I think it would do me a violence, also."

Powl sat next to me, on the floor so I could not see his face. "Well, that is certainly how I see it, too, Nazhuret. I was afraid I would have to tell you as much, and then maybe all hell would break loose. People don't like to work as hard as you have worked without a reward."

I laughed. "Then," Powl continued very calmly, as though not interested, "what will you be?"

The rain on the roof was like a cavalry. The rain in the pots was like cavalry drums. "I don't think I'll be anything, Powl. I have lost the art of being things. I will instead do things. Make breakfast. Grind lenses. Wash clothes."

Powl nodded. "Infinite freedom."

"And infinite teaching," I answered, not meaning to flatter.

Powl was biting his hand; I could see that, from behind and above him. "What is it I have taught you?" he asked me.

I had my answer ready. "You have taught me to be still, so that I could move properly. You have taught me to listen, so that I can speak properly. You have taught me to see, so that I might not always *be* seen."

My teacher crowed. "Glib! Glib, Nazhuret, but entirely

accurate." He slapped his knee, but still he did not turn his head to mine. "I shall have to remember that one. But let me be serious for a moment.

"Lad, out of my own experience let me advise you to avoid . . . to avoid grabbing on to things: ideas, possessions, even other people. Anything you own is going to cut into your perfect freedom."

I held my soggy, coarse shirt away from my body. "Possessions, Powl, do not seem to be my most threatening temptation. So I am to stay a beggar?"

"You have that honor, yes," said Powl, in all his fine linen and piping. "And another thing: I repeat you must stay out of the reach of officialdom, for with what you now know it will be deadly to you. Do not touch the police, the military, for even with your innocent heart you will wind up hanged. Especially with your innocent heart!

"Someday, too, the world's respect is going to try you."

"I'm sorry?" He looked so sorrowful saying these words.

"It will . . . try to seduce you, even you. Eschew it, Nazhuret. You are as much a lord as any man can be, sitting there in your homespun, teaching your teacher philosophy."

I had opened my mouth to reply, but Powl was up and walking. My abrupt, eccentric teacher was through the outer door without another word. I still had not seen his face.

Two days later I knocked Powl unconscious and I could not wake him up for long, anxious minutes. As I looked down at him lying in the mud of the last rainstorm, it came to me that my teacher was not a strongly built man, and not very young, either. I dragged him inside and undressed him and began to wash his clothes.

Powl sat up as I was wringing out his pleated shirt. The first words he said were, "Nazhuret, I have never desired any personal ascendancy over you."

I giggled, partly from relief that he was not dead. "I know.

I know. But it is inevitable, you know, master."

"I will not permit "masters." You know that."

He lay down again, stifling a groan. "I have worked three years to awake in you an inner... an inner authority that no other can supersede. Only one man in ten thousand possesses that. It is perfect. It is deadly."

He rolled toward me. "You cannot not give your allegiance to anyone, Nazhuret: king or prelate or..."

"Or teacher," I concluded for him, and I arranged his shirt on a hanger. "What a joke," I muttered aloud. "My problem all through life was that I was *incapable* of committing this authority of mine to anyone. That's why I hung on at the school for years, unwilling to take a master."

"I will not permit masters!" he repeated. I think he had a bad headache.

"Until I came here." I looked over at the man on the bed, who had refused for so long to allow me to be owned by him. "That particular incapability ended here. And, Powl, don't denigrate me too strongly for my humility. I think you would not have liked it had I argued, contradicted you, and refused your instructions."

"Of course not," said Powl. "I would have been insupportable. You were just an ignorant boy."

After that he took a long nap.

That summer, Powl taught me to hunt. By "hunting" I do not mean the sport of venery, but rather the job of putting meat in one's mouth: snaring rabbits, for example. Venery is a grand passion among the great. Snaring rabbits is mostly against the law, but beggars will always do it, as it is preferable to starvation.

Powl had no particular feeling for the chase, but he was remarkably efficient at it. His skill with twine and with the small, light bow was hardly credible; it made me doubt for the first time that the man was mansion-born.

It would have been simpler for me had I been brought up in the country, or had the man not first taught me for three years to observe the forest world harmlessly. The shock I received each time a rabbit screamed, lung-pierced, tended to depress my appetite.

In the warm weather we went on a vacation, or at least for me it seemed a vacation. We bivouacked for weeks unbroken, carrying only sticks, sacks, and dowhees, looking like peasants except that Powl wore neat doeskin breeches that kept out every sort of thorn. Our walking sticks were of imported tropical grasswood, which around Sordaling City was the latest rage among laborers in easy circumstances, its gold- and black-mottled weightlessness being much admired. Ours were slightly heavier than the usual because they had had the walls within the length hollowed out, and within them rested slim little bows made of foil-blade billets: Powl's invention. These were lighter and more concealable than wood, and needed only to be kept oiled. It amused him sardonically that it was considered a freeman's right to carry a sword to pierce men, whereas for carrying a bow to pierce the beasts of the field a man could forfeit both hands.

One art Powl never mastered nor tried to master was that of cooking, so I slit, gutted, butched, and roasted the victims of our morning's or night's effort while Powl lectured me on the subject of national politics.

On this subject I was as ignorant and as fascinated as is a well-raised maiden about copulation. I had felt myself more informed of events at school than I did now, years later, but after Powl opened up the court world to me, I saw I had always been a chick in the egg.

He had a story about each of the (then) four dukes: Garmen of Hight, who kept a small army of pretty boys at his side; Andermit, with his palace where all furniture was red and white; Shandaff, who was not enough of a peasant at heart to be an effective noble; and Leoue of the bee colors: yellow and black. The Duke of Leoue had been King Ethelbhel's field marshal and now was that of his son. Leoue always was first in the reckoning.

My teacher spoke no direct criticism of most men, and very little praise of any sort, unless there is criticism inherent in reporting that a man favors small children, or has execrable taste in domestic design.

I knew already that Leoue had a reputation for using his men's lives rather liberally, and I asked whether Powl considered him a good and just commander. In reply he told me, at unnecessary length, how Eydl, late Duke of Norwess, and he had despised one another so thoroughly that their anger had spiced the court for twenty years.

I realized I had once again asked the wrong sort of question, the sort that only leads to others.

About the late king, Powl spoke more directly and with more respect. King Ethelbhel had been a magnetic leader, with high ideals and a great concern for the position of his country amid the civilized nations. His love for Velonya was jealous, like a man's love may be for a beautiful wife. Perhaps Powl implied that like that sort of love, Ethelbhel's jealousy caused his inamorata difficulties, or perhaps I only imagined he implied that.

Ethelbhel had had more touch of the student than was usual among Velonya's monarchs, and he had both endowed universities and sprinkled his own court with scholars. His favorite study, however, was Old Velonyan history, and he was firmly contemptuous of both science and foreign influence. Actually, he had drawn little distinction between the two.

King Ethelbhel would have liked to conquer for the sake of Velonyan grandeur, but as Felinka was savage and Rezhmia a source of contagion, he could not have loved what he had conquered, and Powl suggested that was why his campaigns usually had failed.

I let Powl nibble his grouse breast clean before I suggested that it was simpler to admit that the Rezhmian Red Whips and the Rezhmian leadership might have been better at the time than ours. I knew little enough about the Felink campaign, except it had lost us many ships and men, but I had studied the southern fiasco.

"Perhaps," said my teacher, wiping his lips on the napkin he carried, a magical napkin that never seemed to get soiled, however often used, "though you expose your ignorance in speaking of the Red Whips as being in any sense obedient to Rezhmia. But still I think the personal analysis is meaningful. In the new king, Rudof, we have in a way the blossoming of Ethelbhel's intellectual striving." He folded the napkin, although he would use it again in only ten seconds.

"Velonya has never had a ruler as broadly educated as this young man. He can read fair Allec, and at court he keeps (so I have heard) a Rezhmian translator. He acted very cleverly in the matter of closing the sea war with Felink, though a lesser man might have dug in his heels out of wounded pride. Rudof does not curl up like a bug dislodged when his ideas are challenged."

This was slippery: implicit criticism of the old king in the form of faint praise of the new. I grinned behind my roasted parsnips, more certain than ever that Powl had cut his teeth on state documents. "What a fine monarch, Powl," I said, straight-faced. "You yourself might have had charge of his education!"

Powl's gray eyes, flat as a fish's, looked at me. "Yes, Nazhuret, you have discovered me. Every afternoon when I leave you, I hotfoot it west to the city of Vesinglon and review with the king his multiplication tables. It is the reward of my life."

As I had predicted, he now unfolded his napkin and used it again. "And I do not mean to paint you too rosy a picture of the new king. Like his father, he is a man with a temper, and being the only son, he has been terribly spoiled. Cross his will at your peril."

I denied any intention of crossing the will of the King of Velonya, and I took a second helping of boiled vegetables.

The new king, I now learned, did not get along with his wife, Chelemut of Low Canton. Between them it was not merely the lack of sympathy common to youngsters who were wed sight unseen. They really could not get along together, according to Powl, and had not had a moment's communal peace since their wedding six years before. Powl insisted that the situation was beyond remedy, for one could not mix the swarthy pride of Merecanton with Velonya's redheaded temperament. He chewed his dinner thoughtfully and gazed at the fire, as though he knew a lot about Low Canton. Or about temperament.

But now there was a son and heir, a crawling mite named Eylvie after his grandfather, and Rudof's chain might be loosed.

I mentioned my old black letter, Baron Howdl, hoping for the truth finally about the disappearance of his daughter, or at least for some nasty gossip to validate my dislike of the man, but Powl only sighed and tossed into my plate all the bones for picking and the roots he had found not worth his while. (This was our habit, at my instigation. I hated to see food wasted when I was hungry. I was always hungry.) "No, Nazhuret, I have not bothered myself with barons," he said.

More than once, on that summer holiday, Powl reminded me that our ignorant insularity regarding the Rezhmian people was more than equaled by their passionate dislike of us, on no better grounds. And about the Felink he said that it was unlikely any treaty between our peoples would be a lasting success, because we had never tried to understand the way they thought, nor had they tried to understand what six months of snow do to a people. He walked on, laughing at the thought. Powl had a rich laugh, slightly edged in effect. "If you thought that Zaquash was an odd way of speaking, lad, you ought to investigate the Felink tongue."

As on this trip we had drifted back to our birth language, I suggested that we do that, but Powl only shook his head. "I haven't the skill for it," he said, but I knew he was lying, and under the late summer sun I felt cold all through.

When we returned to the observatory, Powl was bronzed and I had stripes of red and brown all over my face. (It is my curse to spend all summer sunburned and all winter snow-burned, my king, thus adding an unusually garish coloring to my unusual appearance.) I spent all of one day on a thorough clothes-washing and then moped through a day of heavy rain, perfecting my calligraphy.

Next day was cool and breezy, with a very bright smell in the air. Powl came up the hill rather late and set me one of my tasks of contemplation.

This time I was to understand how grief comes to the freeman as well as to the slave. I nodded, and politely I went out into the oak copse, which was not as green as it had been, and I sat with my back against a tree, though I could hear everything Powl was doing in the observatory, and when he left, my ears followed him down the hill.

After he was gone, I came in and was not surprised to find the tables of the observatory bare, except for my winter shirts and trousers; my walking stick; my out-of-fashion gentry clothes; my dowhee; and the sword I broke three years before, now rebladed.

There was a letter:

My dear Nazhuret,

Please lock the place and leave the keys on the root where you have so often sat outside. I will fetch them before they have a chance to rust away, but I will not be back here soon. Live carefully, my son. You have been the best thing in my life.

Powl

Obedient to the last, I left the key on the oak root. I also left him my bag of marbles, for it was all the gift I could make. As I started away, now red-nosed as well as burned red, I remembered that there was a half regal buried under that same oak root and that Powl had left me no money. I dug it out of the soaked earth and then, remembering my teacher more clearly, I placed it on the bag of marbles.

After I wrote those previous words, sir, I crawled out the window and ran away. I don't know why it is that when one (read "I") dredges up some old and private loss it is exactly those persons he feels closest to whose presence he cannot bear. After scratching down the substance of Powl's dismissal of me—sweetly worded but still a dismissal—I left a message of five words on a scrap of paper and took myself to a stranger's grainfield under a high, gray, dribbling sky, where I gathered in the amaranth crop as though my future depended on it. The poor tiller must have thought I was desperate for coppers.

When I came home again I had determined to write no more in this history. I had good excuses: I was occupied, the story was well finished where I had left it, my king already had heard the rest anyway, it became unacceptably ambiguous from this point....

A hundred good excuses.

Today came the first snow, and my spell of temperament has cooled with it. I am ready to continue.

Never before the day I left the observatory had I been free of command: not at school and not with Powl. But in the last six months of my training, control had so softly drifted from my teacher to myself that I suffered now no uncertainty, no panic, no decay into playing marbles and talking to myself. I slept in the woods and continued to head south, the direction in which I had been going on a day's promenade three years before.

I was alone, though—as alone and untouchable as a bubble in glass—and I was unhappy. To say true, I grieved. I remember that wet maple autumn as particularly glorious: bright conflagration, with the gold leaves and the leaves of that bluish red that is the color glass turns when gold is added to it. The time was as quiet as glass, too—as though I had put a glass cup over each ear and heard only the noise of my own blood.

For two days I did not hunt—finding it a harder thing to release the bowstring for my own belly alone than I did when I was feeding my teacher as well—but in our northern woods there is nothing in the autumn but meat and perhaps cattails, if one can find them, so in the end I was forced to hear a rabbit scream for me alone.

It rained a very chilly rain and I cut pine boughs and heaped them in order like shingles, as Powl had taught me. I got wet anyway. The little vine maples under the trees made red stripes, their layers as cleanly horizontal as so many small horizons, and among them wandered fogs like little living things. Like slow birds, perhaps. Many times in those first days I found myself with legs tucked in and hands hid in my woolen shirt, lost in the black wolf of Gelley. It was not by my will that I sat like that, taut and empty, any more than a sick man babbles by will or an old man talks to himself. My self-collection began to stretch a shadow over me, and I wondered if I should not fight it, as Powl had had me fight most of my natural inclinations.

He was not there to ask.

I skirted a number of villages as a wild beast might have done, though the smell of bread in the air drove me mad. I was not finished with grieving, not finished with staring at nothing, and I had nothing to say to any human being.

On the third day the rain and mist let up. I was walking through very low country, where the road was crossed by waterways as often as by deerpaths. The mud envied me my clogs and strove mightily to remove them with my every step.

Odd enough, the sound it made each time I broke its grip was dry and hard, like a stick snapping. That percussion followed me through the morning until noon, when the sun stiffened the road's fabric.

I smelled horse, I smelled leather, and I smelled great shovelsful of disturbed soil, much like the smell of Powl's earth closet. Around a forested corner the road slanted down, and as I followed it the air lost the sunlight and grew wet again.

There I saw the beast itself, blowing and moaning, trapped past its chestnut belly in mud. It was fat, squat, and short-legged for its mass, and laid out flat on the road, its long face glistened with terror sweat. Where it had struggled against the sucking, remnants of its harness were flung out in the morass like water snakes. The cart it had been pulling was half gone behind it, with only one yellow, mud-caked wheel rising free. There was no human form in sight.

I could see the great crack across the left of the road, where a plate of earth, hard above but mucky under, had broken and canted and sailed off entirely into the ditch, dropping the beast into sediment more than a yard deep and without solidity. For a man it would have been a sloppy, infuriating sort of joke. For a light horse it would have led to panic and perhaps injury getting out. For this cobby, stub-legged fellow, it was slow death.

It had been there a while already, by the pale, dried earth speckling its back and by the immovability of its defeated head. The breath whistling in and out of the horse's nostrils made me think of thirst; though it was trapped in treacherous water, there was nothing for it to drink. Nor had I anything to give it; in this desolation of rain and puddles, I had not thought to fill a bottle.

There on the yet-solid bank were the marks of sticks or shovels, where someone had tried to dig the beast a path out. Behind it was a black-soaked heavy rope, with which perhaps they had tried to rope and pull it out. Now there was no one.

I wondered where they had gone and what new attack they would attempt next. I looked at the horse, the tilted cart, and the broken harness, and I mused.

He grunted at me like a pig, very sadly.

There was an ax in the cart as well as a load of root vegetables; the driver must have been very certain no one would rob him in his absence. Or very distraught.

I took the ax and went into the low woods, where the trees were so thick few got enough light, and they clawed at one another's branches and rose too thin. I picked a spindling pine and I hacked it through at my waist level, and then had ten minutes of dangerous work shaking it to free it from its neighbors so it would fall where I wanted.

It fell in the opposite direction, actually, but I was out of its path smartly. I had underestimated the tree's bulk and was forced to chop again to remove the heavy end of the bole, and then raise another sweat cleaning off the biggest branches. In the end I could drag it and lift one end (the light end) off the ground. I hauled it to the road and lifted the light end over the floor of the cart, extending it like a blackboard pointer over the mud-trapped animal, which lifted its head dully to look. I took the rope with me and found it to be very heavy, stiff, and hard to grab, with all the grime. I climbed the tree to its end, which bobbed but held up my weight, and I lowered myself the three feet to the horse's back.

The creature sank no farther; evidently it was standing firm under all that mire. I attempted to run the rope under the big brown belly, but it was too wide, and the mud was not firm enough to dig. I had to settle for tying a bowline around its neck. I ran that rope over the trunk end and wrapped it once. Inch by inch I shortened the line between the horse and the sapling until the heavy end rose over the road and the horse was half choked with the tension.

Like my patron spirit the monkey (though I had never seen a monkey), I climbed four-legged to the other end of my lever and then began to leap up and down on it. The natural spring of the sapling made this an interesting occupation, and the beast's strangled screams added urgency.

I thought perhaps I was only hastening the horse's demise, for that neck now looked as long as any blood horse's and the tongue seemed to be swelling in its gaping mouth, but then it began to thrash as well as scream and one front hoof broke surface, looking improbably round and delicate for a beast that size. It struck and splashed and was joined by its fellow, and then the mud released with a sound of great bad humor, and the horse was up on its hind legs and crashing forward again onto the edge of the road.

It gave way. Like the piece beside it, it proved treacherous, and the horse sank into mud again. This time the undercut was not so deep, however, and the fragments of wagon-compressed earth remained underfoot, where they could be of use. The horse swam its front legs and heaved its rear and was out on the roadway, steaming.

The tree was bobbing up and down like a fishing pole, and with each bob it pulled the horse's head up. I went to release it and found the rope hopelessly jammed. I had to hack it apart at the knot with the ax.

Now what? The beast was free but in trouble still. It shivered, and each of its knees had a tendency to buckle. It was important to get it home, to the amenities a cart horse expected (so much more than the amenities I was used to expecting): blankets, mash, clean straw, and possibly a roof overhead. But which way was home?

If the cart had been going away, then home was the way I was going. If the cart had been returning, then home was behind me. But there was nothing behind me for many miles, and besides, the load of roots indicated it was on its way to market. No one buys mangel-wurzels in that quantity for personal consumption. I was at least three-quarters certain the direction was south, but if I were wrong, the poor exhausted beast might not have it in it to do the walk twice.

As I mulled the problem, the horse began to walk, dragging me behind it.

It had immense strength for a horse so weary and so badly treated by life. I could no more turn or stop it with my rope tied to its headstall (to the best of my memory the bit was broken through) than I could have pulled it out of the muck by hand. I could have left it to its journey, but having so far taken charge of the horse, I felt reluctant to let it go.

Not many miles along, where low woods of maple and sumac gave way to plowed fields, I met a party of men coming toward me. There were four of them, walking two by two, three dressed much as I was, in light woolen the color of sheep and one in a linen apron much stained. This one also led an ox and cart. The two in front stopped as they saw us: muddy horse and muddy man, and they gaped like baby birds. Their next reactions were very different, for the peasant on the left pointed, hopped, and ran at me, shouting, "That's my horse! It's mine! Mine!" while the other—the fellow in the apron—cursed, threw aside what looked like a saw, and turned his back on the whole scene.

"I don't doubt this one's your horse," I answered the farmer, and instinct prompted me to speak the broad Zaquash idiom of the territories. "I found it in a sinkhole."

"'Deed! Indeed! In a hole he was, and neither man's brain nor ox shoulders could get him out." The owner spoke better Velonyian than I had expected. He took the mud-slick rope from my hand, and so it was he who was dragged at a good foot's pace along the road. I liked the change.

"I got him out," I said, and then realized it sounded like boasting. The peasant and both his retainers stared at me, fish-blank. The aproned fellow spat in my direction.

"Don't min' him. He thought he was going to get to take

Rufon out piece by piece and keep the pieces. He's butcher-man." This peasant spoke the heavy Zaquash I had expected. Probably he was the owner's hired man.

"How'd you get him, then?" asked the farmer. "We couldn't pull him nor pry him."

"I used a class two lever, with the cart as fulcrum and myself as weight." When none of the four congratulated me or even nodded comprehension, I began to add, "A class two lever is one where—"

The farmer cut me off. "He musta worked his way mostly out by himself," he said, and as far as their party was concerned, that finished the matter. I stood in the road and allowed the horse to drag them on, for truth to tell, I was slightly miffed. After a minute the hired man ran back, puffing, to inform me that his master didn't really think I had been trying to steal the horse and that I was invited to dinner.

To have it granted that I was not trying to steal was not as satisfactory as being thanked for returning a valuable animal otherwise doomed to rendering, but it occurred to me that there probably would be things to eat on the farmer's table that I would not find by the side of the road. I had had nothing but my own cooking or Powl's (horrific thought) for three years.

The walk to the farmstead was one long argument between Farmer Grofe and the butcher over the latter's disappointed hopes. He felt that since he had closed his shop for a half day for this effort, he should receive recompense in the shape of a sheep or goat at least. After all, he remarked, the doctor doesn't give back his fee when the patient dies, so the butcher ought not to be penalized when the victim does not die. Grofe was no sophist. He told the butcher that it was the luck of the draw, and if he found any of his livestock, large or small, hanging in the village shop the butcher himself would join it.

The two attendants rolled their eyes at this, indicating that Farmer Grofe's threats were rare and to be taken at face value. Next, the butcher suggested that I be held for the cost of a new cart, since my trick with the class two lever (he remembered that part) probably had broken at least an axle. No one replied to this, but I began to wonder if my being invited to dinner was entirely a friendly gesture.

It was a very uncomfortable journey, and an uncomfortable meal afterward. I had been away from groups of men a long time.

There were marrows in butter, and there was Mistress Grofe: a thin woman much smaller than her husband and seemingly angry. She did not inquire about the conditions of my visit, and that seemed to me odd, but neither did she fear to take the butcher's part in the argument. I felt she believed the man's goodwill to be of more future benefit to her than the services of one chunky plowhorse.

There was fresh mutton passed about the table, and that liberally, for it was the beginning of slaughter season, but the dishes that caught my eye and set me drooling were the great tureen of bright soup, with red beets and white parsnips floating amid a speckle of green herbs, and the poppy-seed pastry, glazed in syrup.

The smells of the table were overpowering to one who had been so long on plain stuffs, but overpowering in a different manner were the odors of the diners: Grofe, his wife, two sons, one daughter, the man I'd met earlier, and one maid-o'-work. Three years of militant washing, in the company of Powl only, had made me more delicate-stomached than a deacon. The warm smells of the food mixed with the still warmer smells of sweat stink and well-aged sweaty wool, and that kitchen smelled worse to me than the fresh guts of a rabbit.

Adding to this the natural shyness of a man who never knew, when he opened his mouth, which language or mixture of languages would be coming out, and the Grofes had a very quiet dinner guest who breathed through his mouth. Perhaps they thought I had a cold. They did not ask me anything of who I was. It was obvious to look at me that I was a nobody.

The Grofe farmstead had much heavy woodwork in the dining room, and a clock that announced the hour by the antics of a wooden man who left his cottage on the wall and hit a tiny triangle with a mallet as many times as the hour allowed. The ringing was not made by the triangle, of course, but the effect was still amusing, at least for the first few hours. The furniture was black with beeswax and the cushions plump and the room very tidy. Mistress Grofe sat at her end of the table and glared her anger at all of us.

After dinner, at Grofe's request, I scratched out a picture of the affair I had created to liberate the horse from the sinkhole; it was done on the back of a bill of sale for wheat in the shock, I recall. Grofe was literate, at least to the point of signing his name. He seemed to understand the principles of my deed (I have learned since that most farmers far surpass me in that sort of cleverness), and I found myself miming how I had jumped up and down on the butt end of the sapling, and how the beast had looked being hauled up by the neck, almost like Zhurrie the Goblin of North Dormitory, Sordaling School. I was terribly bucked up to find I could make these people accept me, even if only to laugh at me, and that I slid into their accent and idiom as cleanly as Powl might have wished.

I said that Grofe and his wife had a daughter. Her name was Jannie and she was sixteen years old. She had covered the walls with samplers of trees, flowers, houses, alphabets, all sorts of usual things, and now she took up a position at the right of the fireplace, engaged on an embroidery of adult scope. It made her squint a little and couldn't have been pleasant work, but perhaps she needed the excuse of work to remain in the parlor with a male guest.

When the hired man returned from his evening call at the barn to say the old horse had made light work of his oats and looked ready for five more years, Grofe broke out a bottle of very potent cider and poured for me the very first glass. Jannie glanced up, hidden from all eyes but mine by the frame of her needlework, and when she met my glance she was not squinting at all.

Most sixteen-year-old girls are pretty, and I can remember nothing more about her than that she was at least as good as the average, that she was slight as her mother, and that she had brown hair in ringlets.

Already I was less bothered by the nearness of humanity and by its odors. The cider, atop the mass of lamb, soup, marrows, and pastry, made me very warm, and the company's laughter had softened my mood further. Without becoming talkative, I had come to be at ease and to wonder at this strange unity that was a family household.

To most men I suppose there is nothing to wonder at: People live in households, in family. But I had lived first in some sort of castle, then in a school, and lastly in an observatory, and to me this was exotic. Attractive. The red cushions, the little wooden man, the beeswax shining by firelight. Even with Mother glaring in the corner.

Until that glance, without squinting, that no one in the room could see except myself.

In my hand my glass slipped, but I did not drop it. I had to pretend to my host that I had not heard his last remark, for certainly I had made no sense of it, and then I excused myself shortly, as though I had the usual evening errand. I had left my pack outside the back door, and I scooped up the pack and walked out the rutted path, the farm dogs following but offering no obstacle. As it was a night of no moon, I didn't go far but spread my blankets within distant sight of their houselamps, and I watched them all go off, one by one, with the one in the kitchen being last.

The air was sweet and my privacy sweeter. If Master Grofe and his men had seen the look his daughter had granted me, and had they further known the effect it had had on me, body and mind, I was firmly convinced they all would have risen up and slain me.

The troop on horseback that descended on the Grofes' came along the road a quarter mile from my bed under a walnut tree, so I became aware of them only as a shudder in the earth and a dream of the chestnut horse's ineluctably muddy progress. I was awake but unprepared when I heard Jannie's scream, and then I was running for the roadway. I am no great runner, because of the length of my legs, but I can go on, barefoot or no, and barefoot was how I chased the six men who rode from Grofe's farmstead. I reached the road before they did and hid beside a hedge, knowing a horse's night vision exceeded even mine.

I had no thought that the Grofes had taken it into their heads on impulse to flee their homes in the middle of the night. I doubted very much that they owned as many as six riding horses: luxuries on a farm. These riders had to be those notorious things, Zaquash avengers: ill-content young troublemakers who strike at the well-to-do landowner of Velonyan blood. I remembered Master Grofe's lack of accent, and his unusual education, and it became obvious to me. Also obvious, by the lumpy appearance of one man in the middle of the riot, they had raided Jannie Grofe herself. As I became aware of the position of that rider, I sprang across the road, close enough to startle the horses. The men were wearing bag masks, the trademark of the Zaquash avenger. The man holding the girl, however, rode not the Zaquash flat pad, but the old Velonyan saddle, cross-pommeled and long in the stirrup. The horse was tall and the road high-crowned, so the only part of the fellow I could reach was his straight knee, which I hit with the heel of my hand as heavily as I could. I thought to make him drop the reins so I could take control of the horse. Howling, he dropped the girl instead. As I was standing below, I caught Jannie, threw her over my right shoulder, and ran.

Four of them followed us, thrashing over high crop and stubble fields, and though the riders could not see us, the horses could, and they knew what they were chasing. As once before in my life, I made for the line of darkness that was trees.

Jannie was shouting for me to put her down. I don't know if she even knew who had her, though later she said she had known, but I had not the time to follow her dictate, even if her legs had not been tied together.

Very soon I could see the animal's noses out of the corner of my eye, growing larger and closer, and I gave up this rabbit game. I threw Jannie sideways as far as I could and bounced out of the path of the leadmost horse.

It was startled, and it plunged forward. As the near front hoof circled up in the canter, I caught it and helped it further up and out. The horse fell away from me, and I nearly took the force of its rear legs' convulsive kicks as it toppled into the next two beasts behind it. I did nothing more heroic after that; I hefted Jannie Grofe in my arms and pounded on.

We made the wood line and the creek it concealed, where horses could not follow. We were very quiet, and I untied her with my hands and teeth. After a while we heard the raiders give up, cursing, and depart the way they'd come.

Jannie took a large splinter out of my instep, where I had trodden a branch end-on. She was very collected. More than averagely pretty, for a sixteen-year-old. We walked the fields home cautiously, hand in hand, and in my young pride I refrained from limping.

I learned more of human nature that early morning, which is to say, I became more confused. The victor's welcome I received from the Grofe household (and that in truth I had expected to receive) was cut through by a strain of its own opposite. The old wife who embraced her lost daughter cuffed her also, without explanation and at regular intervals. She demanded of me what my whole role in the damned business was, as though both Jannie and I hadn't related it in detail already, and turned her back to rail at Grofe once more before I could reply.

Grofe himself was less accusatory and less distraught, but again and again he made me repeat that I had not known the raiders, their horses, their words, the place from which they had come, or the place to which they vanished. More than once he asked me about a small box, not much larger than a loaf of bread. I had not noticed such a thing, but he didn't want to hear that.

Their disbelief was understandable, for the story told by Jannie was one of great drama, with massive struggle against armed men and the tossing of a horse and rider over my shoulder. I tried to reduce the narrative to human proportions, but the hired man, whose name I now remember to be Quaven, stared and glared at me in the light of the single lamp, with black shadows of the black chair backs climbing up and down the walls.

Mistress Grofe had woken first at the sound of the approaching horses, but (she repeated more than once) had not been able to rouse her old man. One raider had broken the front window, crawled in through the mess of slats and panes, and had drawn the bolt for the rest of them, and by the time the elder son had reached the bottom of the stairs, they were standing in possession with torches, swords, and a primed harquebus pointed right up the stairway.

They grabbed the boy and began ransacking the house for valuables, and when that proved time-consuming, dragged the girl from her bedchamber instead and offered to trade her person for the proceeds of the early barley crop. It was not "all your gold" or "your silverware and jewelry." I inquired after this, since it seemed to speak close knowledge of the farmstead or at least of the area. Grofe repeated that it had been the proceeds of the early barley crop they demanded, and that is what he gave them, in a box not much larger than a loaf of bread.

And still they took her, tying her hand and foot, and they rode off with Jannie, the harquebus, the box, and all.

Grofe sat at the black table, with one hand clutching at the hair of his forehead and the other making angry flat thumps against the wood. With every thump the smell of beeswax rose and mingled with the smell of the smoky lamp.

"We can go after them, Daddy," said the younger boy, a child of perhaps thirteen who was already taller than I. Grofe looked up absently and continued to thump.

"Do you have horses?" I had to ask. "I mean, not like the chestnut, but road horses." If they had horses, they should already be on the road and riding, instead of damaging the woodwork and burning oil.

"A few saddle mounts," answered Grofe, shooting me one of his untrusting glances. "Not fast, but good for a long way. But it wouldn't do to go haring off, not knowing after who or where."

I remembered the sound of their retreating hooves. "They went north, on the plain road, with one horse lame and a man with a broken leg."

"So *you* say." Quaven did not bother to conceal his suspicions of me.

"The road is dry already," answered Grofe. "They'd make sure of that before riding out on us."

"Not so dry as that, only two days after a rain. There's a heavy night dew this season; I have cause to know that."

They all stared at me, even Jannie.

"I can track for you," I told him, all the while knowing Powl would call this a mistake.

• • •

Quaven had fetched me my boots, for I didn't want to do any more treading on my bare, wounded foot, and the rest of my gear was spilled out on the kitchen table as security (I suppose) for my good behavior. I could not ride and track, so I had to trot before them, while Grofe, Quaven, and the elder boy used my white, moonlit head as a beacon.

The farmer had heard my name as Zural, which would be at least a good Zaquash sort of name, and I let him call me this. Now, finally, he asked me what I did for myself and I told him I was an optician. He let that be, though I imagine he thought it to be some minor territorial religious sect.

The place where the riders had left the road after me was unmistakable, as was the place where they had scrambled back on. One horse stepped unevenly, while another, with larger feet, wandered from one side of the road to the other, seeming to be imperfectly controlled.

A few miles on, they turned right into the forest, on a path that was between a cow trail and a wagon road.

"Commerey," stated Grofe.

The tracks in this damp wood were unmistakable, and with my attention relaxed, my mind became aware of how weary I was, having walked all the previous day, then sprinted, then run with a heavy weight. A soft, heavy weight, very pretty, and of a certain shape. Only sixteen.

My foot slipped in the muck, and in the sudden awakening I remembered who was behind me and that they did not trust me.

The land opened again, and ahead was heard a wailing and a weeping that announced itself to be no trivial matter. "Commerey," said Grofe again. He quickened his horse and trotted by me, followed by the others. When I caught up with them they were on the large porch of a house built to their own plan, and another man was hammering his fist on the wall harder than Grofe had pounded the table, while a woman more generously built than Mistress Grofe hung over the rail, weeping. Small children hung upon her or huddled on the steps.

Grofe was striding back and forth, adding his anger to theirs.

"You's avengers got their boy. Killed him as he stood," said Quaven to me. This insistent, deliberate connection of myself with the thieves and murderers, added to my tiredness and my sore foot, caused me a moment of blind anger, and I had to catch myself with my hand already launched. All I could do was make myself miss his face entirely, so only the wind made him blink, and then I held guard for another half second, until I was certain I had myself in rein.

I don't think he was sure what had happened, but his brown, Zaquash face set in belligerent wrinkles. "I wouldn't try that against a man, you great monkey," he said, as though I had only raised a fist to him. Perhaps that was all he saw.

There had been four of them—I could account for the other two—and they had been angry. They had taken two silver candlesticks and a naming bowl, and the life of an eighteen-year-old boy, though he had not opposed them in any manner. None of the Commereys had.

"I can tell you why them's hot about," said Quaven, speaking loudly into Master Commerey's grief. "It was 'cause this fellow 'mong us."

Briefly Grofe described my part in the business, leaving out the episode of tossing the horse over my shoulder. I climbed the stairs, stepping around the children, and allowed Commerey to peer out at me through blank eyes, and through the door I saw the body of the boy laid out on two chairs, with a basin and rags below him and one candle for light.

"You can track them?" he asked me, and I could only say that I had so far.

He was a big man, square-faced, with less Zaquash about him than Quaven but more than Grofe. "Then track for me, too," he said.

At about dawn Commerey called my attention to a hemispherical stone, knee-high, set into the earth beside the roadway. "Ekish Territory line marker," he said. The other riders at my back grunted as though he had said something of real meaning.

I sat down on the meaningful stone. "Territory line marker? How does that affect our chase?" I asked the big man. "We had no legal authority before, so we haven't less now." Commerey got down from his horse and stood beside me. He looked down sharply.

"More tired you get, less you sound like a local man, Zural. Where you come from?"

I felt chastened and foolish as well as bone-weary. The farmer was right, so I dropped the accent entirely. I told him I had been raised in Sordaling City, and when that didn't suffice, that I had been raised as a servant at the Royal Military School. There was no lie in that, and it was enough.

Grofe answered my question. "Beyond this marker, lad, Satt Territory gives way to Ekesh. It was Ekesh avengers struck us, so we're going in the right direction, that's all."

"How do you know they were Ekesh, Master Grofe?" I asked him. Grofe spoke with energy, but his back was wilted and his hands heavy on his horse's withers.

He snorted, and so did the horse. "Would have to be! Don't ask idiot questions." He pushed the beast forward again.

The differences among the various Zaquash territories are not obvious to outsiders, and their inability to hold common cause is still less comprehensible. If it were not that way, I imagine Velonya itself would remain a small country on the middle-western border of the continent.

Forgive my impudence, my king. This paper will not easily

erase, and my manuscript comes too slowly for me to toss the page. I am forced to rely on impulse and honesty.

It was bright morning, and our grim troop cut through populated neighborhoods. I wondered if our errand was written across our faces and what the Territorial Guard would do with us if they found us out. If we found the avengers, we could either turn them in to their own constables or perform a forced extradition, carrying them back across the line. Either way, I knew Powl would not approve of my role in this, but I felt pressed by the situation.

Ekesh is the Zaquash word for lake land, and on that morning we passed by many of the waters that made the place famous: cool, finger-shaped, hemmed in iris and cattails, and of the same clear green as fine glass held edge-on to the light. The panfish of Ekesh (called that because they are the shape of a pan, complete with long handle) have orange-red spots over their gills, and in the translucent waters they looked like sparks darting. Dragonflies of many metallic colors crowded the air in their last attempt that year to do whatever it is dragonflies do, and the hummingbirds, looking much like the dragonflies, fought each other over the season's last twinberry blooms. In the daze of my constant walking, I forgot my errand, I forgot the banging of the horses' hooves behind me, I forgot even that my foot had been pierced and now was well inflamed.

I can see why your forefathers lusted to possess little Ekesh Territory, my king, though Satt is richer and Morquenie has the port. Though I felt neither the strength nor the desire to conquer these round fields (for they plow in circles), green waters, and all the armored dragonflies, still I wished even then to return to Ekesh, on any other errand than man-hunting.

It was many years before that happened.

We passed a town, the name of which eludes me. The

roofs, however, were of clay, orange-red, the color of the spots on the panfish. We spoke to no one. No one prevented or delayed us.

The tracks I was following did not leave the road as we passed the town, though there were signs that the lame horse stood in one place awhile, and water was spilled on the earth. Two or three miles beyond there rose a birch wood, not too heavy or dark, and there our avengers finally showed some individuality, for the horse under imperfect control went off onto a slim path to the left, and none of the others left the road this time to bring it back.

I told the riders I thought we were near the end of the hunt, and five men looked down on me with faces white and expressionless as the moon. They swayed in their saddles. Commerey's eyes were fixed on nothing.

I had thought I was the weariest man there, having jogged while they rode astride. But I was young, and also I had lost neither cash crop nor family the night before. Politely as I knew how, I asked for two men to take the wood's track while I led the rest forward. Grofe's son and Quaven did so, the Zaquash under protest.

Under broad noon we came to a declivity so sharp the road itself tacked left and right for the safety of carts and wagons. Down below was a palisade town all of wood, of no great age by the looks of it, and in the center of the town lay a lake like a mouse's eye, perfectly round, perfectly brown. Most riding horses left the road here and scuttled down quickly through the grass, but the lame horse I followed had taken the slower way. At the bottom they formed together again and entered through the open gateway of the town.

"Shelbruk," Commerey named the place, and he sat on his horse as though he were broken of his last idea.

I leaned against the wood of the palisade. "Well, there it is, good men. The avengers are in Shelbruk, unless they've already left again, and I doubt that. I have tracked for you

110

night and day, and shown you the tracks as I went. I cannot also decide what you are to do about them."

Grofe and Commerey looked down at me and said nothing.

"Well, can I? I know neither your laws nor your customs."

The hired man looked at Grofe and Commerey and shifted his buttocks on the saddle. Then they pushed past me through the gateway.

I had nothing—not my blankets, not my change of clothes, not my optical blanks or grinders. I sat by the clean well that overlooked the lake that Shelbruk Town had dirtied, and I dared to look at my foot. The wound had begun to seep and looked like it would be grateful for the sun, so I sat on the stone curb, that foot cocked up on the other thigh, and watched the poorer housewives and maids-o'-work draw water.

Most had carts with little donkeys, a few had carts with large dogs, and the unfortunate few had only strong backs. They carried their supplies in metal buckets of the sort used elsewhere to store milk. The lake well was so popular on this fine day that I was convinced there was no piped water in all of Shelbruk, a conviction I now know was false. Very few of the women accomplished their errand without much stopping for fan-waving and talk, and even a beggar with a silly face and an ugly foot was not beneath their notice. I learned that the cabbage worm was very bad and the price of worsted impossible and heard four separate guesses as to the father of the baby of some lass named Nishena. One old lady returned to her home and prepared me a sage and rosemary compress to draw the pus and keep the flies off. I decided that day that I liked the company of women, and I have never changed in that.

My pack, poor as it was, was a territory away, and I had run all night and all morning. I could smell myself. I borrowed a small bucket from one of the lakeside laundresses, filled it with water, and took myself down a lonely alley to wash in a spot of reflected sun. In lieu of soap I used the compress.

I had finished upon the person of Nazhuret and was assaulting his shirt and trousers when I heard hoofsteps approaching around the corner of a brick building. Hurriedly, I donned the trousers and before I had time to do more, a man led a horse my way.

The horse was a shining gray of quality, somehow familiar. The man was lean and dark and dressed in grimy velvet, too warm for the day. He recognized me as I recognized him as the fellow who had stopped me on the road the previous summer.

He stopped, his face hidden in shadows, then led on again, until he and the horse's head shared my square of sunlight. He slid down the wall, regardless of his clothing, and, squatting on his heels, pulled out a long pipe. This he filled and lit: a laborious process. I went back to squeezing herby water through the wool of my shirt.

"Smells good," he said, though the stink of his smoking overwhelmed all other odors. Then, as I wrung the shirt out, he added, "So. No more the goblin, Zhurrie?"

Wetheaded, dressed in rags, and with one boot off, I can't imagine that I ever looked more like a goblin than at that moment. I looked into his face for irony and could not decide whether I had found it. I put the wet shirt back on and stood up. So did he.

I asked him who he was, and he answered, "You don't remember Arlin, Nazhuret? No? Well, it was a very long time ago. You were young."

"Then so were you, sir. Were you at the school? I don't remember an Arlin. But there were so many boys." I carried my dirty water out with me, lest I muddy the fine horse's hooves. Arlin followed.

"But I remember you, despite those numbers," he said.

The alley was narrow, and I was forced to lead. "I think

I am hard to forget," I told him, and behind me I heard both a squeak of leather and a sharp laugh.

"How vain we have become," said Arlin. He was mounted already, and as I turned to explain that my remark was the reverse of vanity, he pushed past me and trotted off.

In deep chagrin I spilled the water on a stretch of pavement that looked in need of it, and I considered how good I was at embarrassing myself. If I never spoke again, I would never feel the need to apologize.

I went looking for my Satt territorial flock, wondering if I had done right in abandoning them at the city gate. They might have met their enemy and been killed by them. They might have fallen asleep in their saddles and be sitting at the end of some blind avenue, all three of them and their horses, snoring.

I decided I would try the offices of the Territorial Guard in case Grofe and Commerey had decided to trust to that authority. I inquired of a grocer, and passed three sleeping dogs and a well-attended puppet theater in which two dolls were engaged in hanging another by the neck. The unfortunate victim was raised clean off the stage platform by the suspending rope, and the hand supporting him was withdrawn (in fearful symbolism for the vital force, I suppose).

The effect was unsettling, and discovering that the guard office was on a quiet street immediately behind the puppeteers turned it into an omen. Though Powl had no faith in omens, he had had less faith in policemen, and again I wavered, a few feet from the gold letters spelling EKESH.

As I stood there, too tired for decision, a man came stumping and sighing along toward me. He yawned. He scratched a stubbly face. Though I could not trace my memory back to Arlin of the gray horse, I had no trouble with this man, for I had seen him only twelve hours ago—or had seen his boot, his breeches, his jacket, and his hand as they pursued me over fields of stubble, and the lungs that now yawned and sighed had been screaming as his horse went up and over.

His hair was as new-chick yellow as my own. I hadn't expected that, but then a bag over the head will conceal a great deal. His eyes were blue, and he was very tired. So was I.

I felt a great reluctance to be the tool of vengeance, even of a very justified vengeance. At the same time, I could not forget the weeping of the Commerey household over the body of a boy not yet grown. It was true I had been the cause of the Zaquash avengers' murderous anger, but had I not acted, perhaps it would have been Jannie, not yet grown, who was dead now.

I took a middle line. I stepped in front of the yawning fellow and said to him, "I recognize you."

He recognized me at least equally well. He squawked, swung a random fist, and turned to run back the way he had come.

I had gone two steps in pursuit when his mood changed on him and he skidded and tripped on the cobbles, turned, and came straight at me with a dagger that was half a sword in length.

The attack had neither art nor science, but at that moment I would have traded a great deal of art and most of science for two sound feet or even an hour's sleep. I watched my right hand parry the blade near the hilt and the left help carry it out beyond my body. I had my left hand over his, so I continued my spinning motion until I had taken him around and into the wall of the Territorial Guard itself. He smashed the timbers with face, elbow, and knife together, and the dagger stuck firmly into one black firwood upright. Because I was not sure of my footing, I slipped and broke his arm at the elbow before I thought to release it. He stood where he had been slammed, howling of the pain.

There, in the doorway, stood a man in the green, epauleted uniform of a captain of the Territorial Guard. Powl's words

to me rang loud in my mind: "Do not touch the police...
for you will wind up hanged." He looked down at me coldly
enough, and I—like the man I had just injured—considered
the chances of turning and running. I had twisted my sore
foot on the cobbles.

"You were very lucky, lad," said the captain, and his mouth
spread in a chilly grin. "If you hadn't slipped sideways he
would have spitted you."

I knew immense relief, and felt called upon to explain.
"Captain, this man kidnapped a woman from Satt Territory
last night. I believe his friends also—"

"What is that to me?" asked the captain, and his grin shut
down. "My authority is Ekesh. You'll have to get the Satt
Guard to file for extradition. If you have names, residences,
occupations, all that." The Territorial Guard captain was very
large, as usually they are, and casually he reached over and
lifted the avenger by the hair and looked into his face. "Edd
Gellik," he said. "I am not surprised." The man chose to leave
some of that hair behind as he staggered off, clutching his
broken arm.

The captain put a silver whistle in his mouth, and within
ten seconds the fleeing man was surrounded by guards as large
as the captain.

"There is no legal impediment, however, in arresting him
for deadly assault." The wintry smile came back. "Nor, for
that matter, for destruction of official Ekesh territorial property."

They had pulled him down, with no regard for his injury,
and he screamed as they bound him and dragged him into a
doorway. I felt faintly sick, and faintly sorry I had allowed the
day's events to progress to this. But I could not plausibly have
explained away an armed attack with a captain of the Territorial Guard as witness to it.

I followed them in and wrote out for them my account of
what had happened. All present seemed surprised that I could

write. I stated that I had approached the man, uttered the words "I recognize you," and was immediately assaulted with a dagger, which I evaded to the detriment of my ankle. No more than that was required. To me it seemed an inadequate document, but the Guard captain was pleased enough to dismiss me with the advice to let the Satt Guard take care of Satt business from now on.

I took to the streets again with very little peace of mind. I knew enough about law in the Velonyian-controlled Zaquash territories to guess that the penalty for armed assault was likely to be more than a few years in confinement. The man called Gellik might go to a labor gang. Might die in a labor gang was almost to say the same thing. Or he might die at the end of a rope.

Had the Guard captain blinked at the wrong moment, or had I not had the fortune to appear to have slipped, it might have been myself awaiting one of these ends. A short result to Powl's long labor.

The puppet show in the market had folded and gone. The grocer and his fellows were packing. I asked a baker if I might help him load, in exchange for one of his unsold bread rolls. He was a portly man, and it was obvious he didn't think I had enough size to be of real help, but he allowed me to amuse myself, and I spent the middle of the afternoon in the odor of brown crusts and raisins. He gave me six large poppyseed rolls in a bag made from a single sheet of folded white paper.

Though poppyseed rolls are a specialty of Ekesh, I had never seen such a container before, and was as taken with its simplicity and cleanness as I was by the speckled treasure within. I ate of one and examined the other's cleverness while I looked for some place to rest my abused foot.

The sign proclaimed the place to be an inn and the door was open, though no sound of activity leaked out. It came to me, fresh from my success at the little market, that I might be equally able to lift things over my head in here and win a glass of something to go with the bread rolls. I was very thirsty.

Though it was quiet inside, it was not empty. Both the inn residents' bar and the locals' bar had groups of men sitting over ale, and the barmaid, slouched in the doorway between the two, stared out toward the street, oblivious to both sets of customers.

I entered the shadow of the front hall and glanced at the two doors before me, unsure which was which. No sign informed me, of course. It seems to be a rule of territorial hostels that the stranger must guess which room was designed for his use, or else inquire of the spirits of the air.

Three dull-looking men occupied the right-hand chamber. None was eating, so it was impossible to tell whether they were residents of the inn or locals desiring a glass. One had his head in his hand, while the other two were drawing in beer spillings on the bar itself. I turned to the other door.

It was almost the same group, dull, drinking, composed of three men, although there were dirty plates piled at the bar's end. It took me more than a glance to realize that these three were the men I had led from the maple woods of Satt to these Ekesh lakes.

In that same moment, a part of my mind spoke up from below (I know no better way to put it, sir) to tell me that I also knew their mirror image across the wooden bar wall. Without moving, I turned my eyes back to the right-hand door.

The shoulders of one of the men gave him away. The tip of a spur, seen out of the corner of my eye as indeed it had been seen before, as I ran for my life and for that of young Jannie . . . I could not be certain, and yet I was certain.

From the left door came a sigh that slid into a groan. Grofe, almost certainly. From the right came some tired laughter. I stood between the two, and what my course of action was to be I had no idea.

117

If I had owed Master and Mistress Grofe anything for their marrows, pastries, cider, and the half acceptance that had come with it, I had paid that debt already. With Commerey, sitting silent and square as a rock behind an untouched ale, I had no connection, though even now he had my sympathy. I had just gotten one man into the hands of the Guard and I strongly suspected he would die in those hands. I wanted no more part of this.

Yet there were the three men who had stolen Grofe's income; kidnapped his daughter, perhaps to kill; tried in a sprightly manner to kill me; and ended by waking a young man from his sleep only to murder him. I disapproved heartily and wished them every sort of unsuccess if only they didn't drag me down with them.

I might have gone quietly into the left side, waked up my Satt friends, and explained to them who their neighbors were, but then I would be committed again. I might have even more quietly walked away.

Instead, I decided to let the moment create itself. I stood and I waited, and I watched the wooden partition and the two doors flanking it with the same aimless attention I had paid to the bricks of the observatory.

My eyes were scratchy. My ankle made itself known.

"Here, boy," said the barmaid, coming out from the bar into the left side and approaching me by that door. "Don't block the door that way. What is it you want?"

Three sets of eyes on the left side of the bar lifted casually, drawn by voice and movement. Three sets of eyes on the right did also, and the door was clear and open between the residents' bar and the locals' bar.

The Satt farmers were quicker to react, though only by an instant. I heard Commerey's chair falling backward and then Grofe's bellow. I grabbed the barmaid by her arm and flung her out into the street.

"They're going to fight!" I told her, and she in turn took hold of my wrist.

"How by perdition do you know that?" she shouted in my ear. "You haven't even been inside!"

I slipped her grip and jumped back into the place, closing the door behind me. When she pounded, I jammed a ladder-back chair beneath the knob. I did not want to have to carry this lass on my back as I had Jannie; the barmaid was bigger than Jannie, and I was not fresh.

The Satt men were over the bar and shoving through the partition door, which the avengers were trying to brace as I had braced the outer door. The little deal pine bar door, however, had no knob, and a blow of Commerey's huge shoulder splintered both it and the barstool. He stumbled into the room and was hit on the head by a one-pint beer crock. The avenger with the spurs was standing on the bar, displaying a knife that looked much like a shaving razor. The third, less limber or more saddle sore, attempted to climb the bar but gave up and decided to enter the fray from behind, through the hallway. Past me.

I did not recognize this fellow, but he must have recognized me, for he took out another of those thin-bladed, Rezhmian-work razors and sliced upward at my groin. I skidded backward so that the thing sparkled an inch from my face, and as my thigh encountered the chair I had used to brace the door, I knew I was in trouble. I kicked his elbow as I came down on the caned seat, but he did not drop the razor; he circled it above his head and brought it down at my face.

Both my hands had grasped the chair arms to control my fall, and I used that support to launch myself, feet first, at his head. The blade sliced my shirt, but I put both boot heels into his chin hard enough to throw him against the end of the partition, which resounded.

Still the man kept his razor and still he flailed it at me. I parried his arm once more, tried to grab the thing, failed, suffered a cut hand and then as he bent with the force of his strike, I saw below my hand the back of his head and his neck. I struck down with the heel of my hand as heavily as I could, and I knew immediately I had killed a man.

Within, the avenger with the other razor still was on the bar, holding off Grofe and his son with his weapon and his feet. The other avenger was flat out on his back, and Commerey was braced on hands and knees, shaking his head like a sick cow. I heard a little silver sound in the distance. A whistle.

"Out!" I shouted. "Guard! Guard! Guard!" I shouted, and by the third iteration of the name, even dazed Commerey was knocking me aside in his hurry. They issued out the door as close as flies in a cloud, and even the avenger with the knife ran with them. I limped along behind.

The Satt men had left their horses in the inn stableyard, but evidently they had left them saddled, for they were charging back again before I had made half the distance. Grofe cantered past me, his son half stopped and then thought better of it, but massive Commerey brought his beast to a halt before me and plucked me up by the neck of my damp, gaping shirt.

Shelbruk went by me at a great rate, with cobbles looming large enough to break a horse's leg or a man's head. I had a mouthful of red horsehair before I found a secure position on the pommel in front of the rider. We flew past the market, empty and echoing, and made a clangor over the flagstones around the well. I heard the Guards' whistles again and again, but I saw no uniforms, and we were out the town gates before any thought to close them on us.

If they had any intention of closing the gates.

"You're bleeding freely, lad," said Commerey. I was surprised that a man so recently brained would have attention to spare for that, and after glancing at my hand I told him it was not a bad cut but that razors make for long bleeding.

I looked behind as we climbed the steep hill over the town. No one seemed to be following, least of all the avenger with the knife.

"Did you kill that man I tripped over in the hall?" Commerey asked me, and I admitted I had. It sounded impossible to me, even as I said it. It felt like a lie in my mouth.

"I'm indebted to you, then," he answered me. "He's the one shot my Coln right through the heart."

He put me down on the road where we had left Quaven and Commerey's boy, and once again I was put to tracking, like a dog. I found signs that the two had come out again, shuffled a while in the roadway, and then pushed their mounts carefully into the undergrowth. There was nothing in these marks Grofe or Commerey might not have seen himself, had they had the patience or the vision to look.

My Satt men's horses did their own share of aimless circles and impatient pawing as the riders discussed whether to wait for the boys or to leave. Grofe's opinion, as best I remember, was that pursuit would come eventually and we ought to ride on. Commerey believed the Shelbruk Guard was glad to have seen the tail of us and that we should wait.

As they disputed the matter (never asking me my opinion, though I was the one who had had to kill, and the one without a horse under me), the two missing members pressed out of the woods, dragging briars. For a moment all the weary men stared at one another. "We got the maggot. We buried him," said Quaven, and for another silent moment all drank in the excitement of this boast and swagger, and their tired eyes glowed. Then they began to laugh and pound each other on the back.

I stood in the middle of the road, the legs of the sweating horses all around me. I called for Quaven to repeat what he had said, to explain what they had done to the man with the broken knee.

121

"We took his Ekesh heart out of his Ekesh body!" The hired man's face was gray, aside from two red circles directly under his eyes. His eyes grinned and glittered, but he was so tired he was leaning backward against the reins, dragging his horse's head in. The beast was even more tired and did not complain.

The boy chimed in, "He was lying on his fucking bed with his fucking wife cluck-clucking over him, Dad, and that's it where we did him. Like a hog, he was. A big, long hog." He was no more than sixteen years old—Jannie's age—and his voice was filled with glee and horror and exhaustion.

Commerey said nothing in return. He was looking instead at me—the only one to do so. "What would you have us do, walk him into Shelbruk, to be patted on the back? They killed my son."

"He didn't kill your son. He had a broken leg. He was helpless."

"It's all the same," he said to me, his heavy face without expression. "My boy was helpless."

Quaven kicked his resistant horse forward. In his right hand was a cavalry saber he had not owned earlier in the day. "I've had enough of this weasel," he said, and he shook the blade in the air at me. The horse, not cavalry-trained, began to dance sideways.

"Fold it up, Quaven, the man's been a friend to us," said Grofe, and he pushed his horse between the steel and myself. The hired man still was drunk on his violent success, however, and though he slid the weapon away, he spat in my direction.

"I won't ride with him. He's another filthy Ekesh and I don't want him following anymore."

Grofe bristled. "Where did you get the power to say who rides and who doesn't, plow-pusher? I hire you to—"

I interrupted. "I haven't been riding at all, as you might remember, Master Grofe. And as for following—I led, not followed you to this day's work, and I'm very sorry I did so, for it's been a nasty one. So I will bid you good day here and hope our ways do not intersect again."

I retraced the path the horses had made in the brush until I was far enough from the road that I no longer heard their many-hooved progress. I followed a narrow path for a few miles, back west and south toward Satt according to the sun, and then my travels caught up with me and I curled where I was and slept.

I awoke cold in the dark of night, with deer leaping over me.

It took me three days to retrace the path I had run in half of one night and a morning, and those three days are of a piece in my memory. I might have been under one of the lakes of Ekesh, so odd was the autumn light and shadow and so poor and unconnected was I. No pack to carry and a foot that reminded me momently how bad I had abused it.

I took my time walking, avoided the traveled road, and when I was hungry I set a snare of birchbark and caught a rabbit. After an hour of trying to start a fire without any tools at all, I gave up, stuffed the beast in my shirt, and went on. I ate cattails from one of the countless ponds instead.

That night I lay on a bed of fir, covered by more branches, but I was a shade too cold to sleep. The moon was first quarter and not yet set, and I wondered if it would be wiser to use the next few hours in forward progress. The straight road was only a mile or so below, and I had no qualms about using it at this dead time. But when that astronomical body finally rolled on and under, it would leave me in greater cold and greater darkness, without even the comfort of a fir bed. I stared out at the white stripe of the path from my hiding, until the stripe took on a life of its own. I had never seen a ghost, but it seemed appropriate I would see one tonight. Perhaps it would have a broken neck.

So weary was I that the apparition inspired very little fear in me, and after I had stared at it for some minutes, the floating glow took on a horizontal appearance. Soon it formed the lineaments of a white dog, and then it had the face of a white dog, very round-cheeked and pointy-eared, and the dog seemed to be laughing at me.

The ghost sniffed, snorted, and took one step closer.

My first thought was that hounds from Shelbruk Town had found me out, but then common sense took over and I realized that people do not track with fuzzy, sharp-nosed dogs like this one: the sort of dog that would have a curled plume of a tail. No, it was the smell of the dead rabbit that drew the beast on.

Even I could smell that odor, both from my clothes where I had worn the carcass like a cummerbund, and from where it lay now at my feet, as useless to me as ever. Dead rabbit grows old quickly.

I picked the corpse up by the hind feet, and with that movement of my white arm, the white dog vanished. I threw the rabbit to where the dog had been, wiped my hand on the fir boughs, and closed my eyes determinedly. In a few seconds I heard the crunch of bones. I must have fallen asleep then, for when I woke again the moon had gone on, but pressed back to back against me was the soft, odorous, and very warm white dog. I did not object.

The next morning he was not there, but the earth was pocked with dogprints half the size of my own hands. A number of the nearby trees, also, had known the dog's attentions.

That day threatened rain, but before it could fall I came to a farmhouse and offered to split wood in exchange for tinder and a flint. I was more wary of the farm wife than she was of me, but in the end I broke so much oak to hearth size that she offered me dinner and a place in the kitchen to sleep as well as the fire tools. I took the dinner gratefully, but so disillusioned about my kind was I that I chose to sleep in the cow byre.

She was a large, kindly woman with many children and a mild sort of husband who came in from the last harvest late and approved of my work without suspicion. They told me they had enough for my hands to do for a good month, and money to take away when I left, but the contact with Satt versus Ekesh had soured me on farm families. I turned the job down.

I wish with all my heart, my king, that I remembered the name of these people, instead of Grofe's.

That night the rain came down hard, but the byre of ten cows was steaming warm. I wrapped myself in straw and listened to the beating on the roof and the breathing of the cows and the squeaking of many mice. Before long one of the squeaks became a squeal, which ended in a snap, followed by butcherly crunching. I crawled up though my bedding and out into the aisle, where I beheld my white dog, catching mice by moonlight. I had to reassure myself that there were no hens asleep on the ground before I returned to bed, and with the dog curled beside me, it was almost too warm.

The next day was wet but not cold, and I steamed like a cow myself, in my coarse woolens. I found with some difficulty my own prints where the cut through to Satt Territory joined the Ekesh southern road, and I was back in Satt by midday.

Behind me down the muddy trail paced the dog again. First I felt him and then I heard him and last I turned and saw him in full daylight for the first time.

He was very dirty, more gray than white, and the tail I had always imagined as a high plume hung sodden behind him, almost touching the mud. (If I had been a dog at that moment, hungry and on a mud road going nowhere much, my tail would have looked much like that.) His feet were large and his legs long, like sticks, but his ruff was very elegant and his eyes grinned.

On impulse I bent to him and made the usual kissing noises

that men make to attract dogs, and the result was that he was gone from the path entirely.

When I could see before me the road down which I had followed the horse and up which I had led the Satt farmers, it was twilight already. I left the path and made a few of my birchbark snares and then a bed of pine branches, the softer fir not being available. I heard a howl and a growl and a snap that told me the dog was yet with me, had discovered one of my snares, and had disposed of it. He was a large dog. The tree I used as a pillow had a squirrel's cache of walnuts and hazelnuts in it, which I robbed and cracked in my hand. The next beast to fall into one of my snares was perhaps the same squirrel that had fed me, and I felt slightly dishonorable about eating it, but almost at the same moment I caught another rabbit in my one remaining trap, so I cooked the rabbit and threw the squirrel to my dog.

My dog, I say, though I could not even touch him.

It was bright morning when I came to the tree where my pack had been laid, and only then did I remember it had been brought to the farmhouse. I went after it.

There were horses and wagons tied in back of the building, crowded as a wedding. I went past them to the kitchen.

Quaven came to the door. I heard voices in conversation behind him, but there was nothing to be seen in that room but tables piled high with food. "We don't need you today," he said, and made to close the door in my face. My temper was almost ragged, and I gave the closing door such a blow that Quaven skidded half across the kitchen.

"No doubt you don't, but I need my pack, if you please," I answered him, and when he came on with his fists waving, I spun him to the floor and sat on him. "My pack," I reminded him. "Optical supplies. Glass blanks. One grasswood stick."

"I don't know anything about a pack," he said, and then he began to call for his master. Grofe came.

"He forced his way in," said Quaven, as loud as he could

with my weight on his stomach. Master Grofe looked at me coolly and without decision.

"Why shouldn't he come in, Quaven? We owe the lad much."

"All I want from you, master, is my pack, which I left here." I stood up. The kitchen was filled with food, as for a wedding.

"I never saw it!" shouted Quaven, standing also. "I never, ever!"

To Grofe I said, "He had it when he brought my boots. Someone has it now."

For a moment the dark man stood still and silent, and I could hear someone laugh in the room behind. As at a wedding.

Was it the older son who was marrying, so soon after the catastrophe of the raid? Or could it be Jannie? Sixteen was old enough for a girl to wed. Barely old enough. Perhaps they felt it important to wed her off now, before the story of her abduction could spread.

If that was so, it was a shame, I thought. Such a girl deserved a long, leisurely, silly wedding.

Grofe said, "I remember it. Not since that night, though. Let's see." He strode out of the kitchen, out of the house. I followed him and Quaven followed me, protesting. We came to the haybarn and Grofe went up a ladder. As I came up after, Quaven gave a yank back on my leg. I kicked him in the face.

There, in the man's crude cubby, were all my possessions. They lay in disarray but not too badly damaged, although the jeweler's rouge was smeared experimentally around the inside of the linen bag. The glass blanks had been too incomprehensible even to destroy, and the secret of the bow stick was intact.

Grofe said he was sorry for the inconvenience. He offered to pay—in kind, not cash—for whatever was broken. I gathered it up and told him I needed nothing except my knife, which had been appropriated. He went down the ladder to Quaven, and there were words between them. When Grofe came up again, he had the knife, slightly blade-nicked but otherwise usable.

He watched me pack all away, with measure in his eyes. "I'm sorry my man did that," he said. "You can't trust anybody these days."

I didn't reply.

"For instance," Grofe continued. "We owe you a lot. I admit it. But still, I don't trust you at all."

I waited for him to go down the ladder first, expressing somewhat the same sentiment. "It is not necessary that you do trust me," I said at last. "Or that I trust you, thank the Three. All I want is to be quit of you people."

"You'll take food, though," he said. "I like to pay what's owed, and all we have to pay now is in food."

I thought of the kitchen heaped with plates, and I remembered Mistress Grofe's buttered marrows. I followed the man back into the kitchen. Quaven was nowhere around.

Grofe made me up a large napkin filled with things that would travel—hard sausage, breadsticks, and cheese—and as I was tying it onto my pack a young man of about my age came from the front room into the kitchen, slamming the door in his excitement and sliding on the tiles. "Twelve," he said. "We have twelve men and twelve good horses, to leave at moonrise, day after tomorrow."

He was waving a bag—a small bag with three holes cut into it as eyes and mouth are cut into a pumpkin.

Grofe didn't look at me immediately. The young man did, with dawning uncertainty. He put the bag into his pocket.

I cleared my throat. "How long have you people been doing this to each other?" I asked Master Grofe as controlledly as I could. "I mean, raiding and killing each other at harvesttime?"

The tall farmer glowered but still didn't look at me. "Ekesh has been raiding *us* for years outa count. And, of course, we retaliate. We have to." Then he did look at me. "I have to. I'm broken. Destitute. Without cash I won't make it through another year."

I dropped the wrapped napkin on the floor and turned to go, but though I was through with him, he wasn't through with me. "By God's Three Faces, you jug-handled ass! You got a right to be holy about it, don't you? You didn't have anything to start with. And you could have got my money back—you had the chance and you didn't."

I hadn't known about the money then, of course, but what I said to him was, "I couldn't run with that and your daughter, too," and then I closed the door behind me.

Later, after a dry day without a job, a handout, or a wood to snare in, with the dog following behind me as hungry as I was, I wished I had dropped my pride instead of the napkin of food.

Between the last work and this, my king, has fallen a freeze, the late corn harvest, and what I am tempted to call a plague of religion. You know the sort of event I mean—it begins with the revival of old prayers and ends with villagers cutting the fingers off their own children to bury beside the old circle "altars." It is very Zaquash, this periodic eruption of bloodletting, and deep-rooted in the peasantry. They feel that the little digit will stand for the child itself and that the parent who is willing to sacrifice his own get to the earth will encourage the spirits of nature to reciprocate. The year has been so unlucky that the people are desperate, and I fear that this season there have been more than fingers put under the earth.

Though I feel myself to be in some senses a personification of Zaqueshlon, still I have stood against this blood excess for all my adult life. It is against the law, against religion, and against the essence of Nazhuret, inside and out. I am sick of it, sir, and sick of opposing an ignorance as limitless as the ground I walk on. I don't know if all my philosophy, my science, rhetoric, vehemence and slapdash heroics have changed one thing. Not in twenty years.

Forgive me one more dramatic digression, sir. And please don't send troops to cut the fingers off the fathers in retribution. That was my first impulse, too, and it is exactly the wrong response.

It is my own belief that the earth spirits need no special propitiation. Having only to wait, they receive us all in the end. Even more ironical is that I have dug amid the circle ruins myself (thereby reinforcing in the local minds the conviction that old Nazhuret is both spirit-touched and simple besides), and beneath the good grass and the sad little digits I have uncovered old bits of weaponry and grommeted leather, which lead me to believe that the altars were no more religious in nature than are the fortifications of Settimben Harbor. By the angle of the blades and the size of one little horsebit (you see, I theorize from very little evidence) I am inclined to date these structures from the last strong Rezhmian occupation of the area, no more than five hundred years ago. I cannot believe that whatever dark southern soldiery happened to die in these places have any possessive interest in the fingers of Zaquash babies. I know very little about the last occupation, but I do know something about the dead.

It seems to me sometimes that this whole territory with its suspicious people and all their condemnable customs are only the offspring of Velonya's and Rezhmia's mutual and faithful hate: children a man is ashamed to have engendered.

My pen runs on about children today because they are dancing under my window. In the mud. They are loud and not well kept—three of the four were orphans too convenient for the public mood, and the last had a father who was very willing to trade her for a spell of good luck. What I shall feed them I do not know, unless I return to my earlier habits and go poaching in the royal preserves.

I cannot believe I ever made as much noise as these creatures.

I did not walk south with the deliberate attempt to outrun the snow. Every Velonyan born knows the winter is inevitable; I believe that knowledge makes of us the stolid, sour people we are. I went south because I had started out south, and nothing I did or saw on the road was so pleasant that I wanted to turn back and experience it over again.

During that dark end of autumn I fitted my first pair of spectacles for a wealthy farmer's wife who had been reduced to touch to tell corn flour from bean flour. Her cooking was thereby much improved, and with the money I thereby made I was able to buy more blanks in Grobebh Township, multiplying my material wealth. I seem to remember, however, that the expenses of food and lodging while in that metropolis just about returned me to my natural state of indigence. I could formulate a natural law from this.

That year, like this, had its late-autumn madness, and its theme was werewolves. I sat in the inn along Brightwares Street, toasting my feet at the fire and attending to rust along the blade of my hedger (and yes, I had used it to cut hedges more than once this season; I am no Rezhmian warrior to think I keep my soul in a stick of metal, but if I did think so, I hope my soul would be sturdy enough for work), and I listened to four men discuss the nature and habits of the wolfman.

Two opined that he had hair all over and two thought not. Three agreed that he had rather the shape of both creatures—man and beast—and had the choice of human or animal locomotion at will, but the dissenter was firm that a werewolf was a wolf in all respects except when he wasn't, when he could not be told from a man. That his teeth were immense, strong, and pointed there was no arguing against, nor did any dispute the fact that he ate meat, and human meat by choice.

I added nothing to this discussion, having never seen a werewolf or even a wolf, but as a stranger to the neighborhood I felt a certain relief that my own teeth were small, blunt, and slightly irregular along the bottom row.

The small kernel that sprouted all this fancy was that three people from around Grobebh had disappeared since harvest. One, the twenty-year-old son of a goldsmith, had vanished from this same inn only a month before and never made it the four blocks to his home. On that same eventful night the wife of a rental cart man disappeared from her bed, leaving her husband and a young child behind. The consensus was that the monster had eaten the man and buried the young woman to consume later, or vice versa, for it could scarcely be supposed that even a werewolf could consume two grown people in one night.

My own opinion was that the people of Grobebh Township were a naive lot and that these simultaneous disappearances could be explained much better without recourse to a werewolf at all. I felt no need to disabuse them, however. I wrapped the blade again and toasted the soles of my boots in the ashes.

The other disappearance had taken place only a week before, and as it was singular and involved a much-loved grandmama who sold sweets every market day, was not subject to the same explanation. Still, it seemed to me that in a place the size of Grobebh, people would fall out of sight now and then. If they had not had their hearts set on a monster, they would have been dredging the canals for the old dame by now.

I was considering buying a pint of hot ale, knowing it would be the end of my evening if I consumed it, when the door was dramatically thrown open and a lean figure stepped into the light and announced that there were wolfprints on the wet pavement all around the building.

The voice and figure belonged to Arlin, my friend of the

elegant horse and dirty haberdashery, and my heart sank with his every word, for I knew or thought I knew what had made those prints. They were made by my poor, faithful, fearful dog, who would neither leave me nor let himself be touched, and would come under no roof but that of a barn. By the time I reached the door it was pressed solid with bodies, all of them taller than I. There were many loud exclamations, and I heard men stepping out left and right from the door. Then I heard them returning, more quickly than they had gone.

"The size of a man's foot" was said, and another added, "And the scrape of its claws, did you see? Like iron."

The potboy came trotting out from behind the bar, and when faced with my own problem, he leaped lightly onto a tabletop and peered over all heads. I followed him.

There they were, a few soppy dogprints surrounded and obliterated by the booted feet of the men. The day's rain was turning to snow. As it didn't seem likely I would be able to elbow my way through, I leaped for a crossbeam and swung out the door, coming down in the middle of attention.

"I think that's only my dog's prints you're looking at," I said to the innkeeper, who stood nearest me. "He . . . follows me."

The innkeeper rubbed his hands on his apron while snow fell on his bald head. I was a stranger and badly dressed, but I was a paying customer. "Your dog? The brute that made those tracks must be larger than you are."

I considered this and answered that he was. Upon being further questioned I explained that he was the sort of dog with a curly tail and fuzzy face and was very timid. White, or nearly so.

The snow was falling harder, and my explanation had dampened the crowd's enthusiasm. We returned within, where Arlin had ensconced himself in a chair by the fire and was amusing the potboy with dagger tricks, and spinning a saber blade around his fingers.

I did such things when I was a boy; we all did at the school, but I had given them up back in the days of the swan boats on Kauva River. I certainly had never been as good as this young man. He watched me watching him.

"Do you remember me now, Zhurrie?" he asked through a wheel of spinning steel.

I admitted I did not, but that I remembered the period in my school career when we had all been crazy for such dangerous games as this. He grinned in return and answered that some stayed crazy.

Arlin had a face of some character and elegance, but starvation was written over it, perhaps merely of food, perhaps of a more subtle sort. His were the classical features of Velonya, overwritten by black eyes and sallow skin. My own coloring belonged with his features, to create in him the image of aristocracy.

Unlike myself, he did not temper the accent of Velonya when traveling in Zaquash territories, and that face, that voice, and those spinning blades all together served to make him an impressive figure to the peasants. They gave him room.

I told him I couldn't thank him for what he had done upon entering the inn, that with the autumn hysteria upon us, he might have caused a poor dog's death, and all for his own amusement.

The dagger came down in the wood of the table between us and stuck. "So you don't believe in werewolves?" asked Arlin, with no expression in face or voice.

It was not a question I could answer. Powl had disbelieved in werewolves, blood-sucking foxes, and witches of all variety, but I thought his attitude inconsistent for a man of science. "I have never seen a werewolf," I said to Arlin, over the knife. "I have seen a dog."

The thin man stared at me for a good count of ten, as though he could make no sense of my words. Slowly he worked the dagger out of the wood of the table. "You have become something strange as a werewolf yourself, Nazhuret," he said, and then turned his attention to the next table, where a game of Does-o was being set up. He put away all his cutlery and slid down the bench and into the game.

I did not have that pint of ale after all, for the discovery of the pawprints had worried me, and I might simply have risen and left the inn, hoping the dog would follow, had it not been that to leave now, after having paid for my bed (by the hearth), would have been to raise suspicion that I myself was a werewolf. Instead I sat alone and paid attention equally to the sounds of the tap and of the card game and to the silence of snow outside. Perhaps half an hour later Arlin leaned over again and whispered in my ear, "There is a gray wolf outside in the street, staring in at the door with his tongue hanging from his mouth."

I looked over his shoulder and out the window, not moving my head. "That's he. That's only my dog."

Arlin examined his cards, gave a bid, and answered me quietly, "No sign of a curly tail."

I had to admit there wasn't. "It curls only when he's happy," I whispered.

The man sniggered. "It's a wolf," he said for my ears only and returned to the game. Shortly after this I saw the dog dart away, white against the white snow slop, and a heavy horse came by pulling the town's snow drag to clear the street.

Arlin was talking to—no, lecturing—the townsmen on the subject of the court of our young king. He would have us know that things had changed in the few seasons of Rudof's monarchy: that new titles had risen and old blocks of power had been broken. He had created three earldoms out of the ruin of the old House of Norwess, to which there had been no heir, and was ennobling dozens of hot-handed young blades and sending them out on missions of discovery: some north, to the Seckret fur routes; some south, to study at the schools of the walled city of Rezhmia; and some past the Felinkas to find for Velonya new islands to stamp on the maps.

I had a strong sympathy with the man whose deeds Arlin was recounting, for it seemed to me he was employing men to do all the things a healthy youth would want to do himself.

And further (according to this lean and grimy authority), the king had put his court on wheels, or even horseback on the rougher roads, and insisted on obtaining the latest information with his own ears and eyes, through Old Velonya, across the territories and to the dry-land borders, where the Red Whips had broken his father's expansionary drive. Six weeks in the springtime and six in the autumn. Free as a lark.

It was great fun, and not only for the young king. Great opportunities for young men with ambition—young men after the young king's heart.

Arlin was calling my name now, asking me why I did not go forth and find my king an island.

As I had not spoken to any man or woman in the room since the incident at the door, and as I was not dressed in a manner that suggested I had easy intercourse with swords and velvet and blood horses, there was a general public startlement, and a dozen pair of eyes were turned down to the ashes. To me.

I had not been paying strict attention, trying instead to bring together into one image Arlin's view of King Rudof and my teacher's. I closed my eyes and heard the question again from memory.

"I would have more success at *finding* an island than some, I suppose," I answered. When Arlin merely pulled his brow and stared at me, I thought to add, "Having a knowledge of telescopes—being an optician, I mean.

"But though adventure is all well and good, I'd rather be at peace with my wife—if I were a king. If I were Rudof."

My explanations seemed only to make things more murky and the public attention closer, so I put the question back to

Arlin. "Why is a young hotblood like yourself, sir, not engaged among the king's progress?"

"Oh, I am," he said very lightly. "Off and on, I am." And he dealt the cards.

I didn't know the rules of Does-o; then and now card games have only served me as a cure for insomnia. I watched the men idly, noting only that Arlin was a great bluffer, and when he bet gold the others abandoned their silver to him without matching him to see his hand. Perhaps it was the influence of the spinning blades, or the knowledge that this man had seen King Rudof face to face.

I could not tell the strategy nor the plays, save when coins were shoved from one side of the table to the other, but at the same time my ignorance of the game freed my eyes, so that I noticed when the red trey fell into his lap instead of joining the others slid across the table to the sorter. With four men playing Does-o, the absence of a card is not immediately evident, and with the various rounds of picking and discarding, its subsequent reappearance as part of a favorable hand caused no comment.

It certainly caused none from me, though I was shocked to the bottom of my young soul to find that one of our old students had devolved into a card cheat. Cheating at games at Sordaling was a crime that meant immediate expulsion, even when the stakes were marbles and lacquered acorns. But I had no doubt Powl would have informed me that this game and these three strangers and indeed Arlin himself were none of my business. All none of my business.

Arlin had seen a wolf and found it to be none of his business, too.

I withdrew to my purchased hearthstone and settled for the night, and when the game was over I tried not to hear the manner in which the old student crowed over his winnings, excited as a boy—an obnoxious boy. The others, townsmen all, grimly exacted from him the promise that he would return the next night to allow them revenge.

I learned something that evening: If one is going to deal doubly, it is wise to be exuberant about it. Nobody suspects enthusiasm.

I feigned sleep, but Arlin sank down with a great cracking of knees and rubbing of palms against his trousers. "You're not asleep—don't think you can fool me. Not with all this clattering about out here. Not you." He poked me between the ribs as he spoke.

I was forced to look at him, and he took immediate offense at what he saw in my face. "What's the difficulty, Zhurrie? Got a tick up your ass?"

"Not a tick, but a red trey, and on your lap," I answered before I could think whether it was wise or not, lying as I was flat on my back and wrapped in blankets.

Arlin's sallow face flushed, or at least the fire made it seem so. "The last man who accused me of cheating—" he began.

"Had eyes at least as good as mine," I finished for him, and I turned over. The man was unchancy, but I did not think he would stab me in the back. I had a moment's peace and then Arlin grabbed me by the shoulder, or tried to. He was not a heavily built man, and he came down flat on the hearth-stones with the wind shot out of him. For some time he stared at me in surprise, his face upside down to mine. His temper seemed to have dispersed as quickly as it had built.

"So. You're not the complete optician after all," he said when he could. "There's a bit of the soldier about you still."

"I'm not the complete anything," I answered, and I sat up in my blanket. "But how would you know what the complete optician would be like? Do you even know what optics is?"

"Lens grinding," he replied. "I'm not an ignoramus." And he pulled himself off the stones before adding, "You didn't say anything? To anyone? About the cards?"

"You didn't say anything? About the wolf?"

He smiled: a fierce grin on that narrow face. Much like that of a wolf. "So now you admit it is a wolf."

I paraphrased myself. "I never have seen a wolf. I have seen a dog. It looks like any dog to me."

Arlin gave me the glance of one who withholds judgment. "And you say its tail curls over its back?"

"When it is happy."

Still he wouldn't let me be. "How often . . . is the creature happy?"

I found myself inclined to giggle. "Any day now, I expect to see it so." At that moment, I did not know myself whether my pitiful white dog was a grandmother-devouring monster or not, and worse, what means I had to control it if it were a wolf. I leaned over and poked Arlin in the floating ribs, as he had done to me, and he let loose a wild swing at my face that was only half in fun, and then the kitchen girl, a plump thing of fifteen or so, was pushing us apart with her ample charms.

"No wrestling here, lads," she said and deposited herself on the hearthstones much closer to Arlin than to myself, with the exposed top third of her bosom placed only inches beneath his nose.

This was no surprise to me. My size, my face, and my evident poverty made a barrier between myself and all but the most discerning women. Arlin's reaction, however, surprised the girl thoroughly. He smiled at her so maliciously, with such evident understanding of her motives and such complete contempt, that even a servant at a middling-price territorial inn had to take offense. She flounced back behind the bar through the taproom, closing and bolting us officiously away from the ale kegs, and I could hear her clogs rattling down the stone hall and up the wooden stairs at the rear of the building.

"Well, that puts us in our places," I said to cover the embarrassment I felt.

139

Arlin's grin had faded, but he kept his dark eyes locked on me. "I don't . . . appreciate women," he stated. "Or perhaps you had already guessed that."

I hadn't given the matter any thought, and I told him so.

"But you needn't worry, little goblin. I'm very picky about the men I appreciate also," he said, and he rose, his silver scabbard and his dagger glistening in the firelight, and he went to his room.

The inn hearth had a good fire, but I slept poorly and left at first light, followed by my white dog, who was turning into a gray wolf before my very eyes.

I had hoped to be settled somewhere before the snows fell, if not grinding lenses then chopping wood or tending cattle, for the winters of the northern territories are no easier than those of Velonya. Grobebh Township, however, already had a lens grinder, who had to turn his attention to other work at least half the day to feed his family, and as I considered making the circuit of the public stables, I passed the brick front of a printer's house, where a small newspaper, still ink-damp, was being tacked into a glass-fronted case on the wall. There I read of the disappearance of a laundrywoman's child from her bed in the middle of the previous night.

I marched smartly out of Grobebh in the falling snow, looking neither left nor right and especially not behind me.

I could never be reasonable about the first snow of the year: As it heartened me this year, so it was then, except that then I was wilder. The sight of so much simple whiteness awakes in me a similarly simple spirit. It is not that I have never had to shovel walks or coach drives, sir. It is not that I have never greeted the winter with a cough and a runny nose. I have suffered these things like other men, and still the snow exalts me.

When I am cold to the bone, underfed, and oppressed by

circumstance, as I was for my twenty-third celebration of the first falling, I remain cold, hungry, and miserable, but still I must run, plunge, dig, and fling the stuff about like a happy cross between a squirrel and a lunatic. When the first fall is a wet one, my personal eccentricity can be dangerous to my health, but on that white day when I was twenty-two, it was cold enough and dry enough that I was in no danger except of being put in a hospice for my own good.

Luckily I was alone, save for the dog, or wolf, or what-have-you, whom I led farther from human habitation as the white, padded day wore on. He was too rational a creature, or too old, or too suspicious to encourage me when I clambered up a tree and shook down the snow on him. He did not seem to know how the blanket of snow both hid him and revealed his footprints. Once the snow ended and men came out to look at the world, he would be easy to track.

Powl's attitude would have gone beyond laughter at this behavior of mine—not the exuberance, but the fact that I was letting the beast's need dictate my own, when he was no good to me and I had never sought out his company nor derived any great good from it. He had taken rabbits from me and given me none in return. He had never allowed me to touch him except back to back, for the warmth of it. I could not even say I was fond of him.

Perhaps he was a wolf after all. Perhaps he was a were-wolf—after all, I had first thought he wore the face of the avenger I had killed.

It was bright noon when this memory knitted itself in my mind, and for the rest of the day I kept a wary eye on the dog, who kept a wary eye on me.

I was no longer talking to the beast, and that was really his only use to me: to have a better excuse to be talking than to hear myself rattle on.

Hunger is more fierce when it is cold out, and especially when it is snowing. I crossed the fences of farms and barged among the coppiced trees that shed a white dander, but nowhere could I find a rabbit's run or a badger's den in a spot concealed from man to set me a snare.

In the blue light of afternoon I began to realize that this business of living from day to day off the woods had its limits and that I had hit them. As much as the rabbit or the badger I needed protection from the winter, and being a man, I would find it among men.

There was a farmhouse only ten acres or so away; I could see it by the light of its windows. After the day's exertion and the lack of sustenance, the yellow glow seemed holy, seductive, irresistible. It brought tears to my eyes; the tears then froze in the lashes.

I heard a scream and a snap, in that order, and turned to find that my dog had taken a white hare from the middle of the white, stubbly field. White dog, white snow, white hare with a red stain spreading. It was a large animal and as plump as a hare ever gets outside a pen.

Perhaps I was not reduced to beggary yet. I went down on my knees and called the dog, dropping my pack to the snow and feeling with numb hands for flint, knife, and tinder.

The dog put back both his ears, tucked his tail between his legs, and took his dinner as far away from me as his four long legs could take it.

It was not one single light but many, within the large house and without, hung from poles and winking through the falling snow. I stumbled starved and blue-fingered into a wedding, and my coming was so welcome to the assembled party that I might have been the bridegroom.

Their beggar had fallen through, you see: The hired beggar, who by requesting admission first after the vows were completed, ensured that the marriage would be prosperous. The man had been arranged for, but snowfall did not stop to argue, and by the time the bride's uncle harnessed up to bring the old man in from the next village, the wet roads had set their ruts as firmly as steel bands and there was no coming or going out by cart or carriage.

Lucky the festivities had begun that morning with the bride's procession and the groom's, and the priest had come early to bless the butchering (earning two gratuities and saving one trip in rough weather), so the blizzard was too late to stop the festivities. It served instead to enforce them, since no one could go home.

From the blue silence and cold I was flung into a smell of spices strong enough to make a nose bleed, and red fire and red velvets and pies of fresh apple, dried peach, poppyseed, and onions, all brown and shining with egg. For entertainment we had a man with a three-string fiddle and three children on a table of tuned bells, which grew so sticky and covered with grease that their resonance was sensibly diminished.

I remember that the bride was black-haired and the groom half bald, but they disappeared very soon after filling my cap (borrowed, for the purpose) with bread and sausage, and the wedding was not for their amusement anyway.

As none of the fifty guests dared leave and no great number of us could be supplied with bedding, it was decided to dance the night through with lines, squares, and heys, to keep ourselves warm—but no one was very cold, with fifty bodies and a great fire blazing.

Though I had perfected seven courtly dances at school and a great number more with Powl outside the observatory, I think this night was the first night of my life that I learned what it really is to dance, and it was the bride's mother's younger sister who taught me this lesson, along with others, later in the course of the night, after our dancing had brought us down into the cellar, where the cider and cider vinegar were aging.

Her husband was away in the militia.

When it appeared that the back of the storm was broken

and the stars as visible as the floating snow in the sky, I went out into the empty yard to breathe, still wearing the red velvet and rabbit ermine of the beggar guest, and there I did the sword dance by myself on the frozen ground, using my Felinkan hedger in place of a saber.

I ought to have asked Solinka—her name I remember, alone of all I met that evening—to witness my performance, if only in gratitude for the double education she had given me, but I had been alone with myself for so long that feeling of all sorts called out for solitude, and I was overful of feeling.

And then this young matron of two babies gave me no reason to suppose she had an interest in my overful feelings, or that she was anything other than lively at parties. And kind.

By dawn the guests had puddled down in corners, five or six under a blanket, and the only sound was resin popping in the fire. Solinka was with her sister and her sister's husband and both the little children. I folded my red velvet and walked around for some minutes, seeking a place to put it that was not soiled with grease. At last I inserted it between a sleeping child's head and the heart-stenciled wall. I left nothing in payment, for any gift or any work done will break the good spell of the beggar guest. I took the bread and the sausage, left the borrowed cap behind, and went out along the road again, chasing werewolves.

The next town but one had lost a child three nights before. It took me until evening to plow through the drifts to find the settlement, and I broke wood for tinder at the butcher's house in exchange for warm sleeping, dinner, and breakfast. Afterward, in cold sunshine, I went forth to see what I could see.

She had been four, the butcher's wife had told me, and had shared the room with two older sisters. Neither girl had wakened in the night. Her mother had found the window open on its chain; there was no better clue than that. It was no effort for me to discover the house and even the window that had known this horrid event; I would have had to be determined to avoid being shown what the whole population wanted to show me.

It was a simple set of casement windows with bull's-eye glass, only the middle pane of which opened, and though it was closed I could make out the fastenings of a latch and a chain. Beneath, I found what had been a herbal border, now churned to mush by the feet of the curious.

The bottom of the window was at the level of my shoulder. A tall man might have lifted out a small girl without waking others—if she cooperated. I might have lifted myself in and thrown a child out, but again, not if she resisted. Children, however, could sleep like the dead, once they finally got to sleep.

"They like 'em young like that, four or five. That's when they're really tender."

I turned back to the man who had led me to the place, wondering what sort of creature he was to speak of the vanished child that way below her own family's window. "Who does?" I asked him.

"The wolf people. It's like we prefer young pigs and not slab-sided old sows and boars. And, of course, girls is better."

He was not particularly ill dressed. He looked more presentable than I did. A barman, perhaps, or a baker's assistant. His face was loose and his eyes shiny. "Four-year-old girls are more tender than four-year-old boys? How is it you know that?" I tried to keep my voice neutral, but I had let my accent slip, and the Old Velonya had a flavor of disparagement all its own.

He backed a pace. "Why . . . stands to reason."

The window opened and I was looking in the face of a youngster of about eight or ten. Her expression as she looked at me standing below must have been much like mine as I

145

addressed the ghoul beside me. I, like him, stepped back a pace. She slammed the window again and paid great attention to the latch.

"They think they're special goods now," said the loose-faced man, clenching his heavy jaw left and right, his features lit with resentment and satisfaction together. "But she wasn't better or anyone else. And now she's—"

The front door of the house flew open and hit the wall so hard that the door's small window cracked. The sound of breaking glass makes me sick, for I have heard it too often in my work, and I watched the large, barrel-shaped man in the black frock coat come on with great misgivings. My ghoulish friend vanished like a demon of the night.

The big man said nothing coherent but advanced upon me with both arms out and raised, like an enraged bear. Like a bear he flung his great paws at my head and he roared, and I was too busy avoiding his blows to apologize. Besides, what could I say?

For perhaps half a minute I danced a reluctant, bobbing dance with him. He neither punched nor slapped at me. I think his object, as much as he had one, was to grab me and break my back. When he failed in this, he flung himself at the casement window and the wall below so that the latch gashed his chin bloody, and hugging that ordinary window, he began to weep.

When I thought he might be able to hear me I told him I was a forest tracker. That I was there to help. I left him with a small circle gathering around him on the street, people with their heads bobbing, making noises like a flock of ducks. It didn't matter if he understood or not. Or even if he hated me or not.

It was always Powl's greatest criticism of me that I allow myself to become involved in things around me. One event, be it a wedding or a dog's defection or a man weeping into a window, sparks me on into three others, each of which demand their own loyalties and attentions, until I am like a ball bouncing down a steep street from cobble to cobble. He would say the sagacious attitude is one of distance and indifference. In return I would answer that he went through life fearing the cobbles would hurt him.

Before the day was out my self-proclaimed intention was known throughout the village, and many people took an interest in this ragged man who had claimed (by nightfall the tale had grown to this) to hunt and root out the demon of the woods. I had no trouble finding food and lodging that evening, nor people to show me marks in the snow.

Many of these marks were those of the white dog, though I had not seen its furry face since it denied me a share of its dinner, and I looked at those with an attempt at disdain and pronounced them dog tracks, not wolf tracks. No one asked me the difference.

I did not think the brute could have been here four days before to steal a child. I did not think it had the art of stealing children from high windows. But I wasn't certain.

It took me another two days to discover a track worth following out of the village, and I only knew that success because the snow melted again, revealing what it had held in storage for most of a week.

It was not a wolf track, but it was not that of a man in boots or clogs, either. It looked like feet wrapped in rags, which is no garb for the Zaquashian winters. The steps came heavy on the toes, and each was placed in front of the last, like the gait of a sheepdog, or of a man dancing. There was the bulk of something that fell and was dragged some steps through the muck, and then one perfect, tiny child's footprint, with five toes spread, and then another, and then the tracks went up the back of the road onto drier ground.

It was very little evidence, and seemed less as I quartered the thawing turf above. The road was cleared for safety fifty feet from the public road, and beyond that the forest was allowed to press, a dry strutwork of birch and maple, simple as a block print against the gray sky. There I found a passage among the trees—hardly a path—and more of the formless prints. I followed with the hedger in my hand, though I had no intention of chopping branches.

The day grew older, and the air freezing in my nostrils and ears made a hammer-string sort of music, like a distant clavichord. I saw three deer, and I found the empty skin of a rabbit hanging from a tree. It had been rough-ripped and yanked off the body, and though it was thoroughly chilled, it was nonetheless fresh, for such a tempting thing would not make it through one night of foxes and their like.

Men do not skin rabbits where they are caught unless they intend to eat them immediately, for it is much more convenient to carry the beast in God's wrapping. Beasts do not skin their prey. I stood in the freezing wet and contemplated this sad bit of fur, and I considered it might have symbolic significance. So many of the worst sights do.

I caught no rabbit nor tried to that evening, but ate a hard black loaf I had saved from breakfast, along with a bottle of ale. By twilight it was frozen above the ground, but two days of thaw could not be reversed so quickly, and the earth was nasty wet. Ripping a dozen small limbs from the birch trees, I made a platform high up in a maple, and my leather bootlaces secured the thing in place. My pack and I rested better up there than we might have on the ground, but lying still is not the same as sleeping, and the cold crackles of the woods jarred me awake repeatedly.

Since I found the skin I had not known peace of mind, though I am not sure it was fear I felt. The night sky was obscure and interrupted with clouds like faces, like that of the man I had killed, and that of Solinka, whom I had left curled up with her sister and her sister's husband.

There was a brushing and a crashing below, so noisy that it could be made only by a deer. (It is a popular misconception that beasts are silent in the woods.) I pushed to the edge of my tree fort and made out under starlight the flat back of the doe and her pale breeches. She breathed raggedly and slammed down the path anyway. I waited to see what was chasing her.

Short behind came another set of four feet pounding, but these in peculiar rhythm. For a moment there was the round top of a very hairy head, or perhaps a furred cap, and then the disturbance passed. In the distance I saw a flash of white buttocks. Not a deer's. And I heard a human giggle.

It seemed my mind had lost the ability to do more than witness, but my hair had gained the ability for independent action, for it stood erect and crawled about my head. I told myself to move, if only to retreat more firmly under the covers, when there was another sound, and this time the passerby was unmistakable and familiar: a pale, furry shape with plume tail hanging behind. Even the sound of his panting identified him. So intent was he on his own pursuit (Of the doe? Of the pursuers?) that he did not scent me on the earth below, or did not care to stop if he did.

I sat up, wrapped the blanket around me, and stared into the darkness as though it were a brick wall.

Moonrise came only slightly before dawn, but in the sliver of light I unwound my temporary shelter and followed after the hunt, using the flounderings of the doe in the shrubbery for marker instead of the frozen ground. The sun joined her brother in the sky by the time I had reached the carcass stretched out beside the path. The black-red of the frozen blood was the first color I saw that day. Her throat had been ripped. She had been half carved and half gnawed. The remaining meat had been pissed on, and there was a mound of watery shit on the path. I moved with a greater attempt at stealth after finding this.

The day had brightened considerably and the bare trees were groaning, as though they might be forced into thaw again by the light of the sun. My stomach, too, was groaning with

149

hunger, and my sense of smell sharpened when the path I was following broadened, cluttered with footprints both canine and human. The wind was coming at me from before, and it carried all the most objectionable smells of settlement and some that were merely unknown to me.

The dog had gone this way and not returned, so I had to assume there was one alert creature with a good nose ahead of me. At least one. On both sides the underbrush rose to my hips, with dead briar and vine maple. It would be hard to get off the path quickly. I resisted the temptation to drop to an inhuman crouch myself, and I walked forward until I could see the forest open up ahead. Then I opened my pack, took out my lens case, stuffed it in my belt, and climbed a likely tree.

Two lenses, positioned a certain distance apart, become a telescope. Large or small, the principle is the same, so I had turned my great art into small artisanship and made a hand-held, collapsible telescope out of stiffened leather, held into tube shape by buckles and holding the light-gathering lens in place with leather washers. Into this a small bronze eyepiece slid in and out. Second to the hedger, it was my favorite toy, but I had never had to cling to the trunk of a tree while fitting it together. A standard spyglass is more convenient in the long run.

I was not in clear sight of the place yet, but I was close enough to make out a very tiny triangular hut of saplings roofed in fir boughs (which must have been carried a distance) and backed by a stone-faced hill, which stood out like a gaunt hipbone of the earth. In the area before it there was dead grass, some pointed sticks like crude javelins, a fire pit, and a small cairn of rocks. I could not see significance in the latter, unless it were a grave.

From this angle the entrance to the hut was black; I could not tell if it were a dark wooden door or an opening. Not much could fit into a place that size, regardless.

I dismantled my glass and came down. Nothing changed as I approached the clearing, not even the wind, but as I left the trees and felt the sun on my back, out of the crude entrance to the hut stepped the white dog, or wolf, which I no longer thought of as mine. As though by law of opposition, now that I showed him no affection he put his head down and fawned toward me, wiggling his hind end like a saucy girl.

I did not try to touch him, so I don't know whether he would have let me. I approached the empty doorway with my hedger at the ready.

The hut itself was only a doorway. The living space was under the hill, in a cave that yawned a good five yards deep. There were pots and pans cluttered into a corner, the ceiling was black with soot, and on poles hung skins of deer and larger beasts, badly tanned if tanned at all. There was a cot in the back, against the wall.

All this I saw in a moment without paying it attention, for on the cot was the center and focus of the room. Crouched on that dirty bed was a woman of middle years with no clothes on, and over her, engaged in conjugal rites after the style of a dog, was what might or might not have been a man.

His legs were long enough and his hands (propped against her shoulders) human enough. The hair on his head continued down his back in a thin line, and I saw that it was not merely long hair but instead a large expanse of short, bristly growth. His ribs had a good covering, too, and his ears. He was working away at full intensity at the moment of my arrival, and before I could react—I was as shocked and embarrassed as I have ever been—he reached his satisfaction with a grunt and a groan and collapsed upon the back of the silent, seemingly uninvolved woman. And then he saw me and I saw his face.

His forehead was normal enough, though fashion prefers more height. His eyes seemed human, seen in this light and at this distance, but under them like a mask was a growth of bristle like that on his head, joining with his overgrown beard

151

like a mask cut from a bear's hide. His teeth, which in his understandable outrage were exposed to me, were too discolored and broken for me to say much about their size or shape.

With a howl—again human enough—he vaulted off his partner's back, but was brought up short in a manner I could not understand, and I was about to retreat the way I had come when I saw that he was his own impediment: that he was tied into the woman in the manner of a dog with a bitch. Horror and amazement kept me where I was as he strained and lunged toward me and she cried out in pain, her hands over her head.

The coupling broke by this force, and as the fellow rushed at me, his penis still half stiff, I saw there was a red swollen bulb at the end of it, like the bladder on a jester's wand.

Whatever he was, he was in the right of it at this moment, in his own house and with his lady-wife, and I was aware of my infringement in every atom of my body. I could not turn in time, nor did I fancy being chased through the woods by an angry husband, wolf or man, so I lowered both my hedger and my head and caught his charge to fling him over my back.

In the light he was very pale under the hair, and his skin stank and glistened. I am told certain primitive natives of North Sekret grease their bodies with fat to hold out the cold. I had never been told these people were furry, however, nor that they had fingernails thick as horn, as this one did as he hit the frozen earth and sprang up again.

I swished my blade through the air between us, both as a warning to him and to encourage him left, so that I could exit to the right, away from house and home and all. I heard the woman moving behind me but I still was young and had never taken seriously being hit with an iron frying pan.

It was a good blow. Had she hit with the rim she might have broken my skull, but she went flat-on to the crown of my head.

The world rang like a bell, but I did not pass out. Through long practice at being hit, I have become difficult to knock out. The monster before me took this opportunity to advance, nails raised to rend or strangle—I don't know what—and I found my blade slapping him across the face, flat-on as the woman had struck me. He reeled enough for me to leap through the entrance and past him, and then he spun around, crouching, fingers spread wide.

The white dog was barking, barking and running in excited circles around us. He seemed to be enthused but neutral in his opinions. The woman threw the pan at him.

I hesitated among flight, attack, and apology, but my resonant head decided on none of these. I danced from one foot to another over the dead grass, blade toward my naked enemy, and I said, "Is that a grave of a child over there?"

He did not rise from the crouch nor speak to me, but the woman let out a howl between grief and outrage and sank into the doorway, head in hands. Then the man spoke.

"Yes. It died. They all die." His voice was rude, but rude according to the mold of peasant Zaquash, not beast-rude. The woman behind him looked ordinary of face and form, though loose and stretched out. I had not seen many naked women.

Again my tongue spoke without consulting my mind. "It was yours? Not stolen?"

At this he leaped for me again, his expression frightful, and I was forced to kick him in the jaw. As he lay there I asked, "What are you, fellow? What is your nature? Is it . . . magical?" I felt myself blushing at the question, as though Powl were behind me.

"I am not a beast!" he bawled out, his face in the earth, his pointed horn-talons digging into the earth. By instinct I dodged the heavy iron pan, which had been sailed out after me and which was a more deadly assault than any the werewolf had offered. The woman shrieked and called me murderer and claimed I was there to kill them all.

I was not sure myself why I was there, and my enemy was

153

down and blinking with watery eyes at the sunlight. I found myself retreating, and what my own face looked like I have no idea. Around me frisked the dirty white dog, more trusting than he had ever been to me. At the edge of their pounded clearing I stopped and pointed at the creature. "Tell me one thing!" I shouted back at the man. "Is it wolf, or dog? If you know, tell me!"

Without looking, the man set up another keening. *"I am not a beast!"*

I nearly tripped over my pack where I had left it. The wolf-dog followed me, its tail up but not curled. It took me three days of heartfelt effort to discourage it.

In those three days my mind spun between two shames: that I had left a monster in the woods when children were vanishing, and that I had intruded with force upon a pair of very unfortunate people. At last I was able to let these two conflicting disgraces strangle each other, and I was left admitting that I did not know what had happened, or what it was I had seen.

Eighteen years later, I have become more used to admitting that.

One month later I was in the city of Warvala, the largest in all the territories and the first real city I had seen since Sordaling. There is snow in South Territory, but it is not the unbroken five months of cover I was used to, and I was so far protected against the climate as to be sleeping in the basement of the Territorial Library as janitorial assistant and stove minder.

This was a time of lordly comfort: warm, fed, and surrounded by books in three languages, which I had to myself all evening and night. I earned some small money and spent a larger sum of the library's funds in lamp oil.

It was an enlightenment to me to discover that I could

read the titles on the exquisite, calf-bound books that had found their way north from Rezhmia's fortress capital. The language of mysterious significance taught to me by Powl in the last year of my residence was nothing other than Rayzhia. Even more important was the content of these volumes, for the intricate flow of history, poetry, and fantasy I discovered had no counterpart in my own language. I could hear it all in Powl's voice, for every nuance echoed my teacher's own floridity when speaking in that florid tongue. I found I liked such stories greatly, and the naughty ones opened my eyes in many ways.

The janitor, a semilettered man, discovered me chuckling over one scandalous jewel, and when he found I was not merely cherishing the pictures, he had the idea I might earn some extra money by hiring out as a translator for the foreign quarter.

This I did, more out of a spirit of adventure than from any particular need for money—my job plus the occasional production of spyglasses or spectacles had left me wealthier than ever I had been—but my first glimpse of the market in the foreign quarter of Warvala was more than adventuresome. It was the most important event that had happened to me since meeting Powl.

In the foreign quarter were merchants of other territories, and a few daughter shops of Vesinglon itself, as well as a scattering of Falinks selling bright cloth and touristware, but the largest single group were the émigrés from the South, from the city of Bologhini down in the plains, where it is too dry to snow, and from Rezhmia itself. In the broad, clattering square of the market I encountered my first real Rezhmians.

I knew what they looked like from pictures, and because there is a trace of Rezhmian blood—or more than a trace—running through every Zaquash peasant. And in first glimpse I saw only echoes of that picture of the light-armored noble Powl had showed me in the library at Sordaling: slight, moon-faced, dark of hair and complexion, and delicate-boned, like a child in adult's clothing.

But not all the émigrés were wearing the styles of Rezhmia, for the waist-length free hair, the bright cottons and silks, and the slippers of molded felt are not convenient clothing in a windy winter with snow up to the ankles. I came around the corner of a saponier—and I remember that in the glass window was a bar of soap into which had been imprinted tiny violets, which still retained a hint of color against the white soap, laid on a scarf of purple gauze—and there was a young man loading barrels onto a cart, and he wore my face.

He was darker. He had brown eyes, I believe, but the resemblance was overwhelming, down to the attentive set of his ears, which were bluish-red from their exposure to cold. Retroactively, all the other images of the people of Rezhmia in my mind (and I had called them monkeylike to Powl) slid over his and were made real, and I knew my own origins.

He smiled at me, companionably. I returned his salute as best I could and walked on. A minute later I was back and said, "Excuse me, sir, but are you . . . were you born in this area?"

"I know where things are, if that's the help you need," he said in an accent heavier than any I had yet heard. I shook my head. "Are you, by any chance, Rezhmian by birth? I ask not out of idle curiosity, but . . ."

As I spoke, his bluff friendliness vanished, to be replaced by offense, which in turn gave way to his own curiosity. He loaded one more empty barrel and sat down on the cart. "I was born three blocks from here. My father is Rezhmian, of course. Why?"

I was too shocked and too sober to say anything but the truth. "Because you look like me, I think."

Evidently this hadn't struck him, or was less a matter of note to him, but he gazed at me critically for a bit and replied, "Except for the yellow hair and a certain spread of shoulder, yes, I do. Why not? Are we related? Who are your people?"

I answered that I did not know. That I hadn't known I was part Rezhmian until that very moment.

The boy or man startled at this admission, and I saw a quick growth of contempt in his eyes. He turned from me and picked up another barrel. "If you don't know your father, it doesn't matter if you're Rezhmian or not," he said.

This statement did not sting me at all, for I certainly did not want to be Rezhmian. "I have much better than family, as a matter of fact," I answered. "I have myself." Though I was not offended, I picked the fellow up and rolled him over on the street. It seemed to be expected of me.

He looked up past the foot that was holding his face down and made the three-finger signal for yield. "Enough. Let me up. Only don't go blabbing . . . that around town or you'll get worse answer than mine." He stood up. Because the street was frozen, he had acquired very little dirt, and this he allowed me to help brush off.

"You ought to know," he said somewhat sullenly, somewhat shamefacedly, "that when you're half-bred especially, family becomes important, because so many babies of mixed parentage are children of . . . of—"

"Prostitutes," I finished for him. "I imagine so. But in my case I don't think that was likely."

No. It was more likely, given my age and upbringing, that my mother was the victim of rape.

Almost certainly it had been my mother's birth that had gotten me into the Royal School at Sordaling, for few men would feel such an obligation to a by-blow by a foreign woman, paid or not. Perhaps my mother was a young noblewoman or gentrywoman seduced by a member of a diplomatic embassy, or by a rich merchant in the foreign quarter of some Velonyan city, but I doubted that. The appearance of a Rezhmian is not prepossessing to gently raised Velonyan females. I thought it rather more likely that she had been one of the numerous wives who had followed the king's last incursion south, thinking it a lark and themselves above all harm, and who had found themselves amid an alien army without protection.

That seemed to explain everything: my family's lack of interest in me; my admission to the school (both by virtue of the woman's blood and her husband's); and my face, hitherto thought by myself to be unique. It only required that I be a few years older than I thought I had been.

Powl had known. Probably from that first odd look he had given me as I entered the room. Certainly from the moment I gave him my name, which he had pronounced quite correctly and I never had. "Nazhuret," I had now learned, was a Rezhmian name, not too common, originally of the God of the Underworld and now occasionally bestowed upon boy babies.

What had Powl called me at first? "The King of the Dead," his words had been. In a way he made me so, but that had always been my name. My teacher had been discreet. Had he thought the information of my birth would drive me to despair, or had he simply thought it in bad taste?

Not the latter, for he had spoken of our hereditary enemies as a very civilized and interesting people, and he had taught me their language with enthusiasm.

It would be significant to me, he had said. He had expected me to come this way. Perhaps coming home. Perhaps his silence had been only one of his dry jokes, and now I had hit the punchline. Or perhaps he had kept quiet because he thought telling me my origins was one more item that was not his business.

I end this long discursion and return to Warvala in winter.

I had a reasonable success as a translator, especially when there were to be records kept of the interchange. There was more demand for such skill than I would have thought, for few Northerners bothered to learn the language, and most of the émigrés were not lettered people. My accent was a matter of amusement, for as it turned out my Rayzhia was courtly, of the South (trust Powl to make sure of that), and very few of the traders of Warvala spoke its like. Neither, however, did they object to having a functionary with such elegant drawling vowels, even if he did have hair like a dandelion.

Yule came and went. I spent the holiday alone, but then we had never marked it out at the observatory, either. I was invited to the Deepyear celebrations of Pasten's silk warehouse, however, and danced the fire dance and the sword dance and drank spirits of cherry, a southern specialty, very soft on the tongue and deadly the next day.

I had so much money I bought lens blanks by the dozen and ground them into spectacles for old men and women who otherwise would have squinted the rest of their lives away.

One of these, a goodwife born in Bologhini and possessing no Velonyan, rewarded me by instruction in all that an educated boy must know, which I had obviously missed by being brought up by the savages of the northern forests. She taught me the proper address to court a girl of rank above, equal to, or below myself. (Certainly there were few in the latter category.) She taught me how to bow, and the techniques of disciplining the mind, which must be learned in various stages to distract the chittering rats that are our thoughts.

In turn I told her my history of the black wolf of Gelley, which Powl had set upon me and which likely would pursue me for the rest of my life, and she retracted everything she had said concerning my education, for this teacher, she stated, had been a master of the mind.

The library let me go in midwinter, for the janitor's son had come up from the country and it was thought proper he have the job. I did not repine, for they left me my reading privileges, and I found new work keeping order in the Yellow Coach, a large tavern in the foreign quarter. I made conversation in two languages and was very polite in showing the door to the overly enthused. It was light work.

It was an evening in early spring, and I was hovering over the table of my sometimes patron, the silk merchant, who was having difficulties with the emissary from Sordaling Tailories. This man made a practice of being rude, whether only to Rezhmians or in general I had not the opportunity to discover. Pasten knew the man was being rude—his Vesting was not bad—but in translation I turned the Tailories man's demands into polite circumlocutions and thus Pasten was able to pretend they had not been said.

There was some dust of snow on the ground still, but the smell of the day's air had left no doubt in mind that the season had changed.

Like all changes of season, this had put me out of context with the affairs of my life. Change was everywhere, and anything had a chance of happening. What did happen was that Arlin walked into the door of the Yellow Coach, complete with his velvets, his dirt, and his jeweled rapier.

The outfit was silver in color, which went well with his dark hair and fair skin and hardly seemed grubby at all. He even had a cape of fur over his shoulders, and his face was weather-scrubbed, if not by water.

I gave him a wave of recognition and he stared at me blankly for some moments before sinking into a chair. I concluded my business as quickly as I could and sat down beside him. My friend the bartender sent over the boy with two glasses of hot ale.

Arlin was much impressed. To the edge of laughter, perhaps. "Zhurrie! Old stoat, do you own this place? And how is it you preside over a convocation of cat yowls like that one?"

I denied ownership of the Yellow Coach entirely and explained my position. I also explained, with my new Rayzhian indirection and delicacy, that I would pay for his drinks as long as he wished to sit here, but that he would not be allowed to gamble in this house. (I had discovered in myself a nose for card trickery in the past few months. I owe that to him.)

His eyes gave one silver glint, but he did not dispute my authority nor my logic.

"And as for the translating, well, I am half Rezhmian after all." I had gotten to the point where I could say this with no outward flinch. "Like many in the southern territories."

Arlin goggled at me but managed to say quite calmly, "Indeed, Nazhuret. And have you always been half Rezhmian, or is this a recent development? I never heard you rattle off in that tongue before."

"I learned it a few years ago."

"After you left the school?"

His curiosity was so pointed it left me uncomfortable. "Yes, of course. After. You must remember Rayzhia is not offered—"

"While you were studying optics?"

"Exactly then," I said in a voice of great finality, which affected him not at all.

"And where did you pick up sorcery, Nazhuret?" He lifted his mug with a complacent smile as I gaped at him. "What did you do about the werewolves?"

"I know nothing about werewolves," I said. It was both true and heartfelt, but I spoke in the intonation of Powl at his most waspish, and as Arlin only looked cunning and answered, "You're keeping something from me, you weasel," I realized I had taken the role and attitude my teacher had taken whenever I had accused him of being a magician. Whenever I had asked him to explain more than could be explained. I felt harried and without patience.

"How goes the king's progress?" I asked in turn, and Arlin let me turn the conversation. "Long over for the year, I suppose."

"It has begun again for the new year, as you can see by my

161

presence in this charming backwater. He goes to assure himself that his territories are secure against southern invasion."

Twice, in the course of the winter, my face and my fluency with Rayzhia had caused young Rezhmian hotspurs to forget themselves in front of me and to utter remarks prejudicial to Velonya, and in particular toward Velonyan administration of the territories. Both times I was forced to floor the fellows before they could commit themselves to anything demanding greater violence on my part. I was well aware there were tensions.

I had not heard anything of an attempt at the border, however. I asked the young gambler what reason there was to expect the Sanaur to break treaty after twenty-five years of peace.

Arlin gave me a superior smile, mouth closed. "Not the High Sanaur, Nazhuret. Worse, for that could be dealt with in civilized fashion. It is the Red Whips who are massing against us." The smile opened out. "As a half Rezhmian yourself, I would have thought you would know that already."

My answer was delayed by a raising of voices a few tables over, where (if I remember correctly) someone had mistaken another man's wife for something different. By the time I returned, I had had time to think on things.

"No, Arlin. To speak of the Red Whips massing is to speak of wildcats banding together or hawks perhaps. They travel and raid in clans, and their hate of one another—"

"Is dominated only by their hate of the North," he finished for me. He pointed his mug in my direction, perhaps for emphasis or to make known that it had become empty. "You do not believe me; only go see."

I filled it from mine, which I had not touched. "What would I see, other than a parade of nobles moving very slowly and a king no older than I am? You can hardly expect an army preparing for invasion to display itself upon the horizon for the benefit of a tourist like myself."

Arlin put the glass down, undrunk. His long face, always elegant, became beautiful when in earnest. "A tourist like yourself? Zhurrie, I remember when you called yourself a blood knight and had best cause to do so."

I had to laugh. Had I ever been such a dewy fool? "At that time, a better word for me would have been 'schoolboy.'"

His mood had changed again. "But anyway, isn't it worth a journey of forty miles to meet the king of Velonya? As a student of Sordaling—"

Now it was my turn to cut him off. "Meet the king? Nothing I'd like less. In fact, the thought makes me want to head north right n·w, without my clogs on my feet."

"Well, then see him at a distance. Every Velonyan must want to see his king, and it could be your only chance, if you insist on haunting the far territories like this."

Arlin hit a chord in me with this suggestion. Powl had talked about the new king. Had been enthused about him. He was very popular, even in Warvala, where Velonyan rule was more theory than fact. He was said to be very handsome, or at least brilliant in color.

And the smell of the season had changed that day.

"I'll do it," I said. "I'll go south with you."

Arlin's long face grew longer in surprise. "With me? That was not my suggestion, schoolmate. I'm very picky about the men with whom I travel."

"So am I," I answered him, thinking of his grime, his smell. "In fact, I am so picky as not to appreciate men at all."

His grin said that he knew a few things I didn't. "You speak out of ignorance."

Evidently Arlin had not shared my early years at Sordaling. I was beginning to place him in time by the things he said. Too old to have been in danger of rape, but too long in the past for me to remember. About the swan boat time, when I was walking abroad a lot. "I speak out of better knowledge than I wish I had. So often was I held down and raped as a boy that I wished my breeches glued on and my backside glued to a bench "

Arlin's face floated between amazement and disbelief. "You, Nazhuret? Forced? You? I can't believe it of—"

"Why not? They did not have to look at my face that way," I said, and thereby embarrassed myself so that I found excuse to leave the table.

We did not travel together after all, because Arlin had a horse and I did not. I tracked him south down the soggy road.

The land changed decidedly in my first day's march, from the rutted lowland and maple ridges of Zaquash to hills rolling like a shaken blanket, going up and down but mostly up. The trees gave way to pine and then gave way entirely, exposing me in openness like that I had never known before in my life. I imagined it was what the ocean must look like: broad, rolling, but without concealment. The sky seemed to reduce me to insect proportions, and I had been small enough already.

I was seeing the beginnings of the plains and seeing them at their springtime best, tinted with yellow eranthis and early lupine. Despite the prettiness, there was something formal and ponderous in so much visible distance. I felt I ought to be thinking in large concepts, and in rebellion I kicked a pebble along the road.

Atop one particularly crested hill I stopped to stretch out and practice my hedger forms, entertaining the huge, cloudy sky. The world was spread out below, and one gray, glimmering dot was Arlin, or his horse at least, trotting easily toward the pale distance. He probably would reach that smudge that was a village before nightfall. I doubted I would.

Left of him and somewhat beyond was a herd of red deer, or perhaps cows shrunk by perspective. I took out my glass and assembled it.

They were men on horses, and much farther away than had appeared. I wondered if I were looking at the king.

I did reach the town (not a village at all), but Arlin had gone on. The inhabitants of the downs seemed to be as crossbred as I was by their appearance, and not a lot larger. This was a pleasant discovery. I went to the homeliest of the two inns and was immediately recognized as the peacekeeper from the Yellow Coach, whereby the landlady stood me to ale, and we exchanged pleasantries of the publican business.

"By your face, coloring, and your name," she said after some minutes, "I'd suppose you to be Fortress Rezhmia. But you talk like North Vestinglon itself. That's a combination we don't get much." There were so many surprises in her one statement that it shut me up for a moment.

I hadn't realized I had let my accent slip, but now it was too late to repair that. In the speech of Sordaling I answered her, "Name and face—maybe face—are southern, mistress, but how can you claim my yellow hair as Rezhmian?"

She brushed her own dark hair out of her face. "Not Zaquash-Rezhmian, of course. I mean the city. There're plenty of blonds down there in the city."

I must have looked disbelieving, for I was. The man seated closest to my right got a laugh out of my expression. "She means because of the slaves. The nobles down there have a fancy for pale-skinned women in their beds. Have so for hundreds of years, so of course the hair crops up now and then."

The landlady cleared her throat mightily. "Lendall, you can turn anything into an insult. I never said a word about this man being no slave."

"Nor did I," said Lendall. "I only said that there *were* slaves, and that's why the hair!" I broke in to say I was not insulted at all, merely amazed, for I had never heard this before.

Lendall had a Velonyan name, but he looked southern and not at all blond. "Oh, it's sure. They took their choice of women, not longer than thirty years ago, didn't they?" The landlady gave him a glance with teeth in it but refused to be drawn to argument, and I went out to lie in the stable and think about things.

The fortress city. I could speak the language. I could go down there and find my exact double. Perhaps. For months previous I had thought that in coming to the territories I had found my natural place, or as close to it as I ever would find. Now I had a new and more colorful vision to pursue.

I had been going south for a long time, anyway.

I followed Arlin for three days, and after the first day I fell no farther behind. His speed on that first day's travel seemed to me designed only to leave me behind, and having accomplished that, he proceeded as his lazy, elegant self. The second night I spent sleeping under that very broad bowl of stars, and on the third the hills had shrunk to ripples on the landscape no larger than houses, and the wind blew through my homespun as though I were naked.

I passed a thing such as I had never seen before: a hamlet of some eight buildings and a cattle pen burned to the ground. Not even the driven palings of the fence had survived the flames. The black ruins had been rained on, perhaps snowed on also, but they were obviously less than a season old. I walked down what had been a street and that now was paved with glossy black bits of charcoal that had recently been carpenter's wood. The stones of the houses had fallen and scattered, and no living creature was to be found except for great numbers of crows.

I was young enough to be fascinated by ruins (I still am), and I wandered in and out of the foundations, hoping to find either an explanation of the misfortune or at least a poignant reminder. I found nothing but the scattered bones of a dog. Passing back to the road, I discovered a patch of broken earth, some four yards square, not mounded but rain-sunk, with a large staff surmounted by the Holy Triangle. It was all very crude. I stepped close, but as soon as my foot touched the loose soil it began to sink, and I chose to go no farther. My hair stood all on end with the knowledge that I was sinking into a mass grave. Below the sacred sign a paper had been tacked, but the ink on it had run the whole thing sky blue. As I walked on, I noticed that something had dug a hole slanting into one corner of the square, something the size of a large dog.

I had never seen so much violence in my life as was implicit in that motionless scene. Pulling the hedger from its straps, I walked on.

Occasionally I pulled out my spyglass to keep the company of horsemen in view. It was indeed the king's men, for I could make out the banner of the castle and swan, and some splendid body armor was winking in the sun. There were perhaps three hundred horses and a good dozen tent and refectory wagons, which made slow going of it in this season of mud. They were proceeding west as I went south, and though I had every intention of intersecting their path, I was very reluctant to be seen by them. Not that anyone of King Rudof's court might recognize Nazhuret of Sordaling in this peasant with a pack. Likely no one would recognize me even in my school uniform, but Powl had spoken forcefully on the subject of my anonymity.

I estimated that we would reach our closest approach shortly after dawn if the horsemen camped at twilight and I walked half the night. Doubtless Arlin had already rejoined them (if he really had a welcome with someone in that high company) and was fleecing nobles left and right.

Marching through the night on a rolling plain is a far cry from night travel in the forests of home. Even under no light but the stars, the grass rippled with light and the road glowed along its drier spots. I felt I must be glowing as well, and my exposedness made me cautious. I left the road, took off my clogs for silence, and avoided the tops of the hills.

I had plans to deal with Arlin, for among his mysteries, his recurrent pointed attentions, and his subsequent rebuffs, he had irritated me. Also, he made me feel much like a schoolboy again, and I began thinking in terms of schoolboy raggs I could play on him. I could bend a little lead fishing weight onto the end of his sword, misbalancing it. That would put an end to his juggler's tricks. Unfortunately, I did not have a little lead fishing weight, nor was there likely one in the entire royal surround, and if I did find one, the joke might end in the man's slicing off his own finger. I could steal his sword and dagger while he slept, but that might end in someone slicing off Nazhuret's head.

I had decided I would paint stripes on his horse with jeweler's rouge. Pink stripes. That would be offensive enough. But I would have to find the horse, and I still might lose my head to the picket sentry. While I was assessing the dangers, I came around the bottom of a hill, heard voices, and saw fires.

I stood startled. I could not have come so far so soon. Could the Velonyans have walked into the night and beyond? Even so, they would not be camped here, in front of me.

I heard a sound from the top of the hill beside me, only a few yards away. A man scratching himself through layers of clothing. Though reflex I ducked down and noted movement on another of the down ripples. There were sentries, but they were prone in the grass, it seemed. This was a very odd way to keep watch, unless one were as interested in concealing oneself as in spying out others.

The camp was in a natural declivity, and the dozen small fires would not be visible from any distance. I lay down myself in the grass and pressed forward.

There was no picket line; the horses were scattered like the men and the little lumps that were tents. No pavilion at all. By the side of one fire a banner stake had been driven into the earth, but it was bare save for a lump at the top. As a breath of wind caught the fire, it illuminated briefly a long white thing with what appeared to be snakes dangling: a horse's skull with whips thrust through the eyeholes. And the voices I heard were speaking Rayzhia.

I was filled with a horror that was near to despair as I realized where my curiosity had brought me, and my mind filled with images of a burned village, and a sunken grave, beast-robbed. I lay motionless, and at times the fires would flare, showing me faces no different from many of those who had drunk and traded at the tables of the Yellow Coach. I had worked for men like these. Their accent was familiar to me, though I could not understand the words, and so were their faces. Perhaps I did know them.

The Red Whips. Children's nightmares. Brutes. Perfect fighters. The force that had broken the back of Velonyan settlement in the South. I had imagined them to be something other in nature than the everyday people of the southern territories. But why did I imagine that, knowing the truth about Zaquash avengers as well as I did?

Either the wind changed or my ears did, for I could hear conversations where there had been only murmurs a moment before. "By his red hair" was said and repeated; another man elaborated "red hair"; and in the first third of the company, "always."

"I will know Rudof by his royal armor" announced one man, and another answered, "He may not be wearing his royal armor, but he will be wearing his royal red hair!" That met with laughter, but the first man topped this with, "After to-morrow he will not be wearing that either. The old horse will have both." He lifted his arm and pointed at the staff and the skull. "And enough gold to break a leather saddlebag."

I found myself in a trembling sweat. I tried to push backward in the grass and I was not in full control of my limbs. I called up the black wolf of Gelley in self-defense while they continued to plan the assassination of the king.

A voice of greater command than the others adjured them to forget plunder. They were to slice in, kill the Velonyan king, and be off before the heavy horses could be brought forward. That was what they would be paid for. Stopping to plunder a troop three times their size would only get them killed for nothing.

Puzzlement replaced terror in my mind, for what pay have the Red Whips other than plunder itself? I listened until the last of the conversationalists went to sleep, and then I began to back away through the grass. I had gone halfway around the hill when movement close by brought me flat again. It was a change of guard, and the new one came within thirty feet of me as he took the easiest way up the watch hill.

It took me another hour to retreat from the camp far enough to cross the road unseen and put a few ranked hills between myself and the open. After this I ran, and I did not stop to breathe until I saw the red remains of King Rudof's own fires winking before me.

There was nothing furtive or disguised about this camp. It stretched along the road for half a mile, and the great wagons had been left right in the hard-packed roadway, where their long eight-horse tongues lay end-propped on blocks.

The dozen or so peaked pavilions were as much portable houses as tents, with roofs of wood and canvas and walls of quilted felt, each panel painted with the arms of the marshal whose headquarters it was. The knights had their own small tents, and even some of the foot soldiers slept under shelters like folded sheets of paper, hung from two poles. Even the latrines were modestly draped. The fires were large and decorated with pots, though most of the fires had burned to red cinders by this late hour.

In the center of the circle of pavilions lay one identical to them but sporting an overly long central pole, upon which hung a flag I did not have to see in detail to understand.

I saw all this in a moment, for my school years had prepared me to identify the parts of a Velonyan military encampment. It was the sort of place I had expected to spend most of my life.

How the sentries could have missed me I do not know, for I was running with all thought to speed and none to secrecy, but I was at the first horse picket without challenge and then I was under it and amid the sleeping foot soldiers, a three-quarter-size, flaxen-haired peasant running with his clogs in his hand and a large pack bouncing on his back and shouting, "Alarm! Alarm! Wake up! Wake the king!"

Some of the men slept lightly and some I had to jump over. My shouts were not as loud as I would have liked, because I had used up all my wind on the road, but they were enough. I set up a buzz of voices that followed me across a company of thirty bivouacked men.

Ahead was the closest pavilion, and in the light of the old moon, newly risen, I could see the outline of a red lion, sword-girt. That was Garman of Hight. The thought flashed through my heated mind that Powl had called the man a pederast. I passed to the left of the great tent, and the door-guard reached out to grab at me like a man after a bothersome cat. He chased a few feet and halted, cursing.

Here I was at last, in the clear space before the leather and brass door of the king of Velonya and all Zaquashian territories. Four guards stood at the circumference of the pavilion, fully armed and ready for me, their swords in their hands. A ring of late- or early-wakeful men surrounded the cooking fire, their faces glowing orange in its light. They, too, had heard me coming. I came to a halt, swaying, and my legs almost decided to let go. "Red Whips west of here!" I announced as the lounging men walked toward me. "Attacking in the morning! Rouse the king!"

Another man began to shout, much louder than I. At first I thought he was echoing my words. "Alarm! Alarm, men!

An attack upon the king! Assassin! Slay that man!"

I spun in place, my exhaustion forgotten. In the doorway of another pavilion, outlined by lamps from within, stood a man in light field armor, and he was pointing at me with his sword.

The king's guard did not obey, but instead moved into a defensive stance between myself and the leather tent flap. The men at the fire were mostly unarmed, and they approached me warily, but the sentry of the lit pavilion came forward willingly enough, his rapier ringing out of its scabbard, and others in a pack joined him from behind the bulk of the tent, half dressed but armed well enough.

My pack is made to slide off in an instant, and I leaped backward over it to make it a burden to my attacker instead of to me. I wanted my hedger but had no time to stoop for it. I threw one of my clogs and hit him over the eyes.

A man in a black-and-yellow house uniform shoved past the stunned sentry. His rapier was needle-fine and well made, like a sliver of light in the darkness. At the same time around the sentry's other side came a man in underwear, trying to spark a flint on his harquebus. I darted toward him, as he was less ready, and used an elbow in his armpit to knock him into the fellow with the nasty blade.

There were many more of them, now, mostly in the black and yellow (I couldn't immediately remember what marshal owned those colors; I couldn't immediately think at all) but some in royal blue and white and many in white linen and bare skin. I remember that I ducked a sweep that would have taken my head and flinched away from another that wanted my stomach, and then I had the chance to bend to my pack, and my hedger was in my hand.

The beautiful rapier was back in action, and the man who wielded it called for room to use it. He got his way, for the mass of soldiers edged back to circle us as he sent that long needle past the end of my short hedger and at my throat.

I moved my throat to the side and felt only the vibration of the slender blade against the skin, and when that blade was at full thrust, I broke it at the base with the hook of my weapon, as once Powl had broken my own rapier blade. The soldier was as astonished as I had been, but immediately the circle that had formed collapsed toward me. I knew I would have to kill a Velonyan soldier to live a moment longer, and even so it probably would be a short moment.

But the squeeze of attackers backed off again, and all glances darted nervously in one direction. There was shouting again, but not in the bass voice this time. Perhaps it had been going on a while. This voice commanded all of us to halt, and as all the rest did, I felt it advisable to do so likewise. It gave me added moments to live.

I heard the words "Let me see him!" and the circle around me began to open. Then the large man from the doorway bellowed, "No! Assassin! Guard the king!"

"Field Marshal, it is mine to say!"

The circle loosened and very reluctantly the guards in blue and white let themselves be shoved aside, and there in his underwear, with his hair in his face, I beheld Rudof, king of Velonya and Satt and Ekesh and Morquenie and the southern territories.

Like the real assassins, I was prepared to know him by his red hair, but I had assumed the red hair of Rudof to be a dignified auburn. Our portrait of the crown prince in Sordaling School's refectory was painted so. Even under moonlight I could see that the king had a head of hair the color of a very bright carrot, orange red and hanging in uneven curls around his face, and that he was inclined to a different tone of red across his youthful cheeks. In my surprise I was silent. I stood and panted and forgot to bow.

"A peasant boy with a brush chopper in his hand" said

173

Rudof, and he looked pointedly over the company at the man with the bass voice. "Quite right to send the entire camp down on him, Field Marshal."

I looked and knew the man for Helt Markins, duke of Leoue. Field marshal of the Velonyan Army. Black and yellow.

The duke cleared his throat. "A chopper is as good a weapon for an assassin as a sword, sir. Better," he said. "And look: This is not merely a peasant, but a Rezhmian peasant."

"What did you expect in these environs, Markins? A Vesting peasant?" The king gestured to his guards. "Try not to hurt him. Tie him and we'll question him in the morning." He turned and lifted the leather flap again.

I found my voice finally. "Sir! My king! There are a hundred Rezhmian assassins after—" I got no farther, for the king's guards were obedient to his word, and the four marched toward me together, eyeing my hedger, their hands on their swords.

I could not begin killing the king's own men, not if I wanted to be believed. I threw my blade down at their feet, and the one who bent to pick it up I kicked hard in the head. He hit the ground like wet clothes falling off a clothesline. I leaped over him to be on the man behind him before he could grab me. I took him down behind the knee, and at that moment the third guard took me behind the elbows, and I let him have the point of an elbow very hard in the bottom ribs and spun him out by his other arm, keeping the last man away with the bulk of this fellow. All the while, I heard King Rudof calling encouragement. To whom, I could not tell.

And then in that night of voices one last voice was raised, and this one was not strange to me. "Sir, that is no assassin nor peasant boy! That is Nazhuret of Sordaling, and you have no more loyal knight in Velonya!"

I turned to gape at Arlin, standing at the edge of the fire, fully dressed in his silver velvets, every inch a gentleman and every inch a civilian. One of the guards took that moment to try to tackle me, and without engaging my overwhelmed brain, my body tripped him and threw him in an arc that ended at Arlin's feet.

"Enough," said the king. Alone he came forward and next to me. He was tall and lightly built. His eyes were pale in the firelight. "You don't talk like a Rezhmian. Nor a peasant. You don't fight like any peasant, nor any soldier either—not one I've ever seen.

"Nazhuret of Sordaling you are called? Never heard it before. The only man I know who can call himself 'of Sordaling' that I know of is Lord Howdl. Son of his?"

With more force than was perhaps necessary I disclaimed all relationship with Baron Howdl. I heard Arlin snicker. Howdl is famous among boys at the school.

"Nazhuret of the Royal School at Sordaling, sir. That is what the gentleman meant. And I'm not even that anymore. But let us not stop here longer like fools discussing my accent and my education when there are a good hundred red whip riders intending to surprise your troop this morning and murder you."

My message widened his eyes so that even by firelight I could tell they were green. Then he gave a small snort and said, "Well, then, Nazhuret of Sordaling School, I certainly won't stand here like a fool any longer. I will have some lamps lit and we can discuss this inside."

I realized what my tongue had done, and stuttering apologies, followed the king into his tent. The field marshal came behind us.

The king listened to me with his chin resting on his fist, a blanket over his shoulders. He did not bother to comb his brilliant hair back. Occasionally he stopped me, to ask how I had gotten past the nomads' sentries, and, for that matter, past his own, and what I was doing playing a peasant when I was at least gentry by birth, as my study and the Royal School proved, and equal to the finest hand-to-hand fighter in the nation.

My ears burned to have the king so compliment me when I had previously (in some sense) called him a fool. I explained that knowledge of my birth was lost and that I had no reason to expect it was much, that I had been as much a servant as a student, and that now I had left that all behind me to become an optician.

King Rudof roared with laughter until his eyes watered and he began to yawn. I was made to prove myself through my pack, and the king was very interested in my collapsible spyglass. Arlin, whom the king at least recognized, was brought in to corroborate my story. He named me the finest fighter at Sordaling, and that made me smile behind my hand, because that seemed now like such faint praise, and his description of my character and reliability brought the blood to my face again. It was a grand repayment for letting the man get away with cheating at cards.

"When did the Sordaling directors begin admitting Rezhmian boys into their military training?" This was the first time the field marshal had spoken since following me into the king's tent. The field marshal stood behind me and his hand was on his sword hilt, waiting for me to make a hostile move over the table at the king.

King Rudof's gaze sank to the table. I think he was embarrassed. "You have no reason to keep calling the man Rezhmian, Marshal."

I told him I could not very well deny that I was of mixed blood, but that I was neither a traitor nor dishonest. I begged again that he prepare for the morning.

The king stood and threw aside his blanket. A lad in royal colors hurried forward with doeskin breeches over his arm and assisted King Rudof to dress.

"Easily done, my talented optician. I will have the poor devils outside awakened, and they will be told. We will travel today but we will not be unprepared, will we, Leoue?"

The field marshal stepped into the light for the first time and I saw he was as dark as he was burly. He stood beside the king and looked down at me with unmitigated suspicion. "Sire, that is what the fellow wants of us."

King Rudof was putting his jacket over his shoulders. It was very closely fitted. Civilian clothes. "Not 'sire.' I am not my father, to find such a term pleasing, and the only one with a right to call me 'sire' is an infant too young to talk. Of course preparedness is what the lad wants, after running all night to warn us. It's what I want, too. There can be no harm in preparing. Or do you mean us to sit tight until scouts can locate these pony-riding assassins for us? You are too careful of me, old friend."

The field marshal did not look away from me, nor did his eyes seek mine. It was as though he were looking at a beast or a book. "At least let me take this one in charge for you, then."

Rudof stood across the table from him, fully dressed and with that red hair half tamed. "That's all I want to hear out of you, Leoue. I believe the lad is honest.

"You tell me, Nazhuret," said the king, leaning to me over the table. "Do you want to go with the field marshal here? I don't mean as a prisoner but as a soldier with us? Or should we leave you here to wend your simple, glass-grinding way?"

I had been thinking myself. My legs were beginning to cramp from the run, but I was otherwise strong enough. "Have you a wig, sir?"

King Rudof guffawed. "If I wore a wig, lad, it would not be this color, nor this unruly."

"I mean, sir, if you could find a wig like your hair, I could dress in your clothes today and ride where they expect to find you. The ponymen have been told to locate you by your hair."

The king stood still and stiff as though he had been slapped. "In my place! As bait? No, Nazhuret of Sordaling, I thank you, but no. I will take reasonable care of myself, but I will not let you ride in my place."

"Thank the triune God for that, at least," said the field marshal.

While the rest of the camp rose, I had an hour or so to lie still, which I did where I was left, beside the map table in the king's tent. When one is as muscle-tired as I was, it makes no difference whether rest is conscious or sleeping; it is enough not to move. When I could bear to stand again, I begged the chamberlain for a pot in which to warm water for washing, and got instead a tin tub, an attendant, and a change of clothes. First the fellow brought me the breeches and tunic of the 3rd Royal Light Cavalry, and though it was only part of a uniform and only a loan, it brought with it one of the largest temptations in my life.

If I put this on I probably would be expected to ride with that illustrious company, and in the impending attack, if I were to acquit myself creditably, or at least without embarrassment, I might be offered a chance to gain the rest of the uniform, or one equally glorious. I had, after all, as good a training as any man in Velonya or the territories, and my wrestling had impressed the young king.

In doing so I would be reclaiming the Nazhuret of three and a half years ago and turning my back on everything Powl had taught me. But the Nazhuret of three and a half years ago had died, and his ghost was not very restless. Besides, it was Powl's Nazhuret who had wrestled and snapped rapiers for the king's amusement, not the boy of Sordaling School, and Powl's Nazhuret could not take the easy option of obedience to rule.

I put the pretty tunic back in the basket and said I could not wear it because of a religious limitation.

And then it was too big for me.

The valet was gone a few minutes and returned with a

spare suit of the cook's boy, which fit my humor (and my frame) much better.

King Rudof ducked into his tent, fresh and energetic as though he had slept ten hours without a dream. My appearance struck his humor as well, and his laughter had a great charm to it, but in a moment he was serious again. "You have taken a vow, I'm told. It sounds like nonsense, after last night's games. Are you a priest or a pilgrim, then, Nazhuret, or did you kill someone in anger, to make such a stupid . . . ? Is all your battle skill to go for nothing? I had hoped the nation would have the use of what you showed last night." King Rudof had donned the blue and white of a simple horseman of his own company, which suited him very well.

I answered in embarrassment that I was more a pilgrim than a priest if I was either one, and that my training had not gone for nothing or I wouldn't have survived to give the warning of the assassins. He paced, staring down at me, obviously wondering whether to call my statement impudence. An aide brought in breakfast, and I was given the uncomfortable privilege of eating at the table of a king who was not pleased with me. Had there not been biscuits freshly baked, I think I would not have had the temerity to swallow.

The king talked while he ate, sometimes with his mouth full. This had been frowned on at Sordaling. Powl had never permitted it. "Don't you call that fighting, when you laid my personal guard on the ground in rows—not to mention abusing the field marshal's own men? Is your vow that you can fight for your own life but no other?"

I had to down my food before replying, not out of manners but to gain time. My throat was painfully dry. "My limitation, sir, is rather that I cannot spill blood on . . . another's command."

What more pointed, more offensive thing could be said aloud to the king of one's own country? I sat with my hands in my lap and waited.

The king's green eyes did not move from my face. For some seconds he, too, waited, for explanation or apology. "But you can spill barrels of the stuff at your own whim, is that it? I can't say I think much of that vow; it's pure self-indulgence. You are saying you can brawl at any moment it appeals to you, but you cannot fight at the king's command, which is the need of the nation." He spoke without heat or bluster, but to get the matter straight between us.

"No, sir, I can't brawl at whim. Or at least I never do have a whim to brawl. But it is true that I cannot offer obedience in that matter. Not even to you, my king. That is why I can't wear the uniform of a soldier."

King Rudof had a face similar in feature to Arlin's: that is to say, long with a thin, high-bridged nose, a face close to the standard of Velonyan beauty. He was heavier-boned than the sword juggler, and the king had the redhead's mercurial complexion, which went waxy pale as he sat upright and said, "It is not only the paid soldiers of Velonya who are bound to fight at the command of the king. Every man not an ordained priest is subject to that duty."

I could think of nothing whatsoever to say.

"I can have you split open and beheaded for refusing me outright." The youth departed from the king's face, leaving a mask with eyes of steel. I had never seen the old king, his father, save in pictures, but I felt I was seeing him now. The two sentries at the entrance had turned their attention to this dialogue, and now they stepped through the doorway. "That is the punishment for a traitor."

"Yes, sir, of course you can. In that I am entirely at your service," I answered him, and my placating words sounded ludicrous even to myself. They made him blink.

King Rudof sat back and ran one hand through his red hair. Heavily he said, "I think, lad, that you'd best call yourself a priest while you are with this company. Of course, we will be parting ways shortly." He rose and, lifting his long legs over the low table, went past me and out.

First the scouts set out in pairs, and half an hour later the entire straggling procession creaked forward. Every man jack of them ignored me, and no cook's boy asked for his shirt and breeches back. I suppose he wouldn't wear them after they'd been on the man who insulted the king. I stood on the highest point of land nearby and watched for the king himself to pass.

I would have missed him entirely, for there was no red hair to be seen. All the Royal Light Horse were riding in leather headgear, which extended down the back of the neck and into a low visor over the eyes. Nor was he beside the field marshal, where I would have expected to find him, but in the middle of the front row of the lower officers. I finally picked him out by the chestnut horse he rode, which seemed a little grand for the commonality of cavalry and which was a color to appeal to any redheaded rider.

The other companies had their own versions of this helmet, and the three marshals were concealed beneath hats or helmets as well. The foot troops went bareheaded, as was standard, but I noticed as they marched that any men of exceptionally brilliant hair color had been moved to the inside of the row and column.

This was a better maneuver than my own "wig" idea. Instead of having a false redhead, they had no visible heads of hair whatsoever.

I hefted my pack from which my own clothes, washed and fullered for me while I rested, hung smelling of wet wool. I was feeling a profound disappointment in myself and in my meeting with King Rudof, and I pulled apart our short, unsatisfactory conversation in my mind, wondering how I might have had it come out otherwise without lying to the King of Velonya.

Had I had more time, or had the situation been less immediate, I might have been able to convince him that my peculiar style of combat was a matter of involuntary reflex, or too peculiar and too primitive to have military application. If I could only have made it to seem that he was rejecting me instead of (horrendous thing) the other way around. But I doubted that at my best and most prepared I could have made the truth please him better than it did. As Powl would have said, the only solution is to stay away from the centers of power entirely. But even Powl would not have had me let King Rudof walk into a trap of assassins unaware.

I saw them all go by me, even to the last heavy wagon of pavilion bracings, and then I trotted off in the same direction but aiming slightly right and off the road, so that in a very few minutes I was even with the Royal Light Horse again and then ahead of them. The fact that I could not be an obedient soldier did not mean I was going to stand by and let Velonya's enemies attack the king.

Behind me I heard hooves splashing mud, and I was mystified as to whom it could be. I was jogging a path that wound amid the hills while the whole troop of the king were down on the flat by the road, except for the sentries, who had gone ahead. There was no hiding in the grass here, for it was sparse and ankle-high, so I stayed where I was, my hedger in my hand. Perhaps the king had decided he could not brook my impudence after all and had sent out soldiers to drag me back, or to kill me where I stood.

When the single rider came into view I felt surprise and an overwashing of inevitability that it should be Arlin again, wearing the one suit he seemed to own and riding his dainty gray. This time, however, he had two horses, the other being a bony chestnut he led without pack or saddle behind him. I waited for him to catch up to me.

"I expected to find you below," he said without preface. "I didn't think you'd be able to walk today, let alone leap the hilltops." He leaned over and put the spare horse's bridle into my hand.

I looked up at the beast in even greater confusion. "Did you . . . steal this horse, Arlin?" I asked him, and he grimaced. "There you go again, little moralist. I did not steal it. It was an extra. Get on."

I did not argue further. Mounting was difficult with the bulk of the pack and my weapon in my right hand, but the beast stood quiet. "It's an old cavalry horse," he said. "Not sprightly, but used to anything. And it'd better be, carrying you."

The horse had the sort of spine that projects above the rib cage a good ways. I would not choose such a creature for bareback riding if I were given the choice. "I'm not such a clumsy rider as that, fellow. It's only that lately I haven't—."

"Believe it or not, optician, I didn't mean that as an insult. Though"—he turned and gave me a disgusted glare—"you certainly deserve a few. And after I vouched for you to the king."

"I am sensible of that." I pressed the horse even with Arlin's. "I owe my liberty to that introduction. Perhaps my life."

"You owe me nothing," he said, reversing his attitude completely. "I think you could have taken them all down. All the Royal Guard and the field marshals, too."

"I think the king ought to be grateful to you as well," I continued over his words. "If I hadn't had a chance to warn him about the attack coming . . . you do believe me about the assassins, don't you?"

"That's where we're going," Arlin said without changing his sullen expression. "You're going to show them to me."

I did not imagine that the Rezhmian nomads had slept late this morning, so to be yawning where I had left them the night before. We saw no sign of activity along the east–west road, but I had not expected them to prepare their assault so close to the king's night camp. In only a few miles we would reach the intersection where that broad road ended and the traveler must turn south and uphill to the broken mountains of the border, or north along the precipitous hills I had walked the past few days. That north–south road was narrower and more uneven, and the ground rose close at either hand.

Assuming the nomads had excellent scouts (or some other information concerning the movements of the king's company), they would have done as I had done to escape their discovery the night before, and traveled parallel to the road behind the first or second ridge of downs—where we were heading now, in fact.

The day was going to be cold and windy, and the white cook's linens were not sewn for warmth. When I began to lose feeling of the reins in my hands I called a halt, dismounted, took off my pack and then my shirt, and put the woolen homespun next to my skin. This caused Arlin to announce that he had changed his mind about my origin, for anyone who could wear such a garment on bare skin had to be base-born. The cook's shirt I put over my head, with the sleeves pressing back my frozen ears and tied at the nape of the neck. I advised my companion to leave me where I stood, lest he suffer the embarrassment of being killed by invaders in the company of a fellow as sartorially backward as I.

We had reached the hill above the intersection of roads, and there was nothing to be seen below except the rectangular outline of an old building foundation. It might once have been a small inn; what other building would stand alone so close to a border between unfriendly nations I don't know. Nor do I imagine the place had prospered or survived very long. I remembered very well the glossy, charred wood of the village only a day's walk from here, and the vandalized grave.

It had been King Rudof's intention to turn north at this

junction and continue his review of the realm with Morquenie and Satt territories, but I had no way of knowing whether the Red Whips knew the king's habits only, or his intentions as well. The former might be learned through stalking, and by the use of spyglasses like mine. The latter meant treachery.

I did not let my horse top the bare hill, but pulled him up a few yards below, on an uncomfortable slope. Arlin stared puzzled for a moment but followed my lead. "You don't want to be seen on the skyline, is that it?" he shouted over the wind.

I nodded and bellowed back, "Neither do the Rezhmians! They'll be somewhere down between the rises, spread out like the trickle of a stream! Hard to see, even from close by!"

"A hundred men, hard to see?"

Again I nodded, and because I don't have a voice for bellowing, I led him down into the shelter of the hills. "They could hide more than that number. It was those tactics that caused the defeat of our army in the last incursion. Remember?"

Arlin snorted. "How should I remember? I wasn't even born then."

"Neither was I, but I studied my lessons." I didn't know why I was continuing to act like an arrogant schoolboy in the presence of this fellow. My manners distressed me, and I determined at that moment to behave myself, especially since I might be about to be cut down by enemy arrows. It would be a shame to die disgusted with oneself.

I turned north and went very cautiously along the path I had run eight hours before. My companion did not object, but he asked how I had chosen this direction, and I replied that if the assassins were working by chance, they would be as likely to be north as south of the crossroads, and if they had information, they would likely be north. That gave north two chances out of three.

It was easier to ride down here, where a seasonal stream

ran over new grass. I let my old horse pick his way, and as Arlin had intimated, the beast was no fool. It also was easier to talk, which Arlin did. He returned to the subject of my vows and limitations, and interrogated me strictly, while his pretty mare danced left and right over the trickling water, wasting a lot of effort trying to keep her feet dry.

Was I permitted to drink distilled liquors? he wondered. To gamble? To wear silk? To fornicate, perchance? To marry? I replied with what restraint I could muster (for the subject had received overmuch attention in the past day) that what I was not permitted to do was to give over responsibility for my actions. Not to another, nor to chance. That in itself was a vow among vows and a limitation encompassing most other limitations. I said this much and then I asked him to leave off, for as we rode I was trying to see through the hills themselves, and hear noises not yet made.

Arlin did leave off, for he was offended. He spat on the ground and prodded his mare over the stream, yards away from me, where he rode on in a pretense that we were two separate travelers with no connection, until his mare squealed and reared and he called out.

My beast stood calmly enough over the two bodies thrown between large rocks. The old cavalry gelding was used to the smell of blood. The uniforms had been blue and white. I said the obvious: "The king's scouts."

Arlin dismounted and turned one of them over. The tailored coat had been pierced many times by a blade. "I knew this man somewhat," he said. He held his sweating horse with a firm hand on the headstall.

Without getting down I could read the tracks coming around the hill from the road and then leading north in our direction. Only hoofprints. No shoes on the hooves, either. I remarked to Arlin that the Red Whips might as well not have feet, for all the walking they did.

He sprang up in the saddle again, and his mare quieted

from the accustomed weight on her back. Without another word I motioned him behind me, for there was movement between the hills to the west, by the road. I pressed the chestnut slowly forward.

Two more riders, dressed darker than the dead scouts, were trotting at the grassy shoulder of the far side. They were so far ahead of us that we could not tell whether they were wearing the black and yellow of the field marshal's personal horsemen or the rough leather and bright silk of the nomads. Fortunately, I had had the forethought to assemble my spyglass before leaving camp, and now Arlin pulled it from the top of my pack and put it to his eyes. "Ours," he said at last. "And a couple of fools, too: riding down the road as though down Barya Boulevard with girls admiring them. We can catch up with them and tell them what we have seen." His mare turned on her hindquarters, leaped back over the stream like a deer, and continued north. I followed on my old gentleman as best we might. I doubted the field marshal's scouts had anything of interest to tell us, or they would have turned back to report. The prints of the enemy embossed the wet ground all around us: dozens of horses. I wondered if Arlin had any notion where he was going. For myself, the hair on my arms and neck was beginning to rise up with fear.

In only two minutes we had come even with the Velonyans, and Arlin followed a path between two grassy mounds to the road. I followed after, glad to see no hoofprints going in our immediate direction.

The scouts were halted together, and one was pointing up and ahead of him. We were so close I could see the horses' breath fogging in the air. Arlin hailed from the other side of the road and both men started in their saddles, put their hands to their swords, and turned to stare at us, their faces empty of any expression except surprise.

Another cry came from the road ahead, and without warning the road two hundred feet ahead was crawling with small, ewe-necked, slab-sided, slope-rumped horses ridden by men no handsomer than they.

Arlin opened his mouth and pointed at the two scouts, who were so terribly close to the enemy. "We can't help them!" I shouted. "Run! Run!"

His mare wheeled, and my horse let himself be hauled around. Neither was a dull brute, and they took off with a will down the rutted road. Through the crisis of the moment I was kept aware of the old gelding's spine.

Arlin looked back over his shoulder. "They'll never catch us, riding those!" he called. Lest he become overconfident, I answered, "They don't have to!" I, too, looked back, just in time to see the first of the stubby arrows of the Rezhmians sail close between us.

Arlin gaped, disbelieving, but Arlin seemed to share the Velonyan contempt for foreign customs and weapons: contempt built on perfect ignorance. Powl had made sure I knew that the Red Whip archers were superior to ours—it was to be expected in a people who both hunt and fight from running horses. Remember, my king, it is not illegal for a common man of that nation to possess a bow.

I had no chance to share any of this knowledge with my companion, for even as I noted the accuracy over distance of our pursuers, one of their shots hit my horse just above the hock. The beast plunged, floundered, and went down on his knees, leaving me standing beside him, watching the assassins come on. They shouted a welcome as they saw me before them.

Arlin committed an act of great stupidity. He skidded his mare to a stop and spun her once more. I screamed for him to go on, I stamped in place, but the gray mare's legs bunched beneath her and she leaped back the way she had come. He was above me, he had me by the back of the collar and was trying unsuccessfully to haul me up in front of him, and then

I saw him flinch, clawing at his right arm. I grabbed his leg and the saddle and I jumped up behind.

The mare took a hit as well, glancing off her croup, which served only to urge her more heroically on. Arrows hissed around us, then clattered at her hooves and then fell too far behind for me to hear. The shouts of the riders also faded, but I could hear them screaming, "Old horse! The old horse!" for five very nasty minutes. I wondered if any had stopped to put *my* old horse out of its agony.

Arlin was rigid with pain, and the hand that held the reins gripped white-knuckled the high pommel of the saddle. His other hand he had thrust into the lacings of his jacket, and the arrowhead through his upper arm looked too bloody and awful to be real. With a word of warning I pressed the arrow farther through. Arlin screamed like a cat in anger, and the horse hopped once and went on. I reached around him with both arms and broke off the triangular steel arrowhead. With the movement of the horse it was a very rough business, and Arlin almost went off the horse. When I could let him go again I pulled the arrowhead out from behind.

The overburdened mare was booming like a drum with every step, and her lungs also were beginning to whistle. We were going slower now, and I looked back to find our lead only five hundred feet. There were perhaps thirty of the nomads behind us, and their ugly ponies seemed to have as good a wind as Arlin's high-bred dancer.

It stumbled, and Arlin cried out from the shock on his wound. Our pursuers cried out also, like hounds who see the hare before them. The mare went on.

Before us was a tiny settlement I could not remember having seen on the way north. But it was not by the road; it was *in* the road, and the houses were on wheels. I was looking at the wagons of the king's company, standing all alone with their draft horses standing placidly in sixes before them. I could not understand, but as we came I shouted a warning, as though our appearance weren't warning enough.

We pulled even with the first wagon, which had wheels that rose above my head and sides of waxed canvas. I reached around and gave the horse a check, for Arlin was too near fainting to do it himself. I looked back at the Red Whip riders; the sight of the king's supply wagons had not daunted them in the least. They would be with us in seconds. In mystification I glanced down left and right at the ground and saw the marks of the king's soldiers leaking away into the hills.

"Behind the wagons!"

I could not locate the voice, but I had a sudden insight, and I let the mare's failing momentum take us down the row of wheels.

We turned behind the last of the abandoned vehicles just as our pursuers came even with the first. They divided, so as to squeeze us between them, and they cantered along each side of the road. I could hear the noises of their horses' breathing, much like the gray mare's but multiplied by number.

Arlin gasped and spoke. "I'm sorry, optician," he said, and he put his good hand over mine. "I should have left you content back in Warvala."

"I still am content," I said, though it was only true in certain ways. I had my hedger in my hand, though much good it was going to do me. Then came a beaten gong, the canvas sides of the wagons all rolled up together, and a dozen primed harquebuses were fired point-blank into the lines of the Red Whips.

The mare was no cavalry horse. Both Arlin and I were in the air, and when we landed, he was on me and I was on my pack. The infantrymen hidden in the wagons swarmed out over what were left of our pursuers, but the eight or ten riders who still were alive and horsed turned with remarkable precision and plunged off the road and into the hills.

I had shrugged off my pack and picked my companion off the road. The infantry lieutenant sent a man to assist me but I brushed by, denying any help. I did not have to be told where the great mass of the king's men had concealed themselves, for the broken grass and chopped earth led me right. In a narrow cleft between hills too steep for horses they had deployed themselves, with horse troops and lancers at either exposed opening and a small brass cannon I had not known they were carrying.

The cavalry opened to let me through with my burden, and there was a well-tailored civilian at my side. "I am the king's physician. As of yet I have no important wounds to attend to, so I will look at the fellow."

His neat jacket and breeches had gold piping at the seams, as Powl had used to wear. Otherwise he did not remind me at all of my teacher. "No, thank you," I said, stepping smartly by him. "This man belongs to a sect that does not admit the services of a doctor." I was looking for a tent, box, or large barrel that would give me privacy to pad and wrap the wound, for Arlin was bleeding too heavily to delay any longer.

"He is hardly in any position to enforce his views," said the doctor with a fruity chuckle, and I explained very firmly to the man that I would do the enforcing.

There was no such thing as real concealment, for this was not a camp, but with the cooperation of the men a canvas tarpaulin was set up on four short tent poles. Someone also robbed the doctor of a quantity of gauze and flannel.

I ripped the velvet sleeve open down the long seam, revealing a shamefully scrawny arm, with the oversized forearm muscles of people who work with their fingers—musicians, sword jugglers, card cheats. The wound had at least bled itself clean, and I had not heard that the nomads poisoned their arrows. I clamped a pad of flannel over both holes and wound gauze tightly over them. "This will have to be loosened every

191

once in a while, or the whole arm will rot off. Can you stay conscious to do that? Can you? Or else I'll have to ask someone else."

Arlin mouthed the word "no." Then he said, "No one else. But I don't think it will matter. I'm gone."

"Very weak, but not gone," I said, hoping it were true. And then I added, "I remember you now."

Arlin smiled wolfishly. "Do you then? Well, I never forgot. Not anything you taught me."

I laughed. "You now excel me by far in tricks, I'll give you that."

The smile went away. "In tricks only. If I die here, Nazhuret, I want you to know that you always have been my ideal of the true knight and gentleman."

I thought then that I might faint from astonishment. "By the Triune God, Arlin, I'm neither knight nor gentleman. You're raving," I said, and went out. It was easy to get one of the infantry officers to place a foot soldier before the makeshift shelter, with a promise Arlin would not be disturbed.

I found the king with his field marshal, and as I had come to find usual, they were bickering. The Duke of Leoue was not in favor of packing the company between precipitous hills. They had neither room to fight, he said, nor room to run if the Rezhmians chose to fling down stones. King Rudof, still with his leather helmet over his orange hair, was in no mind to change his unconventional strategies, which had worked so far to his great gain.

"Thirty years ago my father came south with his head stuffed with such strategies as yours, Leoue, and he left half his men between here and the mountain passes."

Apparently the field marshal had forgotten the hat ruse, for he was holding his cavalry helmet under his arm. "I fear this strategy, sir, will not leave so many to tell the story. You have boxed us in like cattle in a pen."

He spoke with feeling, and I, who had trained for fifteen years in broad lines, vectors, and squares over the walled field of Sordaling School, could understand the marshal's distrust. I wondered if the king knew how far the bows of the Red Whips could accurately reach. I was in a position to tell him.

Both men sat on stools before the same portable table on which I had scrawled my maps the night before. The king's infantry slouched around in a deceptive disarray, while the cavalry horses stood fully geared, pawing or sleeping or lipping the ground as temperament decreed. A line of servants went around the hill to the road and returned, as disciplined ants, bearing burdens from the wagons on their shoulders. A few more were digging the usual trenches a few hundred feet north of the encampment. Aside from the looming slopes there was no shelter, and the wind blew hard down this cleft in the hills.

"At least, Leoue, you now seem to believe in the assassination attempt." King Rudof leaned back over nothing, using his feet locked against the table legs for support. He looked ungainly and entirely at his ease. It seemed to me, as I stood watching, that he was either very used to devising strategies or he had that rare constitution that thrives in an emergency. Either way it would be fortunate for the nation—as long as his strategies were right and the emergencies controlled, of course.

The field marshal was twenty years older than King Rudof and, like most ranking officers in such a situation, looked worried sick. "Oh, I have always believed there was treachery here, sir," he said. "I have only been less trusting as to its source. I think we had the instigator in our hands last night and let him get away."

As it happens, I was directly behind Field Marshal the Duke of Leoue as he was speaking, and by chance the king met my eyes at the instant my character suffered such calumny. I must have been a grand sight, so covered with Arlin's blood

I looked more like a butcher than a cook in my white linens, and a scratch over my scalp that I do not remember acquiring was bleeding down my head with the energy of a much heavier wound. Immediately the king glanced away again and put one finger into his mouth, as a boy will to smother a grin. "I don't think it's fair to say we had him in our hands, Leoue. Not at any moment, as a matter of fact."

The duke grunted and also leaned in his chair, but not so dramatically as the king. "It would have been only a matter of time, sir, had you not forbade it."

Now King Rudof let the grin appear. "Surely, surely. A line of cannons might have brought him down. Or a concerted press of cavalry, though I'm not so certain of the latter. What do you say, Nazhuret? What force would be necessary to overcome you?"

The field marshal followed the direction of the king's gaze and spun to his feet, knocking over the stool, and swung a large, wild fist at my head. I deflected it as respectfully as I could and stepped back from his angry, startled face.

"To . . . overcome me, sir?" I said the first thing that came into my head. "A cold in the chest, or any sad story. Or seventy vengeful Red Whip riders, for that is the number I figure to be left out there." As I spoke, my attention was admittedly on the man before me, as tall as the king and broader and who flexed his hand repeatedly as though he wished it around my neck. "Why did you come back, fellow? Weren't you grateful to escape with your life? Do you dare to speak more impertinence to your king, or does your Rezhmian blood deny him that position?"

I had no idea how to answer, for I could not speak of my respect for King Rudof before his face, as though he were the kitchen cat, and neither did I want to offend further the first officer of the Velonyan military. Fortunately, the young king took the problem from me.

"I think his information is very pertinent," said King Rudof, rising from his seat with a yawn and crackling his spine left and right. "He has done more than any of our regular scouts—so far, at least."

"That, my king, is the other information I have come to tell you," I said. "Four of your scouts were taken by the enemy. Two Royal Infantry my companion Arlin found stabbed, and two men in your livery, my lord duke, were overrun by the same force that pursued us."

The field marshal frowned black at this news, and King Rudof played with the strap of his helmet between his fingers. "That leaves only the four who went south at the crossroads, then. I have to be doubly grateful to you, priest. We might have waited here for news forever, or until the Red Whips chose to ride down on us."

"We still might," said the Duke of Leoue, squinting over the mass of cavalry and the line of harquebuses on their tripod stands. "If there still are seventy of the devils out there. Just because one lot came down from the north doesn't mean the rest haven't circled us already."

"I don't care," said the king. "North gate or south gate, they're welcome to try. Without one of the optician's spyglasses I can tell my preparations are complete. Come beside me, Nazhuret, and I will tell you my plan."

"No!" The duke's roar turned the heads of fifty soldiers from their blade sharpening or boot polishing or whatever little work of hand was taking their minds off their peril. They stared from him to the king to me, as though they wouldn't want to be in my wooden clogs. "Sir, grant me at least this much, that you do not allow this impudent half-breed access to every military secret we possess!" He slapped his hand against the light armor of his thigh, bowed to the king, and stalked away.

The king blinked at this, and as he watched his field marshal go, his redhead's coloring rose, but after one heavy breath let out through his nostrils, he smiled again. "So be it. Nazhuret, you will have to be surprised. I hope it is a good surprise, lad."

He put his hand between my shoulder blades and led me away from the attention of the multitudes. In my ear he added, "The good duke is my bullmastiff, Nazhuret. He hugs my side and growls at all my friends. He played that role for my father before me. What can I do?"

I felt the charm of the King of Velonya, and it seemed excessive that a man born to such authority should also have that undefinable character that makes men follow a leader, whether that leader is born to authority or not. Also, with the king's arm around me that way, I felt myself in equally undefinable danger. Perhaps from that very charm.

We came through the press of men toward the hill that blocked us from the road. The king seemed to be looking for something here that he did not find. The artillerymen who had saved Arlin and myself had been dispatched to the north and south "gates," as the king called them, and he had to summon their lieutenant back again.

While he waited, I took the opportunity to tell him that my friend Arlin bore more of the credit for discovering the hiding place of the nomads than I did, and all the credit for getting us back alive. The king's glance was ironical. Much like Powl's. "So I should reward him—though I am surprised to find that any of these civilian fops who ride our train like peacocks are capable of action. What does he want?"

The question stymied me. All I could think of, where Arlin was concerned, was money, for what else does a card cheat work for? But gold was not the King of Velonya's greatest power of gift. To suggest money would be insulting. What I had recently learned of my old friend caused me only to shake my head. "Not entitlements, certainly. Nor military office. Court position . . . he would also find that difficult.

"I don't know, sir. I think your good regard would be enough."

The king's response was a wide-eyed stare. "You think

that, do you? Has this fellow also taken vows?"

"Something like that," I answered.

King Rudof let that be for the moment, for the artillery officer had arrived. He was asked what had become of the prisoners taken in the wagon ambush. The officer stared, stuttered, and said he would have to inquire.

The idea of interrogating one of the captives was daunting, for they, like many primitives, were loyal unto death to their own packs and had never been known to give over their people's secrets. Still it must be tried, I recognized that, and I wondered if I would be asked to translate. I wondered, also, what persuasions the king would employ.

"You have good Rayzhia?" he asked me, and I nodded.

"Then you can aid me if I become lost, for my language studies are rusty."

No Velonyan of quality spoke Rayzhia, unless it was a few musty scholars and an eccentric like Powl. I must have stared, for with some amusement Rudof went on, "I surprise you. Well, I did not learn it on my mother's knee, as you did. A friend taught me."

Before I could correct the king's misapprehension about me (if it was important enough to need correction), the artilleryman returned. He came over the trampled grass with great reluctance and told the king there had been no survivors.

King Rudof frowned. "Kausan, you are mistaken, for I watched the affair. We took most of them alive, if not intact. I need one rider to interrogate, and it must be now."

The artilleryman was gray-faced and glistening with sweat. He ventured to suggest that the barbarians had killed one another upon capture, and the king, by law of opposites, flushed a stunning red color beneath his orange eyebrows as he inquired whether they had been suffered to accomplish this deed while under military guard.

The officer struggled to reply, and his expression was pitiable, for his career was tumbling to ruin about his head. King

Rudof put his hand on the man's lapel, whether to shake him or thrust him aside I do not know, for at that moment came three staccato barks of a bugle, and the king flung himself past the artilleryman and into the mass of soldiers between himself and the exposed flank.

From where I stood I could see nothing but other men's heads, and the signal meant nothing to me. I floundered in the king's wake, and everyone let me by.

The throat of the valley had been pocked and trampled by Velonyan troops, and untidy heaps of kitchen equipment and rolls of canvas batting had been abandoned on the path that hugged the climbing ridge to the west. Where I had seen antlike processions bearing their burdens were now cantering riders, moving loosely but in perfect control, in circles some four hundred feet away from our line. These were not ants, but dragonflies: creatures with wings.

I spied all this from the tiny elevation that the king had claimed for his headquarters. Five marshals stood awaiting him as his long legs thrust him up the outcrop of stone. He was panting not with effort but excitement.

"Too far, sir," said Marshal Garman. "They don't seem to be ready to engage us yet. There only seem to be sixty or so, and I imagine this sight of us has cooled their ardor for battle."

The Red Whips had known our numbers twenty-four hours before and certainly had suffered no shocks at the vision before them. I kept my mouth shut, however, for the king knew all this, and knew besides what destruction that distant line of dragonflies could work on trained soldiery. I was standing behind the assembled command officers, happily unnoticed and hopping from one foot to another to see over their heads.

"We must not ignore the other end of this bottle," said Leoue. "Their dance out there could be merely a distraction."

"There are sixty riders in sight and we . . . disposed of . . .

twenty-five an hour ago, Leoue," answered the king. "That leaves only ten at the most to be playing tricks. As long as we have men on the ridgetops we are secure."

"Sir, we cannot say there are only about ninety brutes opposing us. I think we should distribute guns and horses more evenly."

King Rudof put his arm behind his field marshal's back, as he had with me. "Too late, old friend. Look, they're coming. Now my trick will work or it won't."

The riders did not turn and charge our guns but instead wove their circles closer and closer. The ponies, so rude in build and trapping, were working by leg signal as finely as any lady's town hack, while the reins were slipped over their pommels and each rider had in his hands the little lacquered bow with its shape like rosebud lips, ready to pucker and kiss death at all of us. I noticed red-lacquered quivers, also, each filled with a dozen arrows.

"Those bows are no use to them yet. It's when they get within two hundred feet of us," murmured the king to Leoue as the other officers strode off to their commands.

"Sir! My king, let me correct you!" I heard myself shouting, to everyone's surprise. "It's when they get within three hundred feet of us they will begin to fire, and by the time they reach two hundred, unless we do something, our front lines will be flat as cut hay!"

The king looked back over his shoulder in amazement. "Three hundred feet?" His field marshal snorted.

"I should know. My horse was hit at about two-eighty, and Arlin at slightly less. You cannot judge their bows by ours, nor their archers. . . ."

The king had left me and the duke alone on our prominence, and a moment later had wrested from his bugler the signal horn and was blasting a sharp retreat. At that same moment I heard cries as the Red Whips let loose the first of their volleys. They were slightly less than three hundred feet from our front lines, and they knew their distance to an inch. Gunners went down, horses rose up, and there was much screaming. The front line of harquebus uttered their terrifying blast almost together and then shouldered the weapon and stand to follow the direction of the bugle.

The ground was moving with men following the retreat, but I wanted nothing so much as to find the battlefront. I clambered up the hill on my hands and feet, skidding and scrabbling forward against the great traffic until I could see what was happening on the field.

There were perhaps five ponies down before our gunfire and another few cantering riderless, but the harquebuses were far less accurate at this distance than the little, wasp-buzzing arrows. The sweeps of the enemy had taken down two or three of our gunners for every one of them lost. The artillerymen could not retreat and fire at the same time, and our cavalry in their blue and white could do little more at this distance than rattle sabers and hold their panicked horses.

Without warning the shot-catapult was released, its twenty-foot arm rising like a sprung sapling into the air. Its load of ball spread and vanished into the gray air and another few riders went down, but it, too, was aimed too close to do major damage. A shrill cry reached me from across the distance, and more arrows hurried the retreat as men and guns and horses fell over one another.

If the king had a secret weapon, he had better deploy it.

Now the arc of riders had reached the first of the abandoned piles, and one reached down, still cantering, and grabbed the steel handle of a stockpot and swung it into the air. The heap clattered and fell into itself, and then a man was running over the ground—a man not in nomad dress nor in cook's uniform but in the sky blue of Velonya, and the rider was after him. It was pitiful and horrifying, but the end was preordained, and I saw the hiding soldier opened across the chest by the touch of Rezhmian steel.

There came a bellow of fury from the valley below me. It was the king, and his face was not good to see. His hand was in his mouth, and he had drawn blood from it.

In a moment I understood both the plan and its misfire. I scrabbled forward on the side of the hill, and when I came even with the rearmost of the retreating gunners I let gravity carry me down. I hit the man with my shoulder and took him down, and while I was atop him I stole both his flint and the canvas gun shroud, which I put over my head as I ran, hugging the ridge of stone, toward the advancing enemy.

From in front I had one brief, perfect view of the destruction. At least a dozen Velonyans lay motionless, while more were carried or dragged back with the retreat. It was a retreat, and not the rout I had feared. I heard the shout of the king, though I don't know what it was he said, and then I turned my eyes ahead.

The nomads were only thirty yards from me: a rumble in my ears and a shaking of the stony earth. Down on my hands and knees, at badger height, I could clearly see the mounds and the divots, the gouges and the streaks in the dirt our Velonyan assemblage had left in preparing their positions. It was obvious to me that there was meaning in the placement of three areas of disturbed earth and piled rubble, but the Red Whips had not overheard what I had overheard from the lips of King Rudof, and nomadic riders have no reason to be awake to the possibilities of black powder.

The crude brown canvas was threatening to slip off behind, revealing my attire of brilliant white. None of the riders appeared to have seen me yet, so I grabbed the gun shroud in my teeth and kept crawling. Ahead of me, flat against the ground, the saber-broken soldier lay in a hump, his blue jacket maroon with his spreading blood.

I heard the riders again, crying the name of their tribe totem. They brandished their delicate little bows, and the circle slid closer to King Rudof's new front line. Closer to me, as well. I pulled from my pocket the flint striker and crawled faster. There were arrows again, and the riders had flawless eyes for distance.

The fallen soldier was not where I expected to find him, and in confusion my eyes followed a smear like a snail's track, but bloody. He was not dead after all, and as I watched he inched himself back into the blind of pots and canvases, digging his way with a clatter unheard amid the sounds of hooves and killing.

I could not imagine a fellow as badly hurt as that succeeding in lighting any fuse, so I scurried behind him, losing my covering on a new sprung thistle. To my right I saw the wall of riders wheeling around, and one detached himself from the rest. It was the man who had discovered the spy before, and he aimed his pony like a weapon at us. I stood and ran for the collapsed blind, knowing it was too late already, but I hadn't covered more than five feet when burned air stung my nose, I saw smoke and heard a hissing like water on fire, and then the world to my right blew up and buried me in a storm of very heavy cookpans.

There was a taste of iron in my mouth, and I believed I was back in time half a year, fighting a werewolf and being crowned with a frying pan by his wife. This danger kept me from passing out entirely, and my eyes focused on a field of smoke, flames, and bodies. What remained of the Red Whip force was riding in panic toward the ranks of their enemies, but as I watched, the ground went up twice more, even nearer to myself than the first charge, and I was flung hard into the hard side of the ridge. I had a glimpse of the Rezhmian nomads lit in orange fire, I saw a horse lifted as I had been lifted by the booming air, and then I did go down into the black.

I came to in a wagon, one of a line of wounded men, less hurt than most. I sat up amid great dizziness and found blood wet on my face and head; it seemed to be coming from my ears.

Outside (it took me long minutes to get out and down the stairs), the camp of the king seemed to be packing up. I heard a man singing, or surmised the sound had that source. My hearing was as greatly disturbed as my balance.

A fellow in civilian clothing rushed at me, babbling something, and he tried to force me back into the makeshift hospital coach. Not understanding and unable to gather my own thoughts, I was forced to pin him against the ground before continuing, and I found it unusually difficult work.

I went to find Arlin, for he had some special need of me, I couldn't remember what. I would remember when I saw him, I thought, and I staggered on.

The little shelter I had created for him had collapsed and been trampled when the entire camp had plunged to the rear. I lifted the grimy canvas and looked under it stupidly, as though he might still be hiding beneath. Two well-intentioned soldiers came to me then with the same intention as the doctor previously. One let himself be waved away, and one had to be hit.

I did not find Arlin, but the king found me. He stood before me, talking energetically, and this time he clapped me on the shoulder rather than the back. Though I could not hear, I could talk, and I told him I was looking for Arlin, who was badly injured and now had disappeared. Perhaps I was shouting.

King Rudof gave me a searching look, then called for an aide, who brought him pen and paper. Against the man's back he wrote to me, "He is not among the dead, nor the wounded. I will have him cried through the camp."

I waited, dizzy and with a roaring of battle in my ears that would not cease. The King of Velonya was drawn away by councillors with their multitudinous needs, but he returned to me in a few minutes.

"Arlin was seen in the hospital wagon before you woke. Looking for you. Immediately after, he took his horse and rode north. No one challenged him."

I read this twice over, and the second time it was no better news. Only then did I notice that the king had written to me in Allec. A piece of cleverness, perhaps? A prying at my past?

Or a prying at my friend's past? I decided that was the case. "Sir," I said to the king, trying not to bellow, "do not fear that Arlin my friend is the traitor who has served you so badly. He had good reason to flee the camp when he did, and none of it is disloyalty. Indeed, I know of his remarkable faithfulness in certain matters... and of his ability to keep his own council, unfortunately. I only fear he will die on the downs somewhere, with no company save that council."

"I can have him tracked," wrote the king, and I rejected that idea—rudely, I fear.

"Not in this hard country, and with him on that horse. I doubt I can track him myself."

The king took my shoulders in his hands and so very clearly spoke that I could read his lips. "Why has he fled? What can this man you describe have to fear in my company?" he demanded of me.

How could I tell the king, bright and magnetic as he was, and willing to forgive my own lawless eccentricity, what I had discovered that very morning, when the lean swordsman hauled me behind him onto his horse—that Arlin had to fear kindness most terribly: kindness, touch, and hence the discovery that he was no sort of man at all, but a woman living all her life in masquerade?

What a game she had played with me, starting on the road above Sordaling almost one year earlier. Arlin or Charlan, daughter of Howdl, certainly my old friend, as she had claimed. It was I who had taught her rapierwork, and to spin a dull knife between her fingers: Zhurrie of twelve years old and a girl no older. She had known me from first glance and

I had failed with her, altogether, though in retrospect I per ceived that she had not changed so much.

I perceived, I am saying to you, but despite three years of training to do little else but perceive clearly, I had not per ceived at all, and the woman had disarmed me at every step, using truth misunderstood as her weapon.

I used that very weapon now to fend off the king. "Arlin . . . ," I said, and though I was deaf I tried to whisper for his ear only. "About Arlin there is an element of physical manhood . . . missing. For many years. I think he would risk death rather than allow himself to be disrobed by strangers."

The king blinked and came out with a sound half guffaw and half snort, quickly smothered. "Well. Physical, is it?" he mouthed elaborately. "That would explain certain oddities. Your explanation pleases me better than my own first sup positions. We must find him, certainly, but we can be discreet about it."

"I will find him," I told the king, and was irritated at the manner in which he shook his head to deny me.

"You will not," his lips said. "You cannot stand without help."

I had not noticed that the king was bracing me by one arm. This was even more irritating, and I shook my head at him as he had at me. In another moment I was vomiting bile all over the king's boots, and then I blacked out for the second time.

When I woke next, in firm possession of my own head, more than a day had passed and the king's force was heading smartly north toward Velonya proper, all its eyes and ears out for signs of repeated assault.

Sixteen men had been buried, among them the engineer I had tried so uselessly to help and who in his death agony had set the fuse of the king's petard. Arlin/Charlan had not been found, and in my desperation I considered revealing her secret to the king, to make it easier to find her. I did not, because I was not sure it would help and because it would be too large a betrayal. Larger, perhaps, than her life was worth.

This time there was no mistake in guarding the captives. We had been left with eight who were sound enough to talk, and with the assistance of a spoonful of tincture of opium I was able to witness the interrogation.

It was not what I would call torture, though it was forcible, and since hanging was the natural end of any attempt upon the king's life in his own country (or what he claimed as his own), baits of clemency seemed of more value than threats.

Seemed of more value, but in the end all was fruitless, for the nomads resisted blows and offers alike with the indifference of wooden posts. Only their eyes moved, straying from the face of the king to those of his marshals to my own. Upon me they glared with a heavier resentment, seeing, I suppose, their own blood in the lines of my face. But why should that have been cause for hate, when these nomads kill other tribes of Red Whips with as much eagerness as they spend upon the Velonyans? More likely it was my own knowledge of my mixed blood that made me sensitive.

They told nothing. All but one were hanged the next morning, and that least lucky of men was shackled about the neck and ankles, to be brought along for more leisurely questioning. Before that death dawn, however, I had borrowed a horse and ridden back the way we had come, looking for Arlin.

I woke on a plodding horse in a field of stones and purple crocuses, where water ran like strands of hair—bright hair. There were a few oaks and bushes of hazel and alder, deer-thinned. I had been following tracks, light scratches of hooves, impossible to identify, and I must have fallen asleep riding.

I could not expect the horse to have continued my job for me, but I slid down anyway and looked over the glorious carpet of bloom for some sign of a horse's passage. There was nothing.

I was shaking with cold though the sun was shining. Bright

air, bright water, and the purple of the flower cups, each holding blood-red threads within. The place and time had that calm sweetness that accompanies funerals and makes them harder for me to bear. I squatted on a stone with needles of pain driving in through my ears, gagging on a dry stomach, and it seemed to me the beauty was telling me that Arlin was already dead.

In my shirt pocket was the tincture of poppy, and I drank from it, taking in my clumsiness more than I had been advised to swallow. I put my hands over my ears and my nose between my knees and made a ball of myself, while the borrowed horse wandered over the flowers, looking for something better than crocuses to eat.

I awoke when a man picked me up and put me over his shoulder. There was little I could do to resent the liberty. Neither did I feel much resentment, for his hands were kindly though large, and he thumped me between the shoulders as though I ought to be burped. He was a large fellow, long-faced, yellow-haired, well-tailored, and no more belonging on that empty prominence on the borders of the southern territories than might a flock of peacocks. Out of the corner of my eye I could see a gown of blue silk with white embroidery, which floated with the wearer's movement, or perhaps it was only a lace of high clouds in the sky that I saw, moving with the spring winds.

He carried me with no sign of effort, and even in my sickness and stupor I thought that here I had come upon a real Old Velonyan, wide as a house and strong as an ox. I saw the stones and the flowers pass under his feet, and then there was the door of a very fine house under the oak trees, where I had previously seen only air, and as the gentleman took me over the threshold (kicking the door open with his foot, I recall), my head lolled and I could see that there actually was a gown of blue silk, and above it rose the face of a young woman—tiny, dark, and very beautiful. There was something more to be noted about her, but as we passed into the house I found that my poor stock of attention was used up.

Again I came to, propped on a grand bed of heavy wood intricately carved, but it was not silk-dressed like such a bed called out to be. Instead it was clad in good white linen, like my bed back at the observatory, or like the beds at Sordaling School. Beside me sat these two unlikely protectors of mine, seated together as calm as a portrait, but less formally. Like couples long married, though neither seemed old. The room, like the bed, was of carved wood, green or brown or golden I cannot remember.

For such an exalted chamber the furniture was very curious; the chairs were solid oak, with their backs in the shape of a heart and a small heart cut into the top of each, and pillows of red broadcloth were tied to the seats, cottage-style. The windows were large rectangles such as are found neither in grand houses nor cottages but in institutions without pretentions to luxury, such as schools, and on the far wall hung—I swear it—the sort of wooden clock that holds a bird.

Here I woke with an idea that I had been fed by the hands of this kind couple, though how that might have been accomplished while I had fainted I don't know. It occurred to me that I ought to explain to them about the injury to my ears, so that they did not think they were befriending a half-wit, and I turned to where the lady sat beside me, to signal somehow or to ask for paper, and seeing her clearly, I stopped and gaped—a half-wit indeed. She was surpassingly beautiful, with a tiny, heart-shaped face, black hair, eyes of the earthy green of the quiet lakes of Ekesh, and despite the eyes she was without doubt Rezhmian.

Behind her the tall blond man met my gaze and said nothing. He put his hands over her shoulders, and his eyes, ordinary blue, met mine. He smiled at me, and though his face was young, I had only seen such a smile on the faces of very old people. She did not smile, but she put out her hands, tiny like bird wings, and touched my face with them, stroking my hair back over my ears. I saw that her fingers came away tinted with blood, and I looked down at their clean sheets with concern. It came to me that I ought to go die someplace else, so as not to bother them. It seemed to me that I had had this thought once before in another context, but I could not recall it exactly. I propped myself up, which deed was no longer difficult, for the dizziness was gone, but when I raised my head again the blond gentleman was standing over me and extending (of all unlikely things) a very young baby.

Except at weddings, a beggar like myself is not asked for blessings, but I found myself taking the child, who kicked in its white wrapping, and saying the traditional words "Grace to you from the Trinity: God the Father, God the Mother, and the God Who Is in Us All." At least I thought I said them; without hearing, it is difficult to know. With tincture of poppy it is difficult to remember.

I let the little one down onto my chest. It had no hair, and its eyes were cloudy baby eyes. It stared at me seriously for a few moments, then wiggled and extended one arm toward my face in the commanding way that babies have, and I felt a great warmth spreading through me.

I thought the little creature had pissed on me; it would not have been the first time such a thing had happened since I had left Powl and become a jack-of-every-trade. This inconvenience was so minor compared to everything else in my day that I laughed aloud while I waited for that quick warmth to turn to chilly wetness. Instead it spread throughout my body and mind, like sudden delight or like the release within lovemaking. When my eyes could see again, the baby had vanished, though my silly arms were still in position, holding nothing but the bright, still air.

Somehow I had lost this fine couple's child, though I had no idea how, and in bewildered remorse I turned to them, but they were missing, too, and as I peered around the room I was no longer even sure of the identity of the cottage chairs. Nor could I say whether the bird I heard calling was from the carved clock on the wall, or a simple feathered cuckoo on a branch of the oak overhead.

At that moment I became convinced I had fallen into events of great meaning and moment, at least to myself, events not yet categorized by Powl's observational methods. I did not know what they were, exactly, but if I somehow had the ear of powers greater than King Rudof's, I did not want to miss my chance. I stood up in the crocuses where there had just now been a tall-post bed, and I called out to the event even as it passed: "Arlin! You must save Arlin, who is actually Lady Charlan, daughter of Howdl of Sordaling City!"

As though the Triune God would not know who people were without my prompting. I heard my words, in my own unexceptional voice, ring over the hills of stone.

As the glitter in the air softened itself into sunlight, I added: "If it pleases Your Graces."

Of the damage to my ears there was no trace, and the pain and dizziness were vague memories. My borrowed horse was rolling over the crocuses, trying to get rid of the saddle. Both horse and gear had been stained gold with saffron. The hillside was wild and empty.

I found the vial of tincture, and it seemed I had downed almost all of it at one gulp. I certainly had no need of it now. By the position of the sun, I had either been amid the flowers for an entire day and night, or for a short time indeed. I don't think the horse would have stayed for a day and a night; he was trying to wander off even as I mounted him again.

I do not describe this incident to you with the intent to convince you that I participated in a miracle, sir. There was material in that vial of mine for a great deal of embellishment upon reality. There is material in my head for even more. But as I perceived it, I have recounted.

And later that day, while trying to recover the lost tracks, I discovered a large yellow stain over the front of my woolen shirt and not at all the color of saffron.

I claim, sir, to deal in clear perception, and using weapons of reason and intuition upon it, to arrive at some understanding of what is true. This is an outrageous claim on my part—an arrogant, offensive claim—and perhaps someday I shall have to pay for my arrogance.

For the time comes again and again when I cannot make a reasonable assumption out of the perceptions granted me. I could put the events of the day together under the heading "Opium Dreams." But then what of the yellow stain? Did something else happen in my delirium that my muddled mind translated into a baby who pissed on me and disappeared? Did perhaps a real family, without faces representing the Velonyan and Rezhmian boundries of my existence and not living in a home made up of bits of places that had been important to me, pick me up and nurse me, and my grandiflorent brain make up the rest? If so, why was I not sick unto death, as I had been, but as well as if I had not been blown up?

If enough time had passed to heal my broken eardrums and the infection they had brought on, then how could I have forgotten the weeks it must have taken to finish the cure, and remembered the first fevered dream alone?

If my brain were that unreliable a tool to me, then how could I hope to sort out my own memories with it? I was lost before I started. I would not know how long I had been gone unless I returned to the king's procession and asked someone.

As with all events of great moment, I had to pull my interpretation from a dark closet behind my eyes. I chose to believe I had had a kindly visit from God in all three faces at once. I decided that there was significance for me personally in the manner in which the blond man had laid his hands over the shoulders of the dark woman, and that the urine stain on the shirt I wore had great meaning for my future.

I also resolved to wash the shirt.

For three days I rode through the sparsely settled countryside, seeking one set of tracks where it seemed half the horses in the known world had trotted by. Arlin's gray mare had particularly small hooves, only differing from those of the local ponies by being less round and regular and by having a longer stride. I did not find these prints, nor anything that looked much like them. Each evening I returned to one establishment, that of a poulterer who raised rabbits for their skins and flesh, and I chopped next year's wood in exchange for oats so I might abuse my poor cavalry horse further. I think I did not eat during those three days, and if I remember correctly I was not at all hungry.

On the evening of the third day I began to believe that I had chosen the wrong style of hunt: that Arlin had returned to the king's procession as soon as he felt himself (or she felt herself) out of danger from loss of blood. In that case it was I who was missing, and it was possible Arlin would start out again after me and make of this entire emergency a great tangle.

I let the horse rest that night, fed him all the oats I had earned, and pointed him north. Such was the difference between the progress of three hundred men and wagons and the progress of one man mounted that I had found the king's men by midafternoon.

My friend had not been found; neither had he returned on his own. I remember that as the field marshal gave me that news—gravely enough and without his usual rancor—I had a distinct presentiment of death. Arlin's, my own, I could not discern, and indeed it seemed to me there would be little difference between the two.

I don't know what there was about knowing that *he* was actually *she* that turned a year's bickering and uneasy cama-raderie into something as deep as the roots of my life. It was not that I was amorous; in the past year I had had brief, enjoyable affairs with three women, all of whom were older than I, all of whom were warm and good company. Arlin I did not imagine approaching sexually, even in daydreams, for she was still too much of *he* in my perception, and besides, he/she had said she was very picky about the men she appre-ciated. I might wind up spitted on a dagger.

And yet he called me his "ideal of the true knight and gentleman." Had he not been serious in those words, the thing would have been a joke. Had he not been a cheating gambler who said it, it would have been mere triteness. Had she not been a person of such solitary purity and courage as to stand alone and unaided against this bloody world for years, I could not have valued the words. As it was, and with her deathly injured, the accolade meant more than my life to me.

Forgive me, sir, my erratic pronouns. Their gender is out of my control.

We had come back to the northern downs, where the hills were sweeter and dotted with trees. Here, almost fifty miles from the border, we would be troubled by no more bands of Rezhmian raiders, and among the slow, grinding wagons the humility of having lost comrades and the gratitude for having survived danger had given way to the boisterous arrogance of having won a battle. I heard the story of the assault and of the king's glorious petard repeated half a dozen times in the public room of the inn—the same inn where I had stopped on my way south, but now glorified by an air bright with narcissus and thyme.

The landlady remembered me and all our talk of blond slaves and southern cities. Since I had no enthusiasm for talk

213

of battle (nor any talk), I sat myself first before the bar and then behind it, helping draw the tap. I also found myself— out of habit, perhaps—evicting those of the royal company who showed excessive energy in their amusements.

The woman had no husband and was kind enough to offer me a great deal of hospitality, most of which I declined as politely as I knew how. I was very disheartened and at a loss for what to do next. I neither saw the king nor asked for audience with him, but the next morning he sent for me.

King Rudof, as a change from his grand and rickety pavilion, had set himself up at the better inn of the town. It was amusing to see the innkeeper himself, parked with his family at the saddler's across the way, staring out goggle-eyed at the glory that had descended on his property. He did not appear to feel abused, however, and his children danced delightedly backward in circles with knees locked together (a local specialty) for the edification of the officers.

Of course, the king had the family's own small suite of rooms, but the paternal bed had been stood on end against one wall and the king's own bed hauled up the stairs and put in its stead. As I came to him, the king was sitting alone in the room with windows yawning wide, making tentative shots from a nomad's lacquered bow into the innkeeper's mattress. Again the king's easy charm struck me, heavy as a blow.

"Nazhuret," he said, "I have to admit these toys are an improvement over our own weapons. Why do you suppose they have never caught on in Velonya? Oh, and do pull those quarrels from the ticking for me as you come by."

I returned the little arrows to him. "They are laminated with fish glues, sir. It could be that the cold and wet of our climate are too much for them."

The king looked straight at me without words for some time. His red hair fell into his face, and one eyebrow rose slowly, like the sun. "You have a speaking countenance, Nazhuret. Odd in a man of your attainments: almost childlike.

It is obvious you have not found your friend and that you are distraught about it."

"It is true I have not found . . . him, sir. I had hoped he would be with you by now."

The king took the time to shoot another quarrel. "By now? You left us in the morning three days ago. If the fellow denned up somewhere to heal . . ."

I listened, feeling very stupid. I had counted three days since the morning after my ambiguous miracle, which would make the time of my absence a minimum of four days.

As though reading my thoughts, the king continued, "But you yourself have done a stalwart job of recovery, lad. Truth to tell, I had more fears of your survival, with your broken ears and staggers, than I had of your card-playing friend. I had thought to stop you for your own good, except that I didn't want to lose that many men while still in peril of the Red Whips."

The breeze through the windows was seductive, the air sweetly bright, and this conversation made no sense. I put my face in my hands and screwed my thoughts together. "Sir, I count at least four days since I left your camp. On the first of these I met with kind people who took me in and cured me. I was not sure but that I had spent added days there asleep. Now you tell me what my reason cannot follow. . . ."

He slouched to his feet, gracelessly graceful in the manner of very tall men, and leaned over to a table under the broad window. He threw a bound book at me. "Here's our calendar. Let your reason ponder that, and while you're at it, Nazhuret, note that we are nine days behind on this patrol."

Patrol. The thought of this multicolored, creaking royal progress as a military patrol took me aback, but I tried not to let my speaking countenance speak. I turned my attention to the calendar, and after a minute of confusion I put it down. "I see. I see but I don't understand. I will not delay you longer, sir," I said, and turned to go.

He called me back again. With the light behind him, the king looked more saturnine than boyish. His profile was sharp. "Nazhuret, we owe you much, and it annoys me that you will take no payment. Also, I want you in my service as I have rarely wanted any man, and you will not or cannot give me what I want. Therefore I am doubly annoyed. Nevertheless, I give you this freely: my promise that I will hold you free to come and go through my court and my kingdom, as far as I can stretch the law to allow. You may speak to me any time that you have need or feel that the nation does; my chamberlain will not bar or question you. This while you live."

He said this much without looking at me. I was dumb— astonished. I had never heard of such a privilege—honor fit to be sought earnestly by sages and wizards—and offered to a creature of no greater moment than myself. I found my hand was in my mouth, which gaped in the most foolish way. "My king," I said, "I thank you. I will try not to abuse such an honor."

I would try to run away and never see King Rudof again; that was the way I would not abuse this privilege, which was too dangerous and deep for me. I tried to bow my way out, but again he prevented me.

"Not yet," said King Rudof, and now he turned full to me. "I want the right to advise you in turn, Nazhuret. About this Arlin fellow, with all his perils and his lacks. I understand your concern. I do not ask you to give up your search. But . . ."

The word trailed off, and King Rudof rolled his weight from one boot heel to the other thoughtfully. "But don't show to the world this desperation I see in your face. Not among these men of the court, of the army. This friend of yours may be as . . . different as you say, and your concern as pure as a nunnery under snowfall, but men will not see it as such. Do not be obvious."

"Obvious about what, sir?" I asked, for at that moment I was convinced the king knew Arlin's secret.

He gave a tight smile. "That you love him. That you have a long loyalty together."

I changed my mind. The king was not omniscient, but instead jealous. Of me. This was more terrifying to know than words can tell. I had difficulty following all King Rudof said after that: to the effect that Arlin was neither popular among the men nor trusted by the officers. That I was not to be smudged by the same soot as he. That I was not to grieve for him in public.

I could feel my ears burning like the side lamps of a coach. I came very close to revealing Arlin's great secret in disappointment that the king should think ill of Arlin. Think ill of him for the wrong reasons, that is. Dirt and dishonesty were enough of a social handicap.

I had a strong notion that once the king knew Arlin was a woman escaped from a monstrous father, both his ire and his jealousy would disappear. But though it was my notion it was not my secret, so I bowed out and let him think what he would.

One more day had passed with equally tender weather, and I knew I had to leave the royal hospitality before the good and regular meals seduced me (or before the king decided to keep me on a chain), when King Rudof sent for me once again. The messenger had difficulty finding me, as I was sitting on new grass outside the town proper, stripped to my trousers alone and staring at the trunk of a beech tree. Sitting in the belly of the wolf, in fact. I had chosen to retreat there because in that state I felt myself outside the rush of time, and time was telling me that I had failed and that Arlin was dead.

I did not appreciate the disturbance, but speaking face or no, I was not such a fool as to show my resentment to the King of Velonya.

Rudof had made a quaint sort of court in the public room of his inn, with no more accouterment than a one-yard-square gilded seal of his authority and a ladder-back chair with arms. In this setting, separated from his military accompaniment, he was dispensing high and low justice to the few territorials who dared approach him.

I found myself amid what had to be a civil case, by the way in which two well-dressed burghers were glaring at one another and by the relaxed interest shown by all but the two involved parties. The king himself had a glint of amusement in his green eyes, like that of a man having to solve a question of precedence between two sleeve dogs. But though he smiled, and though he let rise one eyebrow, still he was being the king, not to be mistaken for any other young man who had an interest in foreign travel and who shot little arrows into the bottom of his landlord's mattress.

I was led through the assembled crowd and past the open space that the king's authority had created around him. He gave me the sort of look one student gives another when in the presence of outsiders. "We have a boundary dispute, Nazhuret. It seems we have had it for three generations."

I had glanced at the two disputants already: One was tall, bald, and dressed in gray woolens, and the other was shorter, heavier, and dressed with a nod toward fashion. Neither bore any stamp of Rezhmian blood. "You desire assist with translation, my king?" I asked him, making a leg as formally as I knew how.

He grinned at me. "A week with our party and already you cease talking like a normal man. No, Nazhuret, it is not translation nor even the eviction of rowdy drunks I demand of you, and certainly not the stilted speech of a chamberlain's assistant."

I wondered how on earth the king had learned I was a tavern bouncer. Was I watched, and if so, how had I not noticed, for I notice most things? Had there been complaints from the men?

Before I had had time to reply, the king startled me further by adding: "It is pure wisdom I want in this case, lad. Wisdom free from the constraints of legal precedent or political advantage. That is why I chose you."

There was a murmur in my ears, likely of astonished voices. Or perhaps it was a growl of outrage from the king's attendants. Or perhaps it was the blood beating in my ears. I shook my head.

"I'm not fit for such matters, sir. I have never—"

"The case is this," said King Rudof, rising from his chair. He spoke well, as for a large audience. He sounded pleased with himself. "These gentlemen own orchards, having inherited them in tail-male through many generations. Until their grandfathers' time, the boundry between their plantations was a small river, called the Newtabank, which also irrigated both properties. This body of water meandered as rivers will, and each year the loops of its meander cut farther and farther away from the straight. As rivers will." The king glanced at me one of his deadly charming glances. He was deep in his judicial role and conscious of his own immersion. He wanted me to know he was conscious of it. His attendants chuckled appreciatively, as though the glance had been for them.

The king ran one elegant hand through his orange hair. "Though this process complicated the boundary, it was agreed that the Newtabank meandered east as much as it did west, and so there was equality in its alteration."

The peasant with the tailoring mumbled, "It is north and south it meanders, Your Majesty," but everyone affected not to hear him.

"Five years ago, the river, for reasons unknown, changed its course altogether and flows entirely on what was Master Grisewode's property."

Master Grisewode, who was the man in gray, looked modestly at the floorboards.

For that reason, a few years ago another . . . judiciary . . . decided that the boundary ought to be set due east from a

particular spot in the river where it is about to change course."
The king folded himself into his ladder-back seat of judgment
once again, glanced at each of us in the court, and continued,
"Do you approve of that resolution, Nazhuret?"

I shrugged and answered that the decision sounded like
an arbitrary compromise, as worthy as any of its breed.

"Exactly, my lad. And again like the usual way with its
breed, it has led to greater strife than the original condition.
For both of these men have paced the distance—which is
something like three-quarters of a mile—holding the village's
one needle compass in hand, and yet when Master Nazeken
essays this, he finds a copse of twenty prime apple trees and
a dozen chestnuts to be entirely on his side of the boundary,
while when Master Grisewode does the same, this valuable
vegetation is found to be inarguably his."

"Have you tried a boundary walker allied with neither
party, sir?"

The king looked at me over his tented fingers, seemingly
bored beyond boredom. I doubted the authenticity of his
expression. "We did, Nazhuret. This morning. He went twice.
Three times, really, if we count the time he got lost.

"And once he replicated Grisewode and once he nearly
replicated Nazeken. So what do we do, my prodigy?"

I felt both peasants staring at my back in wonder as well
as the cold, concealed hostility of a good dozen courtiers. I
wished fervently that the king would remember that though
I was only the height of a standard ground-floor window, still
I had as many years under my belt as he did.

"If the king would deign to walk the course himself," I
said, "then no one would doubt the accuracy of his footprints."

Rudof chuckled and leaned back in his chair. "In other
words, be as arbitrary as the river. No, Nazhuret. I called you
in seeking a solution out of human reason, one we might
extend to other uses in other times. To create a precedent,
in fact."

I felt sweat prickling the back of my neck and I saw the hostility of the courtiers harden into contempt behind their eyes. I closed my own eyes to examine the problem better.

"I understand, sir. First I must go to my pack, and then I must be shown the place in question."

King Rudof opened his leaf-colored eyes wide and for a moment was without act or role. "Bring the man's pack here," he said to no one in particular, and there was a small but intense storm among the onlooking officials to see first, who was low enough in status to accomplish the task, and second, who knew where my pack might be.

The king reclaimed his composure and cleaned one fingernail with another. "Actually, Nazhuret, any solution that may be extended to a generality must be discovered without . . . without recourse to this one, meaningless apple orchard."

"I disagree," I said, more shortly than I should have spoken to the king, but I was already pondering the tolerances of fine glass etching and wondering whether fish glues would attach metal to leather. "Get me a few long, dark hairs," I commanded, probably as haughtily as the king himself. "Straight and not too heavy. Human better than horse."

I had no lenses preground for distance except those of my own collapsible telescope, so I had to sacrifice it. I am sure the loss was good for my soul. I worried whether the lens miter I carried was accurate enough, but it had been good enough to correct vision, so I proceeded, cutting a grove and then another perpendicular to it, into which I inserted the hairs. The fish glue went around the outside of the lens, and then my telescope was remade with a compass mounted on an enclosed shelf below the tube, and a half-silvered mirror superimposing the image of the needle upon the view seen through the lens.

As an effort of workmanship I have to call it a god-awful

piece of shit. I make no apologies for the language, sir. I have never made a worse scientific instrument. Nor have I ever made an instrument with such an audience around me.

When I considered myself done I was respectfully led to the place from which the border was legally defined. To my astonishment it was a large, pointy granite rock in the middle of a river rushing with all winter's thaw. I gaped at Grisewode and then at Nazeken. "Why did you decide on that inaccessible place to define your boundary?" I asked them. "That was stupidity!"

Grisewode winced. "We did not, my lord. It was the lord circuit justice himself who decided the rock was of central importance."

I looked from the man in gray woolens to Nazeken, who nodded with no more irony in his expression than his opponent had shown. Behind us, King Rudof laughed. I paced the bank up and down, figuring how much upstream lead I must give myself swimming in order to arrive at the stone when I reached the center. I guessed I had about a half-and-half chance of surviving the effort.

King Rudof stepped forward. "Build a bridge," he said, not too loudly. Two long hours later, a sturdy wooden footbridge crossed the gap, and I strode over it with my freakish telescope, the cynosure of all local eyes.

The same light that brought in the distant line of trees threw another image over it through the half-silvered prism: that of compass face and the needle that floated on it. Both pictures were dim, but it was possible to align the black hair that cut vertically up the lens with the needle and the scoring on the compass face that indicated east. Once I had found the particular piece of the skyline that met these qualifications, I began to bring the thing down to human level.

Here the images were more difficult, but at last, by holding my breath, I was able to line up needle, hair, and scoring over the image of a broken tree beside a path, which was as far as viewing went from this point, looking directly east.

"I need a man with a hammer and some stakes!" I called out, with no clear idea of to whom I issued this command. As it happened, it was the king, and soon he had job assigned; my opposite on the bank of the river moved to the spot where I pointed him, and when I saw his stake at the juncture of my compass and lens, I bid him drive it. The fellow moved away as I raised my lens, reestablishing my lines and wishing devoutly for a tripod. Every so often I bellowed and he hammered, and I drove him left or right constantly for adjustment. After a few hundred feet it became necessary to institute a system of couriers to relay my corrections and refill his arms with stakes. Twice he disappeared down the bed the river had abandoned and twice he appeared again farther out and drove in a stake at the bankline. After a good hour of labor I had seen him wield his hammer a good hundred times, and each time my needle and hairline and scoring superimposed his stake, and the last one was driven in at the foot of the broken tree.

I put down the telescope, certain that my eyes would remain one bulged and one screwed tight until the end of my life. "If there is farther to go, we shall have to start again at the other side of the tree, for that's the end of visibility in this direction."

The king was standing at my end of the bridge, his arms akimbo, gazing up at me on my rock like the latest in novelties. "We are splendidly amused, lad! Now you must tell me how you did it."

I slid down the side of the rock and handed him the telescope. "Just look, sir. It will explain itself."

The king scuffled up to the rock's rounded top, almost losing the instrument in the process. Long legs were not made for scrambling. I watched him adjust the thing as I had done and replicate the face I had been making all these minutes. Finally he said, "Be kind to me, Nazhuret. I see only chaos here."

"First play with the focal length until you see at least some of the distant scenery, sir, and then you will notice the needle of the compass superimposed upon—"

"I see, I see," he cut me off, and in another moment he began to issue the hoots of a small boy in small boy's delight. "Rare! Marvelous! Tell me, Nazhuret: Just how accurate is this device?"

I answered that I had no idea. That perhaps it was of no use at all. That I had just now made it up, in answer to the problem at hand. I was chivvied and thumped and bullied by the king in his great good humor and practically carried under one arm as he strode out to march the course of stakes and measure them against Grisewode's line and Nazeken's. Mine cut smartly between them.

"This is good evidence of a kind—of the human kind," said King Rudof, bending down to eye the straightness of our new boundary. "And my own decision certainly would have been a compromise between the two advantageous measurements. Just so. I declare your decision true and valid and the matter settled."

Grisewode looked stunned and Nazeken was blinking, but neither of them seemed about to dispute with the king. I felt obliged to lend the spyglass to each man in turn and explain it to him, urging him to look back along the stakes to the rock and noting that the compass showed due west. Each nodded and thanked me and handed it back, and I am sure neither saw a thing nor cared to.

(Though I have used this method since more than once, sir, I still regard it as more of a convenience than an increase in accuracy of measurement, for I cannot be sure of the inaccuracies in the positioning of the compass attachment, nor the stresses along the length of the tube.)

Our little experiment must have used up all the time King Rudof had promised to the village's judicial system, but he was very taken with it. He walked alone with me and played with the telescope all the way back to town.

I had the distinct feeling I was out on a class break with one of my more lighthearted school fellows as the King of Velonya larked about me, telling me that a hawk was coming toward us south-southeast and that our own steps were largely westerly, though very winding. This feeling of camaraderie with the king, though sweet and inescapable, frightened me to the core. I japed and grinned and wished I were anywhere else on earth.

Perhaps he knew it—after all, he claimed to read me so well—for as we came up out of the orchard to where the village lay in sunlight, his tone grew more restrained and he laid his hand on my shoulder. "First, Nazhuret, I thought you an elegant brawler, with the usual small man's pugnacity. I was wrong: You are not pugnacious. I am not even sure you are small. Next, you showed yourself as a monk, and then as a tracker, a translator, a petardist, and finally an inventor. Just what are you?"

The question was affectionately spoken, and I have only reason to be grateful he left out the term bugger-boy, for it seems I showed that as well. The best answer to any such monster of a question is silence, but silence must have offended the king, so I said the first true thing that came into my head.

"I am the lens of the world, sir," I said.

King Rudof had been about to leap off a six-inch prominence of stone when I spoke, and though he finished his leap, he almost came down in a pile of limbs. His comely face, orange-rimmed, stared as though I had just cursed him, or exploded, or turned into stone. He raised a finger and pointed at me. "You . . ."

I was now so terrified that it was only the presence of the rest of our party, coming down the path discreetly behind us, that prevented me from fleeing the king and his damning finger. What could have shocked him so? The sentiment I had expressed was original, but not of the sort to lead to violence.

"Not only I, of course, sir. We are each of us the lens by which the world is able—"

The finger shook and cut off my words. "No. Stop. Let me think."

He thought very fiercely, his anger flaring through his fair face like the colors of certain fish I have seen. Out of the corner of my eye I could see the procession of our followers draw near and then back away again. "The pattern is almost complete. But I should have known the moment you first spoke, man, when your first words were to command me to cease being a fool."

I certainly did remember that but had strongly hoped the king had forgotten.

"And then you told me you would not serve, and afterward taught me my own business in a hundred little ways, and most of all, you made me eat out of your hand while doing it.

"You lied to me, Nazhuret of Sordaling, when you told me you had no master. You wear his brand across your brow for the world to read. Tell me now his name: the man who taught you, who created what you are out of a half-breed peasant boy and called you lens of the world."

Abruptly the terror consumed itself and left me. "His name is Powl, sir."

King Rudof winced, but not as though surprised. A thin, bitter grin spread across his face. "You do not try to hide it, then."

I answered him, "There is nothing worth hiding," which, taken as a general statement, does not represent Powl's teaching at all. "I studied with him for three years, alone on a hill: optics, language, natural science and philosophy, combat... even dance. What offense is there in that, sir?"

The king did not answer, and the morning air was traced with birds' song. At last he said, no louder than a whisper, "I would die to be you."

So strong was my confidence in my teacher's teaching that I felt no disproportion in his words but only a strong compassion for the man, the king.

I tried to smile. "Sir, you would not want to spend three years in a box of brick, sweeping out a faulty oven, with no company save for a high-handed teacher a few hours each day, until you begin to jabber to yourself like a monkey in a cage. . . ."

One glance reminded me that the king was a brilliant man, and no condescension escaped him. He had composed his features when he replied, "Whether I would or not is of no moment, fellow, for the Earl of Daraln, Viscount Korres— your 'Powl'—has refused three times the command to teach me what he knows."

The Earl of Daraln, Viscount Korres.

"My teacher only called himself Powl. It's a common enough name, sir. He dressed as a well-off burgher." Though I had to say this, I really did not doubt a syllable of the titles.

Irony elongated the king's face. "And did he act like a well-off burgher?"

Now the smile came unforced, involuntarily. "Sir, he acted like no one else on earth."

For a quick moment the king's mood matched mine, and then black anger replaced it. "So do you, Nazhuret." He turned his face toward the village again and spoke over his shoulder these words: "I will have him killed. For treason."

"I repeat," Powl had said, "you must stay out of the reach of officialdom, for with what you now know it will be deadly to you."

Powl: in his burgher-dandy clothes. My arrogant, egalitarian, graceful, and complacent scientist and seer. My personal magician and fighting instructor. How I wished he had burned out my tongue before letting me loose upon the world, as the military might of Velonya continued north. Having as its goal, his death.

It is dead of winter and no usual winter, either. Every window in this low oratory opens out into blank white and cold blue light. It is not the wind that has driven ice against the windows, sir; it is simply that the snow is that deep. Yesterday I went out for wood, wearing cumbersome rawhide snowshoes to ride the powder, and I find only the peak of the place visible, like the prow of a foundering ship. Deer are dying in their sleep and frozen upright; I locate them by ears or antlers, or by sad dimples in the snow.

When you will get this chapter of my history I do not know, sir. Are you frozen in your palaces in Vestinglon—a bright court, unsullied, unspoiled, unmoving? In this deep pocket of the year it is difficult to say truly that any of us is alive.

I reside in a blue, cold purgatory: number seven of twelve, if I remember my catechism. I have no distractions now to continuing a horrid tale, except that of numb fingers. I know I shall not escape this winter, or this story except by coming out on the other side.

My king, I hear laughter over my head in the air. Wonder of wonders. The sound is bright as icicles, warm as horses, and it comes from above the slate roof itself. It must be some children or other, playing with the snowshoes as I did myself. I hope none falls off the webs.

The king's progress, which had seemed so slow when it was fascinating to me, picked up a malicious speed now that it had become deadly. The roads in the North of the territory and in Satt above it were much more traveled and better kept,

and in Apek, the town lying suburban to Warvala, they exchanged their cumbersome wagons and pavilions for coaches,
while the sturdy horses suitable for border use were retired in
favor of the mounts with fine paces, which they had left behind
weeks ago on the way south.

As they rode, I ran behind them, for I could neither leave
the progress and its terrible intent nor accept hospitality from
the king. My boots gave out under this treatment, and then
I ran barefoot. For food, when I had stomach to eat it, I snared
rabbits or begged from the householders on the way.

The first day they rode enthusiastically on their fresh
horses, but on the second I caught up. The king was riding
an elegant chestnut, exactly the color of his own hair, and
was surrounded by a mixed party of nobles and favored soldiers.

The shoulder of the road was grassy and wide, and I managed to keep pace, though no attempt at communication was
possible. Three times horsemen in the blue of Velonya or the
black and yellow of Leoue rode out of the line to slap me off,
one with a whip and two with the flat of a sword, but like a
dog running cattle I did the least necessary to avoid the strike
and I came on. It was at the third attempt against me that
the king noticed my presence, and I heard him call the man
away.

I locked for a moment with the king's eyes, and there I
met honest rage, and in the face of Leoue—his bullmastiff—
was written strong disgust. Certainly I was enough to inspire
disgust: dirty, with bandy legs pumping, my ancient woolens
bagged out in sweat. My hair was in my eyes and my pack
was abandoned on the road behind, with blanket, lenses,
tools, all. Only my dowhee remained, slung behind me in my
belt. What use it would be to me against the king's army I
had no idea.

The nights grew cooler so slowly my sweat dried before it
had a chance to chill me. When I was not chasing the king
I spent my time either asleep (when I could) or in the belly

of the wolf. If I tried any other pastime my dreads drove me to phlegm, tears, or fury.

It seemed to me that I had possessed in my life one friend and one teacher. The friend I had left to crawl off to die while I engaged in unnecessary heroics. My teacher I had bragged into a sentence of death. Myself I was not allowed to kill, by commandment of the Triune Monism, and the king, my enemy, would not help me even to die.

This very emotional attitude settled in a few days into a black stolidity, while I ran and watched and concentrated on nothing.

Three days after the king's last angry words to me, I caught up to him as he sat out in the midday sun, at a crude hostelry table holding tea in a porcelain cup. He was surrounded by soldiers, but none of them was of any great rank nor known to me personally. I don't remember if any rose to prevent me access to the king, but I know I soon was seated before him in all my stinking dirt, and I well remember that the differences in our heights made it appear that I was on my knees before him.

"Don't bother, Nazhuret," he began, looking beside, above, and beyond me. "You can only embarrass us both."

I was astonished that he could speak of embarrassment when the subject should have been life and death. "I am beyond embarrassment, my king," I said.

"And you are too late courtly, with your 'my kings.'" Rudof's face sparkled with anger and his long hands pulled slivers of wood out of the table as I watched. "Nazhuret, you only make yourself a figure of fun with this behavior."

The chair beneath me was seductive. I pulled myself out of a slouch. "I have seen no one laughing, sir, but I will apologize for my courtesy if you desire and call you 'my king' no more."

"I never was your king, as you made as clear as glass from the beginning."

I steeled myself not to meet his anger with some of my own. I knew a dozen ears were listening as well. "Then punish me, sir, and not my innocent teacher."

The green eyes elongated and the face went from hot to cold. I thought perhaps he was about to honor my request, or simply have me slain as preprandial to Powl, but the king said, "I gave you my protection completely, lad. I am not one to break my word."

I shook my head as earnestly as I knew how. "I did not ask that from you, sir. What I do want is amnesty for the . . . Earl of Daraln. If that is really Powl's honor and degree."

The long, white face grinned so sharply it was like a stick breaking. "Are you under the impression I care what you want, peasant?"

"Then kill me instead of Powl—the Earl Daraln," I asked him, and his jaw swelled in knots.

"What if I were to take you up on that, Nazhuret? Have you thought about that?" He glared at me some while longer, and then his face went guarded again. He added, "No, I won't trade you, lad. He is the traitor, not yourself."

I heard a repetitive, dull knock against the wooden wall behind the king, and after a moment's confusion I knew some-one was pushing a broom there. Cleaning the hostelry's public room. A job I had done dozens of times, not three months before.

It hit me with killing pain that there was some soul, un-involved and probably without an ounce of dread in his soul, so close. The king's visit was an excitement of a day, and that was all.

It's strange about the mind of a man: that I remember this little noise and yet have forgotten what the name of the town was, and what men were present at this interview. Memory is like torn paper; some inches rip straight with the angle of the force applied, and others, indistinguishable in any way, frill off into a lace of layers and fibers.

231

Not straightforward at all.

I tried another tack. "Since you know I am a peasant—no, not even that, but a nobody entirely—doesn't that explain to you, sir, why the earl would have chosen to practice his techniques on me? I mean—he said himself he had not attempted such a thing before, and surely he would not waste your time on techniques that had not proved themselves."

King Rudof eased his chair backward against the sun-warm wall. "Nazhuret, you appall me. You betray yourself and your master's teachings with this...sophistry. You do not really have any doubts concerning your education, or your skills. Respect my native intelligence also."

My mind whirled for a minute, for the king was entirely correct. I tried again: "Sir, I meant he was uncertain before. A few years ago. If you were to try him again—"

The King of Velonya winced, not in pride but in pain. He rose. "Don't talk like that, boy. I importuned your Powl every day he was at court, from the time he returned last from Felonka, with that barbaric sword you wear on your back. That was what? Six years ago, when my father still was in good health and I unmarried. Don't think I don't know the man and his meaning. He decided that I, and therefore Velonya, were to be without the benefit of his understanding." Rudof rose to his feet, and I tilted my head after him. In my weariness, the angle hurt. The king saw as much, and it seemed to make him happier.

"I don't think you can find him, sir," I said, though I knew it wasn't politic to taunt or encourage such danger. "I doubt I could find Powl now."

King Rudof hung above me and smiled. "There I have the advantage over you, Nazhuret. I know exactly where the earl lives. In retirement, very near the city of Sordalia. And I know how rarely he leaves home."

As King Rudof turned and went into the inn he had requisitioned (and where the man wielded his broom, his broom, his broom against the wall), my pervading fear was tainted with an odd jealousy—for those parts of Powl that the young king possessed and that I never could.

This seems to be a history of jealousy.

I don't believe I noticed when we were back in the forests: back in the North. I was perhaps the fifth day of my running, and I was not fit for much. What brought it to my brute attention were the lamps winking covertly among the trees.

In the dry South one can see houses clearly a long way off.

I lay without a fire some yards from the van of the king's progress. In the new grass, stinking to heaven with sweat and fear. I remember it was the day that food was brought to me: bits and scraps from a foot soldier who spoke not a word but laid the iron plate beside my head. From the looks of it, my meal was apportioned from many men's plates, and some of the pieces were good, not the sort of thing one throws away.

First the food upset my shrunken stomach and then it made me drowsy. I lay as always waiting for a glimpse of the king, so that I might repeat the substance of my first, second, or third interview on the subject of Powl in still different words.

Perhaps this time he would be sick of me and order my death.

What I saw among the boles of the oaks (here it still was too dry for maple or birch) was a fire that burned in no lamp. My brains seemed to have been left along the road with my lenses, for I wondered if we were about to be victims of another nomad raid: here, on the borders of Satt and Velonya, where there had been quiet since King Posln Dekkan unified the first kingdom three hundred years ago, and where many farmhouses had stood unbroken for longer.

After perhaps thirty minutes, I realized that this leaping glow was only a campfire—probably that of some rural person who wanted a glimpse of the king. I wanted to believe it was

Arlin, of course, though even at the time I knew that such ale dreams could do no more than break me further. I rose and followed the fire's light, staggering from tree to tree, but the light vanished before I was halfway toward it, and though I followed the smell of a doused fire, it was too dark to recognize anything besides the embers.

That night the king was staying in the manor of some noble or other. There was a small ancient castle stuffed with oat hay, I recall, and a modern brick establishment next to it. I had the good fortune to step out of the park at the moment Rudof and his field marshal came out for the evening air.

Maybe it was not good fortune. Perhaps they had waited to see me go before deciding to walk, and my quick return ruined a pleasant evening.

I fell in step behind them, like a lackey or a pet dog. It was Leoue who first noticed the movement, and he turned on me with a roar and a cavalry saber.

The king's scream came too late; I was forced to dodge under the hiss of the blade. King Rudof put his hands over the duke's face, obscuring his vision as I backed out of the way.

"I told you! And I told you again, Leoue! You are not to harm the boy!"

The big duke sputtered, "But he . . . he was . . . How was I to know . . ."

I understood his bullmastiff's feelings, for one cannot always stop to ask credentials in the dark. I tried to apologize but was not very coherent. The king ordered him a few yards away from us. It took more than one command to pry the man away from his king.

"What is it, you piece of misery?" With these words King Rudof welcomed me. "I hope you have a new subject in mind tonight."

I thought I did. "Sir, I could teach you. Anything I know, I could teach you."

First he seemed amused, but then his features pulled awry.

"You are expert, Nazhuret, but you are not the Earl of Daraln."

I answered that I knew that, but added, "Once I lay Powl in the dust. I did. So stunned he was that I had to drag him into the house and pull his shoes off. Once."

It sounded so like braggartism. Pitiful braggartism, too.

"Have you?" asked the king. "I am impressed, fellow. Perhaps you can teach me something. But will you still want to after I have killed your Powl for you?"

"You are possessed of a devil," I said to the king, and he hit me across the face hard enough to clear my angry head.

I saw the king by the light of the tall windows behind, and I saw the field marshal ease closer, his dog-dark eyes on his master, waiting for one word.

Rudof himself stared at his own right hand. "You *let* me do that, churl! You stood there and allowed it."

The accusation took me aback. "Of course I did."

"Why?"

I shrugged. "Because you are the king. If you want to hit me, then I'll be hit."

Slowly he shook his head from side to side. "Oh, I am right to avoid you, Nazhuret, and your damned condescension. You let me hit you as you'd let a five-year-old child hit you. Are you amused by me, then? Are you entertained by the King of Velonya?"

"No, sir," I answered. "I am not entertained at all. You have made me want to die."

At this the field marshal stood forward. "I can help him there," he said, his hand on his sword.

There was laughter from inside the big house, bright as the yellow windows against the darkness. (Yellow windows or blue, the sound is uncanny.)

"I think Nazhuret will find the sword a different matter, Leoue," said the king, his words thickened, the hand that had hit me wiping his own face. "A random box to the ear is one thing, but—"

"No, my king," I said in someone else's voice. "If you want to kill me, then I'll be killed."

King Rudof was a dark shadow against the windows as he looked down silently. He turned and the door was opened. The light and the chatter grew much louder for a moment, and then I was standing in the night with Duke Leoue.

I expected him to spurn my company with equal fervor, but the massive man stood for two minutes unspeaking, and I myself had run out of things to say. Finally he cleared his throat.

"I cannot pronounce your name," he stated.

"No matter, my lord. It's a strange name," I answered.

"It's the devil's name," he corrected me, without apparent rancor. "In South language. The King of Hell. The Rezhmian horse troops would shout that name as they cut our knights off at the knees."

I didn't argue with him.

"You did not condemn your earl, you know," he added, and to my amazement the Duke of Leoue sat down on the grass, grunting, and dropped his saber at his feet. "He was a traitor before you were born: parcel with Eydl of Norwess's sedition. If the old king had not been besotted with his . . . his personal charm . . . he would have been eliminated after his return from the Rezhmian incursion."

He turned his massive bear head in my direction. "The Rezhmians conquered us in body, but Powl they won in mind also. He came back their tool."

This was so absurd it did not even irritate me. "Powl is never any man's tool."

The field marshal laughed: a deep rumble. "You have the right of it, boy. Perhaps the Southerners are his tools."

I saw the glint of his eye whites in the darkness for just a moment. There was only the faintest sign of the hostility and contempt that had used to stamp his face when confronted with my own. "I think," he continued, "that though we are in disagreement as to the meanings of things, we can agree surprisingly as to facts."

I wasn't sure what the man had in mind, but before I could question him, the air wavered with a howl like that of some animal; I could not immediately place what kind.

Then I surmised it. "He is still alive . . . the captive? All these miles?"

The field marshal stirred and glanced at me closer. "Of course, fellow. He will be alive until someone is ordered to kill him. The king has him under close guard."

"What a horror," I whispered, and the bulk of the man before me shifted like the shadow of a tree when the wind blows.

"Don't worry, he hasn't revealed a useful thing."

I should have expected this out of the Duke of Leoue, but my mind had been focused on the condition of that wolf in chains, somewhere in the town or in the king's camp. I rose to get away before Leoue managed to goad me again, when I felt his hand brush my arm. "No, excuse me. I spoke maliciously, and I cannot afford to do that. I am no longer so . . . convinced that you had a part in the Rezhmian attack. Not a real, aware part, at any rate."

"I am grateful for that much," I said, and I felt obliged to explain myself to the man. I began: "If you, Field Marshal, were suddenly told now that you had been an infant of Falinka parentage, stolen and sold to the Velonyans, would that information change your life's loyalty?"

The duke chuckled. "If I were a Falonk I would be little and round and brown-skinned. And my soul would be different as well. If I were a Felonk born, questions of loyalty would not bother me. I have fought Felonk corsairs for years, boy. I know."

He had succeeded in rousing me at last, and ironically, it was when the man had no intention of causing offense. As I tried to leave him, he put a large, restraining hand on my

arm. I circled my hand out of his grip before he was aware
what I was at.

"No, Nazhuret, listen to me. Forget our disagreements if
you love the king."

I stopped, out of amazement that he could pronounce my
name after all. I decidedly did not love King Rudof.

"You won't like what I have to say, but hear it anyway."

I stood, not in reach of him, but within hearing.

"I have known Powl Inpres, Earl of Daraln, now for over
thirty-five years. We were boys together."

I could not have left the man now if he had threatened me.

"I know him. I have never met any man who could command loyalty from others so well while seeming to desire it so
little."

The truth of this statement, coming from that black bear
with all his contempt and blindness, made me shudder.

"Even as a boy he was this way: always in command of
himself. Cold. He had questions and answers for everything."

"More questions, I imagine, than answers," I said quietly,
but the field marshal did not reply to or simply did not hear
this.

"Eydl was under his spell for years, though his was the
higher rank and Norwess's the older honor. They were insep-
arable when they went South, and when they came back
defeated, it was dragging a train of goods, concubines, and
hoary bookmen. No shame for their failure at all."

I was trying to imagine Powl with concubines. It was not
such a difficult feat, after all. He would handle them gracefully,
diffidently, without embarrassment or complication. Cold,
Leoue called him. I would have used a different word, but I
knew how Powl's diffidence felt when one was under its power,
and I could understand.

"Yet it was Norwess who suffered the indignity of his failure. Daraln somehow . . . slipped out from under. He remained

in Vestinglon while Norwess took his woman home and endured his disgrace, and within a year the king was besotted again with Daraln, his wit and his stories and his scientific fancies.

"Five years later, when Norwess was accused of treason, Daraln was the unofficial tutor of Prince Rudof. He was very nearly declared regent potential."

"He was tutor? For how long?"

The field marshal did not allow my interruption. "He survived Norwess's disgrace and his flight with his own small reputation nearly intact—through the prince's love for him in large part. Norwess was destroyed. They were the best of friends, and Daraln the spark for their every strange idea. Yet the Duchy of Norwess is no more, and Daraln goes on."

I couldn't make much sense of this history. I wanted five different men's versions before I could hear it and have an opinion as to what had happened. Still, I valued it as a piece of Powl I did not otherwise have.

"King Rudof is a clever man, boy. Don't you think he can review the past in his mind and see where his favor might have been used to protect a man whose own interests superseded those of his country? Don't you think he now has reason to be angry at your . . . Powl?"

I did not think of these matters at all. My mind was full of the news that Powl had been the king's childhood teacher. For how many years? What had he shared with him, and what had he not?

King Rudof spoke Rayzhia. He said he had been taught by a friend.

"Whatever you think of Powl's interests, Field Marshal, surely you admit he is not at all ambitious. Not dangerous."

"Not dangerous?" The black bear rumbled once again. "He had created you, Nazhuret, King of Hell. If there were ten like you, it would kill Velonya."

Having said this, Leoue rose, dusted himself, and turned his back on me.

I saw the sun rise the next morning, and I heard the bustle of the royal encampment as it packed to leave, but looking up and listening out were all I could do. Five days of forced running had so accumulated the weariness, stiffness, and cramps that I was paralyzed, and I lay on the dewy grass wet-eyed from the sun—and from despair.

My secret friend left a new plate for me, rich-smelling but beyond my power to reach. I believe it was eggs spread on black bread. Various people came to stare at me, but I could not turn my head to identify them. A blanket was thrown over me by a servant in livery, and by that sign I believed the king had been by. By the time the sun had climbed from among the tree boles to hide in the leaves, the procession had trampled and creaked its way off, leaving me in the sheep-cut grass at the edge of a village whose name I don't remember.

Shortly after that my blanket was stolen again, and my breakfast was eaten by a dog. I didn't object to either.

A horse approached at a good hand-gallop; I could hear it in the earth. By its angle it seemed the beast might run me over, though there is nothing a horse hates more than flesh beneath its hooves. I lay waiting without much stake in the matter.

I recognized the hoofbeats only after they had clattered still and Arlin had lifted my head in his hands.

I will call him "he" for consistency's sake.

"I had given you up," I said to him, or tried to say. "I searched for days. I thought you dead."

His dark face glowered in surprise and outrage. "Dead? Why dead? You yourself told me very confidently that I would live."

I laughed, which was both painful and exhausting. "I say

a lot of things very confidently. I hope to convince God with my confidence."

Arlin's eyes widened owlishly. "Well, you succeeded. And I doubt I was hurt as badly as you, Zhurrie: exploded all over South Territory. I would have been back sooner, but I had sold my horse in exchange for...services...and I had to wait until I could get her back again."

Arlin's beautiful, passionate, Velonyan features—horse-face, as the Warvalan immigrants would have called it—soothed my pain and misery as no other could have done. No other but one.

"And did you have to steal her back, old fellow?"

Arlin's scowl was fierce, oversized, like all his expressions. "I won her back in a game of three-hand paginnak."

"That's what I meant—stole her," I said, but it was affection: all affection and relief. I asked him to raise me to my feet, which he did with difficulty, remarking how much heavier I was than I looked to be. I hung my arm over Arlin's neck and shoulder, in which position I could have only one foot on the ground, so much taller was he.

There was soot on the back of his hand and arm and on the silver velveteen of his cutaway jacket. The smell of camp grease, of onions, and of horse sweat made a cloud around him. There were unidentifiable smudges on his face.

I turned to him as well as I could and asked, "Do you do that to keep people away from you, Arlin? Roll in dead campfires, I mean. Use your clothes as a horse-wisp."

His long mouth tightened and the ends turned up. "Nazhuret, you are quick slowly. Does my appearance repulse you?"

In answer I leaned my face to where his hand rested on my shoulder, and I kissed it. "Though I know you are picky about the men you like," I added.

My friend gasped, and in my weariness I had no notion

whether it was the sort of gasp that indicated disgust, gratification, or merely surprise. His large eyes glanced around at the grass. "Do you want to be known for a boy-lover, like I am?"

"I already am," I said, and then the time for light talk was over for me; my dread washed back to me, blacker than Arlin's soot stains.

"Help me, old friend." I took his arm clumsily. "I have offended the king, and someone I know will die for it."

Arlin cursed by the Triune, or perhaps it was a loose prayer. He gave me an awkward little hug. "Offended? Die? The redhead is headstrong, yes, but I had not thought him so—so fickle. So two-faced. When I left the procession a week ago, word was you could do no wrong."

Arlin still was helping me stand. Now he held me at the length of his straightened arms. "Did he have you flogged, old friend? Blustering pig that he is, did he do you harm?"

Under his dirt Arlin was livid, and he showed his teeth in the grin of an angry fox.

I explained as I could. As I told Arlin about King Rudof's command that I show discretion in my friendships, Arlin grinned warily, but with some satisfaction. When I described the novel privilege granted me, he gaped. At the mention of the Earl of Daraln, he broke in with a cry of amazement. "Nazhuret, old stumper, you have picked one dangerous friend! Daraln the sorcerer, of all living men!"

I stepped back, standing on my own, for I felt a sudden distance with Arlin. "How Powl would hate to be called that: sorcerer! Reason and restraint are everything to him."

Arlin was quick to pick up my change. "So he is not a magician?"

I laughed. This time it hurt less. "Oh, yes, he is." I waved the issue aside. "Arlin, child of Howdl—"

"Don't call me that. Even in private."

"Arlin, Powl made me what I am. I could ask for no better craftsman, either." Now I found I could walk, if a dragging shuffle is a walk. I walked three paces left and then three paces right.

"You are very attached to him," stated Arlin, smoothing his soiled finery, flicking one of many ashes off his sleeve.

"I love him wholeheartedly," I answered, and at that moment it occurred to me I could not have admitted as much to Powl himself. Not easily.

Arlin's long, lean face creased in amusement. "So you *are* a boy-lover after all, Zhurrie. Like me. That explains much of your behavior, from what I have seen."

I am sure I colored, remembering one winter and a gold half royal. "I haven't really discovered what I am . . . in that regard, sir. But I certainly never had love with my teacher in exactly that manner." I did not speak convincingly, for it was a half truth at best.

" 'Sir'?" echoed Arlin, now grinning hugely.

"What would you have me call you, without endangering the life you want to lead?"

Instantly the grin faded. Arlin stepped over to where his gray mare was waiting, reins at her feet, obediently. "I meant to ask, Nazhuret. After all this, how many people know about my masquerade?" He didn't look back at me.

As he leaned over one of the two worn cantle bags, I noted that Arlin's lean hips projected from his small clothes in a way that was not really masculine. That line of him caught my eye and held it as I answered "Yourself, me, and anyone else you have told."

Now he did glance up. "You kept mum, though you say you thought I was dying? Dead?"

I shrugged, and the pain of it spread nausea through my insides. "I know you would not be able to continue as you are if all knew you were . . . a woman." I whispered the last two

243

words. "Not for all your spinning steel. And your dirt. And you must have lived through dangers before. I thought perhaps you might rather die."

His eyes were startled, almost expressionless. "And you were not tempted to save me despite my own will in the matter?"

I saw she was preparing to mount again, and I answered that I hadn't been sure that betraying her confidence would help find her.

I am sorry, my king; for some reason I have shifted gender. I mean Arlin, of course.

Since he still wore that guarded face, I added, "And, of course, it was your business, not mine."

Arlin took his attention from checking the girth and now looked full at me, not warmly. I thought perhaps he felt that my humility rang false.

"Not your business. Well, of course, that's so. Every man for himself."

"That's not what I meant," I said, and as he seemed about to mount, I blurted out, "Please don't leave me behind! I must keep up with the king!"

For a moment Arlin's Velonyan face was not guarded, sardonic. For a moment it was distinctly a woman's face, and full of compassion. "Zhurrie, you are killing yourself for the privilege of watching this man you love slain before you."

"No." I shook my head violently. In my emotion, the pain and wear of the body vanished. Almost. "I will find some way· Or I will fight beside him."

"Against the king? Against Velonya?"

Arlin leaned against her mare—*his* mare, I am sorry again, sir—and sighed. "If he is like you, together you will kill a regiment. But still you will die. Both of you."

I fell onto my knees, half for supplication, half from terror of being abandoned. "Help me, Arlin. On your horse. I ask no more, but by all our childhoods, by God, by truth, by mercy, don't leave me behind, I beg you!"

As Arlin yanked me to my feet, his lips were white. If I had been a bit lighter he would have tossed me onto the mare's back. He got up before me and gave heels to the horse.

Between clenched teeth he said, "Actually, Nazhuret, I came pelting here for you so you might help me kill a dragon. And I think my project is far more reasonable than yours."

I had no idea what he meant, and my outburst had used the last of my energy—and my curiosity. As the pretty mare trotted off, her hoof crashed against the tin plate of my breakfast—the one the dog ate—and bent it into scrap.

My arms were around Arlin's waist, and as the horse floated her long trot, my hands rubbed up and down over my friend's flat middle. More compromisingly, my face rubbed against Arlin's—sparse bristle against smooth silk—and our lips were only inches away. The pronoun of my thoughts (and so of my narration) suffered a quick, violent reversal, and I knew all my talk of a pure-minded loyalty toward Arlin—gambler, knife fighter, and baron's daughter—was so much horseshit.

This was the only woman who had ever meant to me more than the strictly structured, limited interchange I had found with bored widows. This also was my closest peer and friend. Was her power over me merely caused by the fact she had not *been* a woman to me? Was I a boy-lover incontrovertibly? Born so, or corrupted by a violent past? Possibly so, but I could not be certain, for I had known so very few women, and in my station of life—fixed between the worlds of beggary, scholarship, and war—I was unlikely to prove important to many women in the future.

What matter what Arlin had been, or what I was now; she was necessary to me, and I wanted her with the longing and patient focus of a brute beast. A wolf in late winter. A buck in the fall. A goat at any season. I sat with my weight against her body, and the horse pressed us together, up and down, my thighs against hers up and down, my hands on her belly up and down. Our faces touching. In my madness I considered assaulting Arlin right on the horse's back.

I could have done that. My education had been eclectic, and I could think of a hundred ways to restrain a person from this position without use of threats and with a hand free to deal with bothersome clothing. I spent quite some time, my head resting on Arlin's shoulder, planning how I might overcome her natural resistance and gratify my lust without either of us having to get down from the horse.

Of course, afterward she would be free to throw a knife at me, but afterward I would most likely save her the trouble and kill myself. I had known too much of being raped. And whether I died for my efforts or was spared, Arlin certainly would carry me no farther toward the king and Powl.

And then, to top all, I was Arlin's "ideal of the true knight and gentleman." I could only bow to that and behave myself.

"What are you laughing about?" asked Arlin, turning her head. Now her lips almost touched mine.

I improvised. "I wasn't. I was groaning. My muscles hurt."

Without preamble she said, "I was not pregnant, you know."

I had not time to comprehend her meaning, let alone reply, when she added, "I know what was said. I have spent many evenings in taverns in and around Sordaling, engaged in salacious discussion of the history of Lady Charlan Bannering, daughter of Baron Howdl. I know every nuance of rumor."

"Neither did your father kill you, I expect," I said, with an attempt to match her dry, disinterested tones.

I felt her shrug. "No, but had the man really understood my nature, he'd have strangled me at birth. I merely ran away." The horse trotted on a few paces before she spoke again. "I was almost fifteen. You, Zhurrie, were . . . partly . . . the reason."

"I was!" I sat up straighter, and the shifting of weight slowed the mare to a walk, from which Arlin pressed her on again.

"Father always had ignored my existence, until some piece of household garbage hinted I had a lover in the city. His reaction was what one might expect. Luckily the informer did not also give a name."

It took a few moments for me to understand that the lover so indicated was myself, at age twelve or thirteen. "It is too bad he didn't find out my name, for I could have convinced him how innocent—"

She made a gesture toward looking over her shoulder but didn't meet my eyes. "You would have had no opportunity. He would merely have sent rowdies to catch you in an alley and geld you. But I never told."

"I am very grateful. Did he—beat you?"

Again her answer came slowly. "That was a long time ago, Nazhuret. I spent six months fuming and six months waiting for my imprisonment to relax, and when that failed, I spent a year and more stealing men's clothes from visitors—anything that might come in handy. Anything that might fit. These were my first lessons in stealing. After I had escaped I studied theft in earnest."

With another person, that phrase might have meant only that she began to steal regularly. With Arlin, I'm sure it meant she studied the matter.

"You did not think to get word to me? I could have been some help."

This time she did turn all the way around. "Nazhuret, you could only have ruined yourself and your career."

Her magnanimity astonished me, and the irony of the situation made me chuckle. I held my stinking peasant shirt out from my body. "Yet here I am, old comrade. Ruined anyway."

Arlin didn't respond to my laughter, and I could not read

247

the expression in her face. I said no more, for she had given me much to think on.

The afternoon air was warm, and my mistreated body loosened considerably. When we had stopped for luncheon and I went off to excrete, I noticed that my urine had gone the color of varnish. It burned and stank. I have seen this since, accompanying too hard use of the body, but at the time it seemed to reflect the state of my mind, suspended between lust and despair.

That afternoon I began to talk, and soon I was telling Arlin the whole history of my interaction with the king, including the surveying lens. Her attitude toward my experiment was more realistic than the king's, and she called it a complicated way to validate the usual legal compromise.

Concerning my unwitting betrayal of my teacher, she was less cynical. The "redhead," she said, was thoroughly spoiled and would take all things except obsequiousness as offense.

I remembered what impudence the king had taken from my mouth, and kept that mouth shut. All kings were spoiled, she added, not just the Velonyan one, and after a hundred percussive hoofbeats, she continued, "You cannot rely on the justice of kings, Nazhuret. Or that of nobles."

I admitted that I had heard such sentiments before, and from a trustworthy source.

"In fact," she said, as the mare broke into a spontaneous canter, "you cannot rely on the justice of men. There is a strong smell of the stoat in most of them."

Still I don't know whether she meant the sex or the race. I remembered my criminal desire of the morning and I wondered about the courtship behavior of the common stoat. I also slipped my chin off Arlin's shoulder.

"Duke of Leoue, you said?" Once again Arlin glanced back at me. "It was he who gave you this... brief history? Then,

Nazhuret, you can believe the opposite of what was said, for the man is your wholehearted enemy."

I answered that I knew that and that the duke hadn't pretended otherwise, but that a man might dislike Zhurrie of Sordaling and still not be a hopeless liar.

The horse clopped on, and Arlin was silent for some time. The air was filled with birdsong, and my mind drifted among illicit ideas. It seemed to me that she must know my mood, and the fact was that she had continued to allow me behind her on the horse, though by now time and sunshine had suppled my limbs and I could run again. Instead I rode locked in this embrace: a forced embrace, but a real one. Of the flesh.

Arlin must have known; she had been silent so long. It must have been that she was waiting for me to speak, and I was very willing to speak. Though she was daughter of a baron and I only a human accident, still an optician makes steadier wages than a card cheat. We were good enough friends that if she couldn't return my love, at least she would not throw me off the horse and ride screaming away.

I plumbed my feelings. I rehearsed a declaration. I was considering whether it would be appropriate to open the matter with a chaste kiss (or a kiss, at any rate), when Arlin spoke out. "It won't wash!" she stated. I thought my mind had been read and flushed to the ears.

"I've been thinking and thinking and thinking about this thing with the king and your Daraln and the duke, and it doesn't ring true."

The sensation was that of having ice water thrown into one's face. I had to shake my head and blink. "I would be glad to find it I was in error, my friend, but—"

"Oh, I don't mean that Rudof isn't homicidally inclined toward the earl. Rudof is one of those who makes a good commander but a dangerous friend. His father was much worse. But he wouldn't just hear news of Daraln for the first time in years and decide to do him in. The flames must have been fanned."

I said nothing. Arlin's habit of referring to important people by their first name alone always took me aback. So did her easy analysis of the quirks of those in power. We behaved with more manners in the military school.

"And all this talk about Eydl, almost thirty years ago. Why?" I thought of what I knew of Eydl, Duke of Norwess, which consisted of a hand-tinted print in the Sordaling library used to illustrate contemporary body armor . . . and, of course, what the field marshal had said to me. "I know almost nothing of him, Arlin," I said.

She snorted and shifted her seat on the mare, but it sparked no response in me; my lubricity had been thoroughly quelled.

"He went South on the king's order without a hope in hell of success," said Arlin. "He was captured by the Rezh-mians. Daraln went to the fortress city unarmed and bargained for his return. The Sanaur, in a fit of generosity, released the man without recompense, and he came home, hauling behind him a Rezhmian wife and a Rezhmian warrior-poet."

"Concubines," Leoue said to me. Legal marriage is in the eye of the beholder. Powl never had mentioned this journey of ransom. There was so much he had never mentioned.

I said, "A warrior-poet? What is that? It is a new category to me. What Velonyan general would latch on to a poet of any sort?"

Arlin laughed. "A general made like you, my true knight. You would be sure to pick up a poet. Or an orphan. Or a stray wolf. But call the foreigner a philosopher instead of a poet, if you want. In the schemes of the South, there is little difference. Or call him a magician. Whatever he was, he was high-born, and very well regarded by Norwess and Daraln."

"How do you know?"

Now Arlin sighed, and it was such a sorrowful sigh, I found I was giving her a hug of comfort.

"I know because they came to visit: Norwess and his tame poet. It was in the time before my father became quite the viper he is. I was four, and I was allowed to sit on the foreigner's knee and babble for him. Now that I reflect on the matter, father probably had been asked to produce a child for entertainment, as he had nothing himself to offer an educated guest. The Rezhmian, in turn, tried out his careful Velonyan on me. Very courtly. Outlandish grammar.

"My nurse told me he had been a deadly fighter among his own people, but he certainly gave no indications of ferocity at the table. I think my nurse was enamored of him."

"Of a Rezhmian courtier?" I had to laugh. "Your old nurse must have been taller than the man by six inches."

"As I am taller than you by a few inches, Nazhuret? I can't deny it.

"You know, I don't remember the man's name. Children forget at random, I think." She sighed once again. "I do remember that he looked like you, Zhurrie. Much like you, even to the blue eyes, though his hair was black. Perhaps that was why I sought you out so many years ago."

At that I sat up. "You sought *me* out, Arlin? As I remember, I found you running dirty-faced by the swan boats one summer."

She stiffened, but not in anger. A crow of laughter almost spooked the gray mare. "And you thought it an accident, you poor sod? It was the work of weeks, to arrange my escapes when you were weren't changing beds, or drilling, or scraping rust off stupid boys' ironwear..." Her voice trailed off.

"I always remembered that man's kindness. The poet's."

"More important than a name. What became of him, Arlin?"

Now the rider's stiffness had a colder quality. "Two years after his visit, he died, with much vomiting and hemorrhage, I am told. My nurse wept openly, so perhaps there had been more there than worship at a distance. The December after that, Norwess's Rezhmian lady died, too, and similarly. It was spread about that they had not the sturdiness of constitution to bear our six months of snow. I myself have never seen a man die of cold with exactly those symptoms. Ground glass in the food, now—"

"Glass!" I winced, both because glass had become my teacher and friend and because I knew from experience what glass shavings did to the skin.

"Yes, glass. For what my conclusions are worth. Don't repeat them lest I pass on in the same manner, old comrade."

We rode in silence for a while, until Arlin cleared her throat and spoke again. "Norwess lasted another few years, and then he was accused of treason, convicted and killed in the very original way our government uses in such cases, and Powl, Earl of Daraln, left public life."

Now her cold voice heated. "When Eydl was arrested, he had lived in retirement for five years. What opportunity had he to commit treason?"

I shrugged, and in our close proximity that gesture was a sort of caress. "What I am more concerned with is that Powl, who had delivered him from the fortress city, allowed his friend to die here. Couldn't it be that he tried to defend him in court, too?"

Arlin glanced out of the corner of her large, dark eye. "What court? You have been brought up in a righteous school, Zhurrie. But it could be that he did defend Norwess. How would I know what happens inside the palaces of Vestinglon?"

To my amazement, Arlin leaned back and gave me a kiss. Lip to lip, unhurried, and filled with sweetness. When it was done, we were both pink and gasping. She gave her attention back to the road.

"In lieu of heirs of Norwess's body—for none had the temerity to come forward to declare themselves—Baron Leoue inherited most of Norwess," said Arlin, and her words were dry. That quickly she could shift, from honey sweet to bitter irony.

I myself was breathing hard for half an hour.

This was not the way I had traveled in the autumn, going south. It was hillier, wetter, with a heavier growth of birch and willow. The pounded road itself was more narrow and tended to be lost among the tree boles. We saw no people, though a few crofter cottages stood shuttered not far from the shoulder. The entire landscape reminded me of the low mountains at the southwestern coast of Satt, and of Velonya, for that matter.

I ventured to say, "I thought we'd have caught up with them by now, Arlin. Slow as the coaches go. In fact, I thought we'd be in Grobebh at noon." I laughed, almost without pain. "Remember: This whole affair began in Grobebh, with you lauding the progress of the king. If you had not kept quiet about the . . . dog and I about the red trey . . ."

With no expression in her voice she answered, "Then Rudof would have a little red arrow sticking out of his big red head. He forgets these things quickly, doesn't he?"

I didn't know what to say in turn, for my anger at King Rudof was almost unslakable, yet I knew how acutely he did remember his debt to me. "Well, that would have eliminated the threat to my teacher, at any rate" seemed both accurate and not too treasonous a statement.

But Arlin shook her head, tickling my nose with glossy black hair and sending odors of woodsmoke and crushed grass through me. "How eliminated the threat, when Leoue is regent of Rudof's little baby? The death of the king would be the ruination of many others."

I had seen no evidence that the field marshal was the malignant force Arlin thought him. Bigoted he was, but so was most of Velonya, and almost all of Sordaling Military

School. I knew the trouble such men caused; none better. I also knew their unexpected kindnesses, and their unshakable loyalty.

"What has the field marshal done to disturb you personally? You've the kind of Old Velonyan looks that they worship. The king calls him his 'bullmastiff.' How is it that you have become so set against him? Was it cards?"

Arlin's glance showed me my place very clearly, and still I could not leave the subject be. "Perhaps he is . . . a friend of your . . . of Howdl? I could understand that."

She groaned, cracked her back, and straightened again. Her narrow, black eyebrows crawled upward, and I felt my pretensions effectively depressed. "Nazhuret," she said in that drawling, ironic way of hers (so like Powl's drawling, ironic way), "I have seen the Duke of Leoue spit upon beauty itself, and I have heard him spread dirty rumors to slander the innocent."

I swayed in my seat. "Three Gods, Arlin! You speak like someone's nanny." I had not known she had that streak of prudery in her, behind the marked cards and the spinning knives. I stifled a grin and resolved to be more careful of my language in the future.

I tried to imagine the bearlike field marshal in back-of-the-hand gossip, and I failed. "Comrade, what in this sorrowing world is so innocent that it can be hurt by an old soldier's slander?" She didn't answer, but I wouldn't let it rest.

"This side of our field marshal I haven't seen! Too bad, too, for he sounds more entertaining in your eyes."

Arlin snorted and rubbed her hand under her nose. "You saw. Likely you weren't paying attention."

Being, as she was, the living proof of my failure to act as a clear lens of all around me, she could have said nothing to shut my mouth as well.

· · ·

The afternoon shadows spread. The air was damp between the boles of the willows and it carried the flavors of last year's leaves and this year's coming fungus. Such soft airs dredge up memories, and when one is weary and unhappy, there is little to defend one.

I should say there was little to defend me, for the odors of the composting earth and the sweating horse and the Arlin's sweat and my own had linked themselves with the quarreling of tiny birds, newly returned north from their winter vacations in Falink, and put me back to the year I had spent in heavy duties in stables. It was during the first time my tuition stopped, and it had been the most miserable time in my life, until it was eclipsed by the day Powl threw me out into the snow.

I dragged through those days of heavy labor again, feeling the same failure of my life, the same fear of the future. Then my only mirror had been buckets of water, and I had carried enough mirrors from the pump to the stalls, the water distorting my already odd features. Then I often sought to find the source of my inadequacies in my face, and surely I had not changed, except that I now had the sophistication to look to my racial mixture as explanation for my difficulties. It was the same idea.

But as I stared into this particular bucket (or thought I did), the face that rippled back was not that of Nazhuret. It had my hair, and the eyes blinked back at my own surprise, but it was a regular Old Velonyan I saw, horse-faced, heavy-jawed. He reminded me of someone.

He reminded me of the man—God the Father—whose baby had disappeared into my shirt, leaving a beautiful, sunburst piss stain that would not come out.

I laughed in the sudden knowledge that I had been asleep and dreaming, and the image wavered and changed. Because I had been sleeping with my eyes open, my head on Arlin's shoulder, I saw that my mirror had been the rounded, ornate guard of her rapier, which accounted for all the length and for the sturdy chin.

I lifted my head. To my chagrin I had actually drooled on Arlin's velvet shoulder. The weight of my head must have been considerable, with the horse jogging beneath us.

"Sleep has put you in a better mood," she said. "What were you laughing about?"

The confusion of my dream was exacerbated by waking in a place I had never seen before. It was a village set among trees along the slope of a hill. Every house was of timber, and all looked raw-new. There was a palisade of stakes, half built and already broken in places, the rest of the circle made up with rough balls of thorn tied in place. There were a half dozen wagons being loaded at the side of the road; none of them was an ox-wagon, but the smaller, more expensive horse pairs. People of all village types were running from place to place, dirtying their shoes in the mud of new construction, splashing through the streams that undercut the palisade and ran unchecked across the mucky road. The sounds of water and voices were everywhere.

"This isn't Grobebh." I stated the obvious. "This isn't anywhere near Grobebh."

"No," answered Arlin, and she cracked her neck with the heel of her hand on her chin, first left, then right. "We are far to the west of Grobebh, and a distance north. This is Rudofdaff, though Rudof hasn't shown much interest in it. A new settlement. It is here where the dragon is.

"Slide off now," she said, leaning back to me. "If you can, after all this riding."

I could stand, though the immobility of the ride had begun to freeze my muscles again. Arlin came down beside me.

It took a moment for this all to sink in, and in that moment my anger sparked and glowed and began to burn.

"You knew where I was going!" I rarely shout at people.

I think I shocked her deeply, though her eyes merely closed all shutters and locked all doors against me.

"You were going nowhere, unless up to the sky, for that's where your eyes were directed, Nazhuret," she said, leading her horse to a trough of concrete set at the side of the road.

"When I could have risen, I would have run again. I'd be closer than I am now, at any rate!"

She denied the truth of this—fairly reasonably, I think in retrospect. I wasn't listening to reason. I let my tongue go in ugly rage for five minutes, accusing her of endless things: obstinacy, selfishness, triviality, betrayal—every sin I felt I myself had committed, in fact. And she returned me slash for slash, putting upon my plate blindness, fanaticism, self-conceit, and more. Arlin was white in the face, and the violence of her speech caused her mare's eyes to roll, tired as the beast was. I must have been purple.

There was a small part of myself that was watching this interchange: a tired, disinterested observer. As the squabble went on and (as they will) reached farther and farther for fuel—from the betrayal of the moment to events of the past winter, autumn, early childhood—the observer noticed that the wagons were beginning to move, and each of them had children within and was flanked by young men with iron-headed hayforks. Too early in the year for haying. Months too early.

The small observer grew with interest in this even, even as Arlin had finished cataloging my character deficiencies past and present and was seeking new territory. She had rediscovered the fact that my ears were like jug handles. My small observer heard this and also noticed a small stain on Arlin's shoulder, and further, that that shoulder slumped, along with the whole back, and Arlin was reeling as she stood.

As the observer was doing this work, it heard me hissing, "You had no business to bring me here. No business . . ." It was not a voice that usually came out of Nazhuret's throat.

The horse moved away as Arlin tried to lean against it. "So be it. I had no business, but you're here. If I guess wrong, and we're too late . . . for the earl, then you can kill me in revenge."

As she was speaking, the observer became Nazhuret again and recognized in my companion the child who had taken imprisonment and abuse for my sake, when I had been just twelve years old. I shook my head at my own nauseous behavior.

"No," I said, and blessedly it was my own, not very impressive voice. "That I will not do." I made my eyes focus on her face with difficulty and took my head between my hands and rubbed feeling into it. "I was taught not to behave this way, Arlin. Forgive me," I said, and I walked stiffly over to where the raw palisade rose, and sat down in front of it.

When I got up again, not too many minutes later, Arlin was behind me, in a group of three or four villagers who were all trying very hard not to stare at me.

"Tell me about the dragon," I asked her.

There were three of the creatures, she said, and the women corrected her: two females and a male. Only the male was dangerous. Only the male had the huge horns. They had come from the west, through this narrow dell immediately after the big thaw, and the bull dragon had been enraged to find the palisade in their way.

It had breached the wall in its second charge and run like disaster through the village, trampling and goring four and carrying off the body of a woman in its massive jaws. Since then it had attacked less rabidly but more efficiently, for prey. Night and day were the same to it. It had killed eight people in two weeks.

In appearance, I learned, this dragon was higher at the withers than any horse, and built like a crescent moon or an angry cat, with the withers and hips being the lowest parts of the back. It had four legs, a neck of moderate length, and a heavy head with three horns. It was furry, it stank, and there were mixed reports as to whether it breathed fire.

They had sent a rider to the royal procession, and they had been promised a company of King Rudof's own huntsmen to root the beasts out. There were no huntsmen within a week's travel, sad to say. In a week the village would be flattened.

This very night, it would be empty.

I considered it all, wondering. I asked if the king himself had heard their plea and was told it had not been the king, but a man in sky blue, who took their request and wrote it down.

It made me shake my head. "Had they gotten to the king, Arlin, I think he'd have been down here with the speed of mercury, with all his youngest hotheads around him. Though I know how difficult it is to get *to* the king."

"You should," she answered me. I lifted my eyes to hers and remembered. "Was that the first time you saved my life, Arlin? There have been so many since. . . ."

I could see her eyes flicker in the fading daylight, and then she turned her face away as we both remembered that we were not on the best of terms. I continued, "Did you try, old fellow, to help them reach Rudof? That would have made all the difference."

Arlin drew back and rubbed dirty palms on dirtier trousers.

"I no sooner got back to that 'gentlemen's outing' when I heard how you had been treated. I knew not to show my face, there and then. I came straight back for you, and I met this news on my way."

"That was unfortunate," I answered. "It would have saved a lot of trouble, for the king is not letting his anger about Powl—about the earl—prove contagious. After the battle with the Red Whips he was looking for a way to reward you. He asked what you might want."

259

Arlin scowled and spat. It was very difficult at that moment to remember that I was looking at a woman. "I don't want anything from a man like that!" he said.

I thought to say "But these people do," when a noise cut through our conversation. It was something like the bray of an ass and something like the call of a loon, but it had the volume of a church organ and strange resonances. It came out of the west, where the sun was sinking between the hills.

Arlin's mare was startled in her feed bag, and the horses harnessed to the single remaining wagon plunged and kicked. I heard a woman crying and saw a family rush out from a doorway, all of a piece, and pile themselves in behind the horses. They, too, were gone.

I looked around me to see that we were alone, Arlin and I. "It's too late to talk about the king's assistance, now, isn't it?" I said.

Arlin went to quiet the mare. "We could still be off, with the last wagon," she called over her shoulder.

I followed. "Didn't you tell those people I had come to slay the dragon?"

She didn't turn to me as she answered, "I said you might."

This made me smile. "And were you more specific, comrade? Did you say how I would slay it? I'd be interested to know."

There was both distrust and alarm in her face now. "Surely you have an idea, at least. You are the magician."

"Me? Optician, Arlin. Get the words straight."

I thought a while. "Release the horse. Spank her away outside these walls. We are in less danger than she is. We can always climb big trees."

Arlin glanced from the beast to me and then back again. I got a strong sense of divided loyalty. "She won't go," she said at last. "She sticks to me. She's been known to try to follow me into houses, and the more frightened she is, the worse. If we put her outside the walls, she'll just run around and whinny. She'll call them to us.

"I'll put her in the barn. It's as solid as anything in this place," she said firmly, and before I could object (if I had wished to object), Arlin led the mare away.

While she was on her errand, I played tracker. Having picked out my dormitory tree, I had nothing else to do. There was no difficulty about seeing the prints; these were all over the village, and I could follow the line of them from one break in the palisade to another. They were like nothing I had ever seen, however, being flat and rounded, with two large, horned toes in front and two smaller, one to each side.

As I examined these, Arlin squatted down beside me. She had bowls of rabbit stew in her hands. "Look what I found, Zhurrie. When the squeal rang out, dinner became less interesting to some people. It's still warm."

We ate with our hands, without manners. I only hoped I could hear over my own chewing the sounds of an approaching monster.

"Well, do you think there are such things as dragons?" asked Arlin, dipping her hands in the nearest stream and then wiping where she always wiped them, on her trousers. "I remember you didn't believe in werewolves."

"I said I had never seen one." I cleaned my hands in much the same way. As we were on the lowest branches of the great maple that was to serve as our refuge and observatory, I added "then."

I spoke to offer distraction, not from her fright, but from my own. I had never studied the slaughter of large beasts; it was not one of Powl's fortes. As I expected, Arlin encouraged me to continue.

"After I left you in Grobebh, I tracked something to its home. It was most certainly a man, but perhaps it was other things as well."

Arlin had reached a large branch some thirty feet off the ground, and she lowered herself along it, arms and legs dangling, as I am told lions do. "Did you get its skin?"

"I didn't kill it. I'm not sure I could have. Its wife hit me with a frying pan. I was not certain it had done anything worse than to sire babies that could not live. It was all very confused and ambiguous." I had found a limb level with hers and at not too great an angle, and I was content to sit on it for now, my back to the heavy trunk.

Carefully Arlin reversed herself so that her head was close to me. She poked me with a finger. "Confused and ambiguous, was it? Then I know your story for the blessed truth."

It was as though Arlin had spoken to me in a language that had been private and uncommunicable until that moment. My throat tightened, and I took her prodding hand in mine. "Very wise," I said. She laughed and then stopped laughing and I let her hand go.

I seemed to have gone too far. Odd, that after a day's forced embrace, such a gesture could unsettle us both. I didn't regret it, but in an effort to smooth the situation I said, "Well, could you kill someone who had a wife with a frying pan?"

Arlin snorted and was herself (himself) again. "No doubt. I am not impressed by the fact of wives. Or frying pans."

"How about by the fact of killing?"

She raised her head. The bark had already grooved her face with imitation wrinkles. "I don't know whether I ever have killed anyone. I stabbed a man once and then ran very speedily away, so I don't know." She scraped closer to me. "What about you? Have you ever killed anyone?"

I said yes and then there was nothing more to say for a few minutes.

The arrival of the dragons was not a surprise; they came shuffling and growling along the slough behind the village like a herd of cows being driven home. Occasionally one would emit that alarming soprano bellow and another would join it—not in harmony, like dogs will, but in grating dissonance.

Arlin's mare began to kick the walls of the barn. Arlin raised herself up. "I put her in the bull box," she whispered. "It's safe." And then the four-yard-high walls of the palisade began to bulge inward.

There was still enough light to see, and over the stakes I saw black shapes like large wagons and I heard some very disgusting breath sounds. The racket of the mare became much louder now and she whinnied, as though to call a foal. I heard Arlin groan. She leaned forward against the trunk of the tree and hit the wood hard with her open palm. "Shut up, shut up, shut up," she hissed: at the tree, at the horse.

The earth beneath the palings gave all at once, and the bright raw stakes made a spiked ruff around the thing that entered. I sat astonished by it.

It was tall, thin, and impossibly huge. The three horns on its elongated head glowed ivory in the last daylight. It had no tail.

It was in the compound now, and another was coming behind it. This one was wider and had only two horns. It had difficulty getting in, resulting in the breaking of a few more stakes of the palisade. The first creature stood only forty feet from us, turning that unlikely head left and right, and snorting. The panic of the mare reached a fearful peak, and now the creature was staring down the row of crude wooden buildings toward the cow barn. It gave one of its stallion calls, which shook the tree I sat in, and trotted in that direction, with its stocky legs mincing high, like those of a hill pony.

So fascinated had I been that I failed to notice that my comrade was no longer sitting beside me. She was halfway down the trunk of the tree; no—she was taking the rest in a leap, shouting like a bravo, her sword winking in one hand and her dagger in the other.

I gave up Arlin to death, but as I did so, I was climbing

down behind her, so I suppose I did the same for myself. Disbelieving, I watched her chase after that thing, shouting much as it had shouted, with less resonance but similar tenor and volume. She was a thin shape in the last light, wavering like a slip of paper in the wind, and it was the shadow of a house that turned, sniffed, and came running after her, bounding lightly, shaking the earth, hideously graceful.

The two-horned female had turned tail at Arlin's shouts and was now trying to make its exit through the hole, which was blocked by the snout of the third, trying to make its way in. They both screamed and grunted and the stallion screamed and Arlin screamed and I was running toward her on my bandy legs as fast as I ever have run.

I didn't know to what purpose.

Now Arlin had turned tail and had no more breath for taunting the thing. I myself screamed, for her evasions were useless; the monster might have run down any horse born. There was only a yard between them when she darted behind a tree and it hit the trunk with its shoulder and I heard ripping roots. Again it bellowed and Arlin was at the wall, plastered back against the stakes, with her rapier twinkling so tiny in front of its blunt snout.

I had reached the side of the thing; so tall it rose I could almost have walked under its belly. I had my dowhee in my hands, but the hedger is not much of a piercing implement, and few swords of any kind might have reached through to the heart of the beast. I saw long, bristling hair, bare pink armpits, legs like those of a man with dropsy. I slashed at the pink, to distract it, and not waiting to see if I had succeeded, dashed in around the bulk of the foreleg and slashed twice under the throat, burying the dowhee completely in flesh.

The thing rose up, shrieking. I saw that none of its legs was on the ground and then I saw nothing, blinded and drowned by blood. It came down all of a piece and I knew I was about to be smashed under it, but I heard its snout hit the palisade before its body hit, and the long head held there, braced.

When the weight of the thing struck the ground I was bounced clean off it into the air, and my face struck the fur of the bloody cut throat before I came down again. It emitted its last breath like the bellows of an organ emptying, and the whole mass twitched, only once.

I was being dragged out from under, and I was content to lay passive and let the dragging continue. I heard Arlin scream at the red sight of me, high and wavering, the first altogether womanly sound I had ever heard from her mouth.

In retrospect I think that I had given up all hope she was still alive (though what else or who else was handling me I did not surmise), and the relief of her racket brought tears to wash the blood out of my eyes. I was both winded and numb and quite willing to lie there beside the bleeding beast, when I remembered there were two more, and it became suddenly easy to roll to my feet. "Where's my dowhee?" I cried, my voice cracking. "Quick! What did I do with it?"

"It's in your hand," said Arlin phlegmily, and then she hugged the bloodsoaked package that was I.

It was some sort of swine, we decided by lamplight after dragging more thorn to plug the entrance hole (although it did not seem the sows had the same pugnacity as the boar). Two of its horns were actually tushes, and the third was pale and fibrous. We measured it at six feet at the shoulder, and approximately sixteen inches more in the middle of the back.

It was a very peculiar night, and it occupies a place set apart in my memory, like that spent with the ghostly family, and that of being dead myself.

We could not skin the entire brute, nor could we have carried it on the horse if we had done so, but we managed the skin of the head, with the ears and horn, and we knocked out both tushes with the back of an ax We also took the sole of one foot, with its double hoof and two claws. We wrapped the whole mess in waxed cloth Arlin found in one of the abandoned cottages, then we heated water and spent a good hour washing. We purloined clothing here and there—for everything we had had been dyed in blood, including my precious piss-stained shirt—ate again, and finally lay down together in the stall next to the distraught mare.

I could not stop shaking, though Arlin seemed nothing more than pleasantly excited by recent events. She very kindly explained the difference by the fact that I had been overused this past week, but I opined instead that I was not the adventurous sort.

It is hard, now, to believe that I slept that night and harder to believe that having fallen asleep I woke at first light.

That morning I witnessed the best and the worst that comes with owning a horse like Arlin's fine mare. Few beasts I have ever ridden or tended could have carried double, endured a night like it had, and then carried double at top speed the next day. Fewer would have had the energy still to spook and shy at everything and nothing in its path. It was spooking because of the wax cloth package strapped with my dowhee over my shoulder. Arlin had abandoned all her other gear, as I had before, to lighten the load, but she had a suspicion the proof of the dragon was a card that might prove of value in the next hand. Or the one after.

Arlin held on to cards like that, even when the hand that dealt them was done.

We had not been under way for a half hour, had climbed east, and both seen and smelled the sea behind us when she asked me whether I really wanted to chase the king or go directly to the Earl of Daraln.

The question irritated me. "Three in one, Arlin; I'm after the king because I have no idea where Powl lives!"

"I do," she said, glancing doubtfully over her shoulder. "I mean, I know where his manor lies, in the hills outside Sordaling. Or did you mean another . . . a hiding place?"

I think I started to sob. "No! I don't know. I've never been there. Am I the only one in the civilized world who doesn't know where my own teacher lives?"

Arlin only answered, "There is no civilized world," and squeezed her horse faster.

We went very fast, over hills and running streams that caused the mare to dance; sometimes I think Arlin pushed straight through the woods without a path. Branches of swamp maple and willow scratched my face and must have done worse to Arlin. The mare's breathing made the drum sound of horses that are working to capacity, but so springy she went it was as though she had no weight and we had no weight on her.

We came out of trees onto a road. "Now you know where we are, don't you?" said Arlin, and I stared around me.

"No. Where are we?"

Again she gave me a distrustful glance. "We're on Sankhill, just south of town. Of Sordaling."

"So quick? This took me weeks on South Road."

"South Road is a great loop, and you were walking and working and nosing about, weren't you? Believe me, this is Sankhill."

"I've never been here," I admitted, and as we pressed along the road—a real road this time—self-pity made me add, "I've never had a horse, nor freedom to use my own feet. I've been in walls all my life, Arlin, until my teacher left me last autumn. I've only *been* places for the past six months!"

"Just like a monk," she said over the mare's smooth gallop.

"Exactly a monk," I snapped back. "The level of my worldly ignorance cannot easily be overestimated." Nor that of the damage that ignorance could do, I added silently.

Arlin refused to be drawn into bickering. "Well, we're less

267

than an hour from Daraln House. If the horse holds up."

I almost fell off. "Less than . . . then maybe the king has gotten to him already!"

"I doubt it." She shook her head with confidence. "He's encumbered. He is not Sordaling bred, and he has not a horse like Sabea under him."

After a quarter mile we turned again, and I thought perhaps I had seen this corner, with its collection of cottages and its courier office. "Without the horse, of course, we'd have no hope."

This seemed such an unnecessary thing to announce that I asked what was in her mind to say it.

"I thought perhaps . . . that you might be angry with me for my behavior last night. Flinging myself in front of the great boar like that. Making you come after."

"You didn't make me come after. It didn't occur to me to be angry." The horse rocked us a few more paces and I added, "Besides, I hadn't time."

Now I knew where we were. I had been along this stretch many times. By God, I had been here with Powl, going to the Sordaling Library. To our left was my very own hill, with the ugly square building somewhere atop it, where Powl had found the astronomer swinging in suicide. Where I had seen Powl swinging by one hand from a string, his bright shoe buckles twinkling, a bright button twinkling in his hand.

"It's been six months you've been gone?"

"More like eight," I answered.

"And now you're coming back to your walls. Your teacher. To die with him?"

"That's not what I intend," I answered shortly, but it was only a half truth; my intentions were blank. Arlin gave a big sigh, like one of the mare's breaths, and again pulled us left off the road and into the trees.

This was Velonya proper, at last: wet muck and standing water, pulling the mare's feet with every stride and covering us with spatters. We could not outrun the mosquitoes.

We came upon a man in the uniform of the local militia (born and bred enemies of the Sordaling students) and splashed by him. He shouted and flashed a pike, but neither threw it nor left his position in the wet brush to chase us.

"Daraln seems to be surrounded by the poppuls," whispered Arlin. "The redhead must have sent a courier ahead. You may find . . . he may be . . ."

I said nothing.

The mare took a low fence and we erupted out of the woods onto a sunny lawn, scattering sheep. The house before me—close before me—was rectangular and modern, of red brick. It was not large for an earl's dwelling, even for one of his lesser dwellings. Its garden of perhaps ten acres was fronted by a tall hedge with an intricately worked gate. Arlin took us from the back around the side and to the front door of the neat, symmetrical house. The mare had to be spun in a circle three times, as though she had forgotten how to stop.

I staggered over the grass and through a rose border just coming into bud. As I swayed on the threshold of the double, paneled door (edged by glass surmounted by a fan of glass), the wax cloth burden on its rope slid down the front of me and broke open.

I tried to call out and could not. I raised my hand to pound and the door opened and there was Powl looking at me inquiringly with a very calm face.

"Nazhuret," he said, and the sound of his voice was a dream and a wound to me. "You don't look very good." Then his eyes slid down to the bloody package unrolling at his feet.

"What's this you brought me?" He leaned over and with one manicured nail prodded the monster's horn.

He was dressed in sedate dark blue, with silver piping, and he had a waistcoat of subdued brocade. I noted—or my little observer noted—that I had been right about my teacher. Given idleness, he tended to become plump. But his head was

269

the same: bald back to the center, smooth, and his face and expression and movement smooth.

"Powl, I've betrayed you. Through my stupidity I've betrayed you, and the king has had a fit of rage and you are condemned."

He pulled at the fibrous horn, lifting the skin around it, and he whistled. "This is indeed something different, and you did very well to bring it to me."

"Powl!" I shouted, and my voice cracked. "You must run! He is on his way now!"

Powl stood up again and looked for something with which to wipe his hands. He settled on my shirt. "Nazhuret, you bring me no news. And no, you didn't betray me. I never told you to keep your training a secret."

He stood in the doorway but did not invite me in. "But you told me to avoid officialdom. Especially the court. I didn't know why then, but—"

"And you don't know why now." He had almost raised his voice. "I gave you good advice, but not for the purpose of hiding me from the king. I do not hide from the king." Powl took one step forward in his mirror-finished shoes. "Because," he said, "it may interest you to know that I am not and never have been a traitor to the crown."

My emotion broke free then. "But the crown's certainly a traitor to you, Powl Inpres, Earl of Daraln, Viscount Korres!" I threw the titles at him like insults, because he had never given them to me. "Either you run from him now or you're a dead man. And me beside you.

"We can break the surround easily—hell, they're only poppuls. You and I can do it easily, and in the forest nothing but hounds can find us, and I think in the past year I have even learned to handle hounds."

"No." He shut me up with one word. As always. "Nazhuret, no and no. I am not a dead man, and I forbid you to waste my effort in you by getting yourself killed."

I stepped closer. "Too bad. You can't forbid me things anymore. You finished with me, remember. You said leave the key."

His expression changed, but still I could not read it. "And you resent that, Nazhuret? You do. But I think it was necessary; you needed... other teachers. Tell me this: Is King Rudof after your blood, too?"

My laugh was ugly, and I stared at the messy burden at my feet. "He has refused to let anyone touch me. He has treated me with indulgence, lenience, privilege—I've never heard of the like! It has driven me mad!"

When I raised my eyes again to Powl, his were wide, blazing. In his face was a sort of intent awe. He began to nod.

It was as though my teacher had discovered a new planet in the skies. "He has? Has he!"

He paced the length of the entry stoop and glanced up again. "And who is this with you, Nazhuret?" His gaze, politely inquisitive, rested on Arlin, who was glaring at him and walking her mare.

"That is Arlin. A good friend of mine from Sordaling," I said.

"I am glad to have your acquaintance, madam," Powl said, and bowed gracefully.

Arlin started and snorted and croaked a laugh. "You're right, Zhurrie. He is a magician."

"I never told her to call you that!" I blurted to Powl, but he was down on one knee and into the remains of the beast again.

Arlin came close, the mare's head bending with hers. "The villagers believed it a dragon. Zhu—Nazhuret killed it for them last night. He didn't want to waste the time from coming here, but I kidnapped him and he did it."

"An appropriate action," muttered Powl, who was regarding the foot with delight.

I was made furious by the ease with which Powl had been

271

able to distract her from the need of the moment. Her distraction distracted me. "It's your pig as much as mine, fellow. I remember prying your rapier out of its snout." Powl regarded none of this bickering, and I took advantage of his absorption to look around me.

The garden was simple, largely lawn and roses, and scattered here and there were wooden implements, wheels, and platforms that might be children's toys and might be the instruments of Powl's own playtimes. "In the past winter I have seen some things," I found myself saying, "that might change your ideas of what is real. What is possible."

Powl chuckled, weighing a tush in his hand. "I change those ideas daily, Nazhuret. Probably I don't believe at all what I did when we parted company."

My gaze rested on a particular wood and wheeled contraption that was clearly a child's wagon. It had dried flower heads scattered within it. It made me catch my breath.

Powl noted, without lifting his head, "No, lad. That belongs to the housekeeper's brat. I have no hidden family. And we are alone here today. Not even servants," he said, and as he spoke I heard hooves on the road, followed by the blare of a cornet.

I drew my dowhee and stepped forward off the stones.

"Put that thing away, Nazhuret, or I'll send you off the place," Powl said in his most headmasterly tones. I merely shook my head and caused him to sigh.

"Think of your friend. Is she to perish because you cannot control your temper?"

I looked at Arlin, who had been turning her head from Powl to myself and back again. Immediately she stalked away, the reins in her hand. "Don't think to use me, Daraln," she said, and her arrogance more than matched his. "I'm no part of this and in no danger."

Powl sighed again, and with audible restraint he said, "Nazhuret, I have an idea of what is to happen here, and it doesn't include your attacking the King of Velonya with a gardening tool. You must trust me, because I am trying to save my life, among other things."

I dropped my arm, glared, tried to speak, and only began to cry. Weeping out of fear: I had never heard of such a thing before. I lifted brimming eyes to see that Powl was not looking at me, nor at anything. He was, in fact, standing upright and open-eyed in the belly of the wolf. I put the dowhee on the ground and sat beside it.

Soon I could feel the beat of hooves through the sun-warmed earth, and immediately after that came a pattern of black and white stripes flashing vertically through the scrolls of the gate: legs of horses milling. That pattern resolved into a frieze of sky blue and white, and far away the gate began to open.

There were other vertical stripes at the edge of my vision; Arlin stood with legs braced beside me, somewhat to the front.

"You said you were not part of this," I reminded her without looking up.

"I'm not a tool to be used against you, Nazhuret," she said calmly, bitterly. "Not even by a magician."

"Then you prove a better friend than I ever did," I answered in much the same tones.

The first guardsmen stepped through the gate, walking in the four-abreast formation that meant they were encircling the king, and as I saw them I stood up, and without will in the matter I found myself also in the belly of the black wolf and very calm.

Arlin's hand was at her sword hilt, and a lark was singing, very sweetly, high up. "Will you be guided by me, old friend?" I asked, and she answered doubtingly, "In this I will."

"Then offer the king no violence. Powl does have a plan."

Arlin gave a gasp as though hope had hit her, unexpected and unwelcome. I saw a scattering of black and yellows among the king's guard and knew that Leoue was with the king.

273

Perhaps twenty men entered Daraln, none on horseback. As they strode closer I saw the head of the king, flaming against the green hedge, and then the black smudge that was the duke. Leoue was dressed civilly, but the king had donned the blue and white of a cavalry captain: one of those uniforms he was privileged to, and very simple. It came to me then that a captain's uniform included a saber, whereas that of a commander, or any court official, would be completed with a rapier. It was better to be a cavalry captain if you wanted to cut someone's head off.

Seeing King Rudof approach so dressed, it seemed to me he had wrapped himself up in his own flag to do murder.

As they came within sixty feet I could see the king's face, and it was a strange color, dark and cloudy—more gray than red. The duke raised his hand and I saw his dark eyes intent on me. He called one word and pointed, and the half dozen black and yellow bees in the garden came buzzing toward me, drawing their swords. "No," I said to Arlin, for I had heard the slick of her rapier against leather.

Out of the corner of my eye I saw very clearly the green calyx snap back from a pink rose blossom.

The soldiers had not closed half the distance between us when the king bellowed the words, "Desist, you rioting hounds!" and in that short phrase was rage uncontrolled. The men glanced back over their shoulders, not willingly, and they shuffled still, watching the face of their own lord, not that of the king.

Arlin whined in her throat, like a frightened hound herself.

For a moment the king turned his face to and his anger on the duke, who replied (for all the world to hear), "Sire. Sir. I have told you what—who—that ruffian is!"

"You have shared your ideas with me, yes. And I have commanded you to let him be. Now it will be as I first said. I want all the guards out of here."

274

The guards' captain did not question. In a moment all the men in blue and white were not walking but running back for the gate. Less promptly, the bumblebees followed.

The captain had taken his king's instructions literally. The guards left but he remained, a shadow of blue behind blue.

King Rudof watched them go and squinted to see the gate close. Then he continued walking toward Powl.

The Duke of Leoue showed his teeth and clenched his fingers in his curling, grizzled beard. He shook his head in frustration, but then that expression faded. He gazed down the length of the drive and then at the entryway, glinting with little panes of glass, and ran to catch up with his king.

When they were a few yards away Powl stepped down off the stones and bowed to the king. It was not an impertinent bow, but neither was it the sort by which a man donates his head to the ax. King Rudof stood in front of Powl, half a head taller, with his hand on the hilt of his saber and then with his saber in his hand.

"I can't . . . I can't . . ." Arlin said this much and then rushed from my side. I knew the unspoken word was "watch."

Powl's shoes shone like dew among the grass.

He looked into the king's eyes and was very poised, very alert, whether to dodge or to die I had no idea. He said nothing, and he did not move.

King Rudof was equally intent, but across his face moved storms of changing expression. He had claimed to be able to read me, but I could not return that skill confidently. All I could perceive, as his saber went up and slowly up for a sideways slash, was that the king had no fears this victim would offer violence in return. And yet the king's face was slick with fear.

The saber caught the sunlight and seemed to be shuddering in place.

The falling of this terrible balance I knew only when Powl's face went from cold calm to deep concern, and yet I knew I

R. A. MACAVOY

was seeing the king's expression reflected in Powl's subtle mirror. Powl Inpres leaned toward the king and lifted his right hand gently as the saber fell out of the king's hand, to disappear in the grass.

"Daraln!" cried King Rudof. "How could you do it? How could you reject me so, after all the years? There was no one left of my youth but you. The grief of it!" And in a moment he was sobbing in Powl's arms, sobbing and slumped, bent far over, like a tall child with a short nanny.

With the inevitable human reflex, Powl was slapping his hand against the young king's back, between the shoulder blades, and I was reminded how that hand, using only a slap, had knocked a brigand unconscious—and of how an unknown hand had pounded me in that same silly fashion when I was sick and miserable, though not so desolate as King Rudof was now.

I watched with complete absorption, untouched as yet by any feeling of relief or gladness, and I noticed that the king's face was turned toward the flagstones of the entryway and the bloody pile on it (with the impossible foot sticking up, and the horn). He stiffened under Powl's rhythm, and then, as though neither threat nor tears had happened, he asked, "What on earth is that?"

Powl began to release him, and he turned his bland face to follow the king's glance. "A rat my cat left at the door just now. It will prove interesting, don't you think?"

Behind them, where I could not see, I heard the duke cursing in despair.

Powl took King Rudof's shoulders in his hands and stood him entirely on his feet again. "I had to deny you, Rudof. For Velonya I had to. Should I be playing experiments on the mind that governs the nation? Do you have time to waste cataloging obscure mammals, like this fellow does? Can you afford to dress in rags?"

Wiping his eyes, King Rudof laughed once. "You mis-

276

spoke. The king does not govern the nation. You taught me that yourself."

Powl shrugged. "He does if he is not careful. You, I know, will be a good king, Rudof." Powl gestured with an open hand toward me. "My madman, here, would not be. Not in any world like this one."

The king turned his grieving eyes on me and I started in place, for I had forgotten my own existence. He cleared his throat. "You love your madman, Daraln. You gave him the best and highest and only gave the rest to me."

I did understand King Rudof, and I would have given him my rags, my dowhee, and all my art to assuage the pain I had caused him.

" 'Best and highest' are traps, sir," said Powl, with a shade of his usual manner, which softened again as he added, "I love you, Rudof. I have since you were born."

"My king!" It was Leoue, shouldering his way past the captain of guards to glare with face twisted from Powl to myself and back. "You have permitted him to bewitch you once again! It is his 'best and highest' skill, if you like those words." He pointed not at Powl but at me.

"That creature is walking evidence of his treachery—issued by a traitor tool, out of a woman enemy to our very blood, and nurtured in treason and dishonorable arts by Daraln. He is named King of Hell with good reason!"

I could not understand this talk of blood and tools and nurturance. I found myself walking, bare-handed, from Powl's side toward the duke.

"What he is telling you very poetically, Nazhuret," my teacher called from behind me, "is that you are the child of Eydl, Duke of Norwess, and of his noble Rezhmian wife, Nahvah, and that your maternal uncle and name-father was Nazhuret, poet, scientist, and warrior: cousin to the Sanaur."

In my mind came these things: the picture of a blond noble on a heavy charger, in heavy armor, to which Powl had called

277

my attention "for the quality of the print"; the words "and my nurse wept openly, so perhaps it was more than romance at a distance"; the tiny lady with a dress of clouds who might or might not have existed and whose baby pissed on me.

These visions took no time.

It was Rudof who next spoke. "So all that is true, Powl? About the boy? I heard it from Leoue, but he is a dog with one bone on the subject of mixed blood."

Powl sighed, and I stared at him. "He is not a boy, sir. He is your age exactly. I have known him for who he is almost four years now. Since he . . . came into the observatory on the hill one day. I knew what secret, southern name they had given the child who vanished, and when I saw Nazhuret, there was that in his face, in the flavor of his thought, in his incurable innocent bluntness, that brought my old friend to me in the flesh."

"You did call me," I said to Powl. Out of all that wild tale, that was all I could pick out for meaning. That I, too, Powl had known from birth. Perhaps cared for. "I didn't come to you by accident." He opened his mouth, but said nothing for a long while. At last he smiled and shook his head, but not as for a negation.

Again to Powl only, I said, "I knew most of that: not about the duke and the poet, but the essential part. That I was half and half. In fact, it's rarely out of my mind."

I was standing an arm's length from King Rudof, my back to him, and once again I was behaving as though the king were nobody. His lean, ruddy hand came to rest on my shoulder, and the duke stepped over the grass. "No, sir. Don't touch him. Remember that your father had his father slain!"

King Rudof widened his eyes in alarm. "Leoue! Who exactly is it you want to remind of that?"

Powl scratched his chin as he said, "True, Leoue. One father killed another, though it was not by the royal command that the boy's mother and uncle were poisoned. And if you are trying to use Nazhuret as a tool against the king as you used the king as a tool against Norwess, you are far out of frame. This man is not usable like that."

"Poisoned?" asked King Rudof, glancing around the small assemblage for information. The Duke of Leoue, too, glanced around him, down the long drive to the blur of blue and black and white and yellow behind the gate. Then he raised his voice, shouting "assassin!" and his own sword—a saber, despite his civilian garb—made a single swing, which slit the throat of the incomprehending guard captain and continued toward the head of the king.

I leaped, though I was blocked by the king and could not be in time. Powl leaped, too, with great speed, but could not be in time. King Rudof only had a moment to fix his eyes on the bullmastiff who had turned on him.

Powl could not be in time, but he was after all, because when he slammed the king aside, Leoue's blade was slowing in the air, and his furious stare was at nothing. Powl watched the duke fall at his feet, and out of the back of his bull neck, right at the junction of the skull, protruded the hilt of an effete, jeweled little throwing dagger. The sort of dagger one can spin.

Arlin was three yards away over the grass. She stared at the brilliant little thing in the man's neck, more like a hair clasp in appearance than a tool of death.

She glanced up confused, past the king, past the earl, to me. "Did I do that, Nazhuret?" she asked, and rubbed a sweaty hand on her thighs.

Powl almost sprang to her. "You have no memory of it?" She shook her head vaguely, still looking over to me.

Then King Rudof bent his back and lolled his head, as though he were about to vomit on the body of the duke. But at a sound he stood straight, both hands out—a picture of command—to greet the scrambling guards. "Sheathe your weapons. It is over. No need for you. Leoue only . . . announced his own attempt at murder."

I went to Arlin and took her arm, which was stiff and chill. She glared at me, and I thought she might cry. I feared she might say something unforgivably impudent to the king, for he made third in the trio of men surrounding her, and he shook her shoulder lightly. "Lad. Lad. Civilian!" She met his eyes.

"I owed you already," said the king, "and now my debt is immense. Don't stand there starved and frozen any longer—he was never your friend as he was mine—but tell me what the King of Velonya can do for you."

Though her expression was slightly impudent, it was not unforgivably so. "Thank you, sir. I do ask something." We all waited for her to continue, and I, for one, had no idea what she would say.

"Is the Red Whip prisoner still alive?"

Rudof stared blankly and so did I. "Yes. To my best knowledge. Do you want him freed?"

"No, sir. I want you to take this traitor's body"—she gestured at her own dagger without looking—"and show it to the man. Then perhaps his silence will end."

Now King Rudof took a shuddering breath. "It shall be done, of course. Is that what you think?" He rubbed his hand through his bright hair and began to pace: himself again. "That he was responsible for the attack on us?"

"What attack?" said Powl sharply, glancing from the king to Arlin and back.

King Rudof wore a skull grin. "So there is something you don't know, Daraln?" As he looked at Powl, the expression flowered into a smile.

Powl widened his eyes. "Oh, that attack," he said.

• • •

280

That evening the king stopped his progress in Sordaling, and as we all had followed him, I still had not set foot in Powl's own residence. I had a strong sense of predestination about that.

Three of the richest men in the city turned their houses over to the use of King Rudof's guard and company. I'm sure they were glad for the opportunity, for they said so repeatedly, in nervous chorus. I was given a bath in a gold-rimmed tub hot as soup and with two footmen scrubbing me together, and then—as they did not know what to make of my rarefied accents and earthy appearance and unearthly name—they wrapped me in a white woolen shirt and breeches with a red silk sash around my middle, as though for a peasant's wedding.

I do appear more nearly normal that way than in a skirted coat.

I considered dropping in at the school, to see whether it still stood, but after consideration I found the idea a dead bore. Instead I went to seek out Arlin.

I found her equally scrubbed, though I doubt with footmen. I had considered the possibility (with trepidation) that I might find her stuffed into woman's apparel, sitting sullen and defeated in some corner. I had underestimated Powl, however, either in his sympathy or his strong ideas of what was his business and what was not, and I came upon her (him) slouching on a marble staircase, legs spraddled, dressed in dashing red and black breeches, with a plate before her and a wineglass in her hand.

I sat down beside her, stared at her immaculate tawny hands, and caught a scent of sandlewood.

"You look good yourself," she answered, though I had been silent. "Still tired, and your nose is a little burned. . . ." She pushed her elbows off a stair and sat upright. "The rider still did not admit anything," she said, and it came to me that Arlin had a much more lively interest in the affairs of the crown than I did. I ventured to guess that the prisoner didn't know who had hired them. Arlin cut me off. "The captain of Leoue's personal guard, however, was less obdurate. Leoue was after the regency and thereby the government." Her laugh was pointed. "Civilized people cannot stand against persuasion like barbarians."

I thought about that, resting my elbows on my knees and my chin in the tent of my hands. I wondered aloud how I would act in such circumstances, and she replied "unbreakable."

She slid toward me over the slippery stones and said insinuatingly, "Nazhuret, I don't see why you think you can refuse to be a duke when you *are* one already. I don't believe the title is optional."

I told her, not for the first time, that if Eydl was my father—"He is," she interrupted smugly—and if his marriage to a Rezhmian was legal and valid—and at this her eyes went pale with anger at me—then still his title had been negated and his possessions revoked.

"King Rudof will negate the negation. It probably is already done, if I know the redhead. And the estates that went to Leoue—"

I stood up to leave her in midsentence, and she caught my hand. "No. Forget it. I apologize, Zhurrie. No more talk of dukes. I know better. I know what you are. All along I knew.

"It would be a bad trade for you. It's just that I had hoped for employment with the Duke of Norwess. Sounds so impressive, doesn't it? Very old Vesting."

I did sit down again, and linked my hand in hers. She slipped from it, muttering the word "boy-lover," so instead I linked my fingers around one knee and rocked on the stairs. "I have no way to employ you, comrade," I said, "But I could certainly help you waste your time."

282

She had been drinking and she sprayed wine all over the waxed marble stairs, except that it wasn't wine but brandy. "Besides, Arlin, you have the favor of the king. You don't need more for advancement."

With her face in the glass again, she said, "But I had my heart set on the favor of a duke."

Before I could open my mouth to speak, Powl was climbing up to us. He looked critically at the speckles of wet on the stairs, took out his handkerchief, and wiped dry a place to sit.

"Nazhuret, I have been looking for you." I looked away from Arlin, drawn from what might have been an important moment by this voice I had feared I would never hear again.

He glanced at both of us and continued, "I have been studying medicine this past year. Are you interested?"

"Of course," I said, but to my distress Arlin had risen and was stepping over me.

"It is not the usual curriculum of medicine, though. . . ."

"Of course not."

"I guess I shall just have to find another duke," Arlin was saying, but Powl, without turning, put his hand behind her knee and made it necessary for her to sit down again.

My teacher smiled distantly at me. "You should see your face, Nazhuret. Your father *was* just the same."

Arlin stared, half offended, half perplexed, at the hand on the joint of her knee that had led her down so easily. "I want you to know that Helt Markins was an honest man, after his own lights," Powl said to her. As her scowl blossomed blackly, he added, "He wanted to save his country from a foreign influence that he felt would inevitably drown the culture of his fathers. And he was right in all that. In two more generations this will be a very different realm."

Arlin's expression flickered with something like anger, and also like enjoyment. With an air of producing an unexpected ace she answered him, "Every two generations—no, every

283

one generation—this is a very different realm. There never was any 'old Vesting' culture, except in the packed-away memories of old men."

Powl regarded her intently for some seconds, then spoke. "And you really don't remember throwing the dagger at all?"

She cleared brandy from her throat. "Well, as to that, it seemed more politic at the moment to withhold any . . . commitment to the throwing. . . ."

"Don't lie to me, Arlin," said Powl flatly. "That is one problem I never had with Nazhuret. Besides, you are trying to deny what is likely the finest thing you have ever done. So far."

He turned back to me those eyes, ironic, interested, without disruptive passion. He smiled interrogatively. "This one is already half mad," he said to me.

"No porcelain hands," I stated, probably with my unhappy soul in my face again. Arlin glared at me, confounded.

Powl's concern wrinkled his forehead up to where the hair once had been. "Do you have fears you will be . . . replaced, Nazhuret? You needn't."

I shook my head violently. "Not by her, Powl. By you!"

They both sat and stared at me, like the audience at a theater.

"I took you correctly," said Powl, nodding.

Then Arlin gave a snort and wiped her damp hair from her face. "Zhurrie, you're impossible," she said, but uncertainly. "Penniless, and a monk besides. Are you trying to cut me out of yet another employment here?"

"I'm not a monk," I told her.

"He's not a monk," said Powl in pain, seeing no trust on her face. "He was not a monk when he came to me and I certainly did not create him one. There are no celibates on this staircase, unless you are one, madam.

"And Nazhuret, I have no interest in consuming your friend utterly, no more than I had in doing the same with you. As you remember. Conversation, elucidation to mutual benefit. For more than these, you must go to someone else." He fluttered his hand indifferently. "To each other, for example."

Arlin was scowling in belligerent confusion, her back against the cold marble wall. "What does all that mean?" she demanded. "What is he saying?"

I thought a moment, took my courage in both my hands, and asked Powl for the key to the observatory.

My king, I have been at this memoir all the autumn, winter, and into the first thaw, and though it has grown out of my expectation, I am at last finished with telling you things you already knew. I have learned that too much of seeing oneself through another's eyes is not instructive but destructive, and I hope I have not done you a wrong.

But then, the people of sixteen years ago are not with us now, anyway. Until your command, I hadn't thought to dig the ghosts up again. There's no small amount of pain involved in looking back to one's youth.

(This morning in the grinding room a chance placing of two mirrors showed me the top of my head, and right at the crown there is either an old scar or a spot of incipient baldness. I don't want it to be baldness—my face is original enough— and if I had courage I would ask Arlin how long the spot has been there. No hurry; I will find out sooner or later.)

That you should have asked for this history so soon after the death of our teacher was very appropriate, and it has helped to reconcile me to that shocking lack and emptiness. I would have had little on my mind this past year but Powl anyway, and you have given purpose and structure to my grief.

It was fitting that he should die over a table of laboratory equipment, going out quickly, like a candle. He had used that heart well, though he had not shown it often.

I have carried tremendous sympathy for you, Rudof, all

these years, knowing what you desired and had to sacrifice for the sake of the nation. Once Powl was kind enough to call me "the stone I flung into places I could never go myself" (that was only once, and then after a good dinner), but that seems the greatest irony of all his ironies.

You, Rudof, are an eagle by nature, welded to chains by the responsibility of your birth. I am (if I know myself) a small bird of the sort that collects pebbles and makes nests of leaves (and pecks repeatedly at mirrors; I mustn't forget that), and yet Powl grafted on to me a limitless power of flight.

So now I end. I enclose Arlin's profound respects (they are difficult to win, you well know, and she feels I have treated her shamefully in this narrative), Nahvah's embarrassed courtesy, the various orphans' confused obedience, the horses' whinnies, the buzz of a newly awakened bumblebee over my paper, the bellow of someone's amorous bull in the distance, and all the weathers of Norwess Province, for your enjoyment in Vestinglon.

Do not mourn Powl, or any of your dead too much, old friend. I share your feelings; I see him daily, when I am not looking for him, and I hear his voice.

But I repeat again that first thing Powl or my own madness revealed to me, on the cold stone flags of an ugly brick building, at the raw age of nineteen:

Death is before life and after it and in it all together, suffused with a light as perfect as the rays of the sun. It comes not as an insult, nor a defeat, nor does it serve as a boundary to the free soul.

This I do remember.